KISS TO *Salvage*

MW01623008

ANNA B. DOE

Text copyright © 2022 Anna B. Doe
All Rights Reserved
ISBN 978-953-8511-15-8

Kiss To Salvage by Anna B. Doe
Publisher: Wild Heart Publishing d.o.o.
Lukarišće, Croatia, 2023
Print on demand

Copyediting by Once Upon a Typo
Proofreading by Once Upon a Typo
Cover Design by Najla Qamber Designs
Cover Photography by by Braadyn

Without in any way limiting the author's exclusive rights under copyright, any use of this publication to "train" generative artificial intelligence (AI) technologies to generate text is expressly prohibited. The author reserves all rights to license uses of this work for generative AI training and development of machine learning language models.

This is a work of fiction, created without use of AI technology. Any names, characters, places or incidents are products of the author's imagination and used in a fictitious manner. Any resemblance to actual people, places, or events is purely coincidental or fictional.

No part of this book may be reproduced in any form or by any electronic or mechanical means, including information storage and retrieval systems, without written permission from the author, except for the use of brief quotations in a book review.

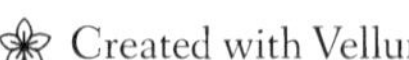

"She was brave and strong and broken all at once." – Anna Funder

To all the people who have fallen so hard, swallowed by the darkness so thick you don't see a way out, only to look at it in the eyes and rise, this one is for you.

CONTENT WARNING

Kiss To Salvage is book two in *Shattered & Salvaged Duet.* In order to enjoy this story, you have to read *Kiss To Shatter* (*book 1*) first.

While *Shattered & Salvaged Duet* isn't a dark romance, the duet contains mature content and dark themes appropriate for readers 18+.

I've included a list of trigger warnings to help readers decide if this book is for you. The list contains some major spoilers, so to avoid disappointing readers who want to go in blind, I've posted the full list of trigger warnings for this duet and my other books on my webpage, and you can find them on my webpage: https://www.annabdoe.com/trigger-warnings.

BLURB

I never expected to fall for my best friend's little sister, and I definitely didn't count on her breaking my heart.

Jade Cole entered my life like a tornado, and I never saw her coming. I should have been strong enough to resist her. After all, she was forbidden, my best friend's little sister, and the bane of my existence.

But the more she got under my skin, the harder it was to resist her. Until I couldn't fight back any longer. One kiss led to another, and the more I had her, the harder it was to let go.

Then she dropped the bomb I never saw coming.

I have cancer.

And it's like I've been sacked to the ground all over again. I've already lost somebody I love to cancer, and I can't do it again.

But I also can't walk away from her.

Because Jade and I? We're like magnets. And no matter how hard you try to separate us, we'll find our way back to each other, regardless of the destruction we leave in our wake.

NOTE: Kiss To Salvage is book two in Shattered & Salvaged Duet. You need to read Kiss To Shatter in order to understand this book. Shattered & Salvaged Duet contains dark and mature themes appropriate for readers 18+. For the full list of trigger warnings please visit www.annabdoe.com/trigger-warnings.

Prologue

JADE

Senior year of high school

She's gone.

Completely, irrevocably gone.

I blink, staring at the dark ceiling. I can hear voices coming from downstairs. People have come to pay respects. How can they be down there, talking and laughing as if nothing has happened?

As if she were still here?

As if I haven't lost the only parent I had left?

Gone, gone, gone…

I cover my ears, trying to muffle the word that echoes on repeat in my mind.

A gut-wrenching sob escapes me. It's so loud it makes my whole body shake. I grab the pillow and cover my head with it, but it's not enough.

Nothing is ever enough to muffle the noises anymore.

Not the sound of her soft wheezing as she was struggling to breathe.

Not the *beeping* of the heart machine as it signaled the moment she was gone.

Not the sound of people mingling around living their life while she is dead.

I grip my head, covering my ears as I let out a frustrated cry.

I have to make it go away.

I have to stop thinking.

Stop feeling.

And just *breathe.*

Shoving the pillow away, I get to my feet, my eyes focusing on the bathroom. Not bothering to wipe away my tears, I cross the short distance to the bathroom while ripping the itchy dress over my head and tossing it on the tiled floor.

With a quick flick of my wrist, the water is on, filling the big, white tub. The one I begged my dad to install when we were remodeling my bathroom.

Before my life fell apart.

When we were still a family.

But it's all gone now.

She is dead, and he left.

Gone.

Both of them.

Gone.

Taking the rest of my clothes off, I don't wait for the water to fill the tub before sliding inside.

The hot water burns my skin, but I barely react. I'm too numb. I just want it all to go away. I want to silence these voices screaming in my head—that damn *beep* ringing in my mind, day in and day out.

So I do just that.

The moment the tub is full, I turn off the water. Sliding deeper into the bathtub, I tilt my head back, closing my eyes.

It's going to be okay, baby girl, my mom's last words ring in my mind, making more tears fall down.

She was wrong though.

Nothing is okay.

Nothing will ever be okay.

She's gone, and she's never coming back.

Gone, gone, gone.

I sink under the water, letting the darkness swallow me whole.

And then?

Then I scream.

Chapter 1

PRESCOTT

You know that moment when you think everything is finally going well, and for a split second, you let yourself believe that this could actually be your life.

You hope.

You hope, and then life shows you just exactly how wrong you are. It smacks you in the head when you least expect it, and nothing will ever be the same again.

That's how it feels as I stare at Jade's tear-stained face.

My ears are buzzing, those three words ringing in my mind on repeat.

I have cancer.

The words I never expected to hear again.

I have cancer.

The words that already wrecked my life once.

I have cancer.

Those blue eyes are big and red-rimmed as they stare at me, her hand covering her mouth as she tries to hold in her sobs.

"Prescott, I'm so so—" Jade reaches for me, but I step back like she will burn me if I allow her to touch me.

"You knew," I whisper, the accusation evident in my voice. "All this time. You knew."

"I'm sorry!"

I shake my head, not believing her words. "You *knew*."

She knew about Gabriel. She knew what had happened, and still. *Still*, she kept this from me. She let me...

No. Another shake of my head. *No, I'm not going there*.

I look around the room. Grace is still standing in the doorway, her hand covering her mouth, while Nixon just stares at his sister, unblinking, as if he's standing in front of a moving train, glued to the spot and unable to move.

"Prescott, you have to—"

"No!" Another step back. "What I have to do is get out of here."

Turning on the balls of my feet, I do just that.

Grace gets out of my way, and I make my way down the hallway, pulling the front door open so hard it bangs against the wall.

I don't stop.

I don't look back.

I run.

But no matter how fast I run or how far I go, I can't outrun her words.

I have cancer.

Chapter 2

JADE

"Wentworth!" Nixon lunges after Prescott. It's like somebody snapped my brother from a dream. One minute, he's standing still, utterly shellshocked by my words; the next, he's moving. Or he would be moving if I didn't stand in front of him, not letting him go.

"No."

Nixon looks down at me, anger and hurt flashing in those eyes that are so much like my own. *Mom's eyes.* "What do you mean, no?! He can't just leave you like that."

I press my palms against his chest harder. "Just like I said, *no*. You won't go after him. You won't bully him or punch him or whatever else is currently going through your head because you're angry at me. *Me,* Nixon. Not Prescott. You're angry at me."

"Oh, trust me, I'm livid with both of you. The one doesn't exclude the other."

I don't doubt it for a second, but I won't let this ruin his relationship with Prescott. They've been best friends since they started college. I won't be the reason why they aren't any longer.

"I know, but I'm here, and we both know it's me who you're truly angry at. I'm the one who lied. So let him go."

"Let him go?"

"I'm going to leave you two to it," Grace whispers from the doorway. My body goes still as I hear the hurt in her voice, and I can't turn to face her.

So many people.

So many lies told.

They'll never forgive me.

And they shouldn't.

"Yes, let him go."

"So what, you're good enough to fuck behind my back but not good enough for him to stick around now that you're sick?"

My cheeks heat from his harsh words. It would have hurt less if he had slapped me.

"I know you're angry, Nixon, and it's completely my fault, but Prescott has nothing to do with this."

"I don't..."

"No, you don't," I snap before he can say anything else. "You don't know what he's been through and why he ran away, but I do. So when I say let him go, you let him go."

"You can't be serious."

"I am. You will let him be, or I swear to God..."

Nixon narrows his eyes at me. I expect him to keep asking about it, but instead, he changes the subject.

"Why didn't you tell me?"

"I-I..." I shake my head, pressing my lips into a tight line to stop them from wobbling. There's a soft sting from the punch I got there last night, but it's nothing compared to the ache I feel in my heart every time I remember the look on Prescott's face.

All this time. You knew.

No, he'll never forgive me.

Not after he opened up to me about Gabriel and what

happened to him. Then again, why should he? So he can watch me die from the same disease that took his brother?

"I just couldn't."

"What the fuck, Jade?!" Nixon yells, the vein in his forehead popping.

I flinch back. It's not even the fact that he's pissed at me. I'll take his anger any day of the week over this utter heartbreak that's written all over his face. That's my undoing.

"Because of this," I force the words out. They're so quiet they're barely audible. "Because of this, Nix. You are happy. You are *finally* so happy, and I couldn't bring myself to break your heart all over again with my suspicions. Not this year, when everything is finally going your way, and you have to focus your attention on footba—"

"Screw football!" Nixon yells, waving his arms around in outrage. "I don't care about freaking football; I care about you. I care that you've been keeping all of this a secret. What the hell, Jade?"

"It's fine."

"Stop saying that!" Nixon yells, running his hands over his face. "It's not fine. You're not fine. You've been a mess for months! For months I've been watching you do crazy shit from afar, unable to stop you. But the pit fight was the last straw."

"How did you even find out?"

"From freaking Instagram! Some of the guys were there last night, and like the idiots they are, they posted it all over their stories. That's how I found out. I thought I was crazy. It couldn't be my baby sister who was fighting in some shitty bar, but something nagged at me to come and check anyway. To make sure that you're okay. The joke's on me, though." He looks at me. *Really* looks at me, his eyes not missing a thing. "How long did you know?"

Wrapping my arms around my middle, I look away, so he won't see the tears burning my eyes.

"For how long, Jade? How much time did we lose?"

A knot forms in my throat, but I swallow it down, pushing the words out. "Back in August. About the time when we moved in here."

"Two months?"

I close my eyes, unable to stand the devastation on his face.

"You've been hiding this for two months?" Nixon runs his fingers through his hair, golden strands sticking up in all directions.

My throat bobs as I swallow, but still no words come, so I just nod.

"At least tell me you've been to the doctor. That you have a plan figured out on how to fight this."

I keep my mouth shut.

There is nothing to say, is there?

Nothing that he'll want to hear.

"Jade?" The little hope that was there dies with that one word. "Fuck!"

He turns around, his fingers curling into a fist.

Shit. I move before I even know what I'm doing, my hands wrapping around his chest and pulling him back before he can slam his fist into the first available thing. "Don't do this. Hitting things isn't going to help. You'll just hurt yourself."

"It'll help me deal with this rage."

"If you hurt yourself and can't play, then all of this was for nothing." I sink my teeth into my cheek so hard I can feel the coppery taste on my tongue. "Please, just..." I shake my head. "Please."

Nixon's body relaxes slightly, so I tentatively let go of him. "It was all for nothing anyway. You lost weeks, Jade! *Weeks*! You better than most should know how precious the time you have is. The sooner you start treatment..."

"I wasn't ready, Nixon!"

My brother takes a step back, his eyes growing wide at my outburst.

I let out a shaky breath, my hand rubbing over my face. The pain meds have stopped working, and I could feel my entire body ache from last night's beating.

"I'm barely twenty, Nixon. I'm barely twenty, and I spent the last year of high school watching Mom deal with this disease. I watched it rip her apart piece by piece. So I'm sorry if I wasn't ready to face the reality of what's in front of me. Sorry for not being ready to be poked and prodded and cut into. Sorry for not being ready to lose *myself* before I even had a chance to find who I am."

"Smalls..." Nixon takes a step forward, his arms wrapping around me. I try to get out of his hold, but he pulls me tight and doesn't let go. "Maybe it's not..."

"It is. I know it deep in my gut, Nixon. The bruises on my side. The inflamed lymph nodes under my arm keep getting worse. The bump on my b-breast..." I suck in a sharp breath, trying to calm myself. "I tried to ignore it. I tried to fool myself that it'll all go away if I just don't panic, but the thing is... The cancer is back."

Four words that ruined my life two years ago, and now they're back. Coming to haunt me. How is this happening? *Why* is this happening again? Why can't we just get a break?

Nixon pushes me back, his hands cupping my cheeks.

"It's okay. We'll figure it out. We have to call your doctor and see what the next steps are. You've lost..."

"I know very well what I've lost!" I snap. The helplessness that's been eating at me since the moment I felt the lump is finally rising to the surface. Taking a deep breath to compose myself, I say softly, "I'm going to deal with this. I just... I need time."

"You don't have time!"

"I know. But I need it anyway." Placing my hands over his, I push him back. "Go home, Nixon."

"You can't..."

"What I can't do is deal with this right now. My head is killing me, and every bone and muscle in my body hurt. I just need..." *To forget.* "I need to sleep."

"What you need to do is call the doctor..."

"It's the weekend. It's not like she'll answer anyway." Taking a step back, I get into bed. The still rustled sheets are from how we awoke earlier when Nixon barged in. I place my hand over the pillow that Prescott slept on. "Please, go home. I'm going to bed."

"Fine." Nixon rubs his hand over his face. "But this isn't done. I'm taking you to the doctor, and I don't care one bit if I have to do it while you're kicking and screaming." He stops behind my back, his fingers gripping my chin and turning me toward him. "I'm still pissed as hell."

"I know."

"But you're my sister, and you're not alone." Leaning down, he presses his mouth against the top of my head, holding on just a little longer than he usually does. "Whatever happens, Smalls. I'm here."

Nodding, I let a tear fall. Nixon brushes it away before taking a step back. Neither of us says a word as he leaves the room, closing the door firmly behind him.

Letting out a shaky breath, I slide under the covers. Grabbing the pillow, I squeeze it to my chest and bury my face into it, inhaling Prescott's scent as I let the tears fall.

I cry.
For him.
For me.
For everything that could have been but never will.
It was all just borrowed time.

Chapter 3

PRESCOTT

I have cancer.

I have cancer.

I have cancer.

I have cancer.

The words echo in my head on repeat. Blue eyes filled with unshed tears and so much sorrow burned into my mind.

I have cancer.

Pushing my apartment door open, I stumble inside and go straight for the kitchen, pulling open one of the cabinets. The door bangs against the other cabinet, the sound ringing loudly in an otherwise quiet room as I grab the first bottle and yank the cap off. I bring it to my mouth and take a pull straight from the bottle.

I have cancer.

Three words.

How can three little words, three short seconds, shatter somebody's life completely?

My eyes fall shut as the liquid burns its way down my throat, making my eyes water.

Fuck, fuck, fuck.

"What the fuck, dude?" Spencer asks as he enters the kitchen. "Are you drunk?"

"Not now, Spencer," I groan, swaying on my feet. I grab the counter to steady myself as the world continues spinning around me.

"Are you shitting me? You enter like Rambo, probably waking up half the building in the process..."

I have cancer.

Turning on the balls of my feet, I throw the bottle at the wall—the glass shatters, amber liquid splashing everywhere. "I said not the fuck now, Spencer," I yell.

Before he can say another word, I grab a new bottle from the cabinet and go toward my bedroom. I slam the door behind me, not bothering to turn on the light. I can hear Spencer calling my name, but I lock the door before falling to the floor.

I have cancer.

"Fuck you, Jade." Uncapping the bottle, I take a long pull. "Fuck you. Fuck your half-truths and pretty little lies."

But no matter how much I drink, I can't erase the look on her face as she admitted the truth.

How long had she known? How long has she hidden it from me?

I look back, trying to see the signs that I might have missed, signs that she's keeping secrets from me, but there is nothing apart from her not wanting me to touch her boobs.

Nothing else.

She knew.

She knew my secrets. She knew my nightmares. She knew about Gabriel. She knew what had happened, and still, she decided to keep it from me.

If I had known...

You kill everyone you love.

Maybe my dad was right after all.

Curling my fingers around the bottle tightly, I drink more.

I drink until the pain dulls to a distant throb.

I drink until the image of her becomes blurry in my mind.

But even falling into oblivion doesn't take the pain away.

And those three little words that slammed like a wrecking ball into my life? They keep up the wreckage even as I sink into darkness.

I have cancer.

Chapter 4

JADE

I stare at the message I sent at some point yesterday, somewhere between living and dreaming the nightmare that's my life. But there is no reply to the four words I sent. The only thing left that I could offer him. Not that I expected one.

Me: I am so sorry.

Letting out a sigh, I turn the phone face down before pushing from the bed. My whole body feels stiff from lying around all day, and my muscles are weak from unuse. Running my fingers through the mess that's my hair, I go toward the door and listen.

The apartment seems quiet, so I open the door and slide out into the hallway, only to come to a stop when I reach the living room and find all my friends sitting there and whispering.

Penny is the first to notice me, so I must not have been as quiet as I hoped for, and all the girls turn toward me, suddenly silent.

"You know I'm not dead yet, right?" I ask, forcing a smile out.

Grace's eyes widen, and Rei's lips part in surprise.

"So it's true? You are sick?" Penny asks, her hand landing on Henry's back, her fingers running over his soft fur.

"Yeah." With a sigh, I look over my friends, my eyes landing on Grace's. "I never wanted you to find out like that."

"Did you ever plan to tell us at all?" Grace asks, her voice harsh.

"Grace!" Rei chastises, but I shake my head. "It's fine. She has the right to feel angry. You all do. I planned to tell you, but..."

"When? When did you plan to tell us? When you were actually dead? 'Oh, by the way, I had cancer. I hope you live a happy life. Love, Jade?'"

"I would have told you."

"Yeah, right. Just like you told us that you're hooking up with Prescott?"

I tilt my head back, the mention of Prescott making the bile rise up my throat. Of course she'd bring that up. It was just another secret I'd been keeping from her, from all of them.

"You and Prescott?" Penny's voice hitches in excitement because only she could ever be excited about it.

My stomach twists with unease. Of the two things, I'd rather talk about cancer than Prescott any day of the week. Cancer was straightforward, you either lived or died, but there was nothing simple or clear-cut about Prescott or the way he makes me feel.

Pushing from the door, I cross the room to the kitchen and open the cabinet. I rummage through it until I find what I've been looking for, tequila. Wrapping my fingers around the bottle, I grab a shot glass and join the girls, sitting cross-legged on the rug in front of them.

"Isn't it a little too early for that?" Grace asks, her brows raised.

I wave her off, opening the bottle and pouring a shot. "It's five o'clock somewhere. Besides, if you want me to talk about this, I'll need some liquid courage."

Tilting my head back, I throw the contents of the shot glass down my throat. The alcohol burns my mouth, making my eyes water, but I welcome it as I refill my drink and force myself to look at my best friend.

We've been inseparable since the moment we were introduced to each other. She was my person, somebody who could discern through my bullshit and see *me.* But just like everybody else, she's overcome her own demons, and the last thing I wanted was to bother her with mine.

"I would have told you," I whisper, needing her to know I'm serious about this. "Eventually. It was never my intention to hide it. I just... I needed time."

Grace watches me for what feels like forever before softly asking, "How long have you known?"

"The first time I noticed something was wrong was when we moved in," I admit.

"Weeks?" Grace's mouth falls open. "You've known for weeks and haven't said anything?"

"It wasn't like that. I didn't *want* to know."

Clasping my fingers around the glass in my hand, I tell them about it all. About the bruises, the lumps in my armpit, the one in my breast, the pain, the uncertainty, the *fear*.

Only when all the words are out, do I allow myself to let out a shaky breath.

There. It's out now. No more secrets. No more lies.

I thought the weight would be lifted off my shoulders, but I still felt empty.

Tired.

I'm so damn tired already, and the treatments haven't even started.

When I look up, I find my friends watching me with trepidation and pity. It's that look of pity that makes me snap.

"I'm not dead yet," I repeat, my voice clipped as I grab the bottle and pour myself another drink, swirling the liquid in the glass. "There's no need for those faces."

"Don't you dare joke about it, Jade Deveny Cole!" Grace chastises, getting to her feet.

"If I don't laugh, I'm going to break, and I don't have the luxury of breaking. Not if I want to face the weeks and months to come."

My words make her stop in her tracks. The reality of what's going on has finally hit her.

"What are you going to do?" Penny asks softly, her hand placed on Henry's back, rubbing his thick fur. It's like the dog can feel her anxiousness, so he's sitting close to her, his head on her thigh. "What's the process here?"

"I have to call my doctor soon and try to set up an appointment for her to get a look at the lump."

"So it might not be cancer?" There is so much hope in Grace's voice, and it hurts me to break it.

"It most likely is. The signs..." I shake my head. "Mom had them all."

The silence settles over the room, making my throat tighten.

This.

This is why I didn't want to tell them anything. It hurts too much to have them look at me like this. Like I'm going to break if they look at me the wrong way, forget talking about it.

"So? What will happen then?"

"I'll get an appointment. The doctor will probably do a biopsy to confirm it and to see how far along my cancer has progressed. Then, we'll decide on the best course of treatment."

The girls exchange a silent look, and it takes all that's in me not to snap. I don't want their scrutinizing, pitying glances. I don't want my friends to feel sorry for me.

Shaking my head, I push to my feet. "It's fine. I'll be fine. Eventually."

"There is no eventually about it!" Grace jumps to her feet and wraps her arms around me. "Why didn't you say something sooner?"

My body stiffens at the sudden nearness, a knot forming in my throat. I swallow, trying to push it down, but it's like the damn thing is stuck. "I didn't want to believe it was the truth. I knew it could be. Ever since Mom became sick again, I've known there was a possibility, but I never thought... I guess I never thought it could happen so soon."

I never thought life could be so cruel.

I should have known better.

"It's going to be okay."

"Grace is right," Rei whispers as she joins us, hugging me from the other side. "We'll be there every step of the way."

Tears blur my vision, and I have to bite the inside of my cheek to prevent them from falling.

"Is there anything you need?" Penny asks, getting to her feet to join us. The girls step back, and she gently places her hands on my shoulders before letting them fall around my waist and hugging me. "Something we can do? Do you need us to go with you to your appointment?"

To go with me and have a front-row seat to this trainwreck? Yeah, I think not.

I shake my head. "Just..." I sniffle, rubbing my nose with the back of my hand. "Please act normal. I don't want things to change just because..." I wave my hand, not wanting to say those words out loud once again. "I need something normal in my life right now. And if you all keep looking at me with those sad puppy eyes, I won't be able to do it."

"Hey, now!" Penny pulls back and frowns at me. "The only puppy eyes you see are Henry's when he's trying to sneak an extra treat."

Henry barks his agreement, his tail wagging excitedly.

"I think he wants a treat now," I chuckle, happy for the distraction and lean back.

"Probably." Penny places her hand on his head, rubbing him behind his ears. "You'll have to wait until we get back home, bud. Sorry."

"Or maybe not." Grace goes to the kitchen cabinet and pulls out a box. The moment Henry hears the rustling of treats in the box, he tilts his head, listening.

"Go on, get one," Penny says with a sigh. Before she even finishes, Henry makes his way to Grace, plopping his butt down as he waits for the treat.

"Such a good boy," Grace praises, giving him a cookie.

He munches on it happily before returning to Penny's side. "He so is," she agrees. "And spoiled to the bones. And while we're on the topic of boys, don't think we forgot about the bomb Grace dropped."

"Right!" Rei looks at me, her brow raised. "You and *Prescott*? Seriously? The Prescott you can't possibly stomach to be in the same room with because you're instantly at each other's throats Prescott?"

Our first kiss flashes in my mind, the memory like a punch to the gut. "Quite literally at times."

"What does that mean?"

I guess today's the day for truths.

It was only a matter of time, anyway. I could probably pretend I don't know what she's talking about. After all, there is nothing going on between Prescott and me. Not any longer.

But I'm tired. So damn tired of all the secrets and lies.

"I told you guys they'd end up together!" Penny clasps her

hands, a smile forming on her lips. "I swear you could cut the tension between them back in Hawaii."

"Prescott Wentworth?" Grace shakes her head; disbelief is clearly written on her face. "Nixon's best friend and Jade's nemesis. I wouldn't have guessed it, not in a hundred years."

"He's not my nemesis."

Not any longer, although I don't think he ever was. Not really.

"So what is he?"

I run my hand through my hair. "We were just hooking up."

"You and Prescott," Rei muses, shaking her head. "I guess now that I look back, things are slowly starting to add up." She sobers. "Does he know?"

"Yeah," I nod. "He knows."

"And?" Penny urges. "What did he say?"

"Nothing. Prescott and I..." I shake my head. "It was just a fling. Temporary. That's all we ever could be. Temporary."

I don't miss the look Grace and Rei exchange.

"I thought we agreed not to make this weird?"

"We did, but..."

"But nothing. Prescott and I aren't together. We never really were, so there's that." I let out a shaky breath. "I'm sorry for snapping. It's just..."

"It's fine," Grace reassures me.

It's not, but I don't have it in me to contradict her.

"Can we please do something normal? Something that has nothing to do with cancer and random hookups?"

Or broken hearts.

At that moment, my stomach decides to let out a loud growl.

"Hungry?" Penny asks, chuckling.

"Maybe a little bit," I admit. "I wasn't really in the mood for food before."

"How about we order something in? And then we can

spend the rest of the afternoon lying here and watching Netflix."

"Yes, please." My stomach lets out another groan. "Although, maybe I should get something while we wait."

"I'll pick the movie!"

With a slight smile, I start to get up. Grace jumps to her feet, offering me her hand.

"We'll get through this," she whispers.

I nod, hoping that she's right.

Hoping by the end of this, I won't break any more hearts besides my own.

Chapter 5

PRESCOTT

"No."

A loud sob follows the statement. I look over my shoulder to partially closed doors where our parents went to talk to the doctors.

Dread spreads through me as the soft whimpers grow louder, making my stomach clench.

I tilt my head to the side, trying my best to overhear the soft murmuring, but it's impossible to do so from all the machines beeping around me.

"There has to be something that you can do!" Dad yells loud enough for us to hear him.

"Mr. Wentworth..." somebody, probably the doctor, says in a gentle voice. It should be soothing, but for whatever reason, it makes the bile rise in my throat.

A loud cough snaps me out of it, making me turn my attention to my brother.

"Gabby!" I slide my hand over his back, trying to keep my trembling hand steady. He's doubled over, his skinny shoulder shaking as he coughs for what feels like forever. "Are you okay? Do you need water or something?"

Gabriel shakes his head. "I don't want to die alone, Prescott."

I grab his hand, squeezing it for all it's worth. "You're not going to die. You're no—"

"We both know that's a lie. I'm not getting better."

I shake my head, refusing to accept it. My brother, my twin, cannot die. "You'll get better, Gabby. You'll get better, and we'll play football together like we planned. We'll go to school and flirt with the girls and..."

"You'll have to do it, Pres." The corner of Gabriel's lips lifts tentatively, but it's a weak smile at best. "You'll have to do it all for both of us."

"No." His cool hand slips out of my clammy palms, so I grab it again. "We'll do it. Together. You have to get better. You can't leave me."

My eyes start to burn with tears, so I close them tightly, not wanting to let them fall. Gabriel is the one lying in bed, the one that's been fighting this stupid disease. Not me. And he hasn't been crying.

"You can't leave me." I grip his hand tighter. "We promised."

When there is no answer, I open my eyes, and it's like I've been sucker punched. Because lying on that hospital bed, hand in hand isn't my brother, but Jade.

"No!" I sit upright and almost bump my head into Spencer's.

"What the fuck, Wentworth?" Spencer asks, watching me warily. "You're still drunk?"

I lean back down, running my shaky fingers over my sweaty face. My heart is still galloping in my chest, my breathing ragged from the nightmare I just had.

Jade.

Lying in a hospital bed.

Thin, weak, lifeless.

I have cancer.

"Fuck," I mutter just as Spencer pulls open the curtains. The sudden burst of light blinds me, making the throbbing behind my temples grow even stronger. "Close that shit."

"I'm not closing anything. It's five in the freaking afternoon," he says, opening the window. "And it freaking smells in here, and that's saying something." He turns to me, eyes wide, as if something just occurred to him. "Did you stay here all weekend?"

I get to my feet, swaying a little from the sudden movement. "I'm going to my room."

"You did, didn't you?" Spencer stops in front of me, crossing his arms over his chest. "What the fuck's going on, dude? First, you storm in like a tornado in the middle of the night, banging and smashing shit before closing yourself off, and now you spent the whole weekend drinking yourself to an early grave?"

Everything fades to the background except his last words.

An early grave.

Gabriel lying dead in his hospital bed.

Jade...

Pushing Spencer out of my way, I run down the hallway. The door to the bathroom is ajar, so I shove it open, drop down to my knees on the tiles, and throw up.

"Fucking hell, Wentworth," Spencer curses somewhere behind me.

My fingers wrap around the toilet seat as all the alcohol I've consumed the last couple of days comes out of me. Cold sweat spreads over my skin, my body shaky as my stomach rolls and tightens, trying to get everything out. That damn image is still stuck in my brain.

I'm not sure how long I stay doubled over the toilet. Once the puking stops, I press my sweaty forehead against my forearm, forcing myself to take a deep breath, which isn't the best option since the wave of nausea hits me all over again. Only this time, there is nothing else left in my stomach.

The faucet starts in the distance. I listen to the water run, trying to focus on it instead of the stench of the puke around me.

"You're a piece of work. You know that?" Spencer mutters before a cold towel hits me on the head.

I grab the towel and wipe my face, the cool cloth feeling good against my skin.

"Couldn't you have waited to be at practice before puking? We won't get this funk out of the bathroom for days."

Shit.

"What time is it?" I ask, already pushing to my feet.

Spencer looks at his wrist. "Five-ten, why?"

"Because Coach said he wants us at the facilities early."

"Look who finally decided to show up!" Sullivan snickers as all heads turn toward me, including the positively murderous glares from my coach and best friend—by now, probably my ex-best friend.

Great. Just great.

I open my mouth, ready to apologize, but Coach is faster. "You weren't so quick when you needed to read the Shark's line earlier, Sullivan."

The sharp words erase Sullivan's smile instantly, his face going beet red even in the dark room. All the murmuring dies down immediately.

"Coach," I say, clearing my throat.

"Get your ass in your seat, Wentworth." Coach turns around and erases the play from the board. "You're already late. You don't have to make us lose more precious time we could spend dissecting our next opponent's offensive line and the best way to breach it."

With a nod, I look around, trying my best to avoid Nixon's probing stare, which is impossible since the only open seat is the one next to him.

My usual seat, but still.

Fuck. My. Life.

Our gazes meet, and I can see the vein in his forehead throb, his fingers clenching and unclenching on the table as he glares at me.

"For every second you spend delaying, we'll add one more round of bleacher drills," Coach says, not even bothering to grace me with his attention.

A collective groan spreads through the room.

"One is not enough? Let's make it two, shall we?" He turns around. His arms crossed over his chest, and he taps his foot as he takes the team in, his eyes finally settling on mine. "Thirty-six, Wentworth."

Shit.

Quickly, I make my way to my seat. My duffle bag falls from my shoulder with a loud *thud* that has me flinching. Although I took some Advil before coming here, my head is still throbbing like a bitch from all the alcohol I drank over the weekend.

"Okay, now that that's settled..." Coach points the remote at the screen, and the play resumes.

For the next hour, we stay in the little room, going over the plays, analyzing them to the smallest of details as we form a plan of attack for our next game.

Stopping the video, Coach flicks on the light. I squint as a piercing pain goes through my skull at the sudden brightness.

"Suit up," Coach says, collecting his papers. "I expect you out on the field in ten minutes."

Chairs scrape against the hardwood as people start to get up and exit the room. I follow suit, my body protesting the movement.

Nixon walks past me, not once looking in my direction.

"What's up, Wentworth? You look a little bit green over there," Scotty chuckles. "Long night?"

"Fuck off, Scotty," I mutter, pushing past him and entering the locker room.

But does he listen? Of course not. He follows after me, going to his locker, and talking like I didn't say shit.

"What? Since when are you so secretive?"

"Lately, Wentworth's too good for us," Nate, our kicker, comments.

"Since he started hooking up with the mystery woman," Sullivan smirks, making my back stiffen.

A chorus of hollers and catcalls spreads through the room, making my headache worse.

Great, just great.

"There is no mystery woman."

"Oh, I don't know. You two seemed pretty cozy at the party a few weeks back."

I open my mouth to tell him where he can shove his assumptions when there is a loud *bang*.

All the voices die down as we turn around to find a pissed-off Nixon glaring at us. "Shut up and get your asses to work." His eyes meet mine and hold. "Thanks to a certain somebody, Coach is annoyed enough as it is, and you don't want to piss him off even more."

"He ain't the only one who's pissed, apparently," Scotty mutters. "What crawled up your ass, Cole? Wife didn't give it up last night?"

Nixon's death glare moves from me to the linebacker. "Scotty, the next time you bring up my wife, I'll make sure there's nothing left of your head to get it out of your ass. Am I clear?"

Scotty shakes his head and turns to his locker. "Whatever, dude."

Hoisting my duffle bag higher, I go to my locker.

"I don't get why you're pissed at us," Sullivan says. "If I remember correctly, we were all there on time. It's not our fault that Wentworth was too busy screwing around to pay attention to time."

"I wasn't screwing around. I was..." My words trail off when I realize saying that I was passed out drunk doesn't sound any better. As a senior and one of the co-captains, I was supposed to set an example for the rest of the team. "Otherwise indisposed," I finish lamely.

"Hear that, boys? Wentworth was otherwise indisposed." Sullivan makes the air quotes and shakes his head. "Will you be otherwise indisposed when we're playing our next game? How about the championship game?"

I grit my teeth. "I was just a few minutes late. *Once*." I put in my combination and yank open my locker with more force than necessary. "I know you'd like me not to show up since that's the only way you'd be able to play, but don't worry, it won't happen anytime soon."

If I dropped a bomb, the silence that followed would be less deafening. But I was so fucking done with Sullivan and his constant jabs. He wants my spot? He better damn well take it because I wasn't handing it to him.

Grabbing the back of my shirt, I pull it over my head and throw it into my locker before grabbing my jersey.

"You sure?" Nixon asks. His voice is soft, so only I can hear it, but I don't miss the edge in his voice.

Putting the shoulder pads on, I slide my jersey over my head before I turn to look at my best friend. "What the fuck does that mean?"

Nixon shrugs, closing his locker. "Just that you're good at turning your back and walking away."

I clench my jaw. I guess it was only a matter of time before he brought it up.

"You don't know what you're talking about."

Nixon chuckles humorlessly, "Don't I?" He takes a step closer, his voice dropping lower. "Because the last time I saw you, I found out you have no problem fucking my sister—*my baby sister*—behind my back, but you sure don't mind walking away when things get tough."

Hushed murmurs spread through the locker room faster than a wildfire, but neither of us pays them any attention.

My fingers ball into fists by my sides. "She let me go."

"So that makes it fucking okay?" He grabs my jersey, pulling me to him and getting all up in my face.

I don't bother fighting him because I know he has every right to be pissed at me. I'm surprised it took him so long to come for me. I was expecting him to come find me that same day and beat the ever-loving crap out of me. I wouldn't have even tried to stop it. I'd relish it, really. Only the knock on my door never came, and a part of me hated him for it, not nearly as much as I hated myself for walking away, though.

Maybe if he had done it, I wouldn't feel this guilty now.

As if that's even possible.

"Say something, dammit." Nixon shakes me, his eyes, that same blue shade of the stormy sky as his sister's, blazing at me. "Give me one good reason why I shouldn't punch you right this moment for breaking her heart."

I have cancer.

I press my lips in a tight line, not uttering a word.

There isn't one. There is no sense pretending there is.

The vein in Nixon's forehead starts to tick, his eyes darkening the longer he glares at me.

I have cancer.

"C'mon, Cole. Do it," I taunt him. *Punch me. Punish me for walking away. For breaking Jade's heart.* "We both know you want to."

Nixon shakes his head. "You're one sick son of a bitch."

I run my fingers through my hair. "One sick son of a bitch that screwed your littl—"

I don't get to finish because Nixon's fist connects with my face. My head snaps back, a coppery taste filling my mouth. I can hear ringing in my ears. My tongue slides over my lower lip. It feels tender to the touch, blood seeping from the split.

Slowly turning around, I find Nixon watching me. He's panting, his fingers clenching and unclenching by his sides as he tries to rein in his rage.

I let out a small chuckle, "That's the best you've got?"

If I weren't living in my own personal hell, I'd have gone there for this.

My words finally make my best friend snap, and he goes at me with full force. His fist connects to my gut, making me double over as Nixon keeps punching me.

I don't bother stopping him or defending myself.

There's commotion in the locker room. I can hear our teammates cursing and see shadows fall over us as guys try to pull Nixon back, but he's like a wild bull.

"What the hell is going on in here?" Coach bellows just as two linebackers haul Nixon away from me. Blinking a few times, I look up at Coach, who's scanning the locker room, waiting for somebody to explain, but all heads are ducked. His gaze falls on me before it shifts to still panting Nixon. "Cole! Wentworth! My office." His voice drops dangerously low. "Now. The rest of you get your asses to the field."

Without waiting for us, Coach turns on the balls of his feet and stalks out of the locker room.

Groaning, I push to my feet, gripping the metal door for support. My stomach is sore, my head is throbbing at full force, and I can feel my eye starting to swell shut.

The guys let go of Nixon. His hands are still clenched, his knuckles bloodied and bruised. We must make a pretty pair.

The locker room is so quiet you could hear a pin drop. Some of our teammates look at us warily as if they're waiting for us to pounce at each other all over again.

With the back of my hand, I wipe my mouth. "You heard the old man. Get your asses out on the field."

With that, I push from the locker and go toward the door. Nixon follows after me, neither of us saying a word as we make our way to the coach's office.

His head snaps up the moment he hears us, eyes narrowing into tiny slits.

"What the fuck was that? Why are my two-star players—the captain and co-captain of my team—at each other's throats, throwing punches like they're in some bar brawl?" he asks, his voice rising with every word until he's yelling, his whole face beet red from exertion.

We both keep our mouths shut, gazes locked on the wall behind him. Coach looks from Nixon to me, his jaw working as he grits his teeth.

"Cat got your tongue?" he taunts. "I should bench both of your asses for the next game. Show you what happens when you fight in my locker room."

My stomach tightens at the idea.

The silence stretches, neither of us budging under his penetrating gaze.

Coach shakes his head in disgust. "But that would hurt the team and me more than it would hurt you." After a few more moments, he lets out a dark chuckle. "Fine, have it your way. You're both cleaning the locker room for the next month. And that's just for starters. But before that, I want to see you out on the field. Bleacher suicides. Two hundred each of you. And you better not stop because the moment you do, you'll start counting again." He shifts his gaze from Nixon to me and back. "*Both of you.*"

Nixon opens his mouth as if he's about to protest but changes his mind at the last second.

Coach lifts one of his brows as if he's daring us to say anything. When we don't, he tips his chin toward the door.

"Off with you two."

Chapter 6

JADE

The black screen of the phone beckons me as I stare at it from across the bed. Like I've been doing for the past thirty minutes. As if it's a snake, and I'm just waiting for it to attack me.

"Don't be a wuss, Jade," I mutter, cracking my neck to relieve the pressure in my shoulders. The tension that's been building there ever since Nixon walked into my room.

Okay, that might not be entirely fair. Yes, Nixon pissed me off and continued to do so over the weekend with his constant calls and text messages, but if I'm completely honest, he wasn't the only reason for this tension, nor the cause.

It was the fact that I have cancer.

Now, if only I could confirm it, and be done with this unknown that's messing with my head.

Inhaling deeply, I force my hand to extend. Wrapping my fingers around my phone, I unlock the screen and go to my contacts, dialing before I can chicken out.

My heart is beating so loudly that I can barely hear the *beeping* as I press the phone to my ear.

"Massachusetts General, oncology department, how may I help you?" asks the perky voice from the other side of the line.

"Can I talk to Doctor Hendriks?"

My fingers are gripping the phone tightly as I wait for the answer. I've been putting this call off for as long as possible, but I can't postpone it anymore.

"Who's asking?" the receptionist loudly asks so I can hear him over the noises of the hospital.

"Jade Cole."

"Wait a second."

"Sure thing," I say softly, but he's already put me on hold.

I let out a shaky breath as I try to calm my nerves.

Breathe, Jade. Just... breathe.

But it's easier said than done. Thankfully, I don't have to wait too long before the line picks up again, and the familiar voice of Dr. Hendriks comes through the speaker. "What can I do for you, Jade?"

"Hey, Dr. Hendriks. Sorry for bothering you, but..." I slide my tongue over my dry lips before letting it all out. I tell her about the bruises and bumps in my armpit and about the lump on my breast. She quietly listens until I get it all out in the open.

"I see. Okay, here's what we'll do..."

There's a soft clicking of the keyboard in the distance. "How about you come and see me tomorrow? I'll have a look, and we'll run some tests, okay?"

"Tomorrow." I nod my head, although she can't see me. "Okay. I'll see you then."

I hang up, my hand shaking as I gently put my phone on the nightstand before running my fingers through my hair.

Tomorrow.

I'm unsure if I'm more nervous now that I have an appointment or when I didn't know anything. Both are a different form of hell.

Shaking my head, I make my way to the kitchen. The apartment is quiet since Rei flew out for her competition, and Grace has a class. This is the reason why I called my doctor now.

I didn't want to risk my friends overhearing my conversation. Silly, since it's not like they don't know. But ever since I told them, they've looked at me like they're either waiting for me to flip out or fall apart. I couldn't deal with their worry on top of my own.

My thoughts trail off as I open the fridge, taking in the contents, which aren't that many. I grab a can of Diet Coke, but my gaze falls on the half bottle of Jack hidden behind it. My fingers tighten around the door handle.

I could pull it out, get shit-faced and call it a day. Maybe that way, I'll actually be able to fall asleep for once. Maybe...

"Jade?"

A hand touches my shoulder, startling me. I jump back only to find Grace looking at me. "Shit. I didn't hear you."

"I figured that out," Grace chuckles. "You planning to take anything else from the fridge, or will you just keep staring at it?" She tilts her head to the side, one short, red lock slipping into her face, but she brushes it away.

I shake my head, closing the fridge and turning my back to the temptation—this time, at least. "I just spaced out for a bit." I force out a smile. "How was your class?"

"Good. Tiring. Remind me why I scheduled my classes early in the morning?"

"Because you are crazy?" I pop open the can and take a sip of Coke, letting the cool drink slide down my throat.

"Optimistic," she corrects. "I usually don't mind it, but this weekend was crazy busy. How are you? Did you—"

I give her a pointed look. "I'm fine."

"I'm sorry, it's just that..." She tucks a strand of her hair behind her ear. "I can't stop worrying."

"See now why I kept quiet? Things change when people

know you're sick."

"*Might.*" She points her finger at me. "When you *might* be sick. You haven't been to a doctor yet, so you don't know for sure if that's true or not."

"It's true, Grace." There were no mights here. Just the delayed truth. "I don't want you to get your hopes up."

I don't want to get *my* hopes up.

"Well, go to the doctor, so we know for sure."

That was the plan. A plan I didn't want to talk about. Finishing my drink, I squeeze the can, making the metal crunch. "I should go get ready for my class." Throwing the empty soda in the bin, I start for the door. "See you later?"

"Call the damn doctor, Jade!"

"Well, look who's still alive."

My back stiffens at the hard voice as I pull to a stop and slowly turn around to come face-to-face with a clearly pissed-off Marcus.

Then again, after what I'd pulled on him the other day, I can't even blame him.

"I'm still standing." I force out a smile, but I can feel the corner of my mouth twitch in pain. My lip was still tender, but at least I could open my eye fully, and the bruises have slowly started to fade.

"The last thing I remember is you were passed out in the passenger's seat of my car." Marcus takes a step closer, his finger slipping under my chin. He tilts my head back, inspecting my face.

I put some foundation on this morning before leaving the house. Lots and lots of foundation. It helped somewhat, but some of the darkest bruises were still pretty visible.

Marcus shakes his head, letting his hand drop by his side. "What the hell were you thinking, Jade?"

I was thinking that I wanted to forget.

It didn't matter how I would accomplish it, or who'd end up hurt in the process. I needed this pain to go away.

"I'm sorry for dragging you into this, Marcus. I should have never done it."

"Hell to the no. If I hadn't been there, who'd have dragged your bloody ass back home? But that was some pretty messed up shit you pulled."

"I'm sorry," I whisper, and I really mean it. The last thing I wanted was to worry my friends. That was the whole point of me keeping it a secret in the first place. Not that it did me much good.

"Well, I'm glad you're in one piece. Just don't do it again."

"No more pit fights. I promise."

"Good."

His phone chimes, drawing his attention. He pulls it out, checking the screen, before sliding it into his pocket once again. "I have to go. James is waiting for me."

"Say hi to him for me."

"Will do. I'll see you soon?"

"You know it."

"Try not to get into any more trouble!" He calls over his shoulder as he starts walking in the opposite direction.

With a shake of my head, I continue toward the cafeteria. The place is filled with students, so I get in line to wait. I pull out my phone, scrolling through my social media, when a hand falls on my shoulder, startling me.

"Have you called your doctor?"

I turn around and glare at my brother. "Hey, Nixon. It's so good to see you too," I mutter dryly. "I'm fine. How are you?"

"Don't be sassy with me, Smalls. Did you, or did you not, call your doctor?"

Huffing, I move down the line and grab a turkey sandwich, and put it on my tray, although I've already lost my appetite. "I've called my doctor."

"And?" he prompts as we continue down the line.

"And," I drawl, looking pointedly around us. "I don't want to talk about it. Not here."

I'd prefer not to talk about it at all, but I don't think that will go over well.

The frown between his brows deepens. "You know you won't be able to hide it forever. If it's..."

"There is no if, Nixon," I interrupt him before he can finish. "Only when. Can't I have at least that under my control? Can't I at least choose when and how I'm going to tell people?" He had already forced my hand once, and I didn't want it to happen again. It was hard enough to have my friends look at me like I might die at any moment.

He shifts his tray into one hand and rubs his jaw, my eyes falling to the scrapes on his knuckles. "Because that went so well with me."

He's right, of course. I knew when Nixon found us that he would have killed Prescott. For being with me. For lying to him. Telling him—telling *them*—I have cancer was rash and reckless, but it did the trick.

None of this was Prescott's fault.

Being with him was as much my choice as it was his, and I wouldn't change a damn thing about it.

Not a damn thing.

Blinking, I return to the present.

"It doesn't matter anyway. What's done is done. I don't want anybody else to know. Not until I have some answers of my own."

Not until I know if I'm dying.

I narrow my gaze at his hands. Not just scrapes, but his knuckles are raw. "What happened to your hand?"

Nixon looks down at his hands for a beat as if he's surprised by the question. "Rough practice," he shrugs before changing the subject. "What did the doctor tell you?"

I let out a frustrated sigh. Sometimes he can be like a dog with a bone. "She told me to come to her office tomorrow. She wants to see me and run some tests."

"Okay, I have a class in the morning, but I think I can skip it, and—"

Skip it?

"Hell, no. You're not skipping shit." With a shake of my head, I turn on the balls of my feet and go to the register.

"Jade," Nixon calls after me, but I don't bother turning around. "You can't ignore this forever."

I can damn well try.

And try I do.

Not that it's easy to ignore my brother's looming height over me, but I'm adamant about doing it. Thankfully he doesn't say anything else—a small blessing since he's known to be a nosey and bossy asshole more often than not.

Aimlessly, I look for an available table, but Nixon nudges me in the opposite direction. "Yas is over there," he tips his chin, and sure enough, Yasmin and Callie are sitting opposite one another, chatting and laughing.

Yasmin is the first who notices us, but the moment she sees me, that smile falls.

"You told her!" I hiss, glaring at my brother in accusation.

"Of course, I told her! She's my *wife.* Besides, it's not like she wouldn't have figured out that something was wrong when I came home upset." Nixon shrugs. "It's fine."

No, it isn't fine, but before I could fight with him about it,

Nixon walks past me and sits down next to her, pressing a kiss to the top of her head. "Hey, babe. Who are you two gossiping about?"

Letting out a shaky breath, I join them at the table, Yasmin's eyes following my every move.

"Nobody."

"Really?" Nixon quirks a brow. "The conversation seemed to die really quickly the moment we sat down. Gossiping about me, wife?"

Yasmin rolls her eyes. "Not everything is about you."

Nixon wiggles his brows. "You didn't say that last night."

I make a gagging noise. "Can we not? Some of us are trying to eat."

"I agree with Jade here," Callie chimes in.

I open my sandwich halfheartedly. My appetite has been down the last few days. My stomach is too wound up to even think about food, much less attempt to eat it.

"Don't try playing nice now. You're just saying that since Hayden's not here."

"Guilty as charged," Callie sighs. "And I just got back."

"Any idea when you'll see each other again?" Yas asks.

"Probably not before Thanksgiving. Football season is in full swing, and with midterms approaching, I don't think I'll have time to drive to his place. But enough about me, what about you, Jade? Found any nice guys?"

I let out a surprised chuckle at her question. "No way."

Nobody would ever describe Prescott as a *nice* guy. Not that he's my guy. Or my anything, really.

My brother lets out a snort. "As if she would ever settle for a nice guy."

I glare at him across the table, but he conveniently ignores me.

Callie looks between the two of us, clearly confused. "Why

not?"

"I don't have time for guys," I shrug, slipping a strand of my hair behind my ear.

Which is true...In a way. I don't have time for guys. Especially for *nice* guys. What would I do with a guy like Maddox? I'm too jaded for somebody like that. Too broken. Too...

I look up, my eyes scanning the busy room. I'm not sure what I'm looking for until I see it.

See *him*.

It's as if the air's been kicked out of my lungs. I would have probably been knocked on my ass if I hadn't been seated.

Days.

It's been three days since I saw him. Since I've heard his voice. Since he walked away. Since I let him.

I wanted to pick up my phone and call him so many times. Hell, I'd even settle for a text. I needed to explain everything to him so badly, but I knew there wouldn't be a point. Knowing what I knew, I understood there wasn't any chance for us.

I don't want there to be a chance for us.

I'm sick with a similar illness to the one that took his brother. Prescott went through too much as it is. He doesn't deserve to do it all over again.

He already saw one person he loved die. He shouldn't have to go through it all over again.

He never said he loved you.

Maybe, but I love him too much to put him through it. I'm not sure exactly when it happened or how it happened, but it's true. I'm in love with my brother's best friend, and there is no escaping it.

Prescott turns his head. It's like there's a pull between us because his eyes find mine instantly like he knew just where to look, where to find me.

And for the second time today, I'm left breathless.

Not because of the piercing heat of those dark eyes as they settle on mine.

But because of the dark bruises marring his face.

One of his eyes is half closed, and his lip is split open.

Nixon's scraped knuckles pop into my mind.

Rough practice.

The same practice where Prescott is every freaking day.

"Nixon?" I ask slowly, my gaze still holding onto Prescott's, unwilling to let go.

"Yeah?"

"What happened to your hands?" I ask once again. My voice is unusually still, almost detached.

Nixon must feel something's off because he turns to me. "I told you, it was a ro—"

"What. Happened. To. Your. Hands?" I ask slowly, forcing myself to turn around and face him. My fingers curl into fists on the table, all the pretense that I'm interested in finishing my lunch gone.

Nixon looks around, searching for the cause of my anger. I know the exact moment he finds Prescott. His shoulders stiffen, lips pressing into a tight line. "Fuck." Nixon runs his fingers through his hair. "Smalls, I..."

"This is the last time I'll ask, Nixon. What happened to your hands?"

He lets out a sigh, "You know what happened."

Of course I do.

"I want you to say it."

"I punched Wentworth." He lifts his hands in the air defensively. "Is that what you wanted to hear? I punched my best friend—my *ex*-best friend—for sleeping with my little sister behind my back and walking away from her. Are you happy now?"

"You had no right!" I hiss, pushing to my feet. The chair

scrapes loudly against the floor, drawing attention to us.

"No right? He was fucking around with you behind my back..."

"I was fucking around with him too!" I yell. "Are you going to punch me too?"

Nixon pulls back, entirely appalled by the idea. "You know I'd never..."

"Then why do the same to him? What's the difference? I told you, Nixon. I told you to leave him out of it. You promised!"

"You are my baby sister."

"And it was my choice. He was my choice. You had no—"

"He left you!" Nixon gets to his feet and tries to reach for me, but I pull back. I don't want him touching me.

"You didn't see me trying to stop him, now, did you? I told you to leave it alone. I told you to leave *him* alone." I shake my head. "You had *no* right."

Tears threaten to escape, so I bite the inside of my cheek. I can feel the coppery taste on my tongue.

"Smalls..."

I shake my head, noticing Yasmin and Callie watching us with wide eyes. "I'm done here."

I grab my backpack and throw it over my shoulder. Before Nixon can say anything else, I turn around and get the hell out of the cafeteria.

But not before I find Prescott watching me. He's standing in front of his table, clearly conflicted about what to do. My steps falter as I drink him in. The need to go to him and curl my arms around him is almost overwhelming. I want to feel those strong arms wrapped around me, feel his familiar scent, and make sure that he's okay. Have him reassure me everything will be fine.

But it would all be a lie.

So instead, I look away and walk out of there without a backward glance.

Chapter 7

PRESCOTT

Letting Jade walk out of the cafeteria is probably one of the hardest things I've ever done.

Even after everything she did, after she kept shit from me, the pull between us was undeniable.

Seeing her completely threw me off. I don't know why. I knew it was just a matter of time. It's not like I could have avoided her forever. We're on the same campus. We live in the same building, for fuck's sake. There was no avoiding her.

I have cancer.

For how long, though?

For how long would she still be here?

Days? Weeks? Months? Years?

How long did she have before cancer took her too?

My gaze darts to Nixon, who's still standing by their table, his eyes locked on the door that Jade just disappeared behind. He must feel me watching him because he slowly turns around, our gazes meeting across the room. My fingers grip the tray tighter as I watch my best friend; defeat, guilt, and fear written all over his face.

I'm not sure how long we stare at one another before Yasmin

elbows Nixon, drawing his attention. Her mouth is moving quickly, and a part of me feels bad for him.

"Wentworth!" I turn around at the sound of my name to find a few guys from my chem class observing me. "You plan on standing there the whole day or what?"

I shake my head, sitting down next to Spencer, who's watching me with interest. He got to the cafeteria shortly after us and managed to charm his way into cutting the line so he could join us.

"Mind explaining what the hell that was?" he asks, quietly enough so only I can hear him. Not that it's necessary since the rest of our group starts talking about the pop quiz we just had—a pop quiz I most likely failed since I hardly opened the book—and barely pay us any attention.

"Explain what?" I ask, digging into my food. I'm not hungry, but it seems like a safer choice than looking at my friend.

"Oh, I don't know. Maybe we should start with the bruises on your ugly mug?" From the corner of my eye, I can see him tapping his finger against his chin. "Or I don't know. Why you've avoided going to your best friend's table?"

There is a beat of silence as he waits for me to answer, but when I don't, he continues.

"Or maybe," he drawls slowly. "How about why you looked at your best friend's sister like a sad puppy waiting for his owner to return?"

My head snaps up before I can think better of it. "You don't know what you're talking about."

"Don't I?" Spencer slowly raises his brow. "Did you seriously think I didn't see the woman sleeping in your bed that morning?"

My stomach tightens at his words.

He knew? All this time, he knew, and he didn't say anything?

"Not that I needed to see your naked asses because it was

plain as day to everyone who looked at you two that something was going on with all the bickering and heated glances across the table."

Were we really that obvious?

"We always fight. It's not like it's something new."

"Oh, you do. You became sloppier in hiding how much it turned you on when you two fought once you started hooking up. Seriously, dude. I don't know how Cole didn't see it at that party. You practically jumped her in the middle of our living room." Spencer shakes his head and dips his fry in ketchup. "I thought you had better moves than that. I presume Nixon finally found out?"

I press my lips in a tight line, refusing to say a word, but Spencer continues without missing a beat.

"I figured as much with you moping around, drinking your weight in alcohol, and all that jazz. By the way, that bottle you broke? You owe me a new one. That whiskey was too good to throw away. Oh, and you'll explain to our landlord the brown stain on the wall also."

"I'll do whatever the hell you want if you shut the fuck up." I jab my fork into the steak with more force than necessary.

"Where's the fun in that?" he chuckles.

I shove a piece of meat into my mouth, chewing loudly, although the beef tastes like rubber.

"Who'd have thought? Mighty Prescott Wentworth was brought down to his knees by his best friend's little sister."

He's not wrong. She did bring me to my knees, just not how he imagined it.

I have cancer.

I stand up abruptly, the fork falling out of my hand with a loud *clack* that has all the heads around the table turning.

"I'm not hungry. I think I'll just go to the gym instead."

"Prescott..." Spencer tries to call after me, but I'm already grabbing my things and leaving without a backward glance.

Cursing silently, I grab the gym towel and toss it into the hamper I'm carrying. There's no way I'll put my hands on another player's shit for longer than necessary. I knew some of my teammates were nasty assholes, but this is another level because I was pretty sure that brown smudge on one of the towels wasn't dirt.

Trying not to gag, I go back into the locker room. The place is quiet since everybody has left already.

The door opens, and Nixon walks in.

Well, except him.

He looks at the hamper. "Done?"

"Just about."

"The equipment is all stored away, so I'm out of here."

A grunt is my only response. Nixon picks up his duffle bag and throws it over his shoulder, disappearing out the door without another word.

Because that's our relationship now.

Talking only when absolutely necessary.

I knew we would have to have it out soon because our game was off, and it showed. Coach was angry and had us running bleacher drills for the second day in a row. Our teammates were pissed, but that was the least of my worries.

Shaking my head, I go toward the washing room, dropping off the hamper with dirty clothes. Then I grab my stuff and get the hell out of there.

A part of me is grateful that I'm the only one around because my leg is killing me. And that's after I've been icing it for a good thirty minutes after practice. Between the gym and training, I'm spent, so I drag my aching body to my car, going straight for the compartment and grabbing the pain meds. I open the lid, one lone tablet sliding into my palm.

"Shit." Running my free hand over my face, I look at the only thing that's my lifeline at the moment. "Shit."

Throwing my head back, I swallow the pill. My hand falls down, and I grip the steering wheel as I force myself to breathe.

I could always take an Advil or something else for the pain.

It's not going to cut it. It never does.

Starting the car, I press my foot hard on the gas, speeding toward home, trying to focus on anything but the pain. The drive takes about twenty minutes, with a pit stop at the store so I can get Spencer off my ass about spilling his precious booze. As I kill the engine, I lean back in my seat, my gaze going straight for the building in front of me, zeroing in on the only open window.

The dim light shines through the curtains signaling that she's home, and once again, I'm hit with that mix of pain and anger at Jade.

Because she lied to me. Because she knew. She knew about Gabriel, and still, she didn't say anything. Because I opened up to her, I told her something that I hadn't told anybody else, and she... she didn't.

She fucking didn't.

She made me feel, she made me open up and fucking feel, and now she'll be gone.

Just like Gabriel is gone.

Gritting my teeth, I reach for the whiskey on the passenger seat and crack open the lid, taking a pull directly from the bottle, my gaze still on that damn window.

On the shadow moving behind it.

Like a freaking ghost.

Chapter 8

JADE

Closing the book, I lean my head back and pinch the bridge of my nose. The headache that's been building for the better part of the day is now in full force, making me wish I could pull my hair out. I should probably call it a day and try to get some sleep before tomorrow's appointment, but I'm not sure I can. I'm not sure I can face my nightmares once again.

A shower.

That's what I need.

A shower to help me rela—

The window rattles as a shadow appears in the frame. No, not a shadow.

Prescott.

My heart kicks up at the sight of him, the ache so strong that it leaves me breathless.

Except for that little glimpse of him I got when I was in the cafeteria, I haven't seen him since he stormed out of my room after I spilled my secrets.

He watches me from across the room, his chest rapidly rising and falling as he tries to slow down his breathing.

He looks awful. His eye is open, but an ugly purple-blue

bruise surrounds it. His lip is still pretty swollen, and the dark circles under his bloodshot eyes match mine. He runs his fingers through his hair, mussing it.

Wild and untamed.

That's what he is.

And I want him.

I want him with all of his wild and broken pieces.

"How long?"

I pull my brows together, surprised by the sound of his rough voice. Surprised by the fact that he was actually talking to me. "What?"

"How long have you been lying to me?"

"Prescott, I..."

"I need to know. I need to know if this was all a fucking game to you..."

I scoot off the bed, needing to be closer to him. Needing to do something to take away his pain. "It wasn't a game."

"What was it then, Jade?" Prescott moves closer, his fingers balled into fists by his sides as he looms over me. "Just a hookup? Screw your brother's best friend behind his back for fun? Well, you screwed me over and screwed me well."

"I didn't hear you complain!" I yell back, shoving at his chest just as the door of my room opens, and Grace appears in the doorway.

"What is goin— Oh." Her gaze bounces from me to Prescott and back. "Wait, how did he get in here?"

"Window," I mutter, still glaring at the man in question.

"Win—" Her green eyes turn into saucers as she switches her gaze to said window. "I guess that explains a lot. Are you okay? I heard yelling and didn't know what was going on. Do you want me to stay?"

I shake my head. "I'm fine."

"Well, if you need me... just yell." She goes to the doorway but holds back, her eyes narrowing on Prescott. "You hurt her; I'll kill you."

Not waiting for his answer, she leaves the room, closing the door behind her.

"Can't hurt somebody who doesn't have a heart," Prescott says softly.

"I don't have a heart?" I scoff, shaking my head. "Then what are you doing here? Why don't you just leave? After all, that's what you're best at."

"Because I can't stop thinking about it. Because that day and your words ring in my head repeatedly, and no matter what I do, I can't push it out of my mind. Because I need some fucking answers so I can move on. I—"

"Oh, you didn't seem to have any problem moving on. You ran out of here before any of us could blink."

"You have cancer!" Prescott shouts. His hands land on my shoulders, giving me a firm shake. "What the hell do you want me to do?"

"Nothing!" I shove his hands away, turning my back to him. "I don't want anything from you, so you can..."

"You're not leaving." He grabs my hand, tugging me back.

Gabriel, don't go. Don't leave me.

I turn around, my chest crashing into his and kicking all the air out of my lungs. His hands slide to my shoulders, fingers digging into my skin as he shakes me. His pupils are dilated, and he looks wild. Wild and scared, and nothing like the man I've gotten to know these last few weeks.

"You can't leave me," he repeats, and something inside me breaks just as his mouth crashes on mine.

The kiss has no finesse, no gentleness, just pure, aching need. He grips my face as his mouth ravages mine. My fingers slide into his hair, pulling him closer to me. Prescott shoves his tongue into my mouth as his hands roam my body. Grabbing my shirt, he tugs it up. We break the kiss, both of us panting hard as he pulls my shirt over my head and tosses it on the floor; I do the same with his. We're a mess of limbs as we get the rest of our clothes off, and then we're on my bed.

He trails kisses all over my body, goosebumps rising in his wake. When his palms slide over my sides, I pull him back up, my mouth meeting his as my legs spread to fit his hips between mine. His hard length presses against me, making me suck in a breath as my hips lift, and I rub against him.

"Fuck, Jade," Prescott mutters as he slides between my folds easily. "We can't keep on doing this."

"No, we can't," I agree. I cup his face, my forehead pressing against his. Neither of us attempts to move back. His hands seize my hips, rolling them against him and torturing us. So close. So freaking close, yet, so far away.

"One last time," I whisper, my throat bobbing as I swallow. "We can't keep doing this, but we can have tonight. One last time."

One more borrowed moment.

Because that's all we'll ever get to have.

Borrowed moments.

"One last time."

With that, he slides into me. My breath hitches as he fills me, a shudder running through me at the fullness.

No matter what happens from here on out, I know for certain there will never be anyone like him. No one will make me feel the way Prescott Wentworth does.

Tears burn my eyelids, so I close them shut, focusing on the pleasure spreading through me as I meet him thrust for thrust. Our mouths lock, tongues tangling together as we chase the high.

And then we're falling, hard and fast.

The sound of our heavy breathing is the only thing that fills the silence. I half expect him to push me away and get the hell out of here, but his arms tighten around me, pulling me closer.

Leaning my head on his chest, I drink in his nearness as my eyelids start to turn heavy.

"I wouldn't have done it," I whisper, the confession slipping from my tongue as I slowly drift to sleep. "If I knew about Gabriel from the beginning, I would have never let this thing between us go so far. It was never my intention to hurt you."

The persistent buzzing wakes me up from a deep slumber. Blindly I reach for my phone, turning off the irritating noise and burying my head deeper into the pillow, that familiar citrusy scent filling my senses.

Last night flashes in my mind.

Prescott sneaking through my window.

Fight.

Sex.

Falling asleep in his arms.

My eyes snap open as my heart kicks into overdrive. I turn my head to the side, expecting to find Prescott's sleeping face next to me, but the bed is empty.

Disappointment slams into me as I run my hand over the cool sheets.

"He left."

He left like a thief in the night, the only sign that he was even here was his faint scent still lingering on the bedsheets.

Another alarm starts to chime, signaling that I really need to get going if I don't want to be late for my appointment. Pushing the thoughts of Prescott to the back of my mind, I get to my feet and quickly go to the bathroom.

Twenty minutes later, I'm dressed and rushing down the

stairs. Letting the door close behind me, I fish inside my bag for the key to Grace's car. She didn't think twice when I asked her if I could borrow it. Now, if only I could find the damn...

"There you are," I mutter to myself as I find them conveniently—of course—at the bottom of my bag. Keys clutched in my hands, I look up and stop in my tracks when I see my brother leaning against the hood of his black BMW.

"What are you doing here?"

I'm still pissed at what he did the other day. He had no right to get into it with Prescott. None whatsoever. Especially after I specifically asked him not to.

"You can be angry with me all you want, Smalls." Nixon pushes off the hood and opens the driver's side door. "But you're not doing this alone."

"I already have a ride." My fingers clench around the key in my palm, the cool metal digging into my skin.

Nixon looks at me over his shoulder. He works his jaw, teeth grinding. I expect him to protest, but he closes the door. "Fine. You can drive then."

I bite the inside of my cheek.

I didn't want anybody to go with me. It felt easier to go on my own and face this on my terms, but I also couldn't deny that a part of me felt relief at seeing Nixon here.

Nixon looks around. "Where's the car?"

Letting out a shaky breath, I walk toward him and pull the key out of his hand. "I guess this will do," I mutter as I go to the driver's side.

"Of course it will," he groans but doesn't try to stop me. Instead, he goes to the passenger's side and slides inside while I finish adjusting the seat.

We don't say much on the drive into the city. My whole body is tense, fingers gripping the steering wheel as I navigate the car through the busy Boston streets. Although I've managed to get a few peaceful hours of sleep with Prescott's arms holding me last night, I'm still bone tired. Keeping busy is a good diversion; I need all the distractions I can get so I don't overthink about what's to come.

As soon as we get to the hospital, I'm hit by the scent of antiseptic and sickness. My stomach clenches with nerves, bile rising in my throat as the memories of all the times I've been here in the last two years come back to haunt me. So many appointments, needles, tests, and trials. All for nothing.

Forcing myself to put one foot in front of the other, we make our way down the hallway to the doctor's office.

I'm not sure how long we wait until the door opens, and they call my name.

Nixon gently places his hand on the small of my back. "It's going to be okay," he whispers.

He's wrong, though.

After today, nothing will ever be the same again.

Chapter 9

JADE

"I have your results." Dr. Hendriks enters the room, a file in her hand. She's in her late fifties, I think. Her light blonde hair, streaked with grays, is pulled in chignon, and glasses are perched on the bridge of her nose. She had been Mom's doctor as she fought cancer.

Fought and lost, a voice reminds me.

With a shake of my head, I push it back, not wanting to go there. Not yet. Not until I find out what's hiding in that file.

I was exhausted from all the probing and tests they ran today, but now was finally the moment of truth.

My throat bobs as nervousness slams into me, making my palms sweaty. I shift in my seat, tucking my hands under my thighs to prevent them from trembling.

"There's good news, and there's bad news." Dr. Hendriks looks up. "Which one do you want to hear first?"

"Bad," I say; at the same time, Nixon interjects: "Good."

We look at each other, and I give him a warning glare. I only agreed to let him sit in on this because I knew he'd drive me more insane with his meddling if he weren't here. But also because some part of me wasn't sure I could do this alone. Not that I'd ever admit it to Nixon.

"Okay," Dr. Hendriks places the folder on her desk, folding her hands over them as she faces me head-on, her dark brown eyes staring into mine. I remember that from all those visits I did with Mom. I liked her directness and no-nonsense attitude, but also her kindness. "The mass in your breast is a tumor, Jade."

My eyes fall shut as her gentle words slam into me like a tsunami.

I'm not even surprised; since the moment I noticed the first bruise and lumps in my underarm weeks ago, I've known it. I tried to push it back and run away from it, but there is only so far you can run before it catches up with you.

"Can we get a second opinion?" Nixon asks, breaking the silence.

"We don't need a second opinion," I say softly. Blinking my eyes open, I bite the inside of my cheek.

I will not cry.

I chant those words, focusing instead on the pain, and face my doctor. "What's the verdict? What are my options?"

"Well, the bad news is..."

"I thought the fact that I have cancer was the bad news," I huff out a laugh. Things were getting better and better.

"It's part of the bad news, yes. The other part is that the biopsy has shown that the mass is malignant."

"Malignant?" Nixon looks at me before switching his attention to Dr. Hendriks.

"That's why it grew since I first noticed it. Not a lot, but..." My words trail off as my voice grows weaker, the emotions swirling back to the surface before I can shove them down. I clear my dry throat, and my tongue darts out to slide over my lips before continuing. "It used to be just a little bump, but now it's more like a pebble."

"Exactly," Dr. Hendriks nods. "I know it all seems very scary, which is understandable. The good thing is you're still in stage one. The cancer is localized in your right breast, and I'm pretty positive we can get this fucker out of your system with the right treatment."

Her words make me choke on a nervous laughter. I don't think I've ever heard Dr. Hendriks curse before. And something about this distinguished, serious doctor saying *fucker* just does it for me.

Nixon looks at me like I've lost my mind, and maybe I have. I don't even have it in me to care.

"Okay, that all sounds promising, right?" Nixon glances at me, but I bite my cheek harder. "So, what are our options? Radiation? Chemo?"

Dr. Hendriks holds Nixon's hopeful gaze before shifting her attention to me.

"Considering your family history," there is a hesitancy in her voice that I'm not used to hearing. I know what she's going to say even before the words are out of her mouth.

A frown appears between Nixon's brows. "You think this is connected to our Mom?"

"She doesn't think that." Nixon opens his mouth, but before he can say anything, Dr. Hendriks drops the bomb.

"Mrs. Cole's breast cancer was genetic. Jade's carrying the gene."

There's a beat of silence as her words ring in the small office. The secret I've been keeping since Mom got cancer is now finally out in the open.

"What?!" Nixon whips his head toward me, his eyes wide as he tries to wrap his head around it. He just stares at me for what seems like forever. "You knew about this." His words are soft, but I can hear the accusation in his voice. I guess I should have thought about this earlier. I should have warned Dr.

Hendriks that she shouldn't mention this little tidbit, but now it's too late.

"I did."

I hate myself for doing this to him.

It wasn't supposed to happen this way.

This soon.

"Before..." I clear my throat, forcing the words out. "Before we found out that it was terminal, they ran some extra tests, and we found out that Mom's breast cancer is genetic. They tested me too."

"You *knew* this," he shakes his head like he can't comprehend it. "Why the fuck didn't you say something?!"

"What was I supposed to say, Nix? Hey, bro, I know Mom's dying, but good news, I'm a ticking time bomb? It's just a matter of time before you lose me too?"

"I'm not going to lose you!" he grits through clenched teeth, his fingers wrapping around the armrest. "I'm not going to lose you," he repeats and lets out a shaky breath before turning his attention to Dr. Hendriks. "Now, what are our options?"

Dr. Hendriks looks at me, and I nod, giving her approval to continue knowing damn well Nixon's not nearly done with this topic.

"My suggestion would be to do a double mastectomy followed by chemo."

"Double..." the word comes out in a rush of air. I thought I was ready for it; I knew it was an option, but I wasn't. Not nearly enough.

Dr. Hendriks places her hands over mine. "I know this is scary, and it's not something any twenty-year-old woman wants to think about or do, but again, considering your family history, I want to be safe, not sorry."

"I know, it's just..."

Double mastectomy.

It shouldn't hurt, not like this. They're just breasts, after all. Tissues. Muscles. A freaking part of my identity.

"You don't have to decide this very instant, Jade. Go home and think about it. There are alternative therapies we could try, but based on my experience, this is the one that'll give us the best chance of success. However, considering what you've told me about how the lump has grown recently, I'd advise against taking too long to make a decision. The sooner we remove the malignant tissue, the better your chances are."

Do a double mastectomy.

Soon.

"Make the appointment," Nixon says.

"What?" My head snaps up. "No."

"What do you mean, 'no'?" Nixon turns in his chair to glare at me. "She just told us that's your best chance at beating this thing."

"But there are other options..."

"How about I give you a moment to discuss this?" Dr. Hendriks asks, getting to her feet.

We glare at one another, but the moment the door closes behind Dr. Hendriks, I pounce at him. "What do you think you're doing? You can't just call the shots, Nixon! This is my body. My disease. My choice."

"The hell I can't!" He pushes out of his chair, running his fingers through his hair. "What do you think you're doing, Jade? She just told you what—"

"She just told me she'll cut off a part of me!"

How can't he see it?

"So you could live!"

"You don't get it." Jumping to my feet, so he isn't looming over me, I wrap my arms around myself and walk to the window.

"Which part don't I get, Jade? That she's giving you a chance to beat this thing? A chance to live?"

"For you, it's about life and death. For me, it's everything!" Tears slip down my cheeks, and I wipe them away. I'm not going to break. "From one day to the next, my life has been turned on its axis, and nothing will ever be the same. Whatever I decide, my whole life will be bound to this hospital for months, *years,* really. I'll be poked, probed, and cut open. Everything I was, everything I am, will be ripped away from me."

"Jade..."

"This isn't my first rodeo with cancer, Nixon. I've seen what it did to our mom. I watched it eat her alive day in and day out. So don't you dare tell me you know what that's like."

Nixon turns me to face him and wraps his arms around me, pulling me into his strong chest. A sob rips out of my lungs, and, for the first time, I realize my whole body is shaking, and big, ugly tears are sliding down my cheeks.

So much for not crying.

I wrap my trembling arms around Nixon's middle, burrowing my head into his chest as I let the admission out: "I'm scared, Nixon."

My big brother soothes his hand down my back. "Me too, Smalls. Me too."

"I don't think I can do this. I don't know how." I shake my head, my fingers clenching around his shirt. "I wish she were here. She would have known what to do."

"I know she would. We'll find a way. I promise you, Jade. We'll find a way," he whispers, his arms tightening around me to the point it's hard to breathe, but I don't ask him to let go.

I'm not sure how long we stay like this, just holding onto one another. Now that all the anger and frustration have left me, I feel empty and tired. So damn tired.

The door creaks open, and I take a step back, wiping away the tears from my face.

"Is everything okay? I'd give you more time, but my next appointment is here."

"Sorry for occupying your space and time." I take the tissue she offers me, wiping at my tear-stained face.

"No problem, these things can get really emotional. Like I said, you don't have to—"

I shake my head. "I'll do it."

"Are you sure?"

"Jade..." Nixon grabs my hand, but I stop him.

"No, I want to do it. I *have* to do it. I just... I just need a little time to come to terms with all of this, that's all." I nod at Dr. Hendriks. "I'll do the mastectomy."

She nods. "How about we schedule you to come in next week? We'll run some more tests and discuss the logistics of it."

Discuss the logistics of it?

That's about the last thing I want to do.

"I don't think..."

"There are things you need to think about, Jade."

"What kinds of things?"

I don't want to think or listen. I just want to be done with all of this.

"Your future. I know it's easy to focus on right here and right now, so easy to get lost in the pain of now that you lose sight of your future. Cancer is a nasty disease, it takes so much out of the person, but it doesn't have to take it all."

I brush the tears away from my cheeks. "I'm not sure I'm following."

"Do you want a family one day, Jade?"

Family?

"I mean, yeah. Down the roa—"

Dr. Hendriks gives me a soft smile, and even before she says the words, I can already see where this is going.

"You're young. It would be good to consider cryopreservation prior to starting the chemo. Look it up, and we can discuss it at our next appointment, okay?"

"What the hell is cryopreservation?" Nixon asks.

"It's a way of preserving the fertility of young women before they start chemo." Dr. Hendriks gives my shoulder a gentle squeeze. "Think about it, and I'll see you next week?"

Chapter 10

PRESCOTT

"That's how you do it, boys!" Scotty yells as we make our way to the locker room.

If you listen hard enough, you can still hear the buzz of the crowd as they leave the stadium after the game. My ears are ringing from the yelling fans and the crushing of the pads, the adrenaline still running high in my veins.

"Motherfucking champs, that's what we are," somebody screams, choruses of agreement going through the room.

I don't bother pointing out that there are still way too many games to play, and everything can change. Even my dark heart feels a flicker of hope that maybe the championship isn't that far out of our reach.

My eyes meet Nixon's, and for a split second, a silent understanding passes between us. Then the reality sets in—everything that has played out in the past week comes rushing back, making him scowl.

"You're still far from being champs," Coach chastises loud enough to be heard over the racket in the locker room. I turn away from Nixon and concentrate on Coach instead. "The Saints surprised us with that interception..."

Somebody groans in the background. "Seriously?"

Coach must hear it, too, because his eyes narrow at whoever said it. "Yes, seriously." One thing's for sure. He doesn't share our enthusiasm. "However, you recovered really well. That doesn't mean you can relax now."

He isn't wrong. Today's game was tough. The Saints didn't want to go down without a fight, and that's exactly what we gave them. We looked like we'd gotten off a battlefield, our black-and-gold uniforms stained with a mix of sweat, grass, and mud. In the end, we won by one touchdown, but it was a close call.

Coach continues talking about the game, dissecting some of the key moments like he always does, but I'm only half listening as I take off my shirt and shoulder pads.

Jimmy, our PT, walks around the room, handing out ice packs left and right.

"Damn, that looks nasty," he says as his eyes fall on me.

I glance down, noticing the shadow of a dark bruise forming over my ribcage.

"Need me to look at it?"

"Nah," I shake my head, grabbing two ice packs, and placing one against my side and the other on my knee. "I'm good."

I sit down, a jolt of pain going through my body. At this point, I'm not sure what hurts more—my knee or ribs.

"You sure?" Jimmy gives me a doubtful look.

"Yup," I try my best to hide my grimace. "Peachy."

There is no way I'd admit out loud that I'm in pain. Especially not in front of the Coach, or the rest of my teammates, for that matter. We're halfway through the season, and the team has a shot at going all the way. I'm not about to lose it all because of a little pain.

"Clean up." Coach looks around the locker room, giving us a warning stare. "Don't party too hard. I'll see you all tomorrow morning so we can go over today's game and start the prep for our next away game."

With that, he leaves us to patch up and shower. Pulling off the ice pack, I inspect the bruise. I got it when a defenseman crashed into me in the fourth quarter. It's going to be one nasty motherfucker, that's for sure.

Placing my hand against my side, I push to my feet.

Holy shi—

Intense pain spreads through me, making my breath hitch and my knees buckle. I'd probably end up on my ass if I weren't expecting it.

Bruised ribs, probably.

"You should let Jimmy look at it," Nixon mutters by my side.

I let my hand drop, not wanting to show any weakness. "I'm fine."

Nixon's eyes narrow as he watches me. "You don't look fine."

"I don't remember asking for your opinion."

Nixon glares at me. "Whatever," things in hand, he slams his locker shut. "It's your funeral."

With that, he marches toward the bathroom, leaving me alone. Or as alone as one can be in a room full of guys. Taking a step closer to my locker, I slide my hand into the duffle bag stashed inside.

"Listen up, assholes," Scotty yells. "There's a party at my place. I expect to see you there. Spread the word."

Tossing my towel over my shoulder, I prowl through the bag until my fingers wrap around the plastic bottle. I flip off the lid, only to find it empty.

Motherfucker.

"Wentworth?"

My back stiffens at the sound of my name. I force myself to

swallow down the knot in my throat before turning around and finding a few teammates watching me. "You coming?"

"Yeah, sure." I lift my shoulder in a shrug. "Gotta shower first."

Dropping the bottle into my bag, I grab my phone and scroll until I find the familiar number.

Me: I need more.

I don't even get to lock the phone before the reply comes through.

Unknown: I'll see you at Scotty's in an hour.

Talk about fast.

"That was one seriously awesome game, Wentworth." A hand slaps me over the shoulder so hard I feel every bone in my body rattle. "Loved that catch in the third. It was a beauty."

"Thanks, dude," I nod at Xander, who's already engrossed in something his date of the night is whispering to him. "Spencer around?"

"I think he went to grab drinks."

God, I need something to drink.

With a slap over his shoulder and a quick thanks, I make my way toward the kitchen.

I scan the space, trying to find Manolo somewhere in the crowd. Every step I make hurts like a bitch, and if I don't take something soon, I think I might puke.

I notice a few of my teammates are already here, solo cups in one hand and girls under the other. I nod in their direction before slipping into the kitchen, where Spencer is flirting with two girls. He notices me first, pulling another shot glass and filling it to the brim with amber liquid.

I guess alcohol will have to do.

"Great game, dude," Spencer grins.

"You weren't even at the game," I point out, tossing down the drink. The alcohol burns its way down to my stomach, leaving warmth in its wake.

"It's the only thing people are talking about. Kind of hard to miss."

"When did you get back?" Placing the glass on the table, I wait for him to refill it.

"An hour ago. Enough time to drop my stuff at home and come find some entertainment for tonight." He winks at the girls. "Right, ladies?"

"Are you charming poor unsuspecting women again, Spencer?"

The hair at the back of my neck prickles at the sound of the familiar voice. Spencer looks over my shoulder instantly. Something I'm not sure how to name flashes on his face before he hides it behind his usual smile.

"They're not poor, unsuspecting women if they don't mind being charmed, Red."

I down the second shot before looking over my shoulder to find Grace standing behind me. Alone.

She's not here.

I'm not sure if I'm disappointed or relieved. I shouldn't want to see her. But I do. I really fucking do.

I couldn't get her out of my head. It's like when she's not here, I can't breathe properly. I couldn't stop thinking about that damn doctor's appointment and how it went. Because maybe, just maybe...

I give my head a shake. *You're not going there.*

It's done.

Jade and I, we're done.

"I guess there is that." Jade's redheaded roommate glances at the girls before shifting her gaze to me. Her eyes narrow disapprovingly before she focuses her attention on Spencer. "Know if maybe they have any water around here?"

Without waiting for an answer, Grace goes to the fridge and looks inside.

"Since when are you not drinking?"

"It's not for me." She crouches down, moving some stuff around. "Found it." Loud cheering comes from the back of the house. Grace looks toward the doorway and shifts from foot to foot. "I guess I better get back." Before they move to Spencer, her eyes meet mine for a split second, and if looks could kill, I'd be gone. "I'll see you around?"

What the hell is her problem anyway?

"Sure," he says as he watches her go.

I grab the bottle from his hand, pouring us both a drink.

"What's that about?" I ask him, tilting my head toward the doorway.

Spencer turns to me. "What?"

"That?"

"Not sure what you're talking about."

"Bullshit," I toss the shot back.

"You wanna tell me what *that's* about?" he raises his brow.

I shrug. "I'm having a drink at a party."

"The third drink in three minutes since you've been here."

Because I fucking hurt, and that's the only thing that's keeping the pain at bay.

"You counting my drinks now, mom?"

"Fuck off, Wentworth."

More cheering comes from the back. I narrow my eyes at the doorway, remembering how Grace was fidgety. I don't think I've ever seen the girl squirm.

"Somebody sure seems to be having fun."

"Yeah, they do," I say absentmindedly, my attention still on that doorway. It's not like I can see through the walls to figure out what's happening. "I'm going to take a piss."

"All those shots getting to you, Wentworth? You're getting old."

"Old?" I huff. "Remind me again, who's the one complaining like a pussy after a rough game?"

Spencer's mouth falls open. "I've been shoved into the plexiglass!"

"In full equipment, which includes *padding*. Talk to me when a two-hundred-plus-pound linebacker runs into you and knocks you to the ground, *old man*," I throw over my shoulder as I make my way into the hallway, where I almost knock into a couple.

I move to the side, letting them pass, my eyes zeroing in on their locked hands. That familiar ache that's been gripping my chest ever since I walked out of Jade's apartment is front and center, but I push it away, making my way into the back of the house where all the cheering is coming from, loud enough to be heard over the beat of the music.

I'm about to head in that direction when Manolo pops out of nowhere, an amused smirk on his face.

"Missed me?"

I look left and right, but by some miracle, we're alone in the dim hallway.

"Are you insane?" I hiss, my back stiffening. "What if somebody sees us?"

"They'll see two guys talking. Chill, dude." He slaps me over the shoulder. "Good game today. I heard you were quite the hero."

"I'm no one's hero."

The dude inspects his nails. "That's not what they're saying."

I clench my teeth. What little patience I had left was swallowed by the pain hours ago. "I'm not interested in playing your games. Did you bring what I asked for?"

Manolo rolls his eyes. "Is that even a question?"

"Apparently," I pull the money out of my pocket. "I'm not in the mood for chitchat."

"Are you ever?" he sighs dramatically.

I let out an irritated growl that has him smirking. "Don't get your panties in a twist." He clasps my hand, exchanging the wad of cash for a bag with pills. "As always, it was nice chatting with you, Wentworth."

My fingers tighten around the plastic, feeling the pills shift in my grasp, and a sense of relief washes over me.

Finally, I'll get some relief.

I could practically feel the effect of the drug, and I hadn't even taken it. Which is all kinds of messed up, but ask me if I care.

A loud cheer erupts from the living room, making me look at the space. There were dozens of people standing in the doorway, obscuring whatever was happening inside that had all their attention.

"What the hell is going on in there? Did somebody order strippers or some shit?"

"Even better," he wiggles his brows. "Coeds are dancing on the tables. There is nothing like some fresh meat to taste. There's this one brunette, and her rack is top-notch. I think I might go for her myself."

Brunette?

My stomach sinks as the image of Grace in the kitchen earlier flashes in my mind. The way she looked toward the doorway as if she was waiting for something to happen. How she disappeared out of the room like the devil was at her heels with a water bottle in her hand.

"Shit."

Turning on the balls of my feet, I go for the door and start pushing through the crowd so I can get inside.

People aren't happy when I shove them out of my way, but I ignore curses thrown at me. A guy that's about my height refuses to budge, so I grab his shoulder and pull him hard.

"Hey, what— Wentworth? What the hell, man?"

"Get out of my way," I bite out, moving past him before he can say anything else.

That's when I see her.

Jade.

I suck in a sharp breath as she appears in front of me, hands raised in the air, her head thrown back, and all that gorgeous hair is cascading down her back.

She's dancing on a freaking table, just like Manolo said.

Some guy tries to grab her, and my fingers clench into fists by my sides.

Fucking hell.

Before I can think of what to do, I'm already moving forward, pushing the last people out of my way until I'm standing in front of the table.

"Get your dirty hands off of her," I mutter. The guy doesn't even have enough time to process what I said before I rip his hand from her and push him back.

"Get the fuck down, Jade," I hiss, looking up at her.

She blinks a few times, her brows pulling together in confusion.

"Prescott? What are you doing here?"

Even in the dark, I can see her dilated pupils. She sways on her feet, the movement having nothing to do with dancing and all with clumsiness—the consequence of her being totally wasted.

"C'mon, Jade, let's go home."

I look up to see Grace standing on the other side of the table, a water bottle in her hand. Our gazes meet for a second before I shift my attention back to the woman who'll be the death of me.

"Oh, she's going home alright. The better question is, what are *you* doing on top of that table?"

Jade must realize I'm pissed because her gaze narrows, defiance shining in her eyes. "I'm having fun." She flips her hair back, the motion making her sway even harder in those heels. "Besides, you're not the boss of me."

Not the boss of her? We'll see about that. The moment I get her off that table, I'm going to strangle her and show her just how much of a boss I can be.

I look around, noticing a few people pointing in our direction. We're making a scene, not that she cares in the slightest. Jade continues to dance, or she tries to, at least. She swirls her hips, but somebody bumps into the table, making her lose her footing.

"Jade!" Grace yells in a warning.

"Fuck."

I step forward, catching her before she falls to the ground. My knees buckle underneath me from the force of the impact. Jade's eyes widen, and my own heart stops in my chest. The stab of pain goes through my leg, making me freeze for a moment, but I grit my teeth, tightening my arms around her as I fight through the pain while trying to keep us upright.

"Damn, that was close," Grace mutters as she joins us. "Are you okay?"

"No, I'm not okay." She tries to wiggle out of my hold, but I don't budge. "Let me go."

"Not a chance in hell, doll."

"Let me go, or I'm going to scream."

"Maybe you should..." Grace tries, but I give her a warning glare that makes her shut up, so I turn my attention to the woman in my arms.

"Since you're already making a scene, I don't see how you can do any more damage, but I invite you to try," I grunt and toss her over my shoulder. Securing my hold, I start toward the door, daring anybody to get in my way or say anything.

"Ugh, I hate you," she punches me in the back.

"You can hate me all you want back in your room."

"You take me home, and I'll just go back out once you leave. Because that's what you do, right, Wentworth? You fucking leave."

Her words are filled with anger and something else that sounds a lot like hurt.

"You're drunk, Jade."

"Not drunk enough to not know what I'm saying."

The cold air hits me as we leave the house. I inhale some fresh air, and I walk us to my car. Only then do I let her slide down to the ground. All those lush curves of hers brush against me as I put her on her feet, making me ache in a whole different kind of way.

She's not yours to have, I chastise myself. *You shouldn't even be doing this.*

But there is no way I'll leave her here like this with a friend who obviously can't get her home safely, like prey for the vultures—vultures like Manolo and the likes of him.

Jade shoves her hair out of her face and glares at me. "You have no right to manhandle me, Wentworth," she jabs her finger into my chest. "I already told you; I don't need you to save me."

"And I already told you. I'm nobody's savior." I pull open the door. "Get in the car, Jade."

"I'm not going anywhere with you. I'm going back inside, where I'm going to get another drink and have fun."

Jade tries to walk around me, but I step in her way, caging her against my car. "Get in the vehicle, Jade."

"Why do you even care?" She stomps her foot, and if things

were different, I might even find it cute. But there is nothing appealing about this situation we're in. "Go back and do whatever the hell is that you do, and leave. Me. Alone."

"I can't do that."

"Why not? You didn't seem to have a problem leaving before."

And there it is, that tone, the crack in her voice, *those words.*

"Jade..." I take a step closer, reaching for her face, but she looks away.

"You should leave, Prescott. Things are only going to get worse from here."

"You don't..."

"I have cancer, okay?" she snaps, biting the inside of her cheek. "This is my life now. I have cancer, and there is nothing that can change that. So excuse me if I want one last night of fun before my life completely falls apart and I die."

Her words shouldn't hurt. After all, it's not like I didn't know already, but I've been trying to convince myself it's all one horrible dream, and eventually, I'll wake up from it, and things will go back to how they were.

Only it's not.

What she said is true. This is our life now, and every time she says those words, a little part of me dies along with her.

I shake my head. "You're not dying."

I'm not accepting that.

Not now, not ever.

Because there can't be a world in which she isn't there.

It just can't.

"I'm dying." Her palms connect with my chest, pushing me away, or at least trying to, but I wrap my fingers around her wrists and hold her tight. "*I'm dying.* And there is nothing that anybody can do to stop it."

"No, I refuse to believe it."

I refuse to live in a world in which she doesn't exist.

She doesn't have to be mine. I can live with that. But she has to *be*.

"Damn, I lost you there for a moment." Grace looks from Jade to me and back. "Is everything okay?"

"Peachy." Jade crosses her arms over her chest. "Prescott was just leaving."

"Prescott is just driving you home." I pull open the door. "Get in."

Jade's eyes narrow on me, and for a second, I think she might try to slap me, but before she can do it, Grace says: "Let's just let him take us home. It's late."

Jade clenches her jaw, that fire burning bright in her eyes. "Fine."

She sways a little as she turns on the balls of her feet, but before I can try and catch her, she's inside the car and pulling the door closed, almost slamming my fingers in the process.

Grace lets out a sigh, "That went well."

I look up, my eyes narrowing on her.

"What? It did." Grace shrugs and makes her way to the back seat. "I didn't expect her to give in this easily. She's been all over the place since... Well, since she told us."

It made sense. When your life is spiraling out from under you, the only thing you want is to have some control, which usually leads to making some pretty bad decisions. I should know firsthand, since I'm a master of making bad decisions.

With a shake of my head, I follow after Grace and slip into my car. My leg still hurts like a bitch, but the pain meds will have to wait until Jade is safe in her apartment.

"You shouldn't be doing this," I say as I start the car and check my rearview mirror as I slowly start maneuvering between the cars. "You'll need all your strength once you start your treatment."

"*Well*, your opinion hardly matters, hotshot," Jade murmurs, her head touching the window. "Want it or not, I'm dying."

My hands tighten around the steering wheel. "Did you go to your doctor?"

She huffs, "Now you sound just like Nixon."

"I'm sure your brother will be happy to hear that." There is a beat of silence as I wait for her to tell me something, *anything*, but there is nothing. "So? Did you?"

"I did. They told me exactly what I told you. I'm dying. Although I'm not sure why you care, you've left before, and you'll leave again."

I press my lips in a tight line. She's right. There is no denying it. I left. Nothing else was an option, not at that moment. Not when the idea of the past repeating itself was right in front of me.

"Everybody leaves," she continues, her voice softer. "One way or the other, everybody leaves. There is no stopping it from happening."

No, there wasn't. We both knew it better than most. Some people have left of their own violation; others who want to stay are ripped from you against their will.

"That's why I promised I'd never fall in love again. The only thing it ever brings you is heartache. Want to know something?" I open my mouth, but before I can utter a word, she continues without waiting for a reply. "I went and did it anyway. Not that it matters. You'll leave anyway, and I can't even blame you. Two sides of the same coin. That's what we are. You and me, Prescott, we're broken. Damaged goods."

My mouth falls open, but no words come out.

That's why I promised I'd never fall in love again. The only thing it ever brings you is heartache.

I went and did it anyway.

I'm pretty sure Jade just told me she loves me, but I'm completely speechless.

What does one say to something like this, anyhow?

If I were a different man, a less damaged man, I'd say it back. I'd do whatever she needed of me. But I'm not a different man.

Damaged goods.

She's right about that.

And she deserves better because I'll never be able to be what she needs. Who she needs me to be. I went through this hell once before, and it swallowed me whole. To do it again... No, I couldn't do it. Not even for her.

Just then, our building appears in front of me. I pull into the parking lot and turn off the car.

"Jade, I—" I turn around to look at her, my mouth completely dry with nerves, but before I can attempt to find the right words to say, I realize that she's fast asleep.

I let out a shaky breath as I stare at her face. Even when she's sleeping, there's a frown between her brows.

I'm dying.

I'm not doing this. Not again. I can't.

"I'll carry her up. Open the door for me?"

Not waiting for an answer from Grace, I get out of the car and make my way to the passenger's side. As gently as possible, I get Jade into my arms and straighten. Thankfully, Grace doesn't say anything as she heads to the building and holds the door open for me.

In silence, we climb up the stairs to their apartment and into Jade's room, where I gently lie Jade on her bed. I skim the back of my fingers over her cheekbone, pushing a strand of her hair out of her face.

"I'm sorry, but I can't be what you need, doll," I whisper softly as footsteps come behind me.

"Stay with her tonight? She shouldn't be alone." Pushing upright, I walk toward the door, but Grace steps in my way, her arms crossed over her chest as she stares me down.

"You don't need to tell me what to do, but we both know who she wants to be here."

I shake my head. "I can't be here."

"Can't or won't?" she challenges, her voice steely.

I grit my teeth, the irritation and pain brewing inside of me. "I'm not doing this with you."

"Fine. But if you're not planning on staying, you should leave. For good. You're just hurting her otherwise."

"What do you think I'm trying to do here?" I yell as I shove past her and make my way for the door.

"Jade was right," Grace calls after me. "Go, that's what you're the best at."

Pushing open the door, I get out and let it slam after me. My leg protests every step I take as I descend the stairs and get outside. My hand slips into my pants pocket, my fingers wrapping around the plastic bag.

I rip into the bag, three pills falling into my open palm. I throw them into my mouth and swallow them in one go. Jade's words still ring in my head as I make my way home.

That's why I promised I'd never fall in love again. The only thing it ever brings you is heartache.

I went and did it anyway.

Chapter 11

JADE

I turn in bed, my stomach clenching uncomfortably as the bile rises up my throat. Groaning, I pull my legs closer to my chest as the stab of pain goes through my skull, making my whole body tense.

"Oh my God..." I bury my head deeper into the pillow, my voice making the throbbing behind my temples intensify.

What the hell happened last night?

"Good, you're awake." Grace's voice echoes in my head, not helping in the least with the headache I'm sporting.

Did I bang my head against the wall?

Because it sure feels that way.

"I wish I wasn't." I grab my head, willing the pulsing pressure to go away.

"I can imagine you do. You drank quite a bit and didn't throw up."

My stomach rolls at the mere mention of throwing up; I try to swallow, but my mouth is as dry as a desert. "It's still a possibility. What time is it?"

"Just past noon. But I figured it would be best to let you

sleep it off for as long as possible. You'll be miserable one way or the other, no sense in hurrying it up."

"Thanks, you're the best."

"If I were the best, you wouldn't feel like shit right now," Grace mutters. There is a beat of silence before she asks tentatively. "Do you remember anything about last night?"

"I..." My brows pull together as I try to search through the fog that's clouding my mind. "A little?"

I rub at my temples as I try to remember what actually happened. I remember the two of us going to the football game. And then somebody posted about a party, the pre-gaming at the apartment, the dancing. Lots and lots of dancing and drinking, dim lights, and loud music pulling me into that familiar oblivion I'd been craving, and then...

Flaring brown eyes flash in my mind, the anger and hurt, and desire swirling inside them as he glares at me.

That's why I promised I'd never fall in love again. The only thing it ever brings you is heartache.

I went and did it anyway.

"Oh my God..." My eyes snap open as my shaky fingers cover my mouth, the words I'm pretty sure I said out loud yesterday ringing in my head. "Please tell me I didn't say what I think I said."

"That you're in love with Prescott?"

My whole body turns to ice as Grace says the words out loud.

"I didn't say that."

I never said those words, not since my mom died and my life fell apart. Not out loud anyway.

"Not in so many words, no."

"God." *Why is this happening to me?* Is there any other moronic thing I can do when it comes to this man? "Why did you let me speak to him?"

"I couldn't stop you. I tried reasoning with you, get you home on my own, but it didn't work, so he hauled you off that table. The only thing I'm grateful for."

"Did he..."

Grace raises her brows. "Did he what?"

I clear my throat, pushing the words out. "Did he say anything?"

Those last few minutes in Prescott's car are extremely blurry. I guess the mix of tiredness and drunkenness will do that to a person.

"Oh..." Grace's face softens, and I know the answer before she even says the words out loud. "No, he didn't. He brought you up because you passed out in his car and asked me to stay with you. That's it."

Of course, he did. Because he's a stubborn asshole, who thinks he can get his way.

"You didn't have to stay the night."

"And risk you dying in your own puke? I think not. I would have stayed either way. I don't need some football player to boss me around and tell me how to take care of my friends." Grace's hand clasps mine, giving it a firm squeeze. "I'm here for you, and I'm not going anywhere."

Everybody leaves. One way or the other, everybody leaves. There is no stopping it from happening.

Grace's hand tightens around mine, turning my attention to her. "You know that, right?"

I let out a shaky breath. "I do."

It's true. I never thought my friends would turn their back on me if they found out about the cancer. Quite the opposite, really, which was why I didn't want to tell them in the first place.

There were two kinds of pain: One from watching people

leave and the other from watching them stay and worry about you. At this point, I wasn't sure which one was the worst.

"Good." Grace nods her head, her free hand slipping under her cheek. "Then will you finally tell me what happened at that appointment the other day? Because that's why you've been acting all crazy, right? I tried giving you time to collect yourself because I know how hard this is for you, but I can't help, *we* can't help, if you don't tell us how."

"How did you know?"

"Oh, please." she rolls her eyes at me. "You never ask for a car, so I figured you were going to your doctor's appointment in the city. You didn't really think you could hide it from us, did you? We failed you once. We're not about to do it again."

"You didn't fail me." My tongue darts out, sliding over my cracked lips. "But you're right; I had an appointment with my mom's doctor. She did some tests which showed I'm stage one."

The corner of Grace's lips turns upward. "That's a good thing, right?"

"Yeah, but..."

"I don't like that word."

I let out a small chuckle, which makes me wince when the jab of pain goes through my skull. "Me neither, *but* because of my family history, she wants to do all she can. I'm going back for more tests and an appointment with the fertility specialist next week..."

"Fertility specialist? Why would you..."

"Chemo." That light dies in my friend's eyes, just like it died inside me when Dr. Hendriks told me the very same thing. "She wants to do six rounds after we do a double mastectomy."

"But that's..." Her throat bobs as she swallows. "Wow... Is that really necessary? You're only twen—"

"It's necessary." Just saying it out loud makes my heart ache, but there is no sense in hoping for the impossible. "I'm carrying the gene for breast cancer, Grace. I've known it since Mom got sick."

Hurt flashes on Grace's face at my words.

"I didn't tell anybody. Mom and Dr. Hendriks were the only people who knew. I didn't want to worry anybody else for nothing."

"It's not for nothing."

"It was. Everything was just so raw back then. Mom was sick. Dad left. Nixon was... well, Nixon. And then they tell me I'm carrying a ticking time bomb inside me. I might have never gotten breast cancer."

"But you did."

"But I did," I agree. "And now Dr. Hendriks is doing everything she can to help me."

Grace nods. "How do you feel?"

"Angry." My eyes burn from the unshed tears, but I blink them away. "Helpless."

Scared.

I feel so damn scared.

"It's going to be okay."

"What if it isn't?"

Grace shakes her head, her eyes shining with unshed tears, but stubbornness is also etched into every line of her face. "It's going to be okay. We'll figure it out—all of it. You're not alone. You have Rei, Penny, Yasmin, Nixon, and me. We'll help you through this."

But not Prescott.

He left, and he wasn't coming back.

Maybe it was better this way. At least one person won't watch me go through hell.

At least one person will be spared the suffering.

No matter how much I need him to be here.

"Thanks, Gracie."

"I mean it." She brushes a strand of my hair behind my ear. "We'll get you through this."

I can only hope that she's right.

Chapter 12

PRESCOTT

"You should have gone on the trip," Gabriel says, his eyes focused on the cards in front of him.

"I didn't want to go on the trip," I shrug nonchalantly.

"Liar," he throws back without missing a beat as he places a draw-four card on the pile. "Red."

"Am not." Rolling my eyes at him, I draw the cards, spreading them wide in my hands so I can see all my options before adding one to the pile. "School trips are boring, anyway."

"Says you. I'd loved to have gone." Gabriel hums as he places a card on top of mine. "What do you think they're doing?"

Of course, he would. Gabriel would love the field trip our teacher, well, my *teacher, has organized. He'd be the loudest on the bus, the first to ask all the silly questions nobody dares to ask in order to avoid sounding stupid. Because if you ask Gabriel, there are no stupid questions, just people too stupid not to ask them.*

"I don't know," I shrug. "Who cares? At least I don't have to be in school, and we can spend the day together."

"You better remember that when..."

"When?" I prompt, dropping my card on the table.

There is a crooked smile on Gabriel's lips as he drops not one, not two, but three plus-two cards.

"Are you shitting me? How?"

My brother smirks. "Luck, I guess?"

The strong vibrating of the phone wakes me out of my dreams. My head snaps up, pain shooting through my neck. I rub the back of it, looking around as I try to figure out where I am.

My room.

Not the hospital.

I'm in my room.

Soft light is peeking through the drawn curtains, signaling that I'd fallen asleep at some point during the night while I was studying. The little lamp is shining dim light over the desk, books and papers are scattered around, and my laptop has long gone to sleep.

The screen of my phone lights up once again as it continues buzzing. I grab it, hitting the answer button as I rub my hand over my face.

"Yeah?" I croak, my voice hoarse from sleep.

"I should have figured you'd still be asleep," Dad booms from the other side of the line.

Letting out a sigh, I lean back in my chair. "Good morning to you, too, Father."

"Morning? It's practically noon! Don't you have a practice to go to? If I were your coach—"

I shake my mouse, glancing toward the screen as I tune out his rant. It's not even seven thirty, hardly noon, except to Benedict Wentworth. Seriously, that man would find something to complain about if he called me at midnight and found me asleep.

"Did you need something?" I interrupt him mid-sentence. "If not, I have to go. I have classes to get to."

"Of course, I needed something! What do you think? That I have time to waste?"

Of course, he did. Because what other reason could a father have to call his son if he didn't need something?

"Did you apply for your MCATs?"

"I—" I look at the top of my screen, noticing the date. *Fuck*, I almost forgot. "No, Dad, I didn't apply yet. The site isn't opening until later anyway."

"Which date will you take?"

I try to hold back my groan. "I already told you, Dad. I'm going to take one of the March dates. It makes the most sense since..."

"What makes the most sense is for you to take the first available date! Knowing you, you'll probably fail anyway because that's what you do. You fail, Prescott. You fail people around you. You fail at football. *You fail.* This way, at least, you'll have the time to retake the test if you want to be able to apply to med schools come spring. Apply for the first available date."

Knowing you, you'll probably fail anyway.

He's right.

I fail people.

I failed Gabriel.

I failed Jade.

And I'll fail my teammates if I'm not able to play.

"Just listen to me—"

"Fine, I'll take the first damn date. Happy?" I yell, unable to continue listening to him go on and on about how big of a disappointment I am. I know that damn well without having to hear him say it on repeat. "Did you need anything else?"

There's a beat of silence. For a moment, I think he might have hung up on me, but then he says: "Your mother wants to know if you're coming home for Thanksgiving."

Home? The word was laughable. There was no more home.

There hasn't been one for a long ass time. Besides, it's been weeks since we last talked. If him coming to my game drunk and punching me in the face can even be considered talking. I see how much they missed me, considering they waited to reach out.

"Coach asked us to stay around because we have an important game."

"Well, you better be home for Christmas. You know how upset she gets."

She'll get upset one way or the other. Mom can barely stand to look at my face these days, not after everything that had happened with Gabriel.

"I'm not making any promises."

"Prescott," there's an edge to my father's voice. Maybe I should care, but I don't have it in me to do so. Not any longer.

"Championship is on the line, Dad. And the Ravens have a decent chance to play in the finals. There's no sense in flying all the way to Michigan if I'll have to be back in a few days. And now I have MCATs to study for on top of everything else. Now, if you'll excuse me, I have a class to get to."

Not waiting for an answer, I hang up. Turning around in my chair, I throw the phone on the bed, rubbing my hands over my face as the frustration simmers inside me like it always does.

The need to go to the gym and work this anger out of me is tempting, but I didn't lie. I do have a class I can't skip if I want to remain eligible to play.

Letting my hands drop down, I push to my feet.

Class first. The gym will have to wait.

"Dude, you look like shit," Spencer says as he joins me. My class just finished, and I've barely survived. I need some caffeine, STAT.

I rub my hand over my jaw, the scruff scratching my palm. "Gee, thanks, dude."

"Hey, I'm just calling it as I see it."

"I need coffee. It's been a long day."

And an even longer night. My class dragged on, which definitely didn't help keep me awake. At one point, I started to doze off, only for my professor to ask me a question. I managed to pull it off, but we both knew I was barely holding on. And that was just class number one. I have to be at the lab in half an hour, so I figured I might as well get some caffeine in me beforehand.

Spencer gives me a once-over. "Have you even slept? The light was still on when I came home around two."

"Yeah," I shrug, pushing open the door to Cup It Up. "I just had some work to do."

One good thing about this particular class? It's barely a few minutes' walk from the coffee shop, making it easy for me to grab the good stuff quickly before rushing to my next class.

The bell chimes as I step inside the coffee shop, only to stop in my tracks when my eyes fall on her.

Jade.

I'm not sure if she heard the door or if she can feel me the way I can feel her the moment she enters a room, but slowly, she looks up, those baby blues meeting mine, and it's like I've been kicked in the nuts.

So close, and yet, so far away.

The last time I'd been this close to her was the night I took her off that table and drove her home, which was ten days ago. I know because I've been counting them off. Ten long ass days, and every one of them, I thought about her, about what she told me that night.

That's why I promised I'd never fall in love again. The only thing it ever brings you is heartache.

I went and did it anyway.

She's standing on the side with Yasmin. Nixon's wife sees me, a sad smile flashing on her face before she returns her attention to Jade and whispers something softly to her, to which Jade nods.

"You're pathetic." Spencer pushes me further inside, the door closing firmly behind him. "Why don't you just go to her?"

I shake my head, forcing myself to look away. "It's not that easy."

The guy standing at the counter moves to the side, so we step forward, placing our order. That prickly sensation at the nape of my neck is as insistent as ever, and it takes everything in me not to turn around and seek her out.

"It's exactly that easy. You go to her. You talk like the two freaking adults you are, and you make shit work."

"Seriously?" I glare at Spencer. "You think you're the right person to give relationship advice? A guy who runs from commitment like the devil is at his heels?"

"Takes one to know one, man."

My back stiffens as footsteps near, my heart speeds up, and I swear I can smell lavender. My eyes fall shut, and I inhale deeply, wanting to fill my lungs with it. Memorize it.

"Pa-the-tic," Spencer mutters as the bell chimes again. A whoosh of cold air sends chills up my spine. Then she's gone.

"Fuck off."

The guy behind the display case places our coffees on the counter.

"If you would listen to me, you'd be singing a different tune."

"Hardly."

There is no amount of talking that could help us, maybe if things were different.

I have cancer.

I shake my head, refusing to go down that road. I lost one person I loved to cancer. I watched him die before my very eyes. I can't do it again. I just...

Slapping the money on the counter, I grab my coffee. "I have to get to the lab. I'll see you later."

Spencer slaps me on the shoulder as I walk toward the door. "Try not to fall asleep, will ya?"

"Fuck off, Monroe."

After the coffee, the rest of my day improves. Or at least I don't fall asleep. Between my classes, I get my ass to the gym, where I sweat off all my frustrations.

I'm halfway through my leg workout when Coach stops in front of me. Gage, our backup quarterback, is a few steps behind him, looking uncomfortable as fuck.

I grit my teeth as I push through the last two reps before lowering the bar back into place. My breathing is ragged, and I'm a sweaty mess, so I grab a towel, wiping some of it away before pulling my earbuds out of my ears. "Need something, Coach?"

"I want you to work with Gage."

I narrow my eyes at the kid, who shifts awkwardly from one leg to the other. Our other backup quarterback transferred schools at the end of last season because he got an offer to play first-string. Our third-string quarterback broke an arm after doing a keg stand drunk. Idiot. So now, we were relying on the rookie to step in if anything happened to Nixon. Not likely, but still.

"Sure," I say reluctantly. It's not like I can tell the coach to fuck off and find a different babysitter for the guy. "Is something going on?"

"Just figured it would be good for you two to work together and get a feel for each other before today's practice. That's all."

Today's practice? I pull my brows together. "And what happens at today's practice?"

"Gage will be filling in for Nixon."

Filling in...

"Why?"

Coach narrows his eyes at me, clearly not amused by my questioning. Well, screw him.

"Nixon had a medical emergency."

Coach's statement draws the attention of a few guys on the team who've been working out, but I can barely hear their questions over the buzzing in my ears.

Medical emergency.

Jade's face flashes in my mind as the dread spreads through me, making my gut twist.

I have cancer.

No, I shake my head, refusing to believe it. It can't be. She was fine. I just saw her a few hours ago. She was *fine.*

You better than anyone knows how quickly things can change, the little voice at the back of my head taunts.

"He's fine," Coach bellows, his words pulling me out of my mind. "It's a family thing. He'll be at practice tomorrow, and all will go back to normal. But today, Gage will take Nixon's place, and we'll use this as an opportunity to improve our team. Now get back to work."

A family thing.

I stumble back.

No, no, no.

"Wentworth?" Coach's piercing gaze meets mine. "Are you okay?"

Okay? How the fuck can I be okay after what he just said? How can he be okay?

I shake my head, taking a step back. "I have to go."

That frown between his brows deepens in confusion. Coach opens his mouth, but before he can say anything else, I'm turning on the balls of my feet and running out of the room.

I barely take time to stop by the locker room, hastily grabbing my backpack and duffle bag before I get out of there. My mind is reeling with possibilities as I sprint across the campus—because today, of all days, I had to park all the way on the other side of the lot—while, at the same time, trying to dig the keys out of my backpack.

Maybe it's nothing. Maybe she's fine. She has to be fine.

But Coach said medical emergency.

She was fine just hours ago.

I'm panting so hard by the time I get to my car, but I don't slow down. Tossing the bags inside, I slide into the driver's seat and start the car.

Usually, it takes about fifteen minutes to get from campus back to our building, but today I made it in eight. The moment I'm in front of our building complex, I just leave my car by the curb. Thankfully, somebody left the front door open, so I didn't have to ring the bell. Instead, I take two steps at a time. My leg protests, but I ignore the pain, focusing on my goal.

Find Jade.

Figure out what's going on.

She has to be fine.

She *has* to.

I'm a sweaty mess by the time I make it to Jade's door and start knocking.

She's here. She has to be here. It's not—

"I'm coming. I'm coming. Hold your horse—" The door opens, and I stop my hand just in time so I don't connect it with Grace's head. "Prescott? Wha—"

"Where is she?" I look over Grace's shoulder as if Jade might pop up out of nowhere, but of course, she doesn't.

"Who?"

"Grace? Is that the delivery?" Grace's boyfriend comes from the bathroom, rubbing his wet hair with a towel. He stops in his tracks when he sees me. "Wentworth? What's up, dude?"

"I'm looking for Jade." I narrow my eyes at Grace, my fingers gripping the doorway so I'm not tempted to push her out of my way and look for Jade myself. "Where is she?"

"I don't think..."

"Where. Is. She?"

"Massachusetts General."

I push from the doorway, my fingers curling into fists before I connect my hand with the wall. "Fuck."

From the corner of my eyes, I can see Grace flinch. Without another word, I turn around and head for the stairs.

"Prescott, it's n—"

I don't bother listening.

No, before she can finish, I'm running once again.

Chapter 13

PRESCOTT

Time moves differently when somebody you know or *care about* is hanging on by a thread. I know that firsthand. Or at least I thought I knew.

But the last time I was in this situation, I was just a kid. Now I'm a grown man. It's the same but different. More intense.

My body is in the car as I drive to Boston, my limbs making all the right moves to get me there as fast as possible, but it's like my spirit is detached from the reality of it all. Like I'm hanging in the air, watching and waiting for what's about to happen.

I thought staying away from Jade would help take away the pain, but the only thing on my mind was: What if this is it? What if the last time I saw her, I was too chicken shit to tell her how I felt? What if—

No, I shake my head, fingers tightening around the steering wheel. *I'm not going down that road.*

Those are the words I chant on repeat all the way to the hospital.

My tires screech as I slam my foot on the break, pulling my

car into the first open parking space I see before rushing out and into the hospital.

The smell of antiseptic hits me the moment the door slides open. I have no idea where I'm going or what I might find. I should have grabbed my phone, but it's somewhere in my bag, back in the car.

"Shit," I mutter, running my fingers through my hair. An older lady gives me a once-over before she pulls away, clutching her bag tighter.

Ignoring her judging stare, I look around, my gaze falling on the map of the hospital and all its departments. I start toward it, trying to form a plan. Maybe I should go to the ER and ask around, although what are the chances of them telling me anything?

I scan the map, my eyes falling on the oncology department. I note the floor number just as the elevator pings. I turn around, taking a step toward it, only to come face to face with Nixon.

I look behind him, needing to see her, needing...

"She's not here," Nixon says softly. It's the first time since this debacle came to light that he sounds like the old Nixon. Like my best friend.

My throat bobs as I swallow, forcing the words out. "Where is she?"

"Surgery."

With one word, just one single word, the ground parts between my feet.

"No," I shake my head.

All the moments we had started flashing through my head.

Not enough.

It wasn't enough.

Nixon watches me for a moment, the realization dawning on him. "She didn't tell you."

"We haven't really been talking," I snap at him. But it's not Nixon I'm angry at. It's me.

I shouldn't have walked away. I shouldn't...

"What happened? Is she..."

Is she all right?

Is she alive?

God, let her be alive.

"She's fine. Or, well, as fine as she can be. Her doctor recommended she do a double mastectomy."

A double...

I run my shaking hand over my face.

She's not dying. She's fighting, fighting to live.

"H-how..." My voice breaks, so I clear my throat before trying again. "How long has she been in surgery?"

Nixon doesn't even bother looking at his watch. "A little over three hours. If we're to believe her doctor, it could be anywhere between four and six hours."

Three more hours.

"I was in the waiting room, but..." Nixon shrugs.

He doesn't have to say anything else. I've been in his place, waiting for some news or to hear that the person I love made it and if they're going to get better. Not that he knows that.

"We can go back upstairs if you want."

Unable to form the words, I just nod.

Nixon hits the elevator button, and we wait in silence. When the elevator arrives, we load in with the rest of the people. It feels like the damn thing is stopping on every fucking floor before we finally make it to Oncology.

"How did you find out, anyway?"

"Coach," I mutter as I sit down. "He came to the gym and told me to babysit Gage because you had a medical emergency."

"Shit."

"Yeah," I agree, leaning back and rubbing my hand over my face. "Shit."

"I just couldn't let her do this on her own. Not after everything that happened with our mom. She always pushed me to put football first, so it all fell onto Jade, and she resented me for it."

I shake my head. "She could never resent you."

Jade loved her brother. Yeah, sometimes he irritated her, but even then, she loved him.

"She did. At least a part of her. She told me so herself after..." He sucks in a breath, taking a moment to collect his thoughts. "After Mom died. Not that I blame her," he rushes the words out. "I should have been there. I should have ignored what Mom told me and been there for her and Jade. Now she's gone, and it's like the past is repeating itself." Nixon leans forward, his elbows touching his knees as he buries his face into his palms. "Apart from Yas, Jade's the only family I have left. I can't lose her."

My throat grows thicker with every word he says, making it hard to breathe.

"I can't *lose* her."

The feeling is mutual.

"I thought it would help," I confess softly.

Nixon gives me a side glance. "Help what?"

"Staying away. I thought it would help me stay detached, but..."

"It's always the unexpected ones that bring us to our knees." Nixon glares at me. "Not that that excuses what you did."

"I never thought it did. But if it makes any difference, I never saw it coming. I don't think either one of us did."

"And yet, you walked away."

I open my mouth, wanting to tell him about Gabriel, about our past, but it's like the words are stuck in my throat.

Nixon shakes his head, clearly irritated. "If you're not planning to stick around this time, go home now. Jade doesn't need another person walking away from her. Not when she's dealing—"

"I'm not going anywhere," I interrupt him before he can finish. The words slipped from my tongue easily, the decision already made before I even had enough time to think about it.

It's too late for that. Because want it or not, planned or not, I'm in love with Jade Cole, and no amount of staying away can make losing her bearable.

Tick, tock, tick, tock, tick, tock.

I watch the needle make its way around the clock, time passing impossibly slowly. It seems to drag on for an eternity, one slow tick at a time.

Nixon and I don't say much as we wait for the doctor to arrive and give us some news on how the surgery went. It feels like it's been years since I rushed to come here, when it's barely been a couple of hours.

The curse of being a doctor or studying to be one? You know exactly what is going on behind those double doors. While Nixon is blissfully ignorant to a point, my mind is reeling with all the information regarding breast cancer and mastectomies. Granted, it isn't much, but it's enough to make me nervous.

At one point, Yasmin arrives. If she's surprised to see me here, she doesn't say anything, just goes to Nixon. He grabs her hand, pulling her into his lap and wrapping his arms around her waist.

A pang of jealousy hits me. I've never, not once, been jealous of what my friends have. Until now. Until I might lose the one person I've fallen for before I even got a chance to be with her.

Jade's not dying.

"Any news?" Yasmin asks, her voice muffled as she returns his embrace.

"Not yet."

She runs her fingers through his hair. "Jade's a fighter. She's going to be okay."

"She has to be." Nixon's arms tighten around her. "You didn't have to come."

Yasmin scoffs, "As if that's possible. Jade's my family too. Besides, I didn't come alone."

As if she called them, Grace, Mason, Rei, and Penny appear in the waiting room.

"There you are!" she says as the group joins us. Grace glances at me before shifting her gaze to Nixon. "Any news?"

"Not y—"

"Mr. Cole?"

Nixon and I instantly look up at the doctor coming from behind the double doors. I jump to my feet, a zap of pain going through my leg from sitting so long.

"How is Jade?" Nixon asks, joining me.

The doctor, an older woman with serious brown eyes, glances over our group before focusing her attention on Nixon.

"The surgery went well, and Jade's currently being transferred to the ICU, where she'll stay for at least the next twenty-four hours so we can monitor her."

"Thank God," Nixon lets out a long sigh, his head falling back as he covers his face with his hands.

My own heart is beating furiously as relief slams into me.

She's okay.

She's out of the surgery.

She's okay.

"How did the surgery go?"

The doctor glances at me, clearly wondering who the fuck I am to meddle, but still, she answers: "The surgery went as planned. Jade was a champ the whole time, and we managed to remove both breasts without any issues. I'll be sending the tissue for more testing, but so far, everything looks good."

Nixon lets his hands drop. "What comes next?"

"Can we see her?" This comes from Grace.

"As I mentioned, Jade is currently being transferred to the ICU so we can monitor her, but if everything continues this way, she should be discharged within the next few days. She'll need some help at first since she won't be able to move her hands a lot, and in a month, I'd like to start chemo." The doctor looks around the group. "If you'd like to see her, you can do it once she's settled, but only two people can be in the room at once."

Nixon nods. "Thank you, Dr. Hendriks."

The doctor offers him a small smile before going back to her job.

Nixon turns around. "She's going to be okay," he says, pulling Yasmin in for a hug.

My eyes fall on the door. She's here. Just mere feet away.

"I—"

"Go," Yasmin gives Nixon a little push toward the door. Her hand falls on my shoulder, startling me. "Both of you."

Nixon and I exchange a look, but we don't have to be told twice. We go toward the nurse's station. It takes a few minutes for her to check if Jade's settled, but then she takes us toward the back.

Our footsteps echo in the quiet hallway, the smell of antiseptic bringing back memories I don't want to face.

The nurse stops in front of the door, pumping some disinfectant onto her hands before she pushes the door open.

Nixon follows after her almost immediately.

Not me, though.

My heartbeat grew faster with every step we took closer to Jade, our footsteps echoing in my eardrums. Sweat coats my palms as the past flashes in front of my eyes, mixing with the present, to the point I don't know what's true and what's a memory.

The shake of the doctor's head.

A loud, almost animalistic cry comes from my mother.

"I'm sorry, there was nothing that we could do."

I swallow hard, brushing my palms against the side of my legs, forcing myself to take a step closer.

Jade's not Gabriel.

She's fine.

She made it out.

She's fine.

Almost on autopilot, I reach for the little dispenser by the door, drenching my palms in disinfectant before I enter the room.

The loud *beeping* of the machines breaks me out of my thoughts. And then, my eyes fall on her. Jade. And it's like I've been hit by a train.

She's lying in bed, covers pulled to her chest and her arms placed by her sides. Different wires and tubes are connected to her. She looks so small, so... *fragile.*

Seeing her like this, she's nothing like the girl I know. Nothing like the girl I fell in love with. And yet, she's all that and more.

Nixon smooths her hair away from her cheek. The dark strands are loose, face free of makeup, and her skin is so pale it's almost the same color as the bed sheets.

So freaking fragile.

Nixon sits beside her, gently taking one of her hands into

his. His lips move as he says something, but that damn beeping is the only thing I can hear.

Unable to look at her, my eyes scan the small room, going over the machines, and looking at her stats. Officially, I still might be a far cry from a doctor, but after years spent in the hospital by Gabriel's side, I knew how to read every single one of them by heart.

Heartbeat, oxygen levels, blood pressur—

A hand falls on my shoulder, snapping me out of it. I look down to see the nurse watching me. "You can go and sit down," she whispers softly.

"Thanks," I rasp, my voice too tight to say anything else.

When she walks out of the room, I shift my attention back to that bed and Jade.

But it's not Jade I see.

Gabriel's small body, too skinny and weak from how the disease ate at him, flashes in my mind.

I blink, pushing the memory back, only to find Nixon carefully watching me. "Are you okay?"

"Yeah." Nodding, I cross the room, taking the chair on the opposite side of the bed, gently putting my hand over Jade's cool fingers. Placing my other palm on top of it to transfer some warmth into her icy skin, I concentrate on Jade willing the demons of my past to stay back, while at the same time knowing it's impossible.

Leaning closer so my lips are pressed against the side of Jade's head, I whisper softly: "Hey, doll. I'm here. I'm here, and I'm not going anywhere."

Chapter 14

JADE

The constant *beep, beep, beep* pulls me out of my slumber. It's a distant noise I can barely decipher, but soon, it grows louder, more insistent.

Letting out a soft groan, I try to shift, but a jolt of pain goes through my body, pinning me to the mattress. My eyes blink open, only to fall shut almost instantly as the bright overhead light blinds me.

Holy hell.

At this point, I'm not sure what hurts more, my body or my head.

Forcing myself to stay still and breathe, I wait until the pain subsides before trying again. Slowly, oh so slowly, I open my eyes. At first, it's only a smidge, barely enough to see anything, but enough to let them adjust before I fully open them, taking in my surroundings.

White ceiling.

The bed.

A hospital bed.

Machines surround me as that *beeping* sound grows louder, more incessant.

Hospital.

I'm in a hospital.

As the realization dawns on me, so does the reason for my stay.

Mastectomy.

I look down at my chest as panic spreads through me, but the blanket is placed over my body, preventing me from seeing anything.

Not like there's anything to see, but...

A soft moan snaps me out of my thoughts, enough to notice the person sitting in the chair next to my bed.

The shaggy dark blond hair and broad shoulders.

Nixon. I want to let out a sigh of relief. He's here. Just like he pro—

"Jade?"

No, not Nixon.

Rubbing the back of his neck, he lifts his head, sleepy dark eyes taking me in.

Brown, not blue.

Prescott.

"W-what..." My voice is raspy from sleep, so I clear my throat, but before I can try again, Prescott jolts upright as if he finally realizes that he's not sleeping.

"Shit. You're awake." He looks around, but we're the only two people in the room. "How are you feeling? Do you need me to give you something? Water? Maybe I should call a nur—"

Noticing the weight of his hand over mine, I tighten my fingers around his. My grip is weak, so painfully weak, but it does the trick, making him shut up and turn his focus on me.

"I'm fine. What are you doing here?"

Prescott's tongue slides over his lower lip. "You're here."

You're here.

As if it's that simple. As if nothing has happened between us. As if these last few weeks didn't exist.

You're here.

"H-how did you find out?"

"Coach. Fuck, Jade, when I heard..." He shakes his head, his face twisting in pain. "When I heard you were in the hospital, it's like something fucking broke inside me."

"Prescott..."

"No," he stops me, the desperation in his tone almost palpable. "I saw it all. All that we were, all that we could be, and then it's like you were ripped away from me before we had a chance to do anything. Be anything. I lost you before I had you because of some stupid idea that if I walked away, I'd be safe. Well, I wasn't fucking safe." Another shake of his head. "I wasn't fucking safe. And when I heard you were in the hospital, I realized I could lose you. Actually, lose you, and you'd never know..."

"You're not losing me," I whisper, my heart breaking a little bit, his pain almost like my own.

His hand cups my cheek, rough calluses skim over my skin as he presses his forehead against mine. "You don't know that."

"Well, I'm damn well trying to do everything in my power to live. I want to live."

I need you to live, Jade. Even to this day, Mom's parting words ring in my mind. They were barely audible as she was struggling to breathe. *I need you to live, baby. Live, laugh, love. Do all the amazing things you want to do. Be happy.*

"I want to live, Prescott," I whisper once again, letting those words out for the first time since I realized I have cancer.

My admission.

Prescott watches me with those dark eyes. I can see the demons in them. The uncertainty. The fear. I can see it all because they're mine too.

We don't make false promises.

It would be just meaningless words, and we both know it.

We've both lived it.

"Jade," Prescott whispers, his thumb caressing my cheek as he just stares at me.

And then his mouth is on mine. Slow and gentle. He kisses me like I'm the most precious thing in the world. As if he might lose me. As if I'll disappear between his fingers like sand, scattered by the wind.

My lips parted, his tongue sweeping inside my mouth. At the first touch, I let out a soft moan.

God, I missed this.

I missed him.

I missed his touch. His kisses. His taste.

I try to raise my hand to pull him closer, but once again, that ache shoots through my arm and chest. The pain is so strong I see white dots flash before my eyes.

I let out a soft whimper, Prescott pulling away almost instantly.

"What?" Panic flashes on his face, his eyes roam over my body. "Are you in pain? I knew I should have called the..."

Sweat coats my skin, my hand shakes slightly on the mattress, but I try to brush it off.

"Damn, when was the last time you showered?" I ask as he grabs the call button, stopping him mid-stride.

"Seriously?"

"What?"

"You're joking? Right now?"

"Hey, it's not my problem you stink. I so don't envy your teammates."

"How can you joke about this shit when you're lying in a hospital bed?"

"I don't see how the two are relevant." I let out a small chuckle, the motion making pain shoot through me.

No laughing. Got it.

Prescott's scowl deepens. "Damn it, Jade. You're in pain. I'm calling the nurse."

"It's not that bad," I try to protest.

I didn't want anybody else to break this bubble we were wrapped in. Not yet. I could suffer through a little bit of pain.

"The fact that you're as white as a sheet would disagree. I swear you dri—"

Whatever he wanted to say was interrupted by the opening of the door.

"That was..." my words die on my lips as Nixon enters the room.

He stops in his tracks when he sees me; his lips parted in surprise. "You're awake."

"She woke up a little bit ago," Prescott fills him in. "I just called for the nurse. She's hurting."

"She's awake and can speak for herself," I protest, trying to push upright, which is a mistake.

The pain must show on my face because both men move into action immediately.

"Dammit, Jade. You shouldn't move."

"What's wrong? Does something hurt?" Nixon asks, placing two coffees on the table in the corner before his tall frame looms over me.

Everything. Everything hurts.

"What hurts is to have you two dumbasses hover over me while I can't do shit to sit upright," I mutter. "Can somebody adjust the bed? I don't want you looming over me like I'm a helpless child."

Both Nixon and Prescott look at me like I've lost it. Maybe I have, but if this is any indication of how the next few weeks will go, I'm already done.

"Hello?"

"Good to see the spunk hasn't left you, Smalls," Nixon says, the corner of his mouth lifting in a smile.

"I've lost my breasts, not my wit."

The words are out of my mouth before I can think better of them, making them stop in their tracks. My tongue darts out, sliding over my lips as I meet their gazes.

"What? It's true," I shrug, trying to play it off, but regret the movement almost instantly.

"You seriously need to stop moving, doll, before I tie you to that damn bed," Prescott growls. He grabs the remote for the bed and presses a few buttons. There is a soft buzzing as the top part of the bed starts to lift.

"Kinky."

Nixon lets out a long groan, "I do not need this shit in my life."

"That's payback for all the mushy stuff I had to suffer through with you and Yas."

Before he can answer, the door to my room opens, and the nurse walks inside. "It seems like somebody woke up," she says cheerily as she stops at the bottom of my bed, looking at the chart before checking the monitors. "How are you feeling?"

"She's in pain," Prescott says before I can even open my mouth.

The nurse moves closer, picking up my wrist and monitoring my pulse, then scribbles something down.

"I'll go and grab some pain meds and call the doctor to give you a look."

"Can't you..." Nixon starts, but I give him a death glare before shifting my attention to the woman. "Thank you."

The moment the door closes behind her, I look at the two of them. "You have to stop this. It's irritating."

"We're just worried about you."

"And I appreciate it, but you're being annoying too. Let them do their job."

"We'll try."

I let out a sigh, "I guess that's the best I can ask for."

Chapter 15

PRESCOTT

"Wentworth!" Coach yells the moment I enter the gym. "My office. Now."

Running my hand over my face, I let out a sigh. Some of my teammates that are in the gym give me wary looks, but I ignore them as I follow after Coach.

I didn't want to leave Jade in the hospital, but she and her doctor insisted that Jade was doing well and she'd probably sleep the rest of the day since they hooked her up on more meds to help manage the pain. So there was no need for us to stay huddled in her room.

Besides, Yasmin promised she'd visit her with her other friends after her classes concluded, and it's not like we can all stay in her room anyway.

"Where the fuck were you yesterday?" Coach bellows the moment I close the door behind me, and then, not giving me a chance to answer, he continues: "I specifically told you to work with Gage, but you up and left without a backward glance. What kind of example does that set? Co-captain ignoring my instructions, fighting with his teammates, and missing practices. I should bench your ass right this moment."

"I went to the hospital."

The man's eyes narrow at me, so I lift my hands in the air in surrender. "It's not an excuse. If you want to bench me, go ahead and do it." It'll suck, but God knows I deserve it. "I wanted you to know where I was."

"What hospital?" His eyes go instantly to my leg. "Don't tell me you messed up your leg again."

"I— no. I went to find Nixon."

"Nixon?" If possible, his frown deepens.

I shift my weight from one leg to the other. "Jade and I…" I feel the heat rise up my neck. Ducking my head, I rub the back of my head and shrug.

Talk about awkward.

There's a beat of silence before Coach murmurs: "I see."

Just that. Two words followed by more silence. I look up to find him watching me. "Does that have anything to do with your and Nixon's brawl from a few weeks ago?"

I press my lips together, not saying a word.

We just stare at one another, and neither of us speaks for a while. After the fight, both Nixon and I kept our mouths shut. There was no sense in pointing the blame, and it's not how this shit is solved anyway.

"Idiots," Coach murmurs. "Get your ass out of my office and get to work."

I nod my head in understanding and turn on my feet to leave, but he stops me before I can make two steps.

"And Wentworth?"

I look over my shoulder: "Yes, Coach?"

"The next time you don't show up for practice without notice, I *will* bench you. Am I clear?"

"Perfectly."

JADE

"You're annoying me."

"I didn't say a word," Nixon protests, stopping in the doorway.

"You didn't have to." Letting out a sigh, I push myself upright, making sure to keep my expression as neutral as possible. People in my life don't deal well with pain. Me being in pain, most specifically. Especially not men. "This is the third time today you're at my place, Nixon."

"Can't a brother check in on his little sister who's recuperating from surgery?"

I roll my eyes at him. "At this point, you might as well move in."

"Well, about that..."

"No," I shake my head. "Don't you even dare go there, or I might call the cops on you."

"First, you'd need to be able to reach your phone."

"I can reach my phone just fine if properly motivated."

Nixon lifts his brows. "So why haven't you answered my texts?"

"Because you're annoying me."

This morning, I was discharged from the hospital with clear instructions to take it easy. No lifting my arms. No carrying heavy weight. Don't do anything with repetitive motions, which includes most housework activities—the only blessing that has come from this.

I was still feeling pretty tired. And in pain. I was itching, and there was this strange pull every time I tried to move my arms, which didn't help.

I had yet to look at myself in the mirror. I couldn't bring myself to do it, though. I couldn't look at my chest. I wasn't ready.

Nixon lets out a sigh as he enters the room. The bed creeks as he sits down. "I'm just worried about you."

"The doctor said everything is fine. There is no—"

"I don't care about what the doctor says," Nixon interrupts me. "How are *you* feeling?"

"I—" I open my mouth, the lie on the tip of my tongue, but the words don't come. Pressing my lips together, I clear my throat and try again, this time settling for the truth. "Tired. And bored out of my mind. At this point, going back to classes and listening to my lit professor talk bullshit about long, dead men sounds appealing."

Nixon lets out a soft chuckle, "Then you must really be bored."

"I am. That's why I've been thinking..."

"No."

"What do you mean no?" I narrow my eyes at Nixon. "I haven't even finished."

"You don't have to finish. The doctor told you to take it easy. So take it easy. You talked to your professors, and they agreed you can hand in the assignments left by the end of the semester and show up for midterms and finals. Am I right?"

"Yeah, but..."

"So no buts. You don't want to end up in the hospital again, do you?"

"I'm going to end up in the hospital one way or the other."

Before she discharged me, Dr. Hendriks told me I should come in a week so she could look at my drain and incisions. If everything is going along nicely, she should be able to take the drain out, and I should continue with the recovery at home before my first dose of chemo, which is coming in less than a month.

One month, meaning just before Thanksgiving.

Happy holidays to me.

Not.

"But if you get some kind of infection, you won't be able to start chemo on time. Please, Jade. Just let it be?"

How can I fight him when he's being so rational? I can't, that's how.

"Fine," I sigh. "Can you go home now? Your wife is waiting for you."

"Yasmin knows where I am. She wanted to come..."

"Of course she did."

Nixon ignores my interruption and continues as if I haven't said anything: "...but I convinced her it's better to give you some space."

I give him a pointed look. "Now, if only you'd listen to your own advice."

"Don't be a smartass, Smalls. There is actually a reason why I'm here."

"Oh, is there?"

Nixon ruffles my hair gently. As if I'm a porcelain doll that'll shatter if he's not careful.

"Always being a smartass," he tsks, but the playfulness that was there only a moment ago slowly disappears. "I wanted to check if you need any help with anything. Drains?" his face turns serious. "Shower?"

My smile falls. "I'm all good. I emptied the drains earlier today, and I can't take a shower until they're out. Plus, even if I could, you'd be the last person I'd call. No offense."

The last thing I needed was for Nixon to help me with the bathroom. He's already treating me like I'm a helpless child. No, I'll deal with the bathroom all on my own, no matter if it takes hours.

"You wound me, Smalls."

"Yeah, well... Now that you've done your brotherly duty,

you can go back to *your* apartment where *your wife* is waiting for you with dinner."

"You wanna come eat with us?" I give him an unamused smile that has him lifting his hands in defeat. "Okay, okay, I'm leaving." He gets to his feet. He interlocks his fingers in front of him, stretching. "Need me to get you anything before I leave? Pain meds? Ice pack?"

"I'm good, seriously, you—"

"Can leave," Nixon finishes. "I know, I know."

"We can go with that one too."

"Tomorrow afternoon, we're going away for a game, but if you text me before I leave, I can bring you anything you need."

"I'm sure I'll be fine. The girls are here. It's not like I'm alone."

These days, between everybody fussing about me, it was hard to get a few minutes of alone time to go to the bathroom, much less anything else.

"I know, but they're not me." Nixon leans down, pressing a kiss to the top of my head. "I'll see you later?"

"I'll see you later." I watch as Nixon walks toward the door. "Nixon?" My brother looks at me over his shoulder. "Kick some ass, will ya?"

The corner of his mouth lifts in a half smile. "You know it."

Once my brother is gone, I pull out the ice packs since they've long stopped doing their purpose, but since I'm too lazy to get up, I just snuggle into the covers and turn on Netflix, my best friend these past few days.

At some point, I must doze off because the next thing I hear is my window being pushed open. I look up to find Prescott climbing inside my room.

"You seriously need to start using the door," I whisper, pushing into a sitting position.

"Where's the fun in that?"

"Oh, I don't know. Not breaking your neck?"

"That's for pussies. Besides, if it were that dangerous, I would have already fallen at least a dozen times." Prescott lets his duffle bag drop on the floor by my desk before he joins me on the bed. He cups my cheek, pushing away a strand of hair behind my ear. "How are you feeling?"

"As good as I look."

"So awful?"

I gently shove him away, but not gently enough because a jab of pain goes through me.

"Fuck, Jade. You're in pain." Prescott's gaze shifts to my nightstand. "When was the last time you put on an ice pack?"

"A few hours ago. I didn't feel like getting up."

"And pain meds?"

"I don't like them. They make me feel dizzy and sleepy."

"That's the point of pain meds." He grabs the bottle and slides two tablets into his palm. He looks at them for a moment before giving them to me along with the bottle of water. "Now take them like a good girl."

"Here you go again." I look at the bottle of water, noticing the intact seal, but before I can even try to open it, Prescott grabs it and opens it for me. "First, you want to tie me to the bed. Now you want me to be a good girl."

Prescott gives me a warning look. "Jade..."

"What?" I bat my eyelashes innocently. "I'm just repeating what you said."

He opens his mouth to protest, but before he can say anything, the door opens, and Grace's head appears in the doorway.

"Hey, are you hun—" The words die on her lips when she notices Prescott sitting on the bed next to me. I see the moment of confusion for a split second before her gaze darts toward the open window and then back to us. "Oh, sorry, I didn't realize you were here."

I give Prescott a pointed look. "I keep telling him he should use the door."

"But this is closer to where I usually park my car."

"Oh-kay," Grace drawls. "You guys wanna eat? I was just about to order some pizza."

"I'm not really..." I start, but Prescott interrupts me. "Food sounds great."

"Good," Grace smiles and disappears before I can contradict her.

"I'm really not hungry," I protest.

"You have to eat. Maybe you'll feel less dizzy if you put some food in you."

I glare at him. "You're extremely bossy."

"Takes one to know one. I'll put these away and come back."

Not waiting for an answer, Prescott gets to his feet, ice pack in hand, and goes out of the room. Sighing, I down the pills he gave me before lying down in time for Prescott to appear with a fresh set of ice packs.

I try to take them from him, but he brushes my hands out of his way and does it himself.

"I smell," I protest, suddenly feeling self-conscious.

"So what?" Slipping off his shoes, Prescott climbs into my bed and pulls me to his chest. "You want me to come straight after practice next time? We can smell together."

I tilt my head back to glare at him. "Don't you dare."

"You sure?" he wiggles his brows. "I think it would be fun."

"I'm not accepting your smelly ass in my bed, Wentworth."

"It's funny you think you can stop me." His arms tighten around me. "Now stop moving, and let's watch Netflix before the pizza gets here."

"Okay," I whisper, trying to relax against him, but it's so

hard when he's near me. My mind turns to mush, and it's so difficult to concentrate with his arms around me.

What are we doing here, really?

Prescott's been around every day since I woke up in the hospital, but a part of me was still worried that something was going to happen, and he'd leave. And as much as I wanted him here now, I wasn't sure I'd be able to let him go again when he changed his mind.

Watching him leave once was unbearable.

Watching him leave twice?

I'm pretty sure it'll shatter something inside of me.

But do I tell him to go?

No.

Like a glutton for punishment, I hold on tighter.

Chapter 16

JADE

"That incision is healing nicely," Dr. Hendriks says as she finishes—well, whatever the hell she's doing. "How are you feeling? Still sore?"

"Not as much as in the beginning, but my arms still hurt when I try to move them too much or make any sudden moves. Like there's tugging. And the itching."

I shudder at the very thought. Since I couldn't take a shower so far, I had to make do the best I could, and let me tell you; it's barely enough.

At this point, my stench was the only thing keeping me cooped up in my apartment.

"That's normal. Your wound is still healing, and the area where the incision is very dense. You should try gently massaging it with some oil. It should help soften the tissue. I also want you to start PT to help with your mobility and regain strength in your arms. The pain?"

"It's there, but it's manageable."

"You don't need to manage it. There is nothing wrong with needing some extra help to relieve the pain."

And risk getting dependent on pain meds? I think not.

"I'm doing good, really. If the pain becomes too much, I'll take some more."

"Okay." Dr. Hendriks steps back. "All done."

"Thank you."

Grabbing the hoodie, I slip it back on and pull the zipper. I've learned early on that if I want to keep some dignity and not call others for help every time I need to get dressed, oversized zip-up hoodies are the way to go.

"Please tell me I can finally take a shower?"

I'm not above getting to my knees and begging. My whole body is one big itching mess, and I'm lucky I haven't clawed my skin off yet.

"You can take a shower. The drains are out, and your incision looks good."

"Finally."

"I'll write down those oils we talked about and recommend a physical therapist who specializes in mastectomy patients."

"Sounds good." I nod my head and hop off the bed.

"I still don't want you to drive or lift anything heavy until the PT clears you. But apart from that, you can slowly get back to normal life."

"Normal life," I huff. The idea seems laughable. My life will never be normal again. "Is there even such a thing?"

Dr. Hendriks places her hand on my shoulder. "It might not seem that way, but things *will* get better." She gives me a reassuring squeeze. "The next time we see each other will be for chemo."

And just like that, she shattered any semblance of normal with eleven words.

Because one day, things might get back there.

But that day isn't today.

Because, first, things are about to get much, much worse.

"You've been awfully quiet," Grace says, glancing at me from the driver's seat. "Did something happen at the doctor's office?"

"Just thinking. That's all."

"About?"

"Life," I let out a soft chuckle. "I'm fine, really."

"You keep saying that, but I'm not sure who you're trying to convince. Yourself or us."

I guess she's right about that.

"It's okay not to be fine, Jade." Grace places a hand over mine, giving it a firm squeeze. "Hell, nothing about this is fine. Young people shouldn't get cancer. You're just twenty. How the fuck is that fair?"

"It's not. But we live in a world that is far from perfect."

"I know, but still. I'm just so angry on your behalf. After everything that has happened with your mom, you deserve some peace and happiness."

Peace and happiness.

I'm not sure I know what those two are anymore.

"I'm sorry," Grace sighs. "Here I'm raging when you're the one who actually has to go through it all, but I'm scared. Scared for you. Scared of what this all means."

"Me too." I lean my head on her shoulder. Turning my hand, I interlock our fingers. "I know I might seem calm, but I'm not. I can't concentrate on that fear because if I do, it'll overwhelm me, and I won't be able to breathe. And with chemo a few weeks away..."

"We'll get through it," Grace nods decisively. "But enough about that. We're almost home, and I have some time before my class. So how about some coffee and scones? My treat."

I let out a soft chuckle, "How can I say no to scones?"

"Dammit," I mutter as the pain slices through me. I drop my hands, closing my eyes to fight the angry tears threatening to come up.

I will not cry.

I will not cry.

I will no—

"Jade?" My whole body freezes at the sound of the familiar voice. I stop, trying to hear over the sound of the shower, hoping I only imagined it when... "Jade? Where are you?"

Shit.

"Jad—"

Even through the foggy glass, I can see the doorknob turn.

"Don't come in," I say quickly before he can push the door open.

I can't have him see me like this. Not...

"What do you mean, don't come in?"

"Just like I said, don't come in," I bite out, the irritation, fear, and unease making me snappy.

"What are you doing? I can hear the shower."

"That's because I'm in the shower. Please just..."

"I'm coming inside."

Quickly, I turn my back to the door, placing my hands over my chest the best I can.

"Jade?" Prescott asks softly. "What are you doing?"

"What does it look like I'm doing?" I ask, my eyes glued to the shower wall. "I know you're used to smelly locker rooms, Wentworth, but I figured even you're familiar with the concept of a shower."

"I mean, what are you doing taking a shower all on your own, not even a couple of weeks after surgery?"

"My doctor gave me the all-clear."

"That's not what I mean, and you know it," Prescott sighs.

"I don't care. Can you just go? I'll be out in a few."

The door rattles, making me jump out of my skin. "Prescott, I told—"

"You'll be out with half of your hair shampooed?" he asks from right behind me.

"W-what..." Goosebumps rise on my skin from his nearness. My tongue darts out, sliding over my lower lip. I peek over my shoulder, seeing the top of his naked chest. I can feel his warmth pressing into me from behind. "What are you doing?"

"What does it look like I'm doing?" He grabs the shampoo from the shelf, squeezing a little bit into his palm. "Tilt your head back."

Too tired to fight him, I do as he says. Soon enough, his expert fingers are massaging my scalp. I let out a soft moan as he shampoos my hair. It feels so nice I want to cry. Or maybe that's my hormones that are all over the place.

"Rinse," Prescott whispers, breaking the quiet.

I step under the spray, tilting my head back and letting the water wash over me. Then he repeats the process once again as if he knows how much I need this.

His body brushes against mine as he grabs the body wash next.

"I can..."

Prescott wraps his arms around my waist, pulling me to him, his lips pressing against the crook of my neck. A shiver runs through me, making my knees buckle underneath. I swear that if Prescott weren't holding onto me, I'd have fallen on my ass right then and there.

"You don't have to hide from me."

"I—" My throat bobs as I swallow the knot stuck inside, my words coming out raspy. "I don't think I can."

"You've seen my scars, doll."

I shake my head. "That's not the same."

"Why not?"

"These are ugly."

"Have you even seen them?" he challenges.

"I just..." Another shake of my head. "Can't. It's too soon."

Too fast. Too soon. Too much.

Just too freaking much.

"Then how can you know they're ugly? You're alive because of these scars."

"We don't know that yet. Not for sure."

He starts to turn me so I'm facing him. I try to resist, but he doesn't let me. So I give in, closing my eyes, so I don't have to see the look on his face when he sees my scars.

Fingers caress my cheekbone; his touch is so tender I think I almost imagined it. "Open those pretty baby blues, doll," Prescott whispers.

I shake my head, refusing to give in. He wants to see me like this? He can suit himself, but I don't have to watch the devastation and pity in his eyes.

"C'mon, I never thought you were a coward."

"This game won't work. Not this time."

Prescott presses his forehead against mine. "I'm not playing games. Never with this."

A promise.

Slowly, I blink my eyes open to find him staring at me. "Was that so hard?"

My throat bobs, but no words come out. Prescott cups my cheeks with both hands. "You've seen my scars, Jade. You don't ever have to be afraid to show me yours. Ever." He presses his mouth against my forehead. This kiss is hard, almost bruising. "When you're ready. Okay? Whenever you're ready, I'll be here to show you just how beautiful you are. Scars or no scars."

He takes a step back, his gaze holding mine. Not moving an inch. "I'll be in your room, so yell if you need anything."

Prescott starts to turn around, but I grab his wrist. My heart is beating a mile a minute as he turns around, surprise flashing on his face. "Jade?"

"Together," I whisper quickly before I change my mind. "Let's look at them together."

Prescott shakes his head. "If you're not ready..."

I clasp my fingers tighter around his wrist, not allowing him to pull back.

"That's the thing. I don't think I'll ever be ready, so I might as well get it over with."

Prescott watches me for a long moment, so long that the water starts turning cold. Still, not once does he lower his gaze. Unclenching my fingers, I let my hand drop. Turning my back to him, I turn off the shower.

"Prescott?" I ask weakly, unable to turn to face him. If he changed his mind...

But of course, he hadn't. Those strong arms slip around my waist and pull me to his chest. "Together."

He turns us toward the door. The glass is still foggy, so he places his hand on it. "Last chance."

I put my hand over his, my heart beating so loudly I could hear the echo of it in my eardrums. We stand like that for a few moments, and then I slide our joined hands over the glass, wiping away the condensation and facing the mirror.

My gaze meets Prescott's in the reflection, neither of us looking away. God, he's beautiful in that masculine, rough around the edges way; that's all him.

His chin leans against my shoulder, that stubble of his tickling my skin as he presses his lips against my ear. "Look at how beautiful you are."

"You didn't even look at them."

"I don't have to see them to know how beautiful you are."

His words... they're my undoing.

He is my undoing.

So I look.

My gaze slides down slowly, taking in this new body I never thought I'd have to face. I suck in a sharp breath when I get to the scars. Matching twin lines are going from my sternum, parallel toward my armpits: red and rugged lines stick out against my otherwise pale skin.

Prescott's arms tighten around me. "Shhh," he whispers soothingly, making me realize I let out a loud sob.

"They look awful."

I try to raise my hands to cover myself, but Prescott doesn't let me.

"They don't. They're telling a story of a survivor."

"They look like a kid took a knife to them."

"A surgeon. And it won't always stay like that. The wound is still pretty fresh, they'll fade away, and you can always choose to have reconstruction after, if you want to."

Unable to look at my reflection any longer, I turn in his arms. "Would you want me to?"

I stare at his face, looking for a sign of... I'm not even sure what. Disgust? Pity? But it's not there.

Prescott's thumbs slide over my cheekbones, wiping away the tears. "It's your body, your choice. But whatever you decide, you'll always be the most beautiful woman I've ever known."

Then his lips press against mine. Soft and gentle at the beginning, but the kiss soon turns hard. His tongue presses against my lips, demanding entrance, which I happily give.

I didn't even realize how much I needed this. His hands on my body, his mouth on mine, and this fire burning between us.

Prescott kisses me strong and hard, his tongue swirling around mine, making me moan softly.

For one blissful moment, nothing else matters. Nothing except the feel of his body brushing against mine, his lips devouring me like this is the only chance we'll have.

Maybe it is. Maybe it isn't.

Right now, I don't have it in me to care.

Because right now, he's mine.

All of our broken pieces fall together in a kaleidoscope of light.

And for a split second, I feel like me again.

Beautiful in my brokenness.

Pushing the door open, I break the kiss. "I need you," I whisper, pulling him out of the shower.

Prescott blinks his eyes open, those impossibly dark eyes of his softening around the edges as he watches me. "Jade, I'm not sure this is the best idea. You're still heal—"

Raising on the tips of my toes, I press my mouth against his, stopping him from finishing. "I don't care. I need you. I need you to make it all go away. I need to feel like me once again."

Gently he cups my cheeks, his forehead pressing against mine. "You'll tell me if it's too much? If I'm doing something that you're not comfortable with or if I hurt you?"

"You'd never hurt me." The words are out instantly, with no doubt in my mind whatsoever. Prescott wouldn't do anything to hurt me. Not now. Not when it comes to this.

There might be a lot of uncertainties about my life and future, but this isn't one of them.

"No," he rasps, his voice tight. "I'd never hurt you, not intentionally. But that doesn't mean I won't do it by accident."

For some reason, it feels like his words have a deeper meaning than just about the physical, but I don't have it in me to care. Not right now.

"Promise me, doll. You won't let me hurt you."

Slowly, I nod. "I promise."

Before the last syllable is out, his mouth meets mine in a slow kiss. Prescott crouches down, his arms wrapping around me as he lifts me in the air.

"What are you doing?" I yelp, bracing my hands against his shoulders.

"I'm taking you to bed."

He crosses the short distance to my bedroom, laying me gently on the bed before he joins me too.

"So damn beautiful."

Prescott traces kisses over my body, down my neck, and over my chest, making sure not to touch the sensitive flesh as his fingers and lips skim over every inch of my body.

"Once these heal completely, I'm going to kiss every freaking inch of your body to show you just how fucking beautiful you are. Erase every ounce of worry still brewing in your mind."

"Prescott..."

"Hmm..." He licks at my navel, my hips buckling underneath his touch as my fingers sink into his hair, and he moves lower, kissing my belly and making his way to my pu—

"Shit," I hiss as his tongue slips between my lips, my legs spreading to accommodate his wide shoulders.

His hands slide under my ass, lifting me off the mattress as his tongue dips deeper, slipping inside me teasingly, the tip of his nose rubbing against my aching clit.

My hands clasp his hair, holding onto the soft strands. "Prescott, I need..."

Sliding his tongue out, he sucks at my clit and plunges two fingers inside me. The orgasm builds in the pit of my belly as he slowly thrusts. And then his teeth graze over my clit. My walls tighten around him, and I'm coming so hard I swear I can see stars.

I'm not sure how long I lie like that when Prescott pulls

back and makes his way up my body. His mouth brushes against mine in a long, gentle kiss.

"Good?"

The corner of my mouth tilts upward. "Better than good."

"Good, 'cause I'm not done just yet."

His fingers intertwine with mine, and he slides into me in one long thrust—my breath hitches at the sudden fullness.

"You okay?" he whispers, his fingers brushing a strand of my hair behind my ear.

"Perfect." I turn my head to the side, my mouth brushing against his. "Make love to me, Prescott."

And that's precisely what he does. He pulls back gently before gliding inside once again. Each movement he makes is slow and measured as we continue kissing like we have all the time in the world.

At this moment, we do. There's no rush, just eternal tenderness. The orgasm builds slowly inside me as I meet him thrust for thrust.

"Jade... fuck."

He presses his forehead against mine, his warm breath tickling my skin as he tries to hold back. I slip my leg around his waist, pulling him closer to me. This time when he sinks deeper, he hits just the right spot, and I feel my pussy tighten around him.

"Together."

Our mouths clash, fingers intertwining as he thrusts once, twice, and then we're both falling. If I weren't already in love with him, this would have been the moment that I'd finally cave.

Chapter 17

PRESCOTT

"I never took you for a geek."

Finishing the equation I've been working on, I look up to find Jade watching me from the bed.

My bed.

It's strange to have her here.

In my space.

Not only do I not bring girls to my apartment, but it's even stranger since we don't need to sneak around like we've done something wrong.

She pulls her legs to her chest and leans her head against her knees. "It's kind of sexy. Do you have glasses?"

The corner of my mouth tips upward. "Who's the one with the kinks now?"

"Hey, you started it." Jade grabs a pillow and tosses it at me, but I catch it before it can hit me in the face. "Seriously? Can't you even let me have this little victory?"

I rub at the scruff on my jaw. "Can't have you damaging this pretty face."

"Of course not. What would your fans say?" She rolls her eyes. "So, glasses?"

"I don't have any fans." I shake my head. "And no to the glasses. Sorry to disappoint."

She purses her lips. "Shame. I think they'd look good on you. Actually, let's try it out."

Jade jumps to her feet and grabs her phone. She's scrolling through and almost bumps into the edge of the desk, but I catch her at the last moment, pulling her onto my lap.

"What do you mean, try it out?" I ask, looking over her shoulder.

"Just like I said, try it out."

She lifts her arm in the air, her phone still clasped in her hand, the camera focusing on us when some kind of filter pops on the screen.

"Seriously?" I scowl at her as matching pairs of glasses appear on our faces.

"I knew it. It's totally not fair how good you look."

"I look ridiculous."

"You look *hot*." She presses the button, capturing the image and bringing the phone closer for better inspection. "So hot. I think this will go to my private collection."

"Like hell, it will." I grab the phone out of her hand.

"Hey, gimmie that. My phone. My photo."

I quickly type over the image and post it before returning the phone.

"What did you do?"

She opens the story just as the picture uploads. My scowling and Jade's smiling faces appear on the screen. She looks small, sitting on my lap, with my hand sprawled over her stomach as I hold her close, the caption "check out the hunk that's my boyfriend" written below.

"A hunk, ha!" she snorts. "Thinking highly of yourself, are we?"

"You're the one who said I was hot," I remind her.

"Also territorial."

I don't even bother denying it. "You ashamed to call me your boyfriend in front of your friends?"

"No way, although these are hardly my friends. Besides, you shared it on the wrong Instagram, buddy."

Rolling my eyes at her, I grab my phone. I made sure to tag myself, so when I open the app, it's the first message waiting for me, making it easy to repost.

"Better?" Chuckling, I shake my head. "I thought we were studying."

"We are, but I'm so bored. I swear, I'm half tempted to throw this book out of the window."

"Not a fan of the classics?"

"If it doesn't have smut in it, I'm out." A smirk appears on her face as she turns to me. "I can totally see my professor's face if I gave her one of the books I read. She'd probably have a coronary."

My brow quirks up. "Smut, you say?"

"Of course, you'd get stuck on that part."

"Hey, can't blame a guy for being interested. The most I've read recently are chemistry and biology, which are not nearly as interesting. So tell me more about these books you're reading in your spare time."

"No way." She gets to her feet. "C'mon, let's go out."

"We're studying," I remind her, but I don't try to resist when she grabs my hand and tugs me upward.

"We studied enough. Didn't they teach you in that fancy doctor school of yours that studying requires substance?"

"I'm technically not in med school. Not yet, which is why I have to study in the first place. You know, so I don't fail my MCATs and can apply to said med schools?"

"We can study later. After a coffee."

"I have coffee here."

"That rusty old thing that filters mud? I think not."

"Fine," letting out a sigh, I get up. "But we're taking our books with us."

Jade shakes her head at me, tsking. "Prescott Wentworth is going all responsible on me. I don't think I ever saw this day coming."

"If you want that coffee, grab your books, Cole, and get your ass moving."

With another roll of her eyes, she starts to turn around, but at the last moment, I pull her back to me, crushing my lips to hers in a hard kiss.

"I thought you said we were going to study," she breathes, her cheeks flushed.

"We are." I slip her hair behind her ears. "This is just an incentive to be a good girl."

"Here we go again with you and your kinks." She places a hand on my chest, giving me a shove strong enough so I fall back on the mattress. "Get your head out of the gutter and grab your books. We've got work to do."

Work, right.

I run my hand over my face, rubbing at my forehead. Letting out a sigh, I push from the bed and quickly gather my stuff just in time to catch Jade grabbing her bag off the floor.

"No heavy lifting," I chastise, tugging her bag from her hand and throwing it over my shoulder.

"Seriously?" Jade props her hands on her hips, and even though she tries, I can see the slight flinch passing over her face at the motion. She tries to act strong, but she's still hurting.

"Seriously." I look around the room, my eyes falling on my chair. *Bingo.* Grabbing the hoodie I took off earlier, I pull the zipper down and open it for her. "Arms."

"You have to be joking."

"Arms," I repeat, putting on my no-nonsense face that has her shaking her head.

"You're crazy." Still, she slides her hands into the sleeves, and I pull the zipper up to her chin.

"You can't get sick with your chemo so close." I take her hand in mine and pull her toward the door.

"We're going out. Need something?" I ask Spencer. He and Xander had gotten home a little while ago and sat their asses in front of the TV.

"We're good," he mutters, barely glancing at us as his hockey player skates over the screen, only to turn around and do a double take. "Well, hello, Jade. Fancy seeing you here."

"Oh shut up, Spence." I pull Jade closer to me. "Let's get out of here."

We say goodbye before grabbing our jackets and heading into the chilly early November afternoon.

"I still think this was a bad idea. I can smell the snow in the air."

She tilts her head back, looking up at the darkening sky. "You think we'll have snow for Thanksgiving?"

"Possibly," I murmur, my thoughts going to all the unanswered calls waiting for me on my phone.

My dad tried calling me a few times in the last couple of weeks, but I've managed to avoid him so far. What was the point of talking? I knew what he'd say, and there was no way I'd agree to go home. I have too much on my plate without dealing with Dad.

"Which is even more of a reason for you to stay home where it's warm."

Jade lets out a loud groan. "Can we not?" She pushes open the door to Cup It Up, the warm air hitting us in the face as we enter.

"I'm just saying..."

"What happened to you taking it easy and staying home?"

"For God's sake!" Jade turns around and glares at her brother, who's leaning against the bar. "Don't you start."

"Maybe if you weren't as stubborn as a mule..."

"Takes one to know one, big brother." She looks at Yasmin, who's standing behind the counter. "Can't you please control your husband?"

Yasmin lifts her hands in the air. "I'm not getting in the middle of you two."

Jade sticks her tongue at her. "Chicken."

"Maybe, but I've learned my lesson the hard way. I'm not doing it again."

Callie glances up from her phone, where she's furiously typing. "One good thing about being an only child."

Nixon huffs, "Have you heard you and Yasmin get into it?"

Callie and Yasmin exchange a look, matching smiles on their faces. "I don't know what you're talking about," Callie says, returning her attention to the phone.

"Of course not," Nixon says dryly. "Hayden coming home for the holidays?"

Callie's face lights up immediately. "He is. They have another game, so it'll be a while, but he should meet us at his grandmother's place."

"While on the topic of holidays." Jade turns to Nixon. "When are we driving back home?"

"You've got an exam on Tuesday, right?" Nixon glances at his wife, waiting for her confirmation.

"Yeah," Yas nods, placing two coffee cups on the counter in front of us. "After that, we're good to go."

"Sounds like a plan. I only hope I won't feel like shit by then." Jade turns to me. "When are you going back home?"

The sip I took suddenly turns sour in my mouth. I swallow

it down, feeling my stomach roll. Unease, guilt, and relief all mix together.

"I'm not going back home."

Surprise flashes on her face. "You're not? So what are you going to do?"

"Stay here, I guess," I shrug. "It's not like it would be the first time."

Jade's mouth opens, the understanding flashing on her face. She knows more about my family situation than anybody else sitting at this table. About my parents, their crazy expectations, and our dysfunctional relationship. About Gabriel.

Sadness flashes on her face, so I slide my hand into hers under the table, forcing out a smile. "Don't look at me like that."

I could take many things, but I couldn't take her sadness. Especially not her sadness because of me.

"I know, it's just..."

"Why don't you come with us?"

Both Jade and I turn toward Nixon to find him watching us.

"What?" he smirks. "Don't look so shocked right now."

A crinkle appears between Jade's brows. "Did you just invite him over?"

"Hey, just because I'm open to the idea of you two together doesn't mean shit. He's sleeping on the couch."

"Like hell he is," Jade protests.

"You can either take it or leave it, Smalls."

"You're being an asshole. If I remember correctly, Yasmin slept in your bed when she was visiting."

"That's different."

Jade crosses her arms over her chest. "Sexist isn't a good color on you, big brother."

"Couch." Nixon points his finger at us. "Take it or leave it."

If possible, Jade's eyes narrow even further. "We'll see about that."

Chapter 18

JADE

I tap my foot, anxious to get this over with. The wait is always the worst.

A hand covers my knee.

I watch it for a while. That big, steady hand that's been my lifeline for the last few weeks. So similar to another one, but not the one I want.

Not really.

No offense to my brother.

"Calm down, or you'll make a hole in the floor," Nixon says quietly. "It's going to be okay."

"Easy for you to say. You're not the one who'll have a deadly medicine injected into your veins in hopes it'll fight off the deadlier disease running in your DNA." I tilt my head back, letting it bang against the wall. "Sorry," I let out a heavy sigh. "I'm just nervous. I want this done with."

"I know. But try to calm down, okay?"

Biting my lower lip, I nod and pull out my phone, checking for any messages. The corner of my mouth twitches upward, my chest relaxing slightly when I see a familiar name written on the screen.

Hotshot: Good luck today! I'm so sorry I couldn't be there with you.

He's not the only one. I want him here too, but he had a lab he couldn't miss that starts in a few minutes. Just because I was excused from going to classes didn't mean I could destroy his future. Prescott wants to be a doctor, for fuck's sake. And not just any doctor. He wants to be an oncologist. So he can try and save little boys like Gabriel and make up for not saving him. Not that there is anything he needs to make up for. He was just a boy himself, and cancer is an ugly, unpredictable disease.

Me: It's okay. I'll see you at home?

Just as I hit send, I hear footsteps coming down the hall. I look up, noticing Dr. Hendriks walking next to a nurse. They're whispering quietly as they come closer. I jump to my feet just as the nurse nods, sliding into one of the rooms and leaving us alone.

"Dr. Hendriks, is it tim—"

"I'm sorry, Jade," she stops me before I can even finish. Her words are gentle, but something about the way she looks at me makes my stomach clench.

"W-what's going on?" I ask, my voice breaking with uncertainty.

Did something happen? Are my lab results that bad? It has to be. Why else would she be looking at me with pity in her eyes? Why wo—

"We can't start the chemo today."

I blink, unsure if I heard her correctly. My heart starts to beat faster, sweat coating my palms.

No, no, no. I shake my head, refusing to believe this is happening. *It can't be happening.*

I might not want to do this, but I *need* it. I need it to beat this thing and live.

"What do you mean you can't start the chemo?" Nixon asks, his arm wrapping around me protectively.

Dr. Hendriks looks at him before returning her attention to me, and for the second time in a matter of weeks, this woman shatters my heart. "We can't start chemo because you're pregnant."

Chapter 19

PRESCOTT

The icy air is beating my face as I hurry across the campus to my car. There is a bite to it, signaling more snow should fall soon, which will make our afternoon practice hell on earth, not that the coach will care. We had four more games, and if we won... I shake my head, not daring to even think about it, so I don't jinx it. Giving up now—hell, losing—wasn't an option.

Four more games.

That's what it all comes down to.

I thought I'd feel different. More unsettled. Sad that the end is so near. Maybe I still will. Maybe it hasn't hit me yet. But somehow, I doubt it. Not with everything happening with Jade. Hell, I was rushing across the campus so I could see her for a few minutes, and then I'll have to hurry back to make it in time for practice, but it'll be worth it.

Today was her first chemo session, and I remember how damn well terrifying that is. And how shitty Gabriel felt afterward. His pale washed-out skin. His hollow eyes. The puking. The shivers.

The idea of Jade going through all that alone makes the bile rise up my throat. My gut squeezes at the mere thought of it, so I hurry my steps. I get to the parking lot in record time and slide into my car. My fingers grip the steering wheel as I try to drive calmly and responsibly. The last thing I need is to get in a freaking accident.

Ten minutes later, I'm parking in the first open spot in front of Jade's building. Thankfully, an older lady is just leaving the building with her dogs, so I hold the door open for her before slipping inside. Bypassing the elevators, I go to the stairs, taking two at a time.

Shouting greets me the moment I get to Jade's floor. Not giving it much thought, I hurry to her door, only to realize the yelling is coming from her apartment. It's muffled enough so I don't hear the exact words but loud enough to be heard through the walls.

"What the—" Grabbing the doorknob, I twist it expecting some resistance, only to find it open. Shaking my head at the idiot who left it unlocked, I push inside, the voices growing louder.

"You don't have a choice!" Nixon yells.

"Says who?" Jade asks, her voice much lower.

"Me! Says me and everybody else who's thinking rationally. You can't—"

I step into the doorway finding Nixon and Jade standing in the middle of the living room. Jade's arms are crossed over her chest defensively as her brother hulks over her, his face red from yelling.

My whole body tenses at the image, fingers clenching into fists by my sides.

"Somebody care to explain what the hell is going on in here?" I ask, my voice deadly low.

What the fuck does he think he's doing, yelling at her like that? As if Jade isn't going through enough as it is. As if—

My best friend turns those murderous eyes toward me. Good, better to have his anger focused on me than on her.

"You fucking son of a bitch." His words are the only warning as he leaps toward me. Before I can blink, his hands are gripping my jacket, and he has me pressed against the wall, those blue eyes the color of a storm throwing daggers at me.

"Nixon!" Jade yells, but Nixon doesn't spare her a glance as he pushes me against the wall again.

"Give me one fucking reason why I shouldn't kill you right this instant."

"Me? I should kill you for the way you were talking to your sister just now."

Jade appears behind Nixon, trying to pull him off me, but it's useless. He's not budging. "Nixon, let him go this minute."

"No way in hell. This is between Wentworth and me."

"Nixon..."

I grip his forearm, trying to push him off me. "You'll have to be more specific than that, Cole."

"More specific? Fine, you want specific?" His forearm digs deeper into my windpipe.

"Don't you da—"

"You got her pregnant, you bastard!"

My head snaps up, my eyes landing on Jade's tear-stained ones as she still tries to pull her brother off me.

"W-what?!" I croak out. It can't be. It's impossible. It's...

All fight leaves me as tears spill down Jade's face telling me what Nixon said is true. A part of me is glad that he's holding me because I'd have fallen to my knees right here and now.

Pregnant.

I close my eyes, letting my head bang against the wall.

Jade's pregnant.

How the fuck did that happen? When? We were so careful. So freaking...

"You had no right!" Jade yells.

Nixon lets go suddenly, and I fall to the ground. Jade shoves her brother away. "That was my truth to tell him."

"Jade..." Nixon says tentatively, taking a step forward, but she pushes him back.

"Mine!" Wiping away the tears, she glares at him. "Get the hell out."

"Smalls, I just..."

"Get the hell out, Nixon!"

Nixon looks at her for a moment longer but does as she asks. Silence settles over the room, nothing filling it except the sound of our heavy breathing, but it's soon broken by a sob.

Taking a step forward, I wrap her into my arms as she cries loudly. Her fingers clasp around me as she buries her head into the crook of my arm and bawls uncontrollably. It's like all the walls that she's been building around herself in the last few weeks have crumbled to the ground.

Completely shattered.

I did this.

Just one more person I broke in the end with my carelessness.

Fuck!

Tilting my head back, I close my eyes to fight the burning behind my eyelids. "I'm so sorry, Jade," I whisper, soothing my hand down her back. "So freaking sorry. If only I'd been there. If only..."

If only what?

If only I hadn't fucked her? If only I hadn't touched her? If only I never gave in that first time? If only I hadn't loved her?

You kill everyone you love, my dad's brutal words come back like a wrecking ball.

I tighten my arms around her. "I'm so, so sorry, baby."

Jade shakes her head, pushing back so she can look at me.

Her eyes are watery and red-rimmed, but she's still the most beautiful woman I've ever seen. "It's not your fault."

"How is it not my fault? If it weren't for me, none of this would have happened. If it weren't for me..."

Jade grabs my cheeks, forcing me to look at her. "If it weren't for you, I'd still have cancer. There is no running away from it. You didn't do this."

"I got you pregnant."

The bile rises in my throat at the mere mention of the words. At their implication. This would be fucked up even if she wasn't sick, but now... now it's ten times worse.

"The last I checked, it takes two people to make a baby. It should have been me who told you. I'm never going to forgive Nixon for doing this."

"He's just worried about you." I rub my hand over my face, pushing my hair back.

She might blame him, but I couldn't. Not when I knew he was right. This is my fault. I fucked up. If she wasn't pregnant...

I let my hand drop down as the realization hits me. "What happened with chemo?"

Jade looks away, her throat bobbing.

No, no, no.

"Jade," I say softly. "What happened with chemo?"

"I can't do it. Not as long as I'm pregnant."

"Fuck!" I ball my fingers into fists, turning around, the need to punch something, to let out all this anger overwhelming me. "Please tell me you got us an appointment to take care of it."

She opens her mouth but closes it swiftly, shaking her head.

"Dammit, Jade!"

"What? What do you want me to do, Prescott? I'm so happy that you and Nixon can jump into solution mode, but I can't! I just found out that I'm pregnant. I can't just unknow it. I can't just wave my hand and schedule the abortion in the next heartbeat."

She can't be serious. She needs chemo. She needs it to live.

"I'm not saying you should do it right now..."

"Oh no?" Those blue eyes shine with unshed tears and anger. "Because it damn well seems like you don't have a problem doing just that!"

"I'm studying to be a doctor, Jade. I know the risks. You said it yourself. They're not going to do the chemo if you're pregnant, and you need the chemo to live."

"Don't you think I know that? But what if this is my only chance?"

"Jade..." I try to grab her hand, try to have her listen to me, try to make her see the risks, but she pulls back.

"No, you're the doctor. So tell me, Dr. Wentworth, what are my chances of ever having a family of my own after chemo?"

I press my lips into a tight line, refusing to give in. We both knew what her chances were. There was no sense in lying to her. There were other ways for her to have a family, but there was only one way for her to survive this.

"See?" Jade offers me a sad smile. "It's not that easy."

"I know it's not easy, but we're talking about life and death here, Jade. *Your life.*" I want to put my hands on her shoulders and shake some sense into her. "The longer you put off chemo, the fewer chances..." I shake my head, unable to finish it. Unable to even entertain the possibility. She's not going to die. I won't watch another person I love die. "You have to do it."

"What I have to do is *think.*"

"Jade, please, you have to..."

"No." Her lips press in a stubborn line I know so well before she turns her back on me. "I'm done listening and having you and Nixon manhandle me like I'm a child. I'm sick, Prescott. I'm sick, not stupid, and definitely not dead."

"Well, if you don't make a decision soon, you might as well be as good as dead, but don't expect me to stay around and watch it all play out," I yell right back at her; the anger, the frustration, and the fear seeping right out of me.

Before she can answer or I can do or say anything else, I turn on the balls of my feet and walk away. I shut the door behind me, the echo following me all the way out, as do Nixon's words.

"You got her pregnant, you bastard."

I move on autopilot, barely noticing that I have less than twenty minutes to make it to practice. Maybe that's exactly what I need. A beating so brutal I won't be able to think, be able to feel...

Pressing my foot on the gas pedal, I drive like the devil's at my heels, making it to the locker room just as the last of my teammates are exiting in full equipment.

But not Nixon.

He's sitting there.

Waiting.

As if he can feel me, he looks up, a tortured expression on his face.

I storm to my locker, tossing the duffle bag in front of it as I rip my shirt over my head.

"Did you..."

"No," I bite back, grabbing my pads and jersey and quickly putting them on.

"Shit. Prescott, I..."

"Don't." Closing the locker, I turn to face my best friend. "Just because I agree with you doesn't mean I'm okay with you treating her the way you did today."

Nixon runs his fingers through his hair, his hand shaking. "She won't listen. I told her..."

I shake my head. "I can't do this. Not right now."

I look away, finishing putting the last of my equipment on, but I can still feel Nixon's gaze on mine.

"What do you need?"

I run my fingers through my hair, chuckling humorlessly at the question. What do I need? "Not to feel." With that, I grab my helmet and go toward the door.

JADE

"You sure you don't want to eat anything?" Rei asks once again, startling me out of my thoughts.

I force out a smile. "I'm not really hungry."

The last thing I want is to worry my friends. I've done enough of that already, but damn, I'm worried that if I eat anything, I'd throw up right here and now.

"Are you okay? You seem off."

"Is it the whole cancellation thing?" Grace asks, joining us from the kitchen and sitting in the armchair next to mine.

"No," I shake my head. "It was just a misunderstanding. She'll call me with another appointment soon."

If I ever make a decision on what to do with this pregnancy.

Fucking pregnancy.

I guess it wasn't strange I missed the signs, not with everything else going on right now. But it still surprised the hell out of me.

I'm pregnant with Prescott Wentworth's baby.

The irony of it isn't lost on me.

I thought about telling my friends what had happened today. But what would be the point? So I came up with a silly excuse about a mix-up and my treatment being postponed. I had two people already looking at me like I was crazy, and maybe, just *maybe*, they were right, but I couldn't add more people and opinions to the mix. I couldn't give more reasons for my friends to look at me with pity in their eyes. I just couldn't.

"Yeah, I know." I rub the back of my neck. "I'm just tired, and it's been a long day. I think I might go and lie down early."

"Okay," Rei places her hand on my knee and gives it a quick squeeze before letting go. "But if you need anything just holler."

I nod, pushing to my feet and wishing them goodnight before making my escape. Back in my room, I slide into my bed and look up at the ceiling, unblinking. How did I get myself in a mess like this?

My fingers itch to slide them down to my stomach, but I resist the pull. Instead, I grip the sheets as the tears gather in my eyes.

Well, if you don't make a decision soon, you might as well be as good as dead, but don't expect me to stay around and watch it all play out.

He's right. I know he is. I know they both are. But how didn't they see it?

How didn't they see how much I'd already lost? How couldn't they see how broken I already was? And taking this little piece? I knew it would leave a wound I wasn't sure would ever heal.

I've given so much already.

So freaking much.

When will it be enough?

Sniffling, I raise my arm, covering my eyes with the back of my hand.

When will it be enough?

When I'm completely broken? When there are no pieces left of me to give? When? When I'm six feet underground, buried alongside my mother?

The window creaks open, startling me out of my thoughts.

The next thing I know, the bed dips as strong arms wrap around me, and the familiar pine and citrus scent surrounds me. I turn to my side, burying my head into his firm chest and let him hold me.

"I'm so sorry, Jade. Sorry for yelling. Sorry for leaving the way I did. Sorry for making you go through this."

I let out a shaky breath, moving closer to him. Like if he holds me close enough, he can protect me from everything that's coming our way. Like he can keep me together, mend my broken pieces, and make me whole again.

"It's fine."

"It's *not* fine. I shouldn't have yelled at you. I should have given you time. I should have held you. I should have just been here. We should have talked about it, but dammit, Jade. I'm scared. I'm scared shitless of losing you. I *can't* lose you, Jade. I will lie and cheat and kill. I'll do whatever it takes to keep you alive. To keep you safe. Because the thought of living in a world in which you don't exist is unimaginable for me."

I squeeze my eyes shut as more tears threaten to fall. His words break me. *He* breaks me. And he doesn't even know it.

That's why I should have stayed away. I knew how this would affect him. I knew it, and I selfishly stayed because I couldn't do this on my own, and now... And now, if something happened to me, he would be left completely broken.

It was one thing for me to break, but Prescott?

Never him.

Closing my arms around Prescott, I cling to him for dear life.

"I know you're right," I whisper softly, my voice muffled by the soft cotton of his shirt.

Prescott's body stiffens under my touch, but he doesn't try to move, so I continue: "I know I have to do it. But it was all just so unexpected."

Prescott smooths his hand down my back, rubbing at my tense muscles. "I know, doll. I know."

"And I know I'm not ready. We're not ready. Even if things were different, I don't think we would be, but for one moment..." My throat closes, and I have to work to swallow the lump that has formed. "For one moment, I could see it. I could see us, and I could see our future. I could see our family. And then it all fell apart like a tower of cards."

"Nobody says we can't have that later on."

I shake my head. "We both know the chances of that are really slim." I tilt my head back, looking at him through my tear-stained eyes. "Why does life have to be so cruel?"

"I don't know, doll."

"I hate this. I hate feeling this weak. I hate everything that's happening. Can't we get a break? Can't we just be happy?"

"I wish I had the answer. I wish..." Prescott lets out a long breath. "I wish I could take this pain away from you, so you didn't have to go through it. I really do. I'd do anything for you, Jade."

I close my eyes, a lone tear slipping away as the fight drains out of me. "I guess it just wasn't meant to be."

Prescott grabs my hand, our fingers interlocking together as his lips brush away my tears. "I'm so sorry."

I shake my head. There is no reason for him to apologize. None of this is his fault.

"Will you go? With me?"

I don't think I'll be able to do it on my own. I'm not strong enough to do it on my own.

"Of course," his lips brush against the top of my head, making shivers run down my spine. "I'm not letting you do this on your own. We're in this together."

The relief spreads through me like a wave. He's here. He's here, and we're going to do this together.

Everything is going to be fine.

At least, that's what I keep telling myself as I cry myself to sleep in the arms of the man I love.

"If the situation was any different," Prescott whispers, tightening his grip on me. "I swear to you, Jade, I—"

I burrow my head into the crook of his neck: "I know."

Tears start to fall, and there is nothing I can do to stop them. I don't have it in me to stop them, so I surrender to them, letting them pull me under like a wave.

"It feels like we're always in the wrong place at the wrong time, doesn't it? Our paths keep colliding for a split second, long enough to cause a wreck but not long enough to last before we're pulled in different directions."

"No, that's not..."

But it is. And we both know it.

So I cry. I cry for him and for me. For our baby, that will never be. For a hope given and hope cruelly taken away from us. I cry for everything that has been stolen, hoping this is finally it —the last piece.

But I should have known it wouldn't be that easy.

Nothing in my life is.

Chapter 20

JADE

"Here you go. You have to take these two pills. First, you take this pill, mifepristone, which will stop the fetus from growing. The second one is misoprostol. It causes cramping and bleeding. It should start in the next few hours. The bleeding can be on the heavy side. It's normal, so don't get upset by it."

Don't get upset by it? Is this woman for real?

I bite my tongue, reminding myself that this is what I came for, and she's trying to help me.

"If you don't start bleeding within the next twenty-four hours, you'll need to come back in."

"How long will it last?" Prescott asks. His clammy fingers are holding onto mine. My lifeline. My safe harbor in the middle of the tempestuous sea.

"It's usually done within four or five hours, but it could be longer. The cramping could also happen on and off for the next day or two. I suggest you wear pads so that you can keep an eye on the bleeding. Other symptoms are also possible."

"What kind of symptoms?"

The doctor looks from me to Prescott, obviously realizing she'll get more from him than from me.

"Mild fever, belly aches, tiredness, dizziness, and diarrhea are some of the more common symptoms."

His hold on me tightens, brows pulling together. He's clearly not happy.

"What can she take for the pain?"

"Any pain medicine will work."

I don't want pain medicine. What I want is to go back home and crawl into bed.

"I suggest you book an appointment in a few days, so we can make sure everything went in order since I understand that time is of the essence."

And then there it is—the pity look.

I stand up abruptly, making the chair sway behind me. "Are we done?"

The doctor blinks, clearly surprised by my outburst, but I'm finished. I need to get out of here. I need to breathe.

"Yes, I..."

I grab the tablets, popping one and then the other into my mouth, swallowing them down.

"Okay, thank you."

Not waiting for an answer, I grab my bag and leave the room.

Air, I need air.

I can feel curious glances on me as I make my way down the hallway and out of the building, but I ignore them until I'm out sucking in gulps of cold November air.

It was done.

Two pills, and it was all done.

Prescott joins me shortly after, his arms wrapping around me from behind as he pulls me into his warm body.

"I want to go home," I whisper softly.

"Okay," he agrees readily. "Do you have pain meds back home?"

I nod, not wanting to get into a discussion with him right now.

"Just take me home."

PRESCOTT

Just take me home.

The look of complete emptiness on her face was like a kick to my gut. There was nothing that I could do to take away this pain—nothing I could do to make it better. Hell, I would have taken the damn pills for her. I would have gone through this for her if only I could.

If only I could...

But I couldn't.

It didn't work that way.

All I could do was stay here, hold her, and watch. I was closed off in my own personal hell while she went through the physical and emotional pain that I couldn't take away. I was powerless, and it was eating at me from the inside out.

Glancing down at my lap, I find Jade staring at the TV, her eyes unblinking. It's the same expression she's been wearing since we woke up this morning. I smooth her hair back gently, watching her stare into nothingness. It's been an hour since we got back home from the doctor's—an hour since she took the pills and ran out of that office.

"How are you feeling?" I ask softly.

Jade stiffens in my arms. I hold my breath but don't stop the gentle stroking motion.

"Fine," she finally answers, her voice all raspy. It's one of the only things she's said today.

Besides take me home, that is.

It was driving me crazy, and I couldn't do anything about it. She needed me, and I wanted to be there for her, but I didn't know what to do to make it better. Not if she didn't want to tell me.

"Do you need—"

Before I can finish, my phone buzzes on the coffee table. I watch it vibrate, not making an attempt to answer it. The screen goes black, but shortly after, whoever it is, calls again.

"You should get that."

Reluctantly, I grab the phone, seeing Nixon's name flash on the screen. I glance at Jade, but her attention is back on the TV, looking but unseeing.

"Hey, man, what's up?"

"Dude, where are you?" Nixon hisses from the other side of the line.

"Home. Why?"

"Because you should be in the strategy meeting in fifteen minutes, or did you forget that? Coach wants to go over the plays before the game tomorrow."

"Shit!"

Shit, shit, shit.

I totally forgot about that.

"Talk about shit, alright. Get your ass over here, or he *will* bench you."

I'm shaking my head even before he can finish. "I can't—" My eyes fall down, only to find Jade watching me. "I'm with..."

"Don't," Jade stops me, her voice harsh.

I asked her if she wanted to have anybody else go with us today, but she just shook her head and said she didn't want anybody else to know.

I get it. I really do. I was the first person who kept quiet about my past so people wouldn't look at me differently. So if somebody understands, it's me, but this is too much for one person to take on by themselves.

"Is that Jade?" Nixon asks.

"Yes, just... wait." I hit the mute button, letting the phone drop down as Jade sits upright. "You should be resting."

"I'm resting." She glances at the phone before looking up at me. "Go."

"What? No."

She can't be serious now, can she? There is no way in he—

"They need you. You should go."

"It's just a strategy meeting," I wave it off. "We've already discussed it, but the Coach is obsessing for—"

"Because just a few games separate you from playing in the playoffs, and you have to win them in order to do that. You have to go."

"I'm not leaving you alone. Not right now. Not when you're—"

"I'm *fine*. I still haven't started bleeding; besides, you heard the doctor. It could take *hours*. Just go do your thing. The last thing I want is for you to be benched because of me."

"Screw football." I grab her face between my palms, pressing my forehead to hers. "This is more important. *You're* more important."

"We both know that's a lie. I'm not going to be the reason you don't keep your promise to Gabriel, Prescott. Go." She places her hands against mine. "Do your thing. And then, come back to me."

"Dammit, Jade."

She's not playing fair, and she knows it. Pulling the Gabriel card out of all things.

"Go. I can't carry this on my soul too, Prescott," her words are just a whisper, pain flashing over her face. "I just can't."

"You call me." My fingers sink into her hair, holding her

close to me. "The moment it starts, you call me, and I'll come back. Promise me, Jade. I'm not letting you do this alone. Hell, I'm half tempted to take you with me."

She lets out a soft chuckle, "I'm sure Coach Davies would be amused by that."

"Fuck him. The only person I care about is you. Promise me, Jade."

There is a beat of silence before she finally nods. "I promise. Now go before you're late."

I sit there, watching her. The need to stay here with her is fighting with the promise I'd made to my brother ages ago, with a promise I made to my team. Reluctantly, I let go and pushed to my feet, grabbing my backpack from the floor where I had dropped it earlier. I stand there in the doorway and watch her, a nagging feeling telling me this is wrong. So, so wrong. But she watches me with a small smile as she mouths: "Go."

With one final nod, I push from the doorway. "Call me."

I should have known better.

I should have seen through the mask.

Because although I pay more attention to my phone, waiting for Jade's text, than I do to whatever strategy Coach is outlining on the whiteboard, her text never comes.

The moment he dismisses us with the instructions to rest and be there bright and early for a light early morning practice, I rush out the door and back to her place.

Grace opens the door, and I move inside without waiting to be invited. "Where's Jade?"

"Her room. What—" her voice trails off as I walk down the hallway. Opening the door, I'm met with darkness, and a small, curled form lying in the middle of the bed.

"Jade..." My voice breaks as I close the door, walking through the darkness until I get to her bed. Reaching out, I flip the small light on her nightstand and am met with Jade's tear-stained face.

The need to scream and punch something is strong, but I push it back. She's in pain. It's written all over her face. Her legs are pulled to her chest, arms wrapped around them, and I can see a red stain on her leggings. *Blood.*

Clenching my teeth, I place my knee on the mattress, wrap my arms around Jade, and pull her to my chest before I get to my feet with her in my arms.

"I know you're angry, bu—"

Angry? More like livid. But not at her.

At myself.

"Shh... I've got you," I whisper, brushing my lips against her temple.

I should have stayed.

I should have been here.

I should have held her as the cramps started.

I should have brushed away her tears as we lost something that could have never been.

Just another sin to add to the long list I'll carry to my grave.

"I'm here now, and I've got you," I whisper those words over and over again as I carry her to the bathroom. I sit her down on the toilet, turning on the water before gently pulling off her clothes, and then do the same to mine before carrying her to the tub.

As the warm water cascades over us, washing away the blood from her, I hold her in my arms, slowly rocking her as she cries.

"Why does it hurt so much? It shouldn't hurt so much."

"I wish I had an answer, doll."

And if I hadn't hated myself up to this point, I do now.

Chapter 21

JADE

The early morning sun is peeking through the window as I'm startled awake. My eyes are all puffy from crying, and it takes me a while to realize I'm in my bed, the memories of yesterday flashing in my head.

Going to my doctor to get the abortion pills, pushing Prescott away and the pain. So much pain. I'm not even sure which one was worse: the physical pain or the emotional one. It was all one big blur.

The moment I felt it, I went back to my bedroom and curled into myself. I didn't want to talk with anybody, and for once, the girls actually listened.

But then he was back. For a split second, I could see the anger flash on his face. I deserved it. I gave him a broken promise. I never planned to call him because I couldn't take his love. Because that's what it was. Love. Prescott might have never said the words, but I saw it. I felt it. I didn't deserve it.

After the shower, he helped me dry up and put on some clothes before we slipped into bed together, where he held me all night long. We didn't say a word. What was really there to say?

Now, I watch the muscles of his back move as he pulls his pants over his hips.

Prescott turns around, his hollow eyes meeting mine.

This.

This is what I've done to him.

Seriously, how selfish can I be?

I should let him go.

I should let him return to his life.

To be happy.

To live.

"How are you feeling?" he asks, sitting down on the bed and gently smoothing my hair away.

"Sore," I whisper, my throat raspy from unuse.

He slides his hand over my forehead and cheeks as if he's testing me for a temperature. "Any more cramping?"

"Are you going all doctor on me, Wentworth?" He gives me a pointed glare, making me sigh. "A little bit, but nothing like yesterday."

That anger that's been simmering under the surface flashes on his face for a split second before he pushes it back.

"Good." He brushes his lips over the top of my head. "You should rest. It's still early."

"Where are you going?" The question slips out of my mouth before I can stop it, and I don't miss the neediness in my tone. So much for letting him go.

"I have to go home and grab my things. The bus is leaving in less than an hour for our game."

The away game.

Shit.

"I wish I could go with you."

"There is always the next one."

But we both know that's not true. There wasn't a next one. If they lost today, that would be it.

"Then you better bring it home, so I can come and watch." I try to push upright, but the pain shoots through my stomach, making me lie back down.

Prescott curses softly. "You really need to rest."

"I'll rest when..." I catch myself before finishing that sentence. "I'll rest, but first..." I beckon him closer. He leans in, and I press my mouth against his. "Good luck today."

"I'll see you soon. Did you call Dr. Hendriks?"

My throat bobs as I swallow. "Yeah, she wants me to come back in a few days. They'll redo the blood tests, and if everything looks good, I should get my first round of chemo before we go home for Thanksgiving. So yay, me."

"It'll be yay the day she tells us you're cancer free. I really should go." With one more kiss, he gets to his feet. "Talk later?"

PRESCOTT

One good thing about the football field? It's the one place where I can battle my demons out in the open, and nobody will blink an eye. In fact, they'd relish it. They'll applaud me for pushing harder, running faster.

I bounce on the balls of my feet as the clock ticks down in the final quarter. Just a few more minutes, and it'll all be done. We were leading by two touchdowns already, so the chances of our opponents winning were slim. But the game has to be played, and nothing was final, until that timer ran out.

The referee blows the whistle.

"Let's go, and wrap this up, boys."

I drop my water bottle in the bin, pulling on my helmet as we run out on the field and line up on the fifty-yard line. Once again, I come face to face with Collins's ugly mug. The dude and I played in middle and high school together, and he was the worst kind of tool even back then. Nothing has changed much since.

Dude cracks his neck and puffs out his chest like a damn peacock. "You're going down, Wentworth."

"You mean down to the end zone like I did the last three times?" I smirk at him, knowing it'll irritate the hell out of him. "Yeah, that sounds about right."

Collins narrows his eyes at me, an evil gleam shining in their depths. "How's that brother of yours doing again? Oh, right he's dead."

My fingers clenched into fists, and I'm about to take a step forward to connect my fists with his irritating face, when the play is called.

It takes me a second to react, a freaking second, but it's enough for Collins to read me and get in my way long enough for Nixon to have to look for an opening. He throws the ball to one of our running backs instead, but the dude is tackled before he passes ten yards.

The officiant blows a whistle signaling 'end of play.'

Nixon curses behind me and gives me a what the hell look, but I just give an imperceptible shake of my head.

"You were saying?" The smug smile Collins gives me makes my teeth clench.

The second time we line up, I don't let him affect me. The moment the play is called, I'm slipping away from him, and conquering twenty yards before I'm stopped.

"You think you're the shit?" Collins spits, his cheeks red. "I've heard some interesting things about you, Wentworth."

The fine hairs at my nape start to rise. *Just ignore him. He doesn't know shit. He's just trying to get a rise out of you.* "I'm sure you did."

"Oh, I did; very interesting things. Like the fact your tastes lean toward flat-chested boys. I always knew you were fucked up. I just never understood to what point. Brother issues, Wentworth?"

His words make me see red.

This time I step toward him, my fingers wrapping around his jersey, but a hand braces around my wrist.

Nixon pulls me back. "He's not worth it."

"Oh, I'm not so sure."

"He isn't worth it," Nixon hisses once again. "Crush him on the field."

I still hold onto Collins, his heavy breaths ringing in my ears.

"Wentworth," Nixon growls, his grip tightening until I let go of Collins.

"Fucking asshole."

I go to our side of the line, inhaling deeply to reign in the rage boiling inside of me.

There are just a few more minutes on the clock. Get a grip.

I line up with the rest of my teammates, tuning out everything except for the sound of Nixon's voice. The moment he calls out the play, I'm running. Collins tries to stop me, but this time I'm faster, I'm angrier, so I do what Nixon told me: I channel it all into this play.

Then you better bring it home, so I can come and watch, Jade's earlier words push me to run faster.

One damn win.

We only need one damn win.

I turn around just in time to catch the ball. The defensive player is there waiting. I duck under him, slipping out of his grasp by mere inches, only to notice another player right at my feet. Completely screwed, I look around for an opening, and that's why I don't see the sack coming.

Not until I'm already falling, my leg twisting underneath

me. The fall kicks all the air out of my lungs as my body connects to the ground.

And then pain.

Hot, searing pain as a two-hundred-fifty-pound body falls over mine.

Chapter 22

JADE

Nixon: Almost there.

I slide the phone back into my pocket, rocking on the balls of my feet as I look up, just in time, to notice the bus pulling into the parking lot.

Biting into my lower lip I wait for the bus to come to a stop, my gaze zeroing in on the door and all the people coming out until I see him. Then, I run.

Prescott notices me almost instantly. I all but throw myself at him, wrapping my arms around his neck. "You're back."

Strong arms curl around my middle as he pulls me closer. "I'm back."

He's here. He's fine.

"The better question is, what are you doing here?"

"What am I doing here?" I pull back so I can glare at him. "Where the hell should I be?"

"Back in your apartment, in bed." He gives me a pointed look. "Somewhere where you're not freezing and risking catching pneumonia."

"That's what I told her, but she wouldn't listen," Nixon mutters.

"I wanted to make sure you were okay."

More like, I *needed* to make sure he was okay. Watching him fall during that game. The utter silence as the players were pulled back, and Prescott's limp body was sprawled on the grass. Those few heartbeats where I was waiting for him to get back to his feet and brush it off. The look of pain when they turned him around before he was swept away.

"What about my warm welcome, Smalls?"

I turn to my brother. "I'm still angry you didn't call me right away."

"I don't exactly wear my phone in my junk cup during the game. I called you as soon as I got to the phone."

I know he's right, but it didn't help with my anxiety. Watching Prescott be tackled to the ground, waiting for him to get up, while I'm miles away and unable to do anything, wrecked me. And not hearing any news for hours didn't help either.

I turn to Prescott and take him in, my gaze falling on the brace holding his leg in place. "Your leg, is it...?"

My words trail off, not even sure how to form the question. What if he's not okay? What if his leg is damaged beyond repair? What if he won't be able to keep his promise to Gabriel and win that title? And most damning of all, what if all of this is my fault?

"It's fine. The doc put my knee back in place after the game."

"Then why are you wearing a brace?"

"Just a precaution." Prescott cups my face, rubbing over my cheekbones before pulling my hood on. "You're all cold. We need to get you inside."

"Fine."

Nixon grabs their duffle bags, and together we make our way to Nixon's car. Technically I still wasn't cleared to drive, but there wasn't anybody else who could come and pick them up.

A loud whistle ripples through the air. "Yo, assholes."

We turn around to see one of their teammates standing with his hands on his narrow hips. Sammi? No, it was something else, Scott, maybe? "Party at my place. Don't make me drag your asses."

Nixon lets out a loud groan.

"I mean it, Cole. You come, or I'm coming for you."

From the corner of my eye, I see Prescott stumble. I grab his hand, trying to steady him. "Are you okay?"

"Fine." He pulls his hand out of my reach, anger flashing on his face. I suck in a breath, not used to seeing it directed at me, but he lets out a shaky breath and schools his features, extending his hand toward me. "Sorry, I just tripped over something."

I slide my hand in his, moving closer to his side. "You sure?"

"I'm sure."

"The same goes for you, Wentworth!" the Scott-guy says, making our heads snap in his direction.

"Yeah, yeah." Prescott rolls his eyes.

I look skeptically at the brace on his leg. "Are you sure you're up for a party?"

"Yeah, I'll manage." I open the passenger side door, and Prescott slides into the car, looking up at me. "The better question is, how are *you* feeling? Are you ready for tomorrow?"

I shrug. "As ready as I'll ever be."

After my failed first attempt at chemo, my stomach was all in knots about tomorrow. A part of me was anxious to get this over with, but the other part? It was terrified of all the things that it entailed.

Prescott grabs my hand, bringing it to his lips. "I'll be there."

My heart does a little flip at the gentle touch.

He's fine.

Prescott is back home, and he's fine.

"And who's going to drive your asses?"

"I drove myself here just fine."

Nixon narrows his eyes at me. "And when were you cleared to drive? Oh, right, you haven't been." You can't miss the sarcasm dripping from his tone. "I could strangle you. You know?"

"It's only a ten-minute drive." With one lingering squeeze, I let go of Prescott's hand and close the door before slipping in the back seat.

"I don't care. You shouldn't have driven," Nixon continues the moment we're inside.

"And how would you get home then? Yas is working."

"One of the guys could have given us a ride."

"Well, I came to pick you up. Can you let it go now?"

Nixon's matching blue eyes meet mine in the rearview mirror. "How are you feeling, Smalls?"

That knot in my throat grows tighter.

We haven't talked about what happened, about what I did. I just told him it was done and that Dr. Hendriks made me a new appointment for chemo. I knew he wanted to discuss it, but I couldn't bring myself to do it. I couldn't think about it, much less anything else. Not yet. Maybe not ever.

I look out of the window, refusing to meet his gaze. "I'm fine."

There's a beat of silence. "If you wan—"

"I'm *fine.* Can we go home now? Please?"

Nixon lets out a sigh but starts the car, and the radio turns on automatically, filling in the silence. From the corner of my eye, I can see Prescott slide his phone into his pocket before extending his hand toward me. The gap is too small for his hand, but he doesn't budge, so I lock my fingers with his as I catch his gaze in the rearview mirror.

So that's how we stay. Eyes locked, fingers intertwined all the way back home.

PRESCOTT

"You sure you're up for this?" Jade asks, brushing her hand over the small of my back.

"Yeah, we don't have to stay long. Just enough, so they don't bitch about me not coming."

My phone buzzes in my pocket, so I slide my hand inside, pulling it out to see the screen.

Unknown: 10:30 the last room on the second floor

Rereading the message, I close it and return my phone to my pocket as we make our way through the crowd. Considering it's just a few days before Thanksgiving and exams were already done, the party was pretty big. Then again, Blairwood loves its football team, and now that we're so close to the playoffs, all eyes are on us. Waiting to see if we'll succeed or fail.

Pain shoots through my leg, my muscles twitching with every step, reminding me of the price I paid to get us here. I'm all sweaty from the exertion, my shirt sticking to my back, but I try to keep my face neutral.

The doc popped my knee back in place. They wanted to do a scan to make sure everything was alright, but I convinced them I was feeling fine, so they let me go with just the brace and the instructions to take it easy and come in after the holidays to have the doc check it once more before they decide on how they'll proceed.

But I won't make it until then. Hell, even if I do, I won't be able to run for the whole game. Not if I can't manage the pain somehow and the pain meds? They're just not cutting it.

Checking the time, I look down at Jade. "Wanna go and grab something to drink?"

"Water is fine."

Nodding at a few people, we make our way to the kitchen, where I get a Jack and Coke for myself and a bottle of water for Jade before going to the game room.

When some of my teammates see us, they make room for us on the couch. I sit down, breathing a sigh of relief the moment my ass hits the cushion.

Jade gives me a worried glance, her fingers tracing my face. "I really think we should have stayed home."

I take her hand in mine, pulling her onto my lap. She tries to protest, but I'm not budging. I'll take all the pain as long as it means I get to hold her close.

I take a sip of my drink. "I'm fine."

She grabs my chin and turns me to face her. "Your face is pale, and you're sweating."

I quirk my brow at her, smirking. "You wanna tell me something, doll?"

"Don't joke about this." She slaps me on the shoulder half-heartedly. "I was so damn worried. You were down, and everybody was moving so freaking slow, and when they finally got up, you didn't."

"I know. I'm sorry for worrying you."

"What happened anyway? I saw you guys talking for a split second, but the camera focused on the play."

Oh, I did; very interesting things. Like the fact your tastes lean toward flat-chested boys. I always knew you were fucked up. I just never understood to what point. Brother issues, Wentworth?

I pull my brows together, my fingers clenching into fists. The rage that simmered inside me yesterday is as hot as ever. "Nothing. Just him talking shit like usual."

Jade shakes her head. "What he did was stupid and reckless. He could have ruined your leg forever."

"You're here!" Yasmin joins us before I can say anything, which I'm grateful for.

Seriously, what's there to say? The last thing I want to do is openly lie to her—for a few more weeks. I have to get through a few more weeks, and it'll be over.

"This place is crazy," Nixon hands Yasmin a drink before looking at me. "How's that leg doing?"

"Fine."

He shakes his head. "Seriously, if either of you says that word one more time, I might be tempted to strangle you."

"Don't ask stupid questions if you don't want stupid answers." I take a decent swig of my drink, cursing myself for not going for straight Jack.

Thankfully, they get the memo, so Yasmin starts chatting about all the things that she has planned for Thanksgiving dinner. My stomach perks at the idea because the girl knows how to cook, and I haven't had a home-cooked meal in forever.

Finishing off my drink, I notice the time. "I'm off to the bathroom."

Jade slides off my lap, and I get to my feet, my leg screaming in protest. I get out in the hallway, and the house seems more crowded than before. Somebody calls out my name, and I wave at them, not stopping to chat as I make my way up the stairs, bypassing all the couples making out or those sitting and drinking.

I glance back to make sure nobody is following me, but only emptiness greets me.

I look at the doors as I make my way down the hallway. The

music isn't as loud here, so I can hear the noises coming from behind the closed doors, until I finally get to the last one. With my hand on the doorknob, I check the hallway once more before slipping inside and coming to a stop.

"Well, hello, handsome," a voice purrs softly as the girl takes me in from head to toe.

"Are you shitting me?" I hiss at Manolo, who's sitting on the bed, the girl sprawled over his lap. Even in the dim light, I can see her cheeks are pink and pupils dilated. She's drunk or high, hell, maybe both.

"Don't worry, Wentworth, Judie's lips are sealed. Right, babe?"

The girl nods her head, her tongue peeking out to slide over her lips.

"I thought you were all about secrecy. This doesn't seem secret to me."

"And to me, it's a perfect ruse." He tilts his chin at me. "What do you need? More of those pain meds you love?"

My gaze shifts to the girl, but she's busy nuzzling her face in the guy's neck.

"No."

Manolo lifts his brows, clearly interested.

"I need something stronger."

As my words sink in, a smile slowly works its way onto his lips. He shoves the girl from him as he gets to his feet. "What are we talking about?"

Five minutes later, walking down the stairs, the bag Manolo gave me is sitting heavy in my pocket. I'm so spaced out that I almost bump into Jade.

"Hey, I was worried, so I came looking for you."

"Sorry, there was a line, so I went upstairs. You ready to go home?"

Jade watches me for a moment before nodding. "Yeah, sure, let's go."

Nixon and Yasmin decide to join us, so they drop us off at our building. Hand in hand, Jade and I make our way up to my apartment. Spencer's probably at one party or another because the place is quiet.

"Wanna use the bathroom first?" I ask Jade, handing her my shirt.

"I'll be back in a few."

I watch her leave the room; my breath is stuck in my lungs as I wait to hear the sound of the door closing. My heart starts beating a mile a minute as I slip my hand into my pocket, pulling out the package Manolo gave me.

Little bottles clink together as I get them out along with the syringe. My gaze darts to the door. I can hear the water running in the bathroom.

Quickly, I undo the brace and remove my pants, shoving them away with my foot. My muscles are quivering with pain, and I hiss softly as I work to lift my leg onto the mattress. Opening the syringe, I stick it into the bottle, pulling the liquid into it. Gritting my teeth, I jab it into my thigh and inject it.

My heartbeat is the only sound I can hear as I pull it out and stare at my leg. My stomach recoils, the bile rising in my throat, but I push it back.

I wasn't sure what to expect, but this was the only solution I could come up with. If I come back after Thanksgiving and my leg isn't doing better, Coach won't let me play. And I have to play.

I *have* to.

The sound of footsteps nearing snaps me out of my head.

Fuck, fuck, fuck.

Panicked, I look around, spotting my duffle bag peeking from under the bed, opened. I drop the bottles and syringe inside, shoving them under the mattress just as Jade appears in the doorway.

"Hey." She watches me for a moment, and I feel the sweat coat my palms. Did she see something? The corner of her mouth lifts in a sad smile as her gaze drops to my leg. "You need any help with that?"

I run my shaky fingers through my hair and shake my head. "Nah, I'm good."

Jade moves closer, sitting on the bed next to me. "Does it hurt? Want me to get you an ice pack? Pain meds?"

"It's nothing I haven't experienced before." I grab the brace, slide it on, and secure the straps as I get up and go to my nightstand, picking up the pain med bottle from the drawer. Sliding two pills out, I pop them into my mouth. "I'm all good."

"Are you sure I can—"

I move closer to her, pressing my fingers against her lips. "I'm sure. The only thing I need is you."

Chapter 23

JADE

"I see you've brought more company," Dr. Hendriks says as she joins us in the hallway.

I don't even bother looking over my shoulder. The hulking presence of my brother and my boyfriend—yeah, that one will take some getting used to—is too hard to miss.

"Yeah, well, at this point, we can run our own hospital," I say, only half-joking.

Dr. Hendriks takes in Prescott, her gaze stopping on his leg brace. "I can see that."

"I'm fine," Prescott waves me off. "I'll be back in the game in no time."

He seems to be doing better today. Not as tense as he was last night, but there are still deep circles under his eyes.

"Well, as long as you didn't get it on my watch..." Dr. Hendriks scans the papers in her hands. "Your results look normal, and we're all set to go. How are you feeling, Jade?"

"Good." I bounce on the balls of my feet. "Anxious to get this over with."

"Okay, let's do this."

Dr. Hendriks leads the way into a room. The space is wide

open with dozens of leather armchairs lined up along the wall, each accompanied by a pole with some kind of machine attached.

A few people are already seated inside. Some look up at us, and some continue to carry on with their own business. Men and women, all different ages, different skin colors, and diverse backgrounds. All of us are fighting some variation of the same nasty disease.

A warm hand touches my waist, startling me. "You good?" Prescott whispers, his warm breath brushing the shell of my ear and making me shiver.

"Y-yeah." I force one foot in front of the other as I follow Dr. Hendriks to one of the available chairs.

"Sit down and get comfortable. As we discussed, you're getting chemo in an IV, and the procedure itself will take a few hours. Every person reacts differently, but there are some side effects. Dizziness, vomiting, a spike in temperature, fatigue."

Appetite loss, weight loss, retching, weakened immune system, hair loss... The list goes on and on and on. Makes you wonder if all of it is worth it in the end.

Brown eyes meet mine, and Prescott gives me an encouraging smile.

It's worth it.

It has to be.

"Yay me," I say dryly, pulling the sleeve of my hoodie up to reveal my arm.

"I want to do three cycles, each one four weeks long. We'll do three rounds, with a one-week break. After three cycles, we'll run some tests to see how you're doing."

Three cycles. Three months. My throat bobs as I swallow.

"Followed by another three cycles?" Nixon asks, saving me from having to do it myself.

"If the results aren't what we're hoping for," Dr. Hendriks

nods, her attention turning to me. "But I don't want you thinking about that. I need you to focus on the right here, right now. Okay? Today is what matters. We're taking one day at a time." Just then, an older nurse joins us, pulling a cart with neatly organized bags. "This is Judy. She'll be your nurse today. I have to go right now, but if you have any questions or don't feel well, you can always call the hospital."

"Thank you, Dr. Hendriks."

Nurse Judy picks up one of the bags and hangs it on the pole by my chair. "How are we doing, Jade?"

"I'll be doing better once this is over."

"We'll see if you think that once you're done," she says, pulling out the needle. I try to keep a serious face, but she must see me flinch. "You afraid of needles?"

"I'm not a fan," I admit.

I've been poked and prodded so much in the last few weeks; you'd think it wouldn't matter at this point. What's one more needle, right? Tell that to my body that freezes every time I see one.

The corner of her mouth lifts. "How about you concentrate on one of those gorgeous men you brought with you today to take your mind off of this?"

"Don't say it too loud, it'll go to their heads." I turn to my left, where Prescott is already seated in the chair next to mine.

"I don't know what you're talking about," he says, placing his hand over mine, his thumb rubbing circles over my wrist.

"Of course you don't," I roll my eyes. "You should have seriously stayed back home. This can't be good for your leg."

"My leg is just fine the way it is. Besides, this is good for me. I can watch and learn first-hand."

"All done," Nurse Judy says, her attention shifting to Prescott. "You a med student, handsome?"

"Pre-med."

"He wants to be an oncologist." I turn my attention to the nurse. "He's studying for his MCATs, so I'll get to quiz him."

Her brows rise in surprise. "Does he now? Well, if you have any questions, let me know." She places her hand on my shoulder. "I'll come back to check on you in a bit. In the meantime, if you need anything, just press this button, and I'll come."

"Thank you."

"You'll quiz me?" Prescott asks the moment she's gone.

"Not like I have anything better to do for the next few hours. And you need to get all the studying in that you can." I extend my hand. "Gimmie."

"Or you could try and rest," Nixon suggests as he brings another chair closer.

I shake my head. "I'm too anxious to rest. So gimme. Let's see what you've got, Dr. Wentworth."

This isn't my first rodeo with chemo. I drove my mom to countless appointments. I sat next to her those first few rounds when they still thought there was something they could do to help her. When she still wanted to fight.

I thought I was ready.

I thought I knew what to prepare for.

I didn't know shit.

At first, I was fine. Nixon and I cross-examined Prescott to help him prep for his MCATs. It was fun, and for a while, I actually forgot where and what I was doing. Nurse Judy came and went, making sure that I was okay, and then, before you knew it, it was done, and I could go home.

Halfway to our house, the chills started. Nixon cranked the heat, and I pulled the blanket out of the duffle bag, wrapping it around myself like a cocoon, but I was still shaking. And then, as we were pulling in front of the house, the bile started to rise up my throat. Nixon didn't even have the chance to stop properly before I unbuckled my seatbelt and stumbled out of the car in time to throw up the little that I had for breakfast.

There was cursing behind me as both men joined me.

"You okay, Smalls?" Nixon asks, crouching down next to me.

"She's not okay," Prescott hisses.

A warm hand touches the back of my neck, the goosebumps rising on my skin and making me shiver.

"Let's get you to bed, okay?"

"Bathroom," I croak, wiping my mouth with the back of my hand. My stomach still feels too queasy, and the last thing I want is to puke in my room.

I try to push to my feet, but the wave of dizziness makes my knees quake. I'd probably fall if steady hands didn't wrap around me.

"I've gotcha," Prescott whispers softly. "Let's get you inside, okay?"

I shake my head. "Your leg..."

"Fuck my leg."

"She's right. You can't mess up your leg, dude." Prescott starts to protest, but Nixon is already picking me up and carrying me up the stairs just as the door opens.

"I thought I heard a car—" Yasmin's voice falters as her eyes fall on me. "Jade? What's wrong?"

"Chemo finally hit her," Nixon says as we get inside the house.

The smell of food from the kitchen hits me as soon as we enter, and my stomach rolls uncomfortably.

"I think..." I gulp down, trying to hold it at bay. "I think I'm gonna be sick again."

Nixon curses but takes two steps at a time, carrying me up

to my room. I cover my mouth with my hands as the bile burns my throat.

"Just a bit more, Smalls."

The moment we're in the bathroom, I push open the toilet seat and start throwing up again. Hurried footsteps come from down the hallway. I hear them talking, but the sound of my vomiting muffles their voices. The awful stench isn't helping because the more I throw up, the worse I feel.

The next thing I know, my hair is pulled out of my face, and a wet cloth is pressed on my neck.

"There, it's going to be okay," Prescott whispers, gently rubbing circles against the small of my back.

"I d-don't..." My words are interrupted by a loud, retching sound. "I don't want you to see me like this," I whisper, pressing my forehead against the toilet seat.

Right now, I don't even have it in me to care how gross this is. I'm all sweaty. I'm hot, I'm cold, and I'm not sure if I threw up everything I had in me or not.

"Well, I'm not going anywhere."

"You're lucky I don't have it in me to throw you out."

"You care about me too much to do that."

His words echo in the small space as we stare at one another for what feels like an eternity.

No, I don't just care about him.

I love him.

That's why I know he shouldn't have to watch me like this.

Nixon clears his throat. "You think you can get to bed?"

"I need to brush my teeth first." There is no way I'm going to bed with this rancid taste in my mouth.

Bracing my palms against the toilet seat, I push to my feet. Somehow Prescott, his brace and all, gets up faster and helps steady me.

"I've got you."

I let myself lean against him, enjoying his strength, his warmth, just for a moment. My throat bobs as I swallow. The bitter taste lingers on my tongue, so I take a few steps toward the sink, where I quickly brush my teeth and splash some water on my face. Even that little thing makes me feel half-human again.

Nixon's head appears in the doorway. "I've got you some Gatorade."

My nose furrows at the mention of the drink. "No," I shake my head.

"You need to drink something, doll." Prescott turns me to face him, his fingers tipping my chin back. My eyes meet his worried ones. "We can't risk you getting dehydrated."

"Water," I croak, giving in. "I can't drink anything that smells or tastes funny."

I'm not even sure if I'll be able to stomach that, but I could at least try. What's the worst that can happen? I end up throwing up again? It wouldn't be the first or the last time.

His brows pull together, but he lets out a sigh. "Fine. Water. Let's get you to bed now."

I force out a smirk. "You're way too eager to get me to bed, Wentworth. I'm really not a good lay right now."

"Seriously?" Nixon groans.

"Jade..." Prescott growls, the warning note evident in his voice.

"Hey, I just say it as I see it."

"Bed, now."

Chuckling, I let him help me into my room. The covers are already pulled away, so I slide into the soft fabric. Prescott pulls the covers over me before sitting next to me and grabs the bottle of water somebody left on the nightstand.

"Water first."

I wrap my fingers around the bottle, tentatively taking a sip. When it glides down easily, I take a few more. "Happy?"

"It'll do for now."

"I don't like it when you're bossy." Putting the bottle on the nightstand, I lean back, my eyelids feeling heavy the moment my head touches the pillow.

"I don't like to see you weak, so I guess we're even." He pushes my hair gently from my face. "Try to get some rest. Okay?"

I hum sleepily. "You'll be here? With me?"

"I'm not going anywhere," Prescott promises.

Soft footsteps move around the room, and finally, I can hear the familiar creak of the door as it's pulled closed, signaling we're finally alone.

"Was it the same?" I ask Prescott. "With Gabriel?"

The silence stretches between us, and for a moment, I think he won't answer me, but after a while he does.

"Yeah."

I nod, pulling the covers tighter around me as another shiver runs through me. "This is just the first one. Things are going to get worse."

I don't know why I expect him to lie to me, but he doesn't.

"They are. That's why you need to rest. Gather all your strength. I need you strong, Jade." His voice grows deeper, rougher. "I need you to fight."

I turn my head to the side, brushing my lips against the fingers still playing in my hair. "For you," I whisper as the darkness slowly starts to claim me. *I love you.*

Startling, I blink my eyes open. I'm not sure how long I've been out of it, but my body is still fighting the chills. The room is clouded in the dim light, the darkness the only thing I can see through the windows.

I must have been out of it for a while. Sliding my hand out of the covers, I reach for Prescott, only to find his side of the bed empty.

What the—

I turn to the side, finding him standing by my desk. No, not standing, more like crouched, his leg propped on the chair.

He's here.

He hasn't left.

He isn't like my dad.

My heart slows down as the realization sets in. I slide my tongue over my dry lips, feeling the chopped skin. My throat is raw from all the throwing up. I should probably get— a glimmer of something flashes in Prescott's hand. I narrow my eyes, trying to see what he's holding.

"P-Prescott?"

He turns around almost instantly, his eyes finding mine. Relief and something else, something that looks a lot like guilt flashing on his face. But what would he have to feel guilty for?

"Hey, you're up."

"Yeah, what time is it?" I ask as I try to sit up.

Prescott joins me on the bed, adding a pillow behind my back. "Almost midnight. You've been out for a while." He touches my forehead. "It doesn't seem like you have a fever any longer, which is good. How are you feeling?"

"Thirsty."

Prescott unclasps a bottle of water and hands it to me. I take a few long sips, letting the cool liquid slide down my throat.

"Better?"

"Yeah, better."

"Wanna try and eat something? Yasmin made some homemade soup earlier."

My nose furrows at the mere mention of food. "I don't think I'll be able to hold it down."

"You'll have to try. You need to get as much energy as you can."

"I know, but... maybe tomorrow?"

Prescott watches me for a moment before reluctantly nodding. "Fine, but tomorrow you're eating something."

"You know it, Doc. Let's go to sleep."

I couldn't believe I was ready to go back to sleep when I barely woke up, but it was true.

Prescott grabs the bottle and puts it back on the nightstand.

"What were you doing up anyway?"

His back stiffens at my question. "What do you mean?"

"You were standing at my desk when I woke up."

"Oh, that. I just got out of the shower and was putting on some clothes. My bag's there."

I look at my desk, and sure enough, I can see the dark shape of his duffle bag on the ground. It makes sense, only... I still remember a flash. Or did I imagine it?

He pulls away the covers and slides into the bed.

"C'mere," he whispers, opening his arms.

Letting go of all the worries, I turn my back to him. Prescott's arms pull me into his chest as his familiar scent lolls me back to sleep.

Chapter 24

JADE

"Don't leave me." I tighten my arms around Mom's frail body. Her familiar scent is gone, overpowered by the smell of disease, medicine, and antiseptic. The mix makes my stomach roll, but even that doesn't stop me from clinging to my mother tighter. "You can't leave me. Not yet."

I'm not ready.

It's too soon.

Too damn soon to lose the woman who has raised me and loved me—the woman who has turned into my whole world.

"It's going to be o-okay," Mom wheezes softly, her voice so low I have to strain to hear it.

I shake my head, refusing to believe it. Refusing to give in.

"It's not okay." It'll never be okay. "I need you. Nixon needs you."

This can't be happening. This can't be our life. Not yet.

"Yo—" She sucks in a sharp breath. "F-fine."

"We won't be fine. We need you."

I need you.

I thought I was ready.

I thought I'd be able to do this without falling apart.

I thought I'd be able to make it easy on her.

But I can't.

She's slipping away, and there is nothing that I can do about it. Nothing that I can do to make her stay.

"Mom..." I try to reach for her, but she's slipping through my fingers. "Mom!"

I startle awake, sucking in a breath. My heart is beating furiously against my ribcage, sweat covering my body.

Running my trembling fingers through my messy hair, I slowly take in my surroundings.

Home.

I'm back home. Sleeping in my room.

I rub my sweaty forehead, feeling the throbbing at the back of my skull.

It was just a bad dream.

Just that.

A bad dream.

I haven't had one of those in a while. It could be that after everything that has happened lately, being home after so long brings the memories of those last few weeks with Mom back to life.

Turning to the left, I see Prescott's sleeping face on the pillow beside mine. His hair is a mess; a frown is etched between his brows as he sleeps.

He's still here.

Prescott has barely left my side since we got home after my chemo. Well, except when I woke up and he wasn't there. What the hell was with that? I try to remember, but everything about yesterday is clouded by the pain.

Thankfully, today I'm feeling better. My stomach doesn't seem like it'll jump out of my mouth, and the shivers have stopped, although I still feel the ache in my muscles. Almost like I have a cold.

The soft light peeking through the blinds falls over Prescott's head, making the gold strands stand out. It's early, too damn early from the looks of it, but there is no way I'll fall asleep again, so I slide my legs over the mattress and get up.

The house is quiet as I make my way downstairs, the clock on the oven showing it's barely past five in the morning. I flick on the small light over the sink and go straight to the coffee machine. There is a soft buzzing sound as the device comes to life, and soon enough, the smell of the dark brew fills the air.

Grabbing the cup in my hands, I take a sip, letting the caffeine enter my bloodstream as I look around the kitchen.

Since I had to reschedule the chemo, Yasmin ended up getting here before us, so everything was already clean, and the house had been aired out since nobody had been here for months. A few pans and bowls were waiting in the fridge, ready to be put in the oven for today's dinner.

Leaning against the counter, my gaze falls on Mom's cookbook.

Nixon and I might have been failures in the kitchen department, but Mom was amazing. I gently pull the notebook out, the pang of longing hits me at the sight of Mom's handwriting filling the pages. Biting the inside of my cheek, I skim the page with my finger, tracing the lines and curves. I flip the page and then another, each new recipe bringing back memories.

Blueberry scones.

My favorite.

The words blur on the page as the memory hits me. Sitting on the bar stool, watching Mom work. The smell of blueberries and sugar as we watched the scones bake—the burning of my tongue as I tried to eat one straight out of the oven. Mom's laughter—damn, I forgot the sound of Mom's laughter until this very moment, and I hadn't even realized it.

Tears gather in my eyes, but I blink them away. Determined, I scan the recipe before pulling out all I'll need.

Putting the bowl on the counter, I add flour, sugar, baking powder, a little bit of salt, and cinnamon, mixing it all together. Then I pull a stick of butter from the fridge and grate it into the bowl before I dip my fingers into the ingredients and start to knead.

Or at least I *try* to.

"Dammit!" I squeeze my fingers, trying to mix all the ingredients together, but my grip is too weak.

I'm so busy cursing that I don't hear the footsteps approaching until bulky arms wrap around my middle. My body stiffens until the familiar smell of pine surrounds me, and I can feel my muscles relax against Prescott's hard chest.

"What are you doing up?" Prescott asks, burrowing his head into the crook of my neck.

The nightmare I had flashes before my eyes, a shiver running through me. How can the same house bring so much good but at the same time so much bad? With a shake of my head, I push the memories away.

"Couldn't sleep, so I went to get some coffee. Figured I might get some work done since I'm already up." I rub the back of my hand against my cheek and tilt my head back so I can look at him.

"I mean, what are you doing up? You should be resting."

"I'm feeling better today," I shrug. "How did you sleep?"

"Good."

"Liar."

Sleepiness still clings to his face, and there are dark circles under his eyes.

"The bed felt empty when you left." He cups my face, rubbing his thumb over my cheekbone. "There. You had flour on it. What are you trying to make anyway?"

"Scones. Now, if I could only make this dough..." I try to squeeze the butter, hoping it'll turn into something, but curse my luck. "Ugh, I hate this!"

"How about you make me coffee, and I'll make scones?"

I turn around, narrowing my eyes at Prescott. "You'll make scones?"

"Yeah," he shrugs.

"Have you ever made scones?"

He raises his brows. "Have you?"

"Well, no."

"Then we're in the same boat." His hands slide down my back, giving my ass a squeeze before he brushes his lips against the corner of my mouth. "I'll knead. You get coffee and whatever else you need."

"Okay," I agree reluctantly. "I guess we'll see if those muscles of yours are of any use." Slipping out of his hold, I go toward the sink. "Wash your hands, and get to work, Wentworth."

While I wait for his coffee to be made, I mix some heavy cream, an egg, and vanilla extract to add to the flour, along with chocolate chips and blueberries. Then, Prescott starts to knead it all together. Grabbing his coffee cup, I take a seat at the counter and watch him work.

Although I don't think he's cooked a day in his life, he's not half bad at it. I watch his biceps flex as he kneads the dough, a look of concentration on his face, and if it isn't one of the sexiest things I've seen.

Suddenly he looks up. "What?"

"Nothing."

"So you're just enjoying the view, doll?"

"Oh yeah, just imagining all the other things I'll have you cook for me."

Prescott chuckles, "If I were you, I wouldn't get my hopes

up." He looks down at the dough. "How about this? Good enough?"

I give the mass a critical look, trying to remember how it looked when Mom made it the last time. "I guess so."

Hopping off the stool, I grab the knife and cut it into pieces, putting them on the tray and adding a glaze over it before popping them into the oven and setting the timer.

"Now we wait," I say, turning around.

Prescott is sitting in the chair I vacated, a coffee mug in his hand. He extends his hand toward me, and I place mine in his, letting him tug me closer. He spreads his legs so that I can settle between them. Placing my hand over the one holding the mug, I lift it so I can take a sip.

"Why were you really up at the crack of dawn?" Prescott asks, tucking a strand of hair behind my ear.

I should have figured out he wouldn't let it go just like that. "I told you. I couldn't sleep."

"Bad dreams?"

I look away. It was unnerving how well he knew me. How easily he could read me. My emotions. My fears. Everything.

Prescott slides his fingers under my chin and turns me to face him.

"It's hard. Being back here, especially after everything that has happened recently."

Prescott nods. "It's the same for me. The moment I step into the house, it's like I'm flooded with memories."

I cover his hand with mine, rubbing my thumb over his knuckles. "I'm sorry."

"Don't be. It's not all bad; more bitter-sweet in a way. Sometimes a memory would sneak up on me, a memory I forgot. Yes, the blow is brutal that first moment, overwhelming in so many ways, but there is also some solace in it. I don't ever want to forget Gabriel, so I'll take any pain I have to in order to keep his memory alive, no matter how hard it might be for me." His expression turns distant as he retreats in his head, lost in his memories. "I wish I could go home more, but my parents... It's just not worth it, you know?"

Yeah, I knew what he meant. There was no way I'd forget the way his parents treated him anytime soon. His dad was a piece of work, and his mom didn't do anything to stop him from bashing Prescott. How can you just stand by and let your husband treat your son so poorly?

"They don't deserve you."

"I didn't make it easy on them."

I shake my head. I'll be damned if I let him talk about himself that way. "The way they treat you isn't your burden to bear. You didn't do anything wrong. You're their child, just like Gabriel was."

"That's the problem, doll. I survived, while he didn't. I exist, I should have been the one who died, and everybody would be happier."

I shake my head. "You're wrong. I wouldn't be happier." Moving closer, I cup his cheeks and press my forehead against his. "You're worthy of love, Prescott Wentworth. Don't you ever doubt that."

Before he can protest, I press my mouth against his, kissing him softly. I move closer, snuggling into his heat as my mouth slides over his. A low rumble comes from deep in his chest as his hands glide down my sides, fingers digging into my hips as he pulls me closer, deepening the kiss.

There is nothing like kissing Prescott Wentworth. It's sweetness and heat, an exciting new adventure, and coming home all wrapped up in one.

I run my fingers through his hair, feeling its softness as I tug his head back, my tongue demanding entrance into his mouth.

Shivers run down my spine as our tongues swirl together, the need pooling between my thighs.

The doorbell rings just as the timer goes off on the oven. Groaning, I pull back. "I'll get the door; you get the scones?"

"It can wait."

"Umm, I don't think you want to eat burnt scones, mister."

He shakes his head, his grip on me tightening. "I don't give a crap about scones."

"Well, I do. Don't be a baby, Wentworth. It doesn't look cute on you."

"Where's your brother when one needs him?" Prescott grumbles, but he lets me go.

Chuckling, I go toward the front door just as the bell rings again. "Coming!"

Damn, I really hope it's not one of those annoying sales—

"Grace?" I frown at my best friend standing on the other side of the door. "What are you doing here?"

"Surprise!" she throws her arms around me, making me stumble a step back.

Instinctively, I wrap my arms around her to steady myself, my gaze darting over her shoulder.

"I don't understand." Her SUV is parked, and more people are coming out. Mason, Penny, Henry, and there, in the distance, is another car driving up the driveway. "Weren't you on your way to New York?"

"Well, about that..." She pulls back, giving me a sheepish smile. "We thought it would be best to celebrate here. With you guys."

I whip my head toward her. "What?"

Chapter 25

JADE

"You didn't have to change your plans because of me, you know," I say to Grace as I place another ornament on the Christmas tree.

"Nonsense," she waves me off. "We didn't change plans because of you."

Taking a step back, I give the tree a critical look before I turn and silently raise my brow at her, she shrugs as her only response.

"We didn't," she insists. "It made more sense. We decided we'll stay here for Thanksgiving and visit our families between Christmas and New Year."

I know she's lying. Ever since I told them about the cancer, they've been around more. Not that my friends haven't been around to begin with, but I knew they could see it too. That subconscious, what if. What if I don't make it in the end? What if cutting myself open and injecting deathly medicine won't be enough to fight my cancer? What if we're living on borrowed time?

People always think they'll have time. They'll see the people they love. They'll visit that one place they always dreamed about. They'll spend the next Christmas with their loved ones. But the sad truth is, we can't know that because there are simply no guarantees. This moment you have right now? It might be your last, so you must embrace it with both hands and cling to it as if it were.

I know that because I've been that person. After Mom told me that the cancer was back, even before we knew it was terminal. We've clung to the moments, hours, minutes, seconds, living them as if those were our last, but it still wasn't enough.

Clearing my throat, I look down at Penny, who's waiting with another ornament ready to be put on the tree. "What about you, Pens? I figured you'd want to visit Kate and Emmett."

"I've seen them recently," Penny smiles, her platinum curls bouncing as she tilts her head, her hand gently touching the box until her fingers wrap around the next ornament in line. "Besides, I think they're excited to celebrate their first Thanksgiving alone."

"They would be happy to have you there."

"Oh, I know that." Her face lights up as she looks down. "Oh, this is pretty," she whispers, her fingers slowly tracing the ornament in her palm.

I blink, the crystal ball coming into focus. It's completely see-through, with different-sized, glittery snowflakes etched into the glass.

"Daddy, you're home!" I run into my father's arms the moment he steps through the door. Wrapping my arms around his legs I bury my face into his thigh. "We missed you."

He had a meeting across the world and couldn't make it back home in time for the holidays because of the snowstorm.

"I missed you too, Princess." Dad rubs my back, pulling me back so he can get to my level. "Were you a good girl?"

I roll my eyes at him with all the sass I can muster. "I'm always *a good girl."*

Dad chuckles, "Of course you are. And that's why Santa left you a present with me too."

I purse my lips. "I wish Santa brought you home on time."

"Me too, baby. Me too." He lifts a brow. "So I should throw the present away?"

"No!" I giggle. "Gimmie."

He hands me a small shimmering bag that I grab out of his hands and open immediately.

"Wow," I breathe as my eyes fall on the ornament in my hands. The snowflakes shimmer as I tilt it this way and that. "So pretty."

"You like it?"

"I love it. I'm going to put it on the tree right now."

The door snaps closed somewhere in the house, yanking me out of my thoughts just as the guys enter the living room.

"Damn, it's freezing outside," Nixon mutters, rubbing his palms together as he and the boys join us in the living room. "Why are we taking these off anyway? They should stay up all year long."

We spent the early morning preparing the Thanksgiving meal while the guys left to get a Christmas tree. Why did that simple job require all of the guys—well, except Maddox—to go. I'll never understand. Now the boys were out, putting the lights on the house, while Yasmin and Alyssa were in the kitchen baking cookies, which left Grace, Penny, and me to decorate the tree.

It was weird, having the house filled with so many people and so much laughter after all this time. And it's not even all of us because Yasmin's parents were supposed to come in a few hours.

Yasmin pinches him. "They most certainly will not. What will the neighbors say?"

"Our closest neighbors aren't in seeing distance," Nixon

points out.

"I don't care. That's not how it's done."

Once again, the doors open, and a few moments later, Prescott is standing in the doorway, his hair disheveled, a few snowflakes clinging to his hair. His eyes find mine across the room almost instantly and hold as he joins me.

"You okay?" he asks softly.

I force out a small smile. "Yeah. I just got lost in the memories."

If he wants to ask more, he doesn't get a chance.

"You wanna put this one on the tree?" Penny asks, returning my attention to the ornament in her hand.

I watch it for a second before shaking my head. "Nah, I think we'll skip it this year."

"Okay."

I glance at the tree, and Grace joins me by my side as we both look at our handiwork. "It looks really pretty."

"Yeah, it does."

"It's still missing one thing," Penny says, holding out a star in her hand. "You wanna do it?"

"Sure."

I take the star from her hand, looking down at it for a moment, before rising on my tiptoes. But even that's not enough since I still have a hard time lifting my arms in the air. Just recently, I've started PT. Thanks to Nixon and Coach Davies, I didn't even have to leave campus to do so. Dr. Snow agreed to work with me so I didn't have to lose time on travel and nag people to drive me to my appointments since I still wasn't cleared to drive on my own. But even so, I was a far cry from being back at one hundred percent.

Prescott must see me struggling because the next thing I know, his hands are on my waist, and he's hauling me up. I let out a little shriek in surprise, making my friends laugh.

"Try not to kick down the tree, Smalls," Nixon teases.

"Well, you could have done this, you know. I'd love to see your expertise."

"Oh, no," Nixon shakes his head. "I've done my job. I bought the tree, got it here, and put on the lights."

I stick my tongue at him. "Poor baby."

"Umm, can you put that star on and then get back to fighting with your brother?" Prescott asks.

"Fine." Letting out a sigh, I turn my attention to the tree, ensuring I don't kick anything as I place the star on top.

My body brushes against Prescott's as he gently places me on the ground. I suck in a breath, feeling each hard line of his body pressing against me.

He opens his mouth, but before he can say anything, Nixon asks: "So about those scones?"

PRESCOTT

Laughter spreads through the backyard as Nixon throws another log into the pit, stirring the fire.

"Scoot up."

Jade tilts her head back, her big blue eyes focusing on me before they drop on the blanket in my hand.

"I'm not that cold."

Stubborn woman.

Seriously, what did I do to deserve this?

Putting the blanket over her shoulders, I wrap my arms around her middle and lift her up. Jade lets out a little yelp of surprise, but I'm already sitting in the chair with her tightly snuggled into my lap.

"You could have warned me, you know."

"I did, but you wanted to fight."

Jade tilts her head back so I can see her roll her eyes at me. "I hardly call that a fight." She glances at my arms. "Aren't you cold now?"

"I run hot all the time."

A lazy smile spreads over her lips. "That you do."

She shifts in my lap, her ass brushing against my dick and making it hard. Jade notices it, too, because she just smirks at me. "Thank God for the blanket because otherwise..."

"If you weren't moving so much, there wouldn't be a problem."

"Jade! Prescott!"

We hold our gaze for a moment longer before shifting our attention to Mason, who's standing in front of the pit, a wooden stick with marshmallows in his hand. "Want some?"

"Yes!" Jade bounces in my seat as she reaches for the stick. I swear she's doing it on purpose. The little witch.

"Wentworth?"

I shake my head. "I'm good."

Jade turns to sit sideways so she can watch me. "You look a little tense."

I tighten my grip around her to stop her from wiggling. She raises her brow at me, taking a bite of her marshmallow, all innocence and whatnot. Moving closer, I press my lips against her ear. "You'll pay for that later."

"Promises, promises."

"Oh, trust me, this is one I'll make sure to keep." Noticing a little bit of white in the corner of her mouth, I lean in and swipe my tongue over it, licking the marshmallow from her lip.

"Hmm... yummy," I murmur, starting to pull back, but Jade's hand cups my face, and she presses her lips to mine, her tongue swiping into my mouth. Sugar and chocolate overwhelm my senses as her tongue twists with mine.

"Find a room already!" somebody yells, and from the corner of my eye, I can see something fly toward us. At the last second, I lift my hand, stopping the pillow from hitting us.

"Sounds good to me!" Jade gets up. "I'll take him..."

"No," Nixon says almost instantly.

Jade glares at him. "You're lucky I can't throw for shit now because you'd have that pillow in your face."

"How about we try not to burn anything down?" Yasmin asks calmly.

"Hey, don't look at me. I'm not the one who has a shitty aim," Nixon says, his teeth flashing in the light of the fire.

Jade grabs the pillow out of my hand, but before she can throw it, I take it from her and toss it right at Nixon's head.

"Who has a shitty aim now, Cole?"

Everybody bursts into laughter.

"That still won't change my mind. Last night was an exception."

"Don't be a shitty loser, Cole," Mason yells, still chuckling.

The front door opens, and Alyssa joins us, her daughter, Edie, in her arms, dressed in a puffy pink jacket.

"What happened?" Yasmin asks.

Alyssa looks down at her daughter. "Somebody's fussy."

"She wouldn't fall asleep?" Maddox asks as the girls join him on the swing.

"No, I think it's her teeth," Aly sighs.

"Poor little Princess," Maddox says in a gentle voice. Edie looks up from the crook of Aly's neck, her face lighting up as soon as she sets her sight on him. "Who's Daddy's best girl?" Maddox nuzzles her cheek as he takes her out of Aly's arms and transfers her into his lap. Aly grabs the blanket and puts it over Edie, who's already dozing off on Maddox's lap.

"I swear you have some kind of magic touch or something."

Aly shakes her head and takes a cup of hot chocolate Yas offers her.

"Right? It amazes me every time."

I shift my attention to Jade to find tears glistening in her eyes. Silently she blinks them away, her gaze meeting mine.

No words are said, but I don't need her to say them out loud to know what she's thinking.

Who she's thinking about.

A vice grip squeezes around my heart as I brush one lone tear that slipped away.

This could have been us.

In a different world.

But that world isn't ours to have.

Brushing my lips against the top of her head, I pull her to me, wishing I could take her pain away.

The conversation shifts, people dividing into smaller groups while I sit here, holding Jade in my arms. She relaxes into me, her head leaning into the crook of my neck, and she listens to Grace talk about her dance students from the center, Penny tells her about her music classes, and then they shift to their plans for the rest of the year.

"Anything you wanna do for the New Year?" I ask so only she can hear me, my lips brushing against her temple.

Jade shakes her head. "As long as we're together, I don't care."

We all stay out for a little while longer, but soon the snow starts to fall stronger, so we gather our things and get back in the house, everybody retreating to their rooms.

Just when I think everybody's gone, I hear soft footsteps padding over the wooden floor before Jade appears in the doorway, two mugs in hand.

"I thought you went to sleep," I say, rising to a sitting position so she can sit next to me on the couch.

"I figured I'd have some hot chocolate to warm up." She hands me a mug, her eyes going to the tree. The lights are blinking softly, making light and shadow play across her serious face. "That last year? We got some hot chocolate, sat here, and watched Christmas movies." She glances at me, the sadness radiating off of her. "I miss her."

My throat closes as I grasp her hand in mine, our fingers locking together. "It's okay to miss them."

"I know." Jade leans her head on my shoulder. "What was something you and Gabriel did for the holidays?"

Taking a sip of my hot chocolate, I give myself a moment to think about it. These days I rarely allow myself to go back to the past. Remembering hurt too much. So did the realization of all the memories that I've lost. But for her? I wanted to try.

"We used to compete to see who'd be the one to catch Santa," I smirk as the memory flashes in my mind, so vivid you'd think it happened yesterday. All these years, I tried to suppress my memories of Gabriel because I thought it would hurt too much. It does hurt, but it feels good, too, remembering him.

"Did you ever catch him?"

"Hell, no," I chuckle. "One year, we thought we got close. We were probably nine or ten. I managed to stay up until midnight. I remember because we had one of those old, big ass clocks in the hallway, and I remember it rang twelve times. I thought that must be it, you know, midnight, it's Christmas. Gabriel must have had the same thought because the next thing I knew, we were both in the hallway."

"What happened then?"

"Mom. She must have heard the floorboard creek, or more likely, she was getting ready to put the presents out because the next thing I knew, she was out in the hallway, glaring at us and silently pointing back to our rooms."

"Caught red-handed."

"We totally were," I chuckle softly.

As the sound dies, we settle into a companionable silence, both of us lost in our own thoughts. I almost forgot how Mom used to be before Gabriel died. Before our life shattered into pieces. Before we were irrevocably damaged. How fun and quirky and loving she used to be. She might not have died, but the part of her that made her the woman she was? It was buried along with Gabriel.

I look down at her to find her already watching me. "That's a beautiful memory."

"It is," I rasp.

Cupping her cheek, I press my mouth to hers, kissing her fiercely.

"Take me to bed, Prescott," she breathes against my mouth, her warm breath tickling my skin. "Make love to me."

How is a guy supposed to say no when she looks at you like you just hung the moon in the freaking sky?

Maybe a better guy could. But I'm not that man.

I don't want to be that man.

I let out a shaky breath and nod. Intertwining my fingers with Jade's, I pull her upright. We don't say anything as we make our way up the stairs and into her room. The moment the lock is in place, we reach for each other, pulling our clothes off.

Maybe it's the memories we just shared.

Maybe it's the reality that nothing is guaranteed. Not this moment, and certainly not tomorrow.

Maybe it's Jade, plain and simple.

Probably a little bit of everything.

I carefully lay her on the bed, my body looming over hers as I show her exactly what she means to me. With my hands, my mouth, my tongue. I love her in the only way I know how. I give her my all and hope it's enough. I hope like hell that we're not living on borrowed time.

PRESCOTT

"Your knee looks good." Dr. Snow frowns at the scan of my leg as she observes it for a few seconds longer.

"That's good, right?" I ask, my fingers intertwined together to stop them from jittering.

"Let me see your knee first, and then we'll talk."

Hopping onto the table, I remove my brace so she can examine my leg.

"The swelling went down, and it seems your mobility is okay. Any pain?"

Before or after the pain pills and steroids? The bitter question pops into my mind, but I push it back, keeping my face neutral.

"Not any more than usual," I mutter, evading. It's not a lie per se. It doesn't hurt more than usual. What she doesn't know is that I've been managing the pain myself for months now.

But seriously, what was I supposed to do? We have three more games. The three most important games of the season, and we have to win them if we want to enter the playoffs. I couldn't let this take away everything I've worked for all this time.

Except... I was almost caught.

Jade saw me.

I thought she was sleeping, which is the only reason why I even attempted to inject the steroids. If I knew… I shake my head. I'll have to be more careful because if anybody were to find out. If I were caught…

Just a few more weeks, that's how long I have to survive.

A few weeks, and then it's done.

"So, what's the verdict, Doc?"

Although we're just a few weeks away from the finals, the gym is buzzing with activity when I get there. I greet a few people as I make my way to the weight benches to find Nixon working with Zane on his arms.

"How's she doing?" I ask, dropping my things on the floor.

Zane glares at me before returning his attention to the bar. Nixon's face's red, his muscles straining as he lifts the weights.

"Two more, c'mon, you can do it," Zane coaches, his hands steadily following the bar, ready to catch it if it falls, but Nixon pushes through, his arms shaking as he finally puts the bar back in place.

Nixon sits upright, and I throw him a bottle of water. He drains half of it first, and I'm tempted to deck him if he doesn't tell me something soon.

Jade had her second chemo session yesterday, and it wiped her out even more than the first one.

It's not anything unusual. I know that firsthand. It sucked watching Gabriel suffer round after round, cycle after cycle and not being able to do anything about it, but somehow watching Jade do it now, left me feeling even more helpless.

I'm not sure if it's Jade or if it's me.

All these years, all the medical advancements, and there

were still too many diseases out there that we couldn't do anything about.

"Yas went to check in on her and told me she woke up for a little bit, tried to eat, but..." his words trail off as a dark expression flashes on his face.

"Dammit." I run my fingers through my hair. I should be there with her. I should—

"I keep telling her that she should move in with us, but she's so damn stubborn."

"As if that's going to change anything."

"Well, at least she'll have somebody to look after her!" Nixon yells.

"Her roommates are there. I'm there."

"And that should make me feel better?"

"Screw you, Cole."

Grabbing my duffle bag from the floor, I go to the other side of the gym. Tucking my earbuds in, I turn on my playlist before hopping on the treadmill. I know I should start slow, but I'm too damn angry for it.

I go through my exercises, pushing until the sweat is dripping off of me, and my muscles are trembling.

Zane appears in my line of vision, his arms crossed over his chest as he glares me down. Sighing, I put the dumbbell in place and pull my earbuds out.

"You have to cut him some slack. He's hurting," Zane says, his face grim.

He's hurting?

"Well, he's not the only one," I bite out.

With a shake of my head, I grab my things and go to the locker room to change. I check my phone, although I'd have gotten a notification on my watch if Jade tried to text or call me.

Nothing.

The locker room is blessedly quiet. I make my way to my

locker, pulling out my duffle. I've wholly overworked myself, and my knee is feeling it. I grab my pain meds, tossing two back just as the door opens. Swallowing, I look over my shoulder to find Nixon watching me from the doorway.

He closes the door and makes his way to his locker.

"I'm just so worried about her," he says, breaking the silence. "You don't know what it's like. We lost our mother to breast cancer not even two years ago, and now all of this."

"You think you're the only one who lost somebody to cancer?" I ask, still pissed at him. "Grow the fuck up, Nixon. People lose their loved ones to cancer all the freaking time."

"As if you know anything about losing people you love."

My brother's lifeless body flashes in my mind.

You kill everybody you love, Dad's hateful words ring in my head.

I shut the locker, the loud *bang* echoing in the otherwise quiet room. "The person who doesn't know shit is you." With a shake of my head, I grab my things. "I'm going to check in on Jade."

My mind is reeling all the way to Jade's apartment. As I pull my car into the parking lot, I'm playing with the idea of going to my place and taking a shower, but I'm too anxious to see Jade, too worried about making sure she's okay to delay this even for a shower, so instead, I go straight to her place.

Jade's given me a key, so I don't bother knocking. The TV is on in the living room, and I can hear voices. Peeking inside, I find Grace and her boyfriend lying on the couch. She looks up. "Hey," Grace sits upright, a small smile on her lips.

"Hey," I glance down the dark hallway. "How is she doing?"

"Still in her room. The last time I checked, she was sleeping."

"Thanks," I glance back at her, nodding my head. "I'm going to check in on her."

"Sure thing." I start to turn around when Grace calls out: "Prescott?"

Reluctantly, I look over my shoulder. "Yeah?"

"We're here for you. If you need anything. You know that, right?"

"Yeah, thanks."

The door to Jade's room is cracked open. I slide inside, my eyes needing a moment to adjust to the dim lighting. Closing the door, I make my way to her bed.

She looks so small curled in the middle of the queen-size bed. The covers are pulled up to her chin. Her face is pale, and dark circles are visible under her eyes.

Gently, so as not to wake her, I touch her face, noting that her skin is dry, but she doesn't have a fever. Gabriel used to get so sick and would stay that way for days after the chemo was over. Each round was harder, each round he needed more time to recover. Until he didn't.

Jade's not Gabriel, I chastise.

I couldn't go down that road because if I did, there would be no coming back from it.

Losing her wasn't an option. Not after everything we've been through.

"You'll be okay," I whisper, brushing her hair away. Just as I pull back, her eyes flutter open, the blue of her irises seeming more intense against her pale skin. She blinks a few times, and I can't help the smile that spreads over my lips.

"Good morning, gorgeous."

"I quite doubt that," she rasps, her hand covering mine. "How was your appointment? Are you cleared to play?"

She's the one lying in bed, fighting cancer, and still, she's worried about me. Swallowing the lump in my throat, I press my mouth against her forehead.

"Yeah, I'm all cleared to play. And you're wrong. You're the most gorgeous woman I know."

"Maybe I'd be more eager to agree if I didn't taste the puke in my mouth. You'd think after brushing my teeth twice, I wouldn't feel it any longer, but..."

Leaning down, I press my mouth against hers. I have every intention of keeping the kiss soft, but her hand slides to the back of my neck, pulling me closer, and I give in. Cupping her cheeks, I kiss her harder, pouring every twisted emotion that I've been shoving back for weeks into it.

My fears, my anger, and my *love,* as tainted as it might be. I give it all to her. I give her my all. She tilts her head back, her lips parting and allowing me entrance as my fingers sink into her hair. A soft moan comes from the back of her throat, and I can feel it in every inch of my body.

Changing the angle, I dive deeper, my tongue twisting with hers. I kiss her until she's the only thing I taste, smell, feel.

Breaking the kiss, I press my forehead against hers. We're both panting, our labored breaths mingling together. Jade slowly blinks her eyes open. Her cheeks are flushed a healthy pink, lips slightly parted, those gorgeous blues staring back at me in all their intensity. If everything else changes, that one thing will always stay the same.

"You taste like home to me," I whisper, sliding my thumbs over her cheekbones.

She raises her hand, her fingers tracing over my lips. "I missed this. I missed feeling this close to you."

Guilt slams into me, but I push it back. She doesn't need my guilt. She needs me to be normal. To give her normalcy. Plastering a smile on my face, I brush my mouth over hers once again. "I'm not really good at the whole boyfriend thing."

"You're better than you give yourself credit for. I know things have been different..."

I shake my head. "You make me want to be better. Only you." With one last kiss, I pull back, disentangling my fingers from her hair. "I should get a shower, I'm pretty sure I sti—"

I look down at my hand, noticing a strand of hair stuck to my fingers. My heart skips a beat as I try to brush it off before Jade notices it, but it's already too late. Her eyes are glued to my hands, unblinking.

"Jade..." I start slowly, not sure how to handle this. Not sure what to say. Yes, we've both known this would probably happen. But knowing something, and seeing it happen, *experiencing* it firsthand are two completely different things.

Her throat bobs as she swallows, blinking quickly a few times to chase away the tears.

"It's fine." She looks away from me. "You were saying something about a shower?"

"Jade, we should ta—"

"No," she shakes her head. "Not now. I can't deal with this now."

I watch her for a moment, unsure of what to do, or what to say to make this better.

Too soon. It's all happening too soon.

But she's looking at everything but me.

Time, she needs time.

Placing my hand on hers, I give it a firm squeeze. "I'll be in the bathroom if you need me. Okay?"

"Yeah, sure."

I open my mouth, hating to leave her like this, but no words come.

You kill everyone you love.

Pressing my lips together, I settle for another reassuring squeeze before I get up. Grabbing a change of clothes from her closet, I go to the bathroom, leaving the door open as I quickly wash up, the smell of her shampoo filling the space.

Once done, I returned to her bedroom to find her lying down, her eyes closed. Carefully, I lay next to her and pull her into my arms. Her body is stiff under my touch, signaling she's awake.

"It's going to be okay, Jade."

She doesn't say anything, not that I expect her to. I don't let go, and eventually, she relaxes against me, but as I'm drifting to sleep, I'm pretty sure I hear her whisper: "I'm not so sure about that."

Chapter 27

JADE

Pulling the hoodie over my head, I hear my phone buzz on the nightstand. I grab it, checking the message.

Hotshot: You don't have to go if you don't feel well.

I roll my eyes and type back, **I feel fine. That's why I'm coming.**

Some days I swear if you were to ask Prescott and Nixon, they would put me in a protective bubble and never let me out. But I couldn't just lay in bed and do nothing for the next few months between chemo sessions. It was already driving me crazy, and it hadn't even been a full month.

Me: I'll see you after the game. Good luck xx

I'm just about to exit my phone, so I can finish getting ready when an e-mail catches my attention. I open it, scanning the message before my gaze flies to the date in the corner of my phone.

"Shit."

Between throwing up and studying for finals, I almost forgot I had less than a week to submit the images for the gallery exhibition. In the end, I decided to go with the couple's photo. Although I wasn't completely happy with it, I had to submit *something*, and it wasn't like I could go around campus and try to shoot something better anyhow.

Setting the alarm with the reminder to send the photos to my professor later tonight, I go to the bathroom, where I put a little bit of makeup on to try and cover the dark circles under my eyes, not that I'm really successful, but it'll have to do.

My gaze falls on the hairbrush. Letting out a long breath, I take it in my hand and look up at the mirror.

For a moment, I stare at my reflection, hating the suffocating feeling tightening my chest the longer I watch.

Slowly, I lift my hand and glide my brush through my hair. My eyes fixed on the mirror as I move my hand in gentle, even strokes.

Glide, glide, glide.

My hair has grown thinner recently, more fragile. I would have been a fool not to notice. I would have been a fool not to notice the amount of hair in the drain after a shower.

Too soon.

It's all happening way too soon.

I'm not ready.

A knock startles me out of my thoughts as the door pushes open, and Grace peeks inside. "Hey, you ready?"

"Just about." Reluctantly, I put the brush down, turning my back to the counter to ignore the number of strands that have fallen off. "You don't have to go with me, you know. Yasmin will be there."

I didn't like feeling like an obligation to my friends, which is precisely what has happened since I started the treatment. My worst nightmare had come true, and there was nothing that I could do about it.

It was the reason why I hid it for so long, why I'm still hiding so many things.

"Are you kidding me? Do you know who my brother is?" she huffs and puffs air at her bangs to get them out of her line of sight. They've grown longer since the last time we cut them, but with everything else, I didn't get a chance to do it.

"I know who your brother is." I roll my eyes at her, my gaze falling to her bangs once again as she moves them aside. "We should really trim those," I comment, my fingers tugging at my own strands.

"I'm ready whenever you are. If I'm being honest, they've been annoying me lately, but I've been too lazy to cut them myself."

"Yeah, how about you don't do that?"

"Why do you think I kept pushing it off? I don't have time to let them grow if I mess something up; besides, it's like you have a magic touch for them or something. Remember when I went to that salon in New York, and they cut my bangs too short? I'd like not to repeat that."

"We could do it now if you want." I look around, trying to remember where I put the scissors.

"Later." Grace waves her hand at me. "We have a game to go to. Jack said he'll come if the Ravens play in the Bowl game, so they better win. Are we going?"

From the corner of my eye, I catch my reflection in the mirror. My stomach clenches, and for a second, I think I might actually throw up. But I've been feeling fine the last couple of days. Exhausted but fine.

Get a grip, Jade. It's just hair.

"Give me a minute. I want to grab a hat."

I see a frown appear between Grace's brows as I move past her and into my room. "You hate hats."

I do. I really do, but what I hate even more is seeing all the thinning and bald spots on my head.

"It's cold outside." I shrug, changing the subject. "What's up with Mason? Is he ready to go back home for Christmas?"

"I'm not sure. You know how he is; he doesn't like to talk about it. I think he still feels weird about going back there, so we'll spend most of the time at my place."

"Is that wise? I can't imagine J.D. being too happy about it."

Jack Daniel Shelton is Grace's older brother. I've spent some time with him since Grace and I started to hang out, and he brought being protective to a whole other level.

I rummage through my closet, pushing away some of my clothes. Seriously, where is that thing? I'm pretty sure—

"He still makes him sleep in the living room! Can you imagine that?"

"Oh, I can imagine," I say absentmindedly as my fingers wrap around the soft material and pull it out.

Got it! Finally. I slip the hat on, frowning at my reflection. The hat looks hideous.

Not as hideous as going around half-bald. I chastise myself. *Deal with it.*

"Like what year it is?" Grace continues, clearly on a roll. "Just because he puts him in the study doesn't mean we're not having sex. Or that I'd want to have sex with my brother sleeping a few doors down from me." A visible shudder goes through her. "Nope, definitely not happening. Besides, it's not like we can even be indecent if we wanted to since you never know when Nicky or Wren might barge into my room. I swear, I think J.D. put them up to it."

"Knowing your brother? Quite possible." I turn around to face her. "How do I look?"

Her green eyes narrow on the hat. "Pom-pom? Seriously?"

"Yes, seriously. Now, are we going or what?" Not giving her

time to protest, I head out of the room, leaving her to follow after me.

"At least it's yellowish."

"Thanks."

The campus is a pandemonium of black and gold. This was it. The game that'll decide if the Ravens are going to the playoffs or not, and people didn't disappoint. We opted to walk to the stadium to avoid getting stuck in the traffic, and most of the students had similar thoughts because it took us twice as long to make our way there. At least we're in the family section.

Yasmin is already seated and chatting with a couple of girls sitting next to her when we arrive.

"This is insanity," I say as I slide into a seat next to her, the cool chair making me wish I have my blanket with me.

"Tell me about it. It's the only thing everybody's been talking about these days." Yasmin gives me a long look, the worry clear in her gaze. "Are you sure you should be here?"

"This game is make or break. Where the hell would I be?" I ask, my eyes trained on the football field and full stands.

"You look pale. And after everything that's been going on lately..."

Great, so much for the freaking foundation, and the time I spent putting on makeup just to avoid these kinds of questions.

"I'm fine. I'm not missing their last few college games."

Nixon's sophomore year, when the team had made it this far, Mom wanted to go so badly to support him, but she'd already been too sick at that point. We watched it online, but I could see the longing on her face. Hear it in her voice when we talked. I wasn't about to put him through that again. No matter how annoying he might occasionally be.

"Do you want to talk about it?"

"Don't even try. She's *fine*," Grace says, her tone mocking as she says the last word.

"That's because I am fine. Can we just watch the game?"

Just then, the music changes, and our opponents are announced. There's some cheering as they run out on the field, but it's nothing compared to the roar of the crowd as the Ravens come out of the tunnel.

"It's game time, baby."

PRESCOTT

"Listen up, boys!" Coach Davies bellows loud enough to be heard over the roaring crowd. "I know you're all tired by now, but we're tied with less than five minutes on the clock. *Five* minutes, that's all you have. Three hundred seconds are standing between you and glory." His serious gaze takes us in one by one, making sure to meet everybody's eyes. "This is it. The final push. Our last stand to show them what we're made of. No matter what happens in these last three hundred seconds, I'm proud of the men you've become, and it's been my honor to train you."

"It's been our honor, too, Coach, but can we all agree to give our best to win?" Scotty asks, cracking his fingers. "I don't know about you, but I really want this W."

He isn't the only one. Guys nod their heads, faces serious as they wait for the game plan.

"Okay then, let's do this."

Coach pulls out his little whiteboard and draws the play. The silence falls over us as we listen to him explain what he wants us to do.

The referee blows a whistle, signaling the timeout is over.

"Ravens on three," Nixon calls out, placing his hand in the

middle of our little circle. More hands join in. "One, two, three..."

"Ravens!" everybody chants as we break apart.

My gaze darts to the clock as we run back on the field.

Nixon slaps me on the shoulder as he jogs next to me. "Run like the wind. The team's counting on you."

A knot forms in my throat as the expectations of all my teammates, and all we've worked for falls on my shoulders, making my stomach roll.

No pressure at all.

No fucking pressure at all.

I look up at the stands, thousands of fans all standing up and waiting anxiously for the last play to be made. Ignoring them all, I let my gaze slide past them to the only person that matters.

Jade.

She's sitting in the family and friend's section, her yellow hat sticking out in the mostly black and gold attire. Her hair's been thinning out, and although she refused to talk about it, I knew she hated every second of it.

Shaking my head, I shift my attention back to the field, coming to a stop in my spot. Nixon and I exchange a quick glance before we get into place. Both teams are even, meaning everything's on the line.

And I mean everything.

There was enough time for the game to go both ways, and we all knew it.

I face the guy opposite me, the fire burning in his eyes as he cracks his neck and crouches down in front of me. I narrow my eyes at him, every muscle in my body tense to the point of bursting.

Nixon calls out the play, and the lines crash in a series of grunts and curses. I try to break through the defense, but they know I'm Nixon's go-to guy, so they're guarding me better than Fort Knox.

The game is brutal, with neither of the teams budging. Every yard won is a war in its own right.

In the third play, I finally find a hole in their defense and win us twenty yards before I'm tackled to the ground.

I shove the guy that's on me away, spitting to the ground as my gaze goes to the clock.

One minute, thirty-eight seconds.

We move the line, getting in position. I don't dare meet the gazes of any of my teammates, knowing we're running out of time.

We're playing to win. They're playing for more time.

And that can't happen.

The buzzing in my ears starts to grow louder, dulling the sound of Nixon's words. But I don't need to hear them. I know them by heart.

I pretend to go right as offense and defense crash together. Then I shift left, shoving through the mass of bodies.

Gritting my teeth, I grip the ball tighter to my chest and run for all that I'm worth. The roar of the crowd matches the pounding of the blood echoing in my ears as I push myself to my breaking point. I can feel the defense running after me, the distance between us lowering with every yard I cross.

I don't dare look back.

Just forward.

Toward the end zone.

Toward the win.

The guy behind me grunts, and I know he's there, just a few inches away, but so is the end zone.

So I brace myself as I extend my hand and leap forward.

It's like all the air is sucked out of space, the voices falling back. Or maybe everything just stopped for a moment. I know my heart did as my body crashed into the ground, another one falling on top of me and kicking all the air out of my lungs.

Groaning, I tighten my grip on the ball as I look up, my heart stuck in my chest.

I blink, my vision slightly blurry from the pain, so it takes me a moment to realize the ball is across the white line, in the end zone.

But even if I didn't, the roar of the crowd would be a dead giveaway.

We won.

"Dude," Scotty slaps me on the back, laughing. "We're going to Moore's to celebrate. You coming?"

"Yeah, I'll be there in a bit," I say, barely lifting my head.

With a slap on the shoulder, he leaves, a few of our teammates in tow.

Letting out a shaky breath, I look up. My leg has finally stopped shaking, and the pain somewhat dulled, although still present. Always present.

Slowly, I push to my feet and take off my clothes before making my way to the showers. Pain shoots through my leg with every step I take, my leg dragging behind me.

As quickly as possible, I rinse off the sweat, grass, and dirt and return to the locker room, towel wrapped around my waist. The room has finally emptied out, leaving only the blessed quiet.

Finally.

Limping back to my spot, I roam around my bag until I find the little bottle I have stashed inside. Taking a glance around the room to make sure I'm indeed alone, I grab the needle, stick it into the bottle, and pull the liquid out before injecting it into my thigh. I feel the sting as the needle pierces the skin, pushing the liquid inside.

It's worth it.

The team has made it to the playoffs.

Just a few more weeks. I only have to survive a few more weeks—a few games.

For Gabriel, and the promise I made him.

"Prescott?"

My body freezes at the sound of my name.

Shit.

Shit, shit, shit.

My heart thunders in my chest as I slowly lift my head to find Jade standing in the doorway, her wide eyes zeroed in on my leg. The needle in my hand. "What are you doing?"

Chapter 28

JADE

"What are you doing, Prescott?" I repeat, looking up from the needle stuck in his leg to his face.

What the hell is going on here?

That night a couple of weeks back, just after my first round of chemo, flashes in my mind again. I thought I was seeing things—that it was all in my head—but apparently, I wasn't.

Prescott only stares at me, eyes wide, lips parted.

"Jade, I—" His tongue darts out, sliding over his lips as he looks around, searching for an out.

Screw this.

I march toward him, grabbing the bottle off the bench.

"No, don't..." He tries to reach for it, but it's already too late. I turn my back to him, pulling the bottle out of his reach as I scan the label on the front.

"*Steroids?*" I turn around instantly, my eyes wide as my fingers grip the almost empty bottle. "You're taking steroids?"

"Jade, I can explain."

"Explain? Okay, then explain it to me. Because the only thing that comes to my mind is, what the hell, Prescott?"

"It's just..." He runs his palm over his face. "It's been hard, okay?"

I stare at him, unsure if I heard him correctly. "Hard? That's the best you've got? It's been hard?"

"Yes, Jade, it's been freaking hard!" He yells, his face turning red. He yanks the needle out of his thigh and gets to his feet. "My leg has been messed up ever since the injury last year. No amount of rehab could take away the pain."

"How long?"

I try to look back and see the signs that I might have missed.

"I've been taking painkillers ever since I rejoined the team. The..." There's a beat of silence. "The other thing, just a few weeks. Ever since I was reinjured in that game."

I shake my head, not believing what I'm hearing. Months. He's been in pain for months, and he hasn't said a word.

And I haven't seen it.

I've been so stuck in my own bullshit that I haven't seen it all happening right in front of my eyes.

"Why didn't you say something?"

"Say something?" he scoffs like the mere idea is laughable. "What was I supposed to say? Hey Coach, I know you guys depend on me, but my leg is killing me every time you push me too hard? He would have kicked me off the team instantly."

"To me! Why didn't you say something to me?"

"To have you judge me like you are now?" He shakes his head. "I think I'll pass. Besides, we were just hooking up."

"I'm not judging you. I'm worried. What if somebody finds out? It'll ruin your whole career."

It'll ruin this whole team. Because there is no way that if something like this came out, that the Ravens would come out of it unscathed. Every single player would be looked at with distrust.

"Of course, you're judging me. Hell, I'm judging myself. Do

you really think I want to do it? Do you think it's easy for me? But it's been the only way. Steroids were my safest option to get back to the game. To be able to play. You, better than anybody, should understand why I need to do this. Why I *need* to play."

I let out a shaky breath. "You can't be serious right now."

"I'm serious. I have to play. I have to win. That's the only way I can keep my promise to Gabriel."

"And you think Gabriel would care more about your promise than about your health?" my voice rises as the exasperation sets in. I can't believe this is happening that we're even having this discussion.

"Well, he isn't here to tell us, is he?!"

I stare at him, our labored breathing the only sound filling the room. "He wouldn't want you to do this, Prescott," I whisper, taking a step forward and trying to reach for him. "He would want you to be happy and healthy. If you keep doing this, you might mess your leg up for good and—"

He shoves my hand away and pulls back, anger flashing on his face.

His rejection is like a slap to my face.

"I don't fucking care, Jade." His fingers slide through his hair, fisting the short strands and pulling at them. "How don't you see it? I have nothing else left. Nothing else but my promise to my brother."

Tears start burning my eyelids, so I close my eyes, trying to push them back.

Just a hookup.

Nothing else left.

"Fine. Destroy yourself. Who am I to say anything, right?"

Prescott's eyes widen as my words set in. "Jade..."

With a shake of my head, I turn on the balls of my feet and get the hell out while I can still keep my cool.

Prescott calls after me, but I don't bother turning around.

The icy breeze hits me the moment I open the door. I gulp in the air, my eyes turning blurry from the cold.

At least, that's what I tell myself as I start walking.

I don't have a destination in mind, but anywhere is better than here.

PRESCOTT

The phone beeps, but the call never connects. Cursing, I hang up and shove the phone back in my pocket as I push the door to the bar open.

Stubborn, infuriating woman.

Moore's is packed when I get there. It's like half the campus appeared to celebrate that the Ravens have entered the playoffs. People slap me on the back as I make my way through the bar, congratulating me on the win. I nod at them as I pass but don't make any attempt to slow down as my eyes search the space for a familiar face.

Why couldn't she have just waited for me outside? Or went with Nixon and waited for me to join them here? But no, she had to come inside just as I was taking care of my leg. She had to see me like that, and a tiny part of me hated her for it.

The other part feels like an asshole for yelling at her.

For throwing those hateful words at her.

She isn't just a hookup, quite the contrary.

She's my freaking everything.

That's why I hate it even more that she, out of all people, saw me like that.

Stopping at the bar, I order a Jack. The shot is in front of me in a matter of seconds, and I down it in one go.

Where the hell is she?

I have to find her and make her understand. If this were to get out… I'd be done. Ravens would be done.

Letting the glass drop on the counter, I'm about to order another drink when the crowd moves, and I spot Nixon sitting with a few of our friends at the table in the back. Pushing from the bar, I shove through the people and make my way to them.

"Hey, is Jade here?"

My best friend's smile falls as he turns to me, his eyes glinting. Between everything that happened with Jade, and our last fight, things between us have been strained to say the least, but if somebody knows where she is, it's Nixon.

"No." His eyes throw daggers at me. "She went to look for you. She wanted to congratulate you on the win. Didn't you see her?"

Shit, of course, he knew that she'd be looking for me. Nixon was like a hawk when it came to his sister these days, and it was driving Jade insane.

So where the fuck is she?

"I did, but she left quickly. I thought I heard her say she was coming here, but maybe she went home instead. I'll go and look for her."

Nixon pushes to his feet. "I'll go with you."

"No, stay. There's no sense in both of us leaving. I'll go check in on her, make sure she's all right."

My stomach rolls with unease.

Make sure she doesn't tell anybody about what she saw.

Nixon looks unsure, and for a moment, I think he'll tell me to fuck off when Yasmin places her hand over his, giving him a firm squeeze. "She probably went home because it's freezing outside, and it's been a long day. You can't micromanage everything, Nixon. Besides," she looks at me, "Prescott will text us when he finds her, right?"

"Of course," I nod. "I'll talk to you guys in a bit?"

With a wave goodbye, I make my way out of the bar. It's freezing outside, and the snow has started to fall in thick snowflakes.

"Dammit, I really hope that she made it home."

Crossing the street, I get into my car. I rub my hands together as I start it, giving it a moment to warm up before driving away.

The campus is relatively quiet as I drive past it, the snow growing stronger by the second.

My headlights illuminate the dark road in front of me. I'm about to turn onto my street when I see a figure walking by the side of the road.

"What the fuck? Are they freaking in—" My eyes narrow as I slowly move closer to the person.

It can't be.

But it is.

Stepping on the break, I put the car in park before I get out in a hurry.

"Jade?" I rush toward her, my eyes scanning her body for any sign of injury. "What are you doing out here in the snow? Are you okay?"

Jade turns toward me, eyes wide. She blinks, a frown appearing between her brows. "I wanted to take a walk. Clear my head."

Clear her head?

"In this weather?"

"It wasn't snowing when I left the stadium. Well, it wasn't snowing this hard anyway."

Her eyes meet mine, usually bright blue color now dull and subdued. Her hair is a tangled mess from the wind and snow, and her cheeks are flushed red from the cold bite in the air.

I close my eyes, letting out a shaky breath.

This is all my damn fault.

Taking a step closer, I face her, my hands wrapping around hers. She doesn't even have freaking gloves, so her fingers are ice cold, the skin slightly blue. "I'm sorry, Jade. I shouldn't have yelled at you. But the whole thing with my knee has me on edge. Everybody is counting on me, and I'm just waiting for the other shoe to drop."

Tears glimmer in her eyes as her fingers tighten around mine.

"You can't keep doing this, Prescott," she mumbles. She blinks her eyelashes furiously. Her usually bright blue eyes now have a hazy, wild look to them. Her fingers dig into my palms so hard I can feel the sting. "Promise me."

"Jade..." My heart starts beating harder as she shakes her head.

"Promise me you'll stop. You can't... Just promise..."

"Okay, I promise," I rush out.

"...m—"

Her words are cut off as she sways on her feet. A shudder runs down my spine as I wrap my arms around her and pull her to me. My heart thunders in my chest as I tilt Jade back to look at her pale face. Her cheeks are rosy, her lips slightly choppy. I thought it was from cold, but when I pressed my hand against her forehead, I could feel the burn of her skin.

My whole body freezes as the chill sets in my bones.

"No." I shake my head as my hand skims over her cheeks and neck. Burning up. "Jade, doll, look at me."

I gently shake her, but she lets out a soft groan, those crystal eyes still closed, and that panic that's been slowly building inside me since the moment I laid my eyes on her reaches the surface.

"Jade, don't do this to me. C'mon, open those pretty eyes for me," I plead with her, but no amount of pleading will help.

She's not waking up.

"You're going to be okay," I whisper, brushing my lips against her hot forehead. I slip my shaky hand into my pocket. It takes me two tries before I'm able to pull my phone out, but somehow, I do it. Unlocking it, I dial the familiar number.

Thankfully, he answers on the first ring.

"I need you," I say before he can even get a word out.

The music is blasting on the other side of the line, signaling that Nixon is still at Moore's.

"Prescott? What the..."

"It's Jade. She's not doing okay."

Chapter 29

PRESCOTT

13 years old

"It's not fair. Why does a dying kid have to be stuck in this place?" Gabriel huffs, crossing his skinny arms over his chest. He lost some weight since he came to the hospital, which is saying something considering, he was skinny even before starting chemo. Nothing tasted good, and he was sick most days. His skin is pale, almost see-through, except for his cheekbones. The bones stand out, a light flush of red spreading over his skin.

"You're not dying," I chastise. "Stop saying that."

"Everybody is dying, Pres."

I grit my teeth, glaring at my brother. He's been so flippant about the whole thing. I get it; things are different for him, but there was a fine line between accepting his reality and giving up. Some days, I think he's doing the latter.

"Well, they're trying to make you feel better, so stop complaining."

"I'd like to see you be stuck here for months on end."

I don't bother correcting him. I might not have cancer, but I was as much stuck here as he was. If I wasn't in school or playing football, I was here.

"Want me to pull out the PlayStation or something?"

Our parents brought it here when Gabriel was hospitalized a few weeks ago so he could play when bored.

"What I want is to breathe." He tilts his head back. "And play football. Damn, I'd kill to feel the rough leather of the football in my hands."

The longing on his face is so intense I can practically feel it in my bones. I hate this. I hate that he has to be stuck here, so far from everything he loves.

"I could go down. We came here straight from practice today, so the ball is in my duffle bag."

Gabriel's head snaps up, his brown eyes lighting up in excitement. "What if we went together?"

"Gabby," I shake my head. "You know what your doctor said."

"I know, but it would be just for a few minutes. How much damage can a few minutes out in the fresh air do?" He clasps his hands together. "Please? Just for a little while."

A knot forms in my throat as I watch him. I should say no. It's for his own good. But seriously, it would be just a few minutes.

My eyes fall on the IV sticking from his hand. "And what are you going to do about that?"

He has me, and he knows it. A smile flashes on his face as he yanks the needle out.

My mouth falls open as I look around, expecting a nurse to pop into the room and yell at us, but nobody comes. "Are you crazy?" I hiss. "What if somebody comes?"

Gabriel waves me off as he slowly gets to his feet, pain flashing on his face. For all his bravado, he's hurting. Has been for a while; that's why doctors wanted him to stay here in the first place.

"It'll be all right. For the most part, they leave me alone if I don't call them since they have much younger kids to take care of."

He grabs the hoodie from the chair and pulls it on. His beanie is crooked, so he tugs it back in place before going to Mom's bag. She left it in the room when she went to call Dad. They had a meeting with Gabriel's doctors, but Dad wasn't here. Lately, he's been working extra long hours, which I think has more to do with his need to stay away than with the work itself. Gabriel grabs the keys and turns to me, that crooked smile of his flashing on his face. "C'mon, let's go."

"I still think this is a bad idea," I mutter as I follow.

"It'll be okay."

He cracks open the door and looks out, making sure the coast is clear before he turns back to me and gives me a signal to follow after him.

My heart is beating a mile a minute as I go after him, expecting to be caught any second now, but by some miracle, nobody comes, and we manage to sneak out of the floor and get into the elevator without anybody noticing.

Once we're on the first floor and out of the building, Gabriel tilts his head back and takes in a deep breath.

I just stare at him, my heart aching for everything that he's lost and had to give up in the last few years.

His eyes flutter open, and he seems a little more relaxed than he was in the room, and some color has appeared on his face.

"You good?"

"Yeah. Let's go grab the ball."

I slowed down my steps so he wouldn't strain himself as we walked to where Mom parked the car. The lights flash as Gabriel unlocks it, and I open the back seat to grab my duffle bag, rummaging through it until my fingers wrap around the football. Turning around, I look for Gabriel to find him a few feet away, waiting.

"Let's see what you've got," he calls out to me.

Reluctantly, I weigh the ball in my hands before gently throwing it at him.

His glare tells me he sees exactly what I'm doing and doesn't appreciate it one bit.

"Did you suddenly grow a pussy since I've been stuck in the hospital, Pres?" my brother taunts as his fingers tighten around the leather. "Grow a pair and throw that ball like a man."

With that, he throws the ball at me, the move so unexpected the damn thing falls out of my hands.

"Shit."

"Damn right. I can't believe Coach is letting you play."

"Well, he does, and I'm the best wide receiver on the team." This time when I throw it, I'm not holding back.

Gabriel catches the ball without any problem and smirks at me. "Only because I'm not there."

That's true. I was good, but Gabriel was better. Two of us together, though? Unbeatable.

And standing here in the parking lot in the middle of November with the chilly air biting our cheeks, I realize how much I missed this. I love football; there is no denying that. But what I love more is playing side-by-side with my brother.

"One day we'll do it, Pres. One day we'll play on the same team again, and there'll be nobody like us. The Wentworth brothers will win it all. We'll become legends."

I could see it as clear as day. A smile spreads over my mouth as we toss the ball for God only knows how long. Until the sky turns dark and the streetlights turn on. Only then do we get back inside.

"This was fun," I say to Gabriel, pushing the door to the pediatrics floor open. "I didn't even realize how much I miss—"

"Gabriel!" Mom yells as soon as we step inside. She shoves me out of her way and goes straight to my brother to catch him as he sways on his feet.

My mouth falls open as Mom calls for a doctor, and more staff joins us, looking over Gabriel.

My mom looks at me, tears glistening in her eyes. "What have you done?" She shakes her head. "He's been fighting an infection for the last two days! And you've just made it worse."

"What happened?"

Nixon must have called Dr. Hendriks because the woman meets us in the emergency room as soon as we get inside.

"She was fine earlier, but she spiked a fever out of nowhere and collapsed," Nixon says, his panicked eyes going to Jade's limp body clasped in my arms.

He wanted to carry her, but I couldn't let go. Because the last time I let go...

This is all my fault.

First, my brother.

Now Jade.

My dad was right.

You kill everyone you love.

"Put her on the bed here so I can take a look at her. Did you take her temperature?"

"No," Nixon shakes his head. "What's happening to her?"

"I don't know yet, but we'll run some tests and find out." Those serious dark eyes meet mine. "I need you to put her on the bed for me now."

Although her tone is gentle, I don't miss the command in

her voice. My throat bobs as my gaze falls to Jade's face. Her cheeks are rosy, and sweat coats her forehead. That awful yellow beanie is crooked.

She has to be alright.

She *has* to.

Gently, I place her on the bed and force myself to take a step back.

One step, but it feels more like a million.

The moment I do, Dr. Hendriks pulls off her stethoscope and places it against Jade's chest.

A soft hand touches mine, snapping my attention away from Jade. "You have to leave so Dr. Hendriks can work and help your friend."

I want to laugh.

Because Jade's not my friend.

She's my everything.

And I could lose her.

When she sees I'm not moving, the nurse takes my hand and leads me out in the hallway where Nixon is standing and holding onto Yasmin for dear life as his eyes stay glued to that damn room and the lifeless body lying inside.

Then the nurse goes back into the room, and the door shuts, blocking us from seeing what's happening inside.

"She's strong," Nixon whispers. "She's strong, and she's going to get through this."

Strong doesn't have anything to do with this.

Gabriel was strong too, and look at where he is now.

"I can't do this," I whisper.

Nixon's eyes meet mine, and I can see all the emotions that are swirling inside me reflected on his face. The worry, the fear, the heartbreak, the love. "What are you talking about?"

I shake my head. "I can't do this."

With that, I turn on the balls of my feet and get the hell out.

Chapter 30

JADE

"So it was just the flu?" I ask, not sure if I understand her correctly. I've been stuck in this damn hospital the last few days because of the damn flu? People don't go to the hospital for those.

"Yes," Dr. Hendriks nods, her eyes scanning my chart. "But thankfully, your brother caught it early and brought you here so we could treat it. Since your immune system has been compromised after the chemo, your body is more prone to getting severe cases of the flu and any other infectious diseases. Unfortunately for you, the flu isn't something you can easily brush off."

"Just my damn luck. When can I go home?" I ask at the same time Nixon appears in the doorway. "You're going home?"

"Nixon!" My heart skips a beat as I look at my brother standing in the doorway of my room, his tall frame blocking my view.

Dr. Hendriks chuckles. "Your labs have come back as good as we can have them at this point, and your fever has been down for the past twenty-four hours. If you promise me you'll behave, I can see about getting you discharged today."

I shift in my bed, my muscles groaning in protest. My fever

might have gone down, but my body is still feeling the consequences of the flu. I feel like a twenty-year-old stuck in an eighty-year-old's body. "Oh, please, please, please."

"And you'll stay indoors as much as possible? I'm afraid there are no more football games for you in the future."

It wasn't the football game, though, not entirely anyhow, but I don't dare correct her. I haven't told anybody what happened after the game, what I saw in that locker room, or how I wandered around campus while I tried to process it all, which landed me in this bed.

It was my own damn fault.

I force out a smile. "Anything to get me out of here faster."

"Okay, I'll let the nurses know to take care of the paperwork, and then I'll see you for your chemo session next week."

"Thank you, Dr. Hendriks."

The woman nods before leaving the room. Nixon lets her pass and then steps inside. My gaze shifts toward the door as my stomach clenches in anticipation.

"He's not here."

My head falls back against the pillow as I close my eyes.

Dammit, Prescott.

He hasn't come since the night they brought me here. The moment I could get my hands on my phone, I tried calling him and texting, but I hadn't heard back.

God only knows what he's thinking in that stubborn head of his.

Knowing Prescott? He somehow convinced himself that the whole thing was his fault.

Nixon sits on the bed next to me, his hand covering mine. "How are you doing?"

"Peachy," I mutter, irritated by the whole situation.

"Really? 'cause you look like shit."

"As if you're any better."

It's not Nixon's fault. He's been amazing through it all. Between classes, studying, football, and staying here, he's been working himself to the bone, and it shows. Dark circles are under his eyes, and his usually clean-shaven face is all scruffy.

"Sorry, that was uncalled for. I'm just ready to go back home."

"I've been thinking about that, and I..."

"No."

Nixon's eyes narrow. "But you haven't even let me finish."

"I don't need you to finish, I already know what you'll say, and the answer is no. The last thing I want is to move in with you and Yas. I love you guys, but nope."

"Jade..."

"I'm fine. I'll do better and try to stay inside or dress warmly when I go out."

"Let's stick to staying inside, shall we? I don't think I can stand another scare like this."

"I'll try my best." And this time, I actually meant it. "Have you seen him, at least?"

"Just at practice, although we haven't been talking much after..."

My brows quirk up. "After?"

Nixon runs his hand over his face. "After everything that has happened."

Here we go again. I let out a loud groan. "I told you, it's..."

"Not his fault," Nixon finishes for me. "Yadda, yadda, ya. He can't keep on doing shit like this. He can't keep walking out on you when things get hard."

I shake my head. "You don't get it."

"Then tell me so I can understand!"

I press my lips in a tight line, looking away. I wanted to tell him; it pained me to see the two of them fighting like this because me of all people, but it wasn't my story to tell, and as long as Prescott didn't want to share about Gabriel, my hands were tied.

Nixon places his hand over mine, his voice gentler this time around. "What's going on with him, Jade? I can't help you guys if I don't understand."

"I can't tell you." He opens his mouth to protest, but I shake my head. "It's not my story to tell. But there is a reason why I let him go that first time. I didn't want him to go through this."

But he came back.

He said he was in it this time.

He said he wasn't going away.

And then he left all over again.

PRESCOTT

From the corner of my eyes, I see the door being pulled open. I turn around, ready to tell Spencer where to shove it, but he isn't the one standing in my doorway.

Jade is.

And she's freaking furious.

"Oh, so you *are* alive. Good." She marches toward me, the fire blazing in those blue eyes of hers. I try to turn around, but her hand lands on my forearm, stopping me from moving an inch. "What the hell, Prescott? What the actual hell? I called, I texted, but what do I get for it? Nothing. Abso-freaking-lutely nothing. For all I knew, you could have been dead in a ditch somewhere."

Her labored breathing fills the room, making my silence seem more pronounced. She notices it, too, because she grits her teeth, the irritation clear in her voice.

"Say something, dammit!"

"What do you want me to say?"

"I don't know, Prescott! Maybe start by explaining why did you take me to the hospital only to dump me there? Maybe explain to me why you left and never looked back!"

"Because it was my fault!"

"I knew it." She crosses her hands over her chest as she glares at me. "I just knew you'd think something so silly..."

"It's not silly. You ended up in the hospital because of me, because of that fight."

"I ended up in the hospital because my immune system was compromised. I ended up in the hospital because, instead of going home after the game, I felt trapped, so I was walking around the campus in the snow. It has nothi—"

"It has everything to do with me!" Prescott yells, running his fingers through his hair. "Fuck, Jade, if we didn't fight, you would have been home, warm, *safe*."

"You don't know that."

"I do know that. I would have made sure of it."

"Prescott, this is silly. It's not your fau—"

She tries to touch me, but I pull back. I can't stand the feel of her hand on mine. "I can't keep doing this," I whisper, shaking my head. "I just... I can't."

You kill everyone you love.

"What..." Jade's brows furrow as she looks down at her fingers before slowly lifting her gaze to meet mine. "What do you mean?"

My throat bobs as I swallow, the words seeming to be stuck, but I push them out. I have to do this.

"This. Us." I shake my head. "I can't do it. You were right. I should have listened to you from the beginning. It's too much. Too hard. I just... I can't."

The silence stretches between us as she stares at me, her

face completely blank. "So you're what... done? Just like that? You're... done?"

"Yes."

I force myself to look at her as I say the word. I need her to see this, need her to understand, and I need her to stay the fuck away from me. I need her to stay alive.

You kill everyone you love.

"I'm done."

Her lips quiver, but she bites the inside of her cheek to stop it from wobbling. "You're joking."

My fingers curl around the armrests, tightening to the point of pain. "I'm not joking. I can't keep doing this. I don't want to keep doing this." Then I go in for the kill, saying the words I know will push her away. "I don't want to keep seeing Gabriel's face every time I look at you. Every time we go to chemo? I remember all the times I sat next to him. Every time you're sick, I see my brother. Seeing you like this brings back so many memories, and I can't keep doing this, Jade. I can't keep on *hurting* like this."

Jade takes a step back, her lips parting, eyes wide like I've slapped her. It takes all of me not to push up and pull her into my arms, tell her I'm a jackass, and beg her to forgive me, but I can't.

You kill everyone you love.

Her tongue darts out, sliding over her lips. "O-Okay."

Before I can react, she turns around. I expect her to dash out of my room without a second glance. I don't know why because every time so far, she's done exactly the opposite of what I expected.

She stops in the doorway, her fingers tracing the wood as she turns to give me one last glance. "Prescott?" She grazes her teeth over her lip. "I'm sorry. It was never my intention to hurt you."

If she planned to deliver a blow, she did it.

With those parting words, she turns around and leaves.

And I let her.

I'm sorry. It was never my intention to hurt you.

You kill everyone you love.

Tilting my head back, I close my eyes, my fingers still gripping the armrests. "Fuck, fuck, fuck."

Out in the hallway, I hear Spencer call out to her, but Jade doesn't say anything.

I wait, holding onto the chair like I'm holding on for dear life. The sound of my heartbeat echoes in my eardrums, battling with the words haunting me. My father's words. Jade's words.

Suddenly, Spencer appears in my doorway. "What the hell have you done?" he asks, glaring at me.

He can be angry all he wants, but it's nothing compared to how angry I am at myself.

"Is she gone?"

"Dude, she was crying. Whatever you did—"

"Is. She. Gone?"

"Yeah, she just..."

Before he can finish, I'm out of the chair and going straight for the liquor cabinet, pulling out a brand new bottle of Jack. Twisting the cap off, I take a pull directly from the bottle, letting it burn my throat.

You kill everyone you love.

It's done. She's going to be okay. She has to be okay.

I take another gulp as I repeat these words like a mantra, hoping it'll burn this ache that keeps growing in my chest, suffocating me.

"Seriously? That's your solution? Drink yourself to death?"

"Fuck off, Spencer."

"No, you fuck off, Wentworth. You just ran off the only girl silly enough to overlook all your flaws and love you. What the hell's wrong with you?"

"You don't know what the fuck you're talking about, so shut up."

"Oh, I don't? I see the way you look at her, dude. Everybody can see the way you look at her. You love her, so why the fuck did you push her away?"

"Because she's dying! I can't watch her die."

You kill everyone you love.

I take a long pull from the bottle. My eyesight turns blurry as I choke on the whiskey.

I can't be the cause of her death.

Not one more person. I can't kill another person I love. I'd rather die than do that to her.

Chapter 31

JADE

On autopilot, I enter the apartment and close the door. I lean against it, the soft *click* echoing in the quiet space as I wrap my arms around myself and let my body slide to the ground.

I can't keep doing this. I don't want to keep doing this. I don't want to keep seeing Gabriel's face every time I look at you. Every time we go to chemo? I remember all the times I sat next to him. Every time you're sick, I see my brother. Seeing you like this, it brings so many memories, and I can't keep doing this, Jade. I can't keep on hurting *like this.*

"Jade?"

Blinking the blurriness out of my eyes, I look up to find Grace watching me with worry written all over her face.

"What happened? Why are you crying? Is it ca—"

"Prescott broke up with me," I whisper, my voice sounding dull even to my own ears.

"What?"

I let out a humorless chuckle at her stupefied face.

"He broke up with me."

I tilt my head back, one lone tear slipping down my cheek. I brush it away quickly, not wanting Grace to see me cry. I was so done with crying.

"But Prescott loves you."

Then why hasn't he said it once?

"He hates me. I remind him too much of..." I let my words trail off. Even after all this time, after everything that has happened, I still can't reveal his secrets to people. Not even my best friend.

Grace sits down on the floor, taking my hand in hers. "You remind him of what?"

"It doesn't matter," I shake my head. "I knew what I was getting into. I told him we shouldn't be doing this. That I didn't want him to go through this. Nobody should be forced to date a dying girl."

Grace grips my hand tighter. "You're not dying."

"But I am."

"You're not." Grace gives me a strong shake. "You're *fighting*. You're fighting to live. You will live. Do you get that? We're not losing you, so I don't want to hear any more nonsense about dying."

I huff as more tears gather in my eyes. "It doesn't work that way."

I wish it were that easy. Wish it, and it'll come true, but those are fairytales for children.

"Well, I'll make it work that way. You're *not* dying. We'll beat cancer's ass. And then we'll beat Prescott's ass." Grace tilts her head to the side, making her locks sway. "Or maybe it's the other way around. After all, I have to return the favor for kicking some sense into Mason last year."

"I don't want you to kick Prescott's ass."

"Well, I want to kick his ass for making you cry."

"I'm not crying," I protest just as another sniffle breaks out of me.

"No, of course not." Grace tucks a piece of hair behind my ear, a few strands falling down into my lap, which only makes me sniffle harder until I'm full-on crying.

Grace pulls me into her arms, and I let her, burrowing my head in the crook of her neck. "I don't think I can do this, Grace."

"You can. I know it's hard, but I know you. I know how strong you are."

"I'm not as strong as you think."

Grace pushes me back far enough so she can cup my cheeks and press her forehead against mine. "Then it's good you have us to help you carry the burden. You're not alone, Jade. You're *not* alone. I'm here. Rei's here. Penny's here. Nixon, Yasmin, and Callie. We're all here."

But Prescott isn't.

And I wasn't sure I would be able to do this without him.

He was my light shining at the end of the tunnel. It didn't matter how dark it got or how hard it was to keep moving; as long as he was there, calling to me, I was able to push through. But now my light is gone. The only thing left is the darkness, and I'm not sure I'll be able to find my way out.

Sucking in a sharp breath, I stop resisting it and let the tears fall.

Grace pulls me to her, stroking my back as I cry, whispering soft reassurances into my ear. I hate myself for being this weak. I hate myself for breaking, but at this moment, I don't have it in me to be strong.

Pulling back, I wipe away the tears, only to notice more of my hair stuck to Grace's shirt.

I reach for it, twisting the hair between my fingers. "I have to shave it."

Grace places her hand on my knee. "When you're ready.

We'll do it whenever you're ready. Hell, I'll shave my hair with you."

My head snaps up. "You'll do no such thing, Grace Danielle Shelton."

The corner of her mouth twitches upward in amusement. "Pulling out the middle name, are we?"

I glare at her. "I'm serious. Nobody is shaving their head for me."

"Okay, okay, no shaving heads. I get it. But seriously, there is still time. It's not that..."

"Bad?" I finish for her, lifting the chunk of hair as proof.

"It's only been a few sessions."

"And things are only going to get worse from here." I hold my friend's gaze, needing her to understand this. "Things will get worse, Grace. Much, much worse. I have to do this. I have to do this *now*. While I still have the choice in my hands."

"Jade..."

I shake my head at her, refusing her consolation. "I've l-lost..." My voice stutters as Prescott's face appears in my mind. The pain in his eyes he was trying so hard to hide. Sucking in a breath, I force the words out. "I've lost so much already. What's one more?"

"Maybe you should wait a few days. Today has been tough on so many levels..."

"No more waiting." I shake my head. "You either help me now, or I'll take the damn scissors and do it myself."

I start to get to my feet, but Grace grabs my hands, stopping me. "Okay, we'll do it now. Just wait a minute. We're not doing this with scissors."

I let her pull me to my feet and lead me to the living room. I curl up on the couch, pulling my feet to my chest as I stare at the screen, my mind reeling as the snippets from the last few weeks pass through my head.

I'm not sure how long I lay like that when I finally hear voices from the hallway. Soft footsteps come closer. "Jade?"

I look up to find Penny standing in the doorway. "What are you doing here?" I ask, forcing myself to brush my tears and sit upright.

"Grace asked me to come." She tilts her head to the side. "Are you okay? Is your flu back? Your voice sounds funny."

"I'm fine. It's just been a long day."

"Henry, take me to Jade," Penny commands, placing her hand on his back.

Although the dog doesn't have his working harness, he leads her around the furniture and to the open seat next to me. She lifts her hand, touching my cheek. "You've been crying. That doesn't sound like you're fine. What happened?"

What's the point in hiding it? Everyone will find out eventually.

"Prescott and I broke up."

"What? Why?"

"Because he's a douchebag," Grace says as she joins us in the living room, a box in her hand.

"He's not a douchebag. He just can't deal with this." Grace opens her mouth, but I interrupt her. "I don't want him to have to deal with this. It's not fair to him. Not after... not after everything that has happened." I tilt my chin at the box. "What's that?"

Grace turns the box so I can see the image on it. "I remembered I saw hair clippers once when I was roaming in Mason's bathroom."

"Snooping around?"

"Of course not! I was looking for my toothbrush, which they stashed away somewhere. Anyway, Mason just brought it here."

My stomach twists as I look over her shoulder, expecting to see her boyfriend's tall form. Although Mason and I have been working through our issues, and our relationship has been better, I didn't want him to see me like this.

"I sent him home," Grace explains. She knows me too well for her own good. "It's just us girls."

"Hair clippers?" Penny's brows furrow. "Why would you... Oh. You're going to do it? Now?"

"My hair's been falling out more and more with each wash and each session. At this point, it's more painful to watch it fall. It feels like I'm losing a part of me with every strand." My eyes close and one more tear slides down my cheek. "I can't keep doing it. I can't keep losing. This way, at least, it's on my terms. The decision is completely mine."

Penny wipes her thumb over my cheek. "Okay, we're doing it then."

"Where do you want to do it?" Grace asks, opening the box and pulling the machine out.

"Bathroom."

Getting up, I grab the chair and walk down the hallway toward my room. I cross the short distance, ready to push the bathroom door open when my eyes fall on my nightstand, more precisely on my camera sitting on top of it.

I stop in my tracks and just stare at it as an idea starts shaping in my mind.

I haven't been able to shoot ever since I did the surgery. The weight of the camera and the fact that I had to lift it all the way to my face didn't go well with the mastectomy.

The e-mail I got the other day flashes in my head. Since everything went to hell, I didn't get a chance to submit my photos yet. The deadline for the project for my photography class is in a few days, and although I've already decided I'd send the photos of the couple, I can't stop thinking about this new idea.

It's absurd. I shouldn't even attempt it. Hell, I never did

anything like it, but... I clench and unclench my fingers, feeling that familiar itch to grab the camera and shoot.

Maybe, just maybe...

If I'm losing so much, maybe I should try and gain something out of it.

Slowly, I move to the camera, my fingers tracing the metal before I pick it up, letting the idea grow in my mind. The poses. The light. The angles.

"Jade?" A hand touches my shoulder. "Did you change your mind? There is no sha—"

"No, I'm doing this." I turn around, my hands clasped around the camera. "But I have to do this alone."

"What?" Penny pulls her brows together as she moves closer, following the sound of my voice. "You don't have to do this alone. We—"

"It's okay, Penny." Grace looks from my camera to me, understanding written all over her face. "We'll be in the living room in case she needs us. Is that okay?"

"We will?" Penny asks, clearly skeptical about it.

"I have to do this on my own." Closing the distance between us, I pull her into a hug and then do the same with Grace.

"Just holler if you need anything."

I nod, although I know there is no way I'll call them.

I have to do this on my own terms.

And this is how I'm going to do it.

I shuffle around my room until I find my tripod. Grabbing it and my camera, I go to the bathroom and set everything up.

I give the setup a critical look. I've never done a self-portrait before. I wasn't one to stand in front of the camera. It was weird. Looking at my own face reflected back at me. I much preferred to take photos of others.

I tried a few different light settings and angles as I got everything ready before going back to the room. Taking off my sweater, I grab the scissors and hair clippers Grace left for me on the bed and bring them to the counter.

Letting out a shaky breath, I lift my head and face my reflection in the mirror. Grabbing the shutter button, I press on it.

Click.

With my free hand, I tug off the beanie.

Click.

I stare at the mirror, for the first time looking at myself. Really looking. The plain black tee hugs me, showcasing my flat chest. Once rich, dark brown hair is now thinned and dry, hanging around my shoulders. I look awful. Defeated. Broken. Dead.

Click.

The beanie slips from my fingers.

Click.

I grab the scissors and bring them to my hair.

Click.

I make the first cut as a tear slides down my cheek.

Click.

I cut strand after strand as more tears fall down until all my hair is chopped as close to the scalp as possible.

Click. Click. Click.

Placing the scissors on the counter, I go to the camera, shifting the angle so it's facing me. I can see the screen reflected in the mirror. Making sure the angle is right, I pull out the clippers from the box and turn it on. The soft buzzing fills the quiet bathroom.

I look right at the camera as I bring it to the top of my head.

Click.

Chapter 32

PRESCOTT

"Where the hell were you this morning?" Nixon hisses as he slides into the seat across from me.

"Can you lower your fucking voice?" I rub at my temples, but it doesn't stop the ache behind them. "My head is fucking killing me."

Nixon narrows his eyes at me. "Are you—"

"Hungover?" Spencer supplies. "Oh, yeah. I think he drank the whole bottle of Jack by himself. You should be grateful he's only hungover. For a while there, I thought I'd have to take him to the ER to have his stomach pumped. Thankfully, at about three, he started to throw up all by himself. Lucky me, huh?"

"What the fuck, dude?"

I let out a groan, "Quiet. You know what that means, right?"

"You should have thought about that before you drank your weight in alcohol. It's all your damn fault," Spencer mutters, biting off half of his burger.

My stomach rolls uncomfortably at the smell of all the food around me. "I don't remember asking for your opinion."

"If Coach finds out about this, you'll never hear the end of it."

"Do I look like I care?" I snap, gritting my teeth. The throbbing behind my temples intensifies.

Dammit, why the hell did I think coming here was a good idea?

Between the noises, my nosy friends, the smells... God those smells.

Nixon glares at me. "What the hell's your problem? We're playing in the freaking playoffs in a matter of days, and you're getting drunk and missing practice?"

"I don't remember needing to explain myself to you," I bite back, shoving to my feet only to come to a halt when I see her.

Jade's walking with Grace and Marcus through the cafeteria, and something one of them says makes her laugh. An actual, deep belly laugh, loud enough that I can hear it all the way here, awakening that ache in my heart. I don't remember the last time I heard her actually laugh.

Mine. Mine. Mine.

My laugh. My smile. My twinkle in those baby blues.

She's not yours. Not anymore, a little voice reminds me. *You made sure of that.*

"Seriously, Wentworth. What the hell's going on with you?" Nixon asks, but I ignore him because I can't take my eyes off of her.

I drink her in from a distance because I know the moment she sees me, it'll be gone. She'll be gone.

You kill everyone you love.

As if she can feel my gaze on her, she looks up, her eyes scanning the space until they land on mine. That beautiful smile falls almost instantly. And that's when I notice it. Her hair. It's all gone.

"No," I shake my head.

"No? What the hell—" Nixon turns around, his eyes

searching for the person who has my attention. "Jade," he breathes out. Her name is a whisper and a curse.

He didn't know.

She did it all on her own.

He didn't know.

Cursing silently, I grab my things.

I need to get out of here. I need—

I almost bump into a couple in my haste to leave the cafeteria to put as much space between us as possible, but no matter how fast I run, I can't run away from the memories.

---

9 years old

"I look hideous," Gabriel says, glaring at his reflection in the bathroom mirror. His hair started to fall out recently, and it's only gotten worse after the last session, so Mom brought hair clippers today to shave the patches that were still holding on.

"You don't look hideous," I lie.

Gabriel sees right through me. "You don't know how to lie for shit, Pres."

"Well, it's not that bad."

"I don't have eyebrows." Gabriel shakes his head. "Everybody will make fun of me when I go back to school."

Some of the kids have been asking about Gabriel and when he'll be back. Out of the two of us, he was the outgoing one. The twin everybody loved and everybody wanted to be friends with. I was just his sidekick—a part of the package.

"If they make fun of you, they'll have to deal with me," I promise, my fingers clenching into fists by my sides.

There was no sense in lying, kids were insensitive assholes, and some of them will tease him about it. Kids like that dumbass

Collins. He saw us at the movies. On one of the rare outings, Gabriel was allowed because he begged our parents to take us for weeks until they finally relented. The next day he started talking shit about Gabriel, so I punched him. We both ended up in the principal's office, and my parents were livid, but I didn't care. He'll think twice before talking about Gabriel that way.

"I hate cancer. I hate chemo. I hate everything," he says, snapping me out of my thoughts. The anger burns brightly in his dark eyes. No, not just anger, but also tears. "I just want to be normal for a change."

My heart twists at my brother's words. I hate this for him. Why do shitty things keep happening to good people? It's not fair. Nothing about this is fair.

"I don't want to be this... this freak."

Letting out a breath I didn't even realize I'd been holding, I move him to the side, grabbing the clippers off the counter, and turning them on. Before Gabriel can say anything, I run the clippers down the middle of my head.

"What are you doing?" Gabriel asks, his eyes meeting mine in the reflection.

"If you're a freak. I'm a freak too."

"Mom's going to kill you."

My parents have been angry at me for so many things I've stopped counting. Stopped caring. The only person that matters is Gabriel, and I won't have my brother, my twin, feel like he doesn't matter. Like he's not good enough.

I shrug. "I don't care."

"Wentworth!"

My head snaps up at the sound of the coach's loud bark to find him standing in the doorway of the gym.

"Why the hell are you still here? Practice will start in ten minutes."

I look down at my wrist, noting how much time has passed since I got here. "I spaced out. I'll be there in a bit."

Slowing down the treadmill, I wipe away the sweat dripping from my face, everything coming into focus. The bright lights, the rock playing in the background, the murmurs of coaches and athletes still working out, and the ache in my leg as the machine finally comes to a stop.

Hopping off the treadmill, my legs feel wobbly from pushing too hard, but I bite the inside of my cheek as I walk toward the door where Coach still stands, his narrowed gaze on me. "Where were you this morning?"

"Overslept."

Which wasn't a lie, but it wasn't the truth either.

"The bags under your eyes would disagree," Coach says, his tone dry.

"I'm here now, aren't I?" I bite back, so done with people getting into my personal business.

Coach's eyes turn into tiny slits, his bushy brows connecting. "I don't care what's going on in your life, Wentworth, but this team is counting on you to bring your A-game and help them win the championship. Your teammates are busting their asses because they know there are no second chances. Every game now could be our last one. Are you with this team or not?"

I grit my teeth, anger boiling in my blood. "I'm with this team."

"Well, then, you better show me." He starts to turn around. "Better yet, show it to your teammates."

With that, he walks down the hallway. Running my hand over my face, I let out a long breath before going to the locker room. The place buzzes with activity as my teammates change into their practice gear. I go to my locker and pull it open.

Nixon looks at me. "Why the hell did you run off like that? Is it Jade's hair? Her doctor said it's one of the common side effects, but it'll grow eventually."

"It's not her hair," I say, my voice clipped as I tug off the sweaty t-shirt to exchange it for my practice jersey.

"Then what the hell is it? It was an asshole move to walk away like that..."

He doesn't know, I realize.

Jade didn't tell him what happened.

She didn't tell him we had broken up.

I open my mouth, but just then, the coach blows the whistle. "You have sixty seconds to get your asses on the field."

"She should have said something. I hate that she keeps shit like this from me. I want to be there for her. She doesn't have to do this all by herself."

Nixon's words are like a blow to my gut. He reminds me too much of myself and who I used to be.

He slaps me on the shoulder. "Hurry up, because Coach will make us run drills."

"Sure thing," I mutter as I slide on my pants, while at the same time, shoving my feet into cleats. By the time I'm done, the locker room is mostly empty, so I turn around, grab two pain pills and swallow them down. Only then, do I join the rest of my teammates.

The practice is grueling, but nobody dares bitch about it, not when we all know what's on the line.

By the time I drag my quivering body to the locker room, the place is already half empty. I make myself go to the bathroom and take a shower. Pressing my palms against the tiles as the cold water crashes at my back, I close my eyes, the image of Jade flashing in my mind.

Even after hours of running drills, she's still in my head, as alive as ever.

Her pale skin and deep circles under her eyes. The way those big baby blues looked at me across the room, the sorrow hidden behind them. I did that. I put that look in her eyes, and there is nothing that I can do to make it better.

You kill everyone you love.

Shoving away from the wall, I turn off the water and grab the towel. The pain meds have started to wear off, and that throbbing is back in full force. I make my way back into the almost empty locker room, the process of dressing slow and grueling. It feels like forever until I'm in the car, heading to the apartment.

Parking the car, I get out, grabbing my duffle bag from the back seat, my eyes fall on the sweater in the corner. I pick it up, letting the soft material slide between my fingertips; that familiar lavender scent still clinging to it makes my stomach knot tighter. Still, I bring it to my face, inhaling it deeply.

Jade's scent.

Soft and sweet, a complete contradiction to the strong woman that she is. A walking contradiction.

She probably left it the last time she was here, the last ti—

I let my hand drop, my fingers tightening around the soft material as I shove the memory back, back, back.

Running my hand over my face, I tilt my head back, inhaling the icy night air, but her scent... still lingers.

It *always* lingers.

I'm about to march inside and find another kind of oblivion when I see it. The light shining through the window I used to sneak through. The shadow standing there. Watching. Waiting.

A lump forms in my throat as her gaze falls on mine and holds it.

I'm not sure how long we stand there, watching each other. It could be seconds, or it could be hours.

That ache inside of me growing stronger, restless.

She was the only person who knew how to calm it. The only person who knew how to bring me peace.

But now that she's gone, there is only a hollow left.

Somebody must call her name because she turns around, breaking our stare.

And I use that moment to slip away.

Chapter 33

JADE

"I can't keep doing this."

"Prescott," I try to reach for him, but he pushes my hands away and takes a step back with a shake of his head.

"I don't want to keep doing this. I don't want to keep seeing Gabriel's face every time I look at you." He takes a step back. "Every time we go to chemo? I remember all the times I sat next to him." And another one. "Every time you're sick, I see my brother. Seeing you like this, it brings back so many memories, and I can't keep doing this, Jade. I can't keep on hurting *like this." And another one. "Don't make me hurt like this, Jade."*

My knees buckle underneath me, finally giving out. Tears stream down my cheeks as he walks away, and this time, I'm not strong enough to let him go.

"Don't leave me," I whisper. "Don't be like him. Don't leave me."

I startle awake, gasping for air. My heart is beating like crazy in my chest, my breathing ragged. I run my hand over my face, trying to even out the rapid rise and fall of my chest.

The same dream has been haunting me for days, ever since Prescott broke up with me.

I understood why he did it, I really did, but a part of me hated him for it. It was torture. Torture seeing him and not being able to talk to him, to go to him, to touch him.

Pushing upright, I feel my bones groan in protest. A few days ago, I had another round of chemo, the last one in this cycle, and my body is still recovering from it.

Worse.

Things had to get much, much worse before they could get better, but I wasn't sure I was ready for it. The only saving grace was that I had a week off, just enough time to feel decent so I could get through my finals, and then it would be over. I've already decided that next semester I'll only take one class. Something to ground me while I go through the rest of my chemo. Something to help me hold onto the future I could have. But I had to beat this thing first.

Grabbing my phone, I notice the time. Today the Ravens are playing their first game in the playoffs. Thankfully it was an away game, so I wasn't tempted to go to the stadium to watch, but I've already talked to Grace, Rei, and Penny, and they agreed to watch it together.

Maybe this will be the final game you'll ever have to watch, a twisted part of me says, but I shove it back.

Getting to my feet, I go to the bathroom to splash some water on my face. With my hair shaved off, my face looks even more hollow than before, the paler skin and the bags under my eyes more prominent.

Letting out a sigh, I shut off the tap and wipe my face before heading down the hallway, where I'm greeted by soft chatter coming from the main space. I follow the sound of the voices, only to come to a stop in the doorway when I see all of my friends gathered in the kitchen.

"We need more color," Grace says. "I think we have another tube here somewhere..."

"Why did we think it's a good idea to do this at home?" Callie asks. She's sitting on a chair, a few foils stuck in her hair.

"The video I watched looked pretty easy," Yasmin says, matching foils in her hair. "Besides, I don't know why you're complaining. You're not the one who has to bleach your hair."

Callie nods. "At least there is that."

"Found it!" Grace yells, lifting a box in the air in victory. "It's been..." She turns around, her eyes landing on me. "Jade, you're up."

They all turn to me, matching guilty expressions on their faces.

"I'm up," I agree, leaning against the doorway. "And what are you all doing?"

"Nothing," they all say in unison, matching guilty expressions on their faces.

"It doesn't look like nothing. I didn't realize we were meeting this early. The game won't start for a few more hours. Besides, if I knew we were having a party, I would have changed."

PJs, or well, my version of PJs, an old pair of leggings with the hoodie I stole from Prescott, is my go-to these days.

"We're not having a party. We're just..."

"I'm done."

I slowly turn around, only to find Penny and Rei standing in the doorway. Rei got back a few days ago and will be staying here for a bit before she has to fly out for a competition, which will decide which skaters will represent Team USA in the Winter Games come February.

"You're up."

"As everybody keeps noticing," I comment, wrapping my arms around my middle as I lift my brow. "Was I supposed to stay in bed all day?"

"Well, no, it's just..." her words trail off. I know what she doesn't say. It's just that I've been in bed for the better part of the last couple of days. That is if I wasn't throwing my guts up in the bathroom.

"I'm feeling better, so I figured I might get some coffee." My eyes zero in on Penny and the towel on her head. "Why are you washing your hair here?" I look over my shoulder to find Grace standing behind me as the pieces start to fall in place. Still, I ask: "What's going on?"

Grace places her hands on my shoulders and pushes me toward the empty chair at the counter. "Now remember, you said not to go shaving our heads..."

"What have you done?"

"We colored our hair," Penny chimes in, tugging off the towel from her head. Her hair spills down, the usually platinum strands now bright pink.

"You did what?!" I look at all my friends. The foils, the smell of chemicals, bleach, the box.

Penny's smile falls as she tugs at one of her strands. "Is it that bad?"

"It's not bad. It's just..." I shake my head, still unable to wrap my mind around it. "Why would you do that?"

"Because we want to," Yasmin shrugs.

"You want to have pink hair?" I ask, not trying to hide the skepticism in my tone. "Since when?"

Grace rolls her eyes. "Since now."

I turn to her. "Pink? With your red hair? Seriously?"

"Yes. I looked it up online. I got a shade called candy for myself, and the rest of the girls have magenta."

Candy and magenta?! They can't be serious.

But even as the thought crosses my mind, I know they can and are. Hell, Penny's hair is already done.

"Why would you do that?"

Grace takes my hands in hers. "Because we see you, and we

love you, and we never want you to feel like you're doing this alone."

My throat tightens at her words, making it hard to breathe.

Yasmin comes behind me, her hand slipping around my shoulders. "Grace is right. You're not alone. You have us. You have Nixon and Prescott and..."

"You haven't told her?"

I glare at my best friend, but it's already too late.

Yasmin looks from Grace to me. "Told me what?"

"Seriously?"

"What's going on?"

"Prescott and I broke up."

My statement is met with absolute silence, but it only lasts a few seconds before I'm bombarded with questions.

Yasmin's mouth falls open. "You what?"

"Are you shitting me?" This comes from Callie. "That little, sleazy—"

"When did this happen?"

"It's not his fault," I slip out of Yasmin's hands and go to the coffee machine. I'd much rather drink alcohol, but as I've learned the hard way alcohol and chemo do not mix. I figured I'd have a few drinks after I was done shaving my head, but I barely finished one shot before I was back in the bathroom, throwing up. Just one more thing that was stolen from me.

"How is it exactly not his fault?" Yasmin asks. "Like, for real, breaking up with your girlfriend who has—"

Her words trail off as if she just realized what she was about to say. Pressing the button on the coffee machine, I turn around and lean against the counter. "Who has cancer. It's fine. You can say it."

"Jade, I didn't mean it like that."

My throat bobs as I swallow. "While I'm grateful that you want to be here regardless of cancer, I don't expect it." I scan the room, meeting the eyes of every one of my friends. "From any of you."

"Jade..." Rei tries to chime in, but I shake my head.

"I mean it. I don't expect anybody to stand by and watch me go through it. I was that person. Two years ago, I was in your shoes, and I hated every second of standing by my mother's bed and watching her die. I hated watching this disease chip away piece by broken piece of her until there was nothing else left."

"This is different."

"Is it, though?" I huff out a laugh. The coffee machine beeps, signaling that my coffee is done, but Yasmin is holding my gaze, and I can't seem to look away.

"It's different because you're not dying. I'm not going to pretend I knew your mother better than you did, but I know the facts. She had stage four cancer; nothing could have been done for her, but you have a fighting chance."

"That doesn't mean any of you have to be here and watch. I've seen myself in the mirror. Cancer is eating me from the inside out, even if we brush away the physical changes. I'm not the girl I used to be. I'll never again be that girl. And Prescott... I don't blame him. Not considering the things I know. Things he's told me." I notice their curious gazes, but before they can ask, I hurry to say: "It's not my story to tell, but remember, I don't blame him. And if I don't, you don't get to either."

"Nixon doesn't know, does he?"

I grab my coffee from the machine and add some creamer from the fridge. "I don't think so. I haven't told him yet." I lift my gaze. "You can't tell him, at least not until the season's done."

"Jade..."

"He can't know." I fix my eyes on Yasmin. "You know how he is; he'll get upset on my behalf and go play my savior, which is the last thing any of us needs. The relationship between them is strained enough as it is, and if they get in a fight..." I let my words hang in the air. "I'm not going to be the reason they don't go all the way."

"He'll find out eventually," Callie says grimly.

"As long as it's not before the game, I don't care." I tilt my chin in Yasmin's direction. "Shouldn't you be washing that off? You'll burn your hair off."

Yasmin sticks her tongue out at me. "You can only wish."

But still, she goes to the bathroom to rinse off. Thankfully, after that, no one brings back the topic of Prescott or our breakup, which I'm grateful for.

Penny blow dries her hair, and I help her style it, while the other girls finish washing the dye off. For all my protests, their hair looked pretty cute, even Grace's, who I didn't believe could pull it off, but somehow did.

"Makes me wish I could dye it too," I say, tugging at the beanie I have on my head. Although it looks ridiculous, I can't not wear it. Not when lately I'm always so cold.

"Did you ever think about getting a wig?" Penny asks.

"I did, but I'm not sure if that's for me. Won't it keep slipping off since there isn't anything to hold it?"

"Let's see what Mr. Google says." Rei slides onto the couch next to me and pulls out her phone. After a few taps of her finger, the results pop up. "Look, there is apparently some kind of band you put on your head that should help you keep the wig in place."

"Really?" Grace leans over to look at the screen. "It looks handy."

"You could always get it to try it out." I look to Callie, who's sitting at the counter, her fingers wrapped around her mug. "It's not like you have to wear it if you don't like it."

"I guess there is that."

"Think about it. It could be fun. You could order a few different styles and colors, see what works, and once your hair grows back, you'll know what looks the best." Grace wiggles her brows. "So, whatcha say?"

"Fine."

They fight over which wigs would look the best on me, and in the end, we order three different ones for me to try out. Just as the order is completed, there is a knock on the door.

"It's probably delivery," Yasmin says, hopping to her feet.

Noticing the time, I switch the television to the game just as the teams enter the field.

My traitorous heart does a little flip as the cameraman zooms in on Prescott's serious face as he listens to something one of his teammates says.

"Please tell me it didn't start yet," Yasmin says as she rushes inside, carrying two big bags of food.

"It's just about to," Rei says, reaching for one of the bags. "Please tell me there are some tacos inside. I decided today's my cheat day, and I'm famished since Alexei has been riding my ass all morning."

"Who orders Mexican and not tacos?" Yasmin rolls her eyes at Rei, just as Grace brings us the plates.

"When is he not riding your ass?" I ask, looking skeptically at the bag. The smell of chicken and spices spreads through the room, and I can feel my stomach roll.

Great, now cancer has ruined Mexican food for me.

"Just a little while longer. It'll all be worth it."

"You plan on doing the Quad at tryouts?"

Rei takes a bite of a taco, humming happily. "No, I'm going all out, though. The Quad Axel is still too iffy, plus if I land it, I want it to be at the Games."

"You will land it. I don't doubt it for a second."

Rei flashes me a smile. "Thanks."

"It's starting!" Yasmin yells, turning the volume up on the TV.

Grace looks at me as she takes her seat on my other side. "You're not eating."

I shake my head. "Not hungry."

An understanding smile flashes on her face. "Need me to open a window?"

This isn't the first time the idea of food caused me to turn nauseous, so they've all gotten used to my picky eating habits.

"Nah, I'm good for now. Thanks, though."

I focus on the screen as the players line up on the fifty-yard line.

The game is a disaster from the very first second. It's like the opposing team is reading our boys like a book. Every move they make, and every play they try, there's someone there to stop it from happening. By halftime, the Ravens are, by some miracle, only down by one touchdown.

"It'll get better," Yasmin says decisively. "They'll figure something out."

But they don't, and the second half is an even bigger disaster than the first. A few minutes before the clock runs out, it looks like the Ravens might get a hail Mary, but Prescott's tackled to the ground, and their opponents win the ball, scoring instead.

And with that, the Ravens' season is officially over.

Chapter 34

PRESCOTT

"It was a tough game, dude. There was nothing that could have been done," Spencer says.

There was so much that could have been done.

I slide my hand over the edge of my glass, staring at the amber liquid.

I could have run faster.

I could have taken a different route.

I could have seen that guy coming.

Nixon could have thrown the ball to somebody else.

Somebody better.

Somebody who could have brought our team a victory.

So many options.

So many different courses that could have given the Ravens a win.

But thanks to me, it was all done now.

We lost, and there was no going back.

No second chances.

"Whatever. It's done now." Clenching my fingers around the glass, I tilt my head back and empty the drink, letting the whiskey burn its way down my throat.

It was all my damn fault.

"What are your plans now? Finals are done. Are you going with the Coles for Christmas?"

Yeah, right. I haven't been talking with either of the Cole siblings, and I was pretty sure they didn't want to see me.

"Nah," I lift my head and signal the bartender for another drink. "I have to go home."

My dad's been on my ass since the loss, demanding that I come home. I didn't see the point. It's not like they want me there. But now that school was done, and there wasn't any more football as an excuse, there wasn't anything that I could do to avoid the inevitable.

"You're going back home?"

"I already told..." The words die on my tongue as I register the sound of the voice.

Abruptly, I turn in my seat and come face to face with Jade. It's like the air's been kicked out of my lungs at the sight of her. "Jade," I breathe as I just stare at her.

She's the last person I expected to find here.

"Sorry," she looks down, tucking a strand of her hair behind her ear. "I didn't mean to listen, but I couldn't help overhearing while I was waiting for my order."

"Your hair."

I reach for it, like the dumbass I am, but stop myself at the very last second.

I have no right to touch her.

Not any longer.

"Gotta love Prime, right?" she chuckles nervously. "Girls convinced me to get a few different wigs. See how I feel about them."

The dark brown wig looks similar to her natural hair, except this one has the first strand bleached platinum. It looks good on her. Then again, even if she put a potato sack on, it would look good on her.

"You didn't need to get a wig."

"I know," she shrugs. "It actually helps. People don't stare as much since I blend in, which makes me feel less self-conscious." There's a beat of silence as we stare at one another. The bartender placed a drink in front of me, but I let it sit. I'm too wound up to drink, to do anything really.

"I'm sorry about the game," Jade whispers. "I know how much you wanted to go all the way."

Of course, she knows. She was there to see me at my lowest, see how much I sacrificed to win, and still, it wasn't enough.

It'll never be enough.

Because everything I touch turns to shit.

Turning back to the bar, I grab the drink, gulping down half of it. "It is what it is."

Jade shifts from one foot to the other. "Well, I'll let you boys be. I guess I'll see you around?"

"Yeah, sure."

She stands there for a beat longer before she finally leaves. I watch her from the corner of my eye as she moves a few feet away and picks up her order from the bartender. The guy flirts with her, and she returns his smile.

My fingers tighten around the glass as I glare at him across the bar. *Back the fuck off, douchebag.*

Not that I have a right to say it. Hell, I don't have a right to even think it. She isn't mine to protect. And there's a good reason for it.

I've destroyed too many people already. Jade won't be another one added to that list.

Grabbing her drinks, she goes off to join her friends.

I sigh and finish my drink, signaling the douchebag bartender for another one.

"Dude, what the hell's wrong with you?" Spencer slaps me over the head. "It is what it is? That's the best you could come up with?"

I shove him away. "What did you want me to say?"

"I don't know. But that was a shitty thing to do. What the hell's even going on between you two?"

"Nothing," I mutter.

Damn, where is that drink?

"What do you mean, nothing? The last I remember is Jade running out of our apartment crying."

I grit my teeth together. "That's because we broke up."

"What?"

The bartender grabs the whiskey bottle and starts to pour.

"Why don't you just add that whole thing to my tab?"

The dude looks from me to the bottle and back. "You sure?"

"Oh, trust me, I'm sure."

I'm going to need all the alcohol I can get to survive tonight. Hell, to survive the next couple of weeks.

"When's your plane?"

I down another drink. "Tomorrow morning."

Spencer eyes the bottle carefully. "You think it's a good idea to get drunk the night before the flight?"

Considering I'll have to deal with my father tomorrow? "It's the best one I've got."

JADE

"I still can't believe she didn't pick your photos for that exhibition!" Grace complains.

"It is what it is," I shrug, tracing the rim of my glass with my finger. "I knew it was risky going with a completely new technique. What bothers me more is that I can't drown my disappointment in alcohol."

That night after I cut my hair, I was so sick there was no way I'd want a repeat anytime soon.

The day Prescott broke up with me.

My glance darts toward the bar where Prescott and Spencer are still drinking. Well, Prescott is still drinking. Spencer has been nursing his Coke for the past twenty minutes and is trying to get him to stop, but with no such luck.

"You're staring."

"Am not," I protest, forcing myself to look away from Prescott and shift my gaze to my best friend.

"You totally are." Grace gives me a sad smile as she looks toward the bar. "He's a mess."

She isn't wrong about that. Prescott is a mess.

"Can you blame him? They just lost the playoffs. He lost his last chance to win that trophy."

I knew better than anybody how much winning that thing meant to him. How much he wanted it. How much he *risked* for it.

"Doesn't make him less of an asshole for acting the way he did and breaking up with you. Especially when he's in love with you."

I look down at the glass in my hand. "Sometimes loving someone isn't enough."

And if that wasn't the saddest part of it all, I don't know what was. If love was the only factor, things would be so much easier, but nothing is that simple. Not really.

"When are you traveling back home?" I ask, changing the subject.

"Tomorrow morning. All my things are in my car, so I'll just stay at Mason's, and we can leave as soon as we wake up. That is if you don't want us to stay."

Ever since the summer before college, I've spent all my holidays with Grace in New York. The idea of going home to an empty house was hard on both Nixon and me, so we haven't been back. Until this year.

"No," I shake my head. "You should go home. I'm sure your brother misses you."

"He does," Grace lets out a sigh. "How about we try and plan something for New Year's? Maybe we could all come to your place to celebrate together."

"Maybe," I say reluctantly. "I'm not sure I'll be up for it since my next chemo session is starting this week."

What's there to celebrate anyway? The fact that I'm slowly dying? That my boyfriend broke up with me because he can't deal with my illness, and it reminds him of his dead brother? Yeah, I think I'll pass.

"We can lay on the couch and watch stupid movies. It'll be just like a middle school slumber party."

"That doesn't sound half bad." I finish my drink and look at Grace's empty glass. "A refill, and then we'll go?"

"Sounds like a plan."

I slide off the stool. "I'll go and grab it."

"I see what you're doing!" Grace yells after me, but I choose to ignore her and make my way through the tables.

The place is quiet tonight, probably due to the fact that most people have left campus by now for the holidays.

The moment I get to the bar, the guy from earlier turns to me, that flirtatious smile back on his face.

"Need another round?" he grins at me, a dimple popping in his left cheek.

"Please," I give him a polite smile. I don't want to be rude, but I'm also not interested in anything more than getting my drinks. Not that the guy notices, or he chooses to ignore it.

"Coke and 7-up, right? You sure you don't want anything stronger?"

"This is fine. Thanks."

"Sure thing." He opens the bottles and places them on the bar in front of me. "You not going home for the holidays?"

"Soon, I have some things to take care of," I say non-committedly as I pull out some money from my bag and place it on the counter. "Tha—"

"What things?"

Gosh, is he serious right now?

But before I can say anything, I hear a low growl come from behind me. "Will you stop flirting with her already? Can't you see she's not interested?"

A warm body connects to mine as Prescott leans against the counter, glaring at the guy.

The bartender takes a step back, a scowl appearing between his brows. "What's your problem, dude? We were just talking."

"Well, go talk to somebody else," Prescott slurs, his arm wrapping around my middle. "She's taken."

"Okay, buddy. I think this is enough," Spencer mutters as he pulls Prescott off of me, giving me an apologetic smile. "C'mon, let's get you home."

Prescott tries to pull out of Spencer's grasp. "I'm not going anywhere. Not as long as she's here."

I turn around and glare at him. "Are you shitting me right now?"

"Don't give me that look, doll," Prescott points at me, swaying on his feet. "I'm not letting you flirt with this dumbass."

"I'm not flirting with anybody, not that it's any of your business."

"Jade, please..." He reaches for me, his fingers brushing against my cheekbone. I close my eyes as a shiver runs down my spine, my stomach clenching.

It's not fair the effect he has on me even after everything that has happened.

I can't keep on hurting *like this.*

Swallowing the lump in my throat, I face him and force the words out. "You should go home, Prescott."

He shakes his head. "Not without you."

"Just go home, Wentworth." Grace joins our little group, throwing her arm around me protectively as she glares at him.

Prescott ignores her completely, those dark, bottomless eyes staring into mine the whole time. "Jade?"

I should tell him to go and leave me alone.

Just like he left me.

I should tell him he has no right to demand anything of me.

I should, but I don't.

"C'mon, let's get you home."

Grace lets out a sigh, "You don't have to do this."

"It's fine. I'm going home anyway, and this way, Spencer can drop me off." I give her a squeeze. "Text me when you get back home?"

Grace nods, and we make our way out to the parking lot. Prescott refuses to take the front seat, so we huddle in the back of Spencer's jeep, his head falling on my shoulder the moment the doors are closed.

The drive back to the apartment is quiet, my heart thundering in my chest at Prescott's nearness. I look down, only to find his eyes closed, lips slightly parted as he breathes.

Unable to resist it, I brush his hair away from his face, feeling that ache inside me grow. It's been so long since we've been close like this, and I missed this. I missed him, dammit.

He's not yours, I remind myself. *He asked you to leave.*

Thankfully, it doesn't take long before Spencer pulls the car in the parking spot and gets out.

I try to pull back without waking Prescott, but his eyes snap open the moment I move an inch, and he grabs my wrist. "Don't leave."

"You can't keep on doing this, Prescott."

"I know, but..."

"No buts. You can't. You wanted this. I did what you asked of me. Now you have to let me go."

He shakes his head. "I can't."

The door opens, interrupting our conversation and turning Prescott's attention to Spencer. I use that moment to get out of the car. Somehow Spencer manages to pull him out of the car and on his feet, most of Prescott's weight on him.

"Where's your key?"

"You don't have to do this."

I just extend my hand. "Keys."

With a sigh, Spencer hands me his car keys, and hanging from the chain are a couple more keys. I walk up the stairs and unlock the front door, holding it open as he leads Prescott's limp body up the stairs. Sliding under Prescott's other arm, I help carry him into the elevator and to his apartment.

Prescott lets out a groan as we drop him onto his bed face first. We take off his shoes but don't even attempt to get his limp body out of his clothes.

"I'm going to grab some water and Advil," Spencer says before slipping out of the room and leaving me alone with Prescott.

I stand there for a moment, watching him sleep. Even in his dreams, it seems that he can't find peace.

Moving closer, I notice the blanket at the bottom of the bed, so I pull it over him. I'm about to take a step back when his hand grabs mine, eyes flying open.

My heart is in overdrive, the fast beat echoing in my eardrums as we stare at one another. His eyes are heavy with a mix of sleep and drunkenness, but he doesn't give in to it.

"I hate you," he whispers. His hand brushes a strand of my hair behind my ear, his gentle touch a complete contrast to his harsh words. "For making me fall in love with you."

I suck in a breath as his words ring in my head. Unsure if I heard it correctly, but I don't get to process it before Spencer returns to the room.

"I found it!" Spencer says, making me jump back. "The damn thing was hidden at the back of the cabinet."

His eyes narrow as he looks between Prescott and me. "Are you okay?"

"Yeah." I wrap my arms around myself to stop them from shaking. "I think I'll go home." I force a smile out as I start for the door. "Thanks for the ride."

"Jade, wait!" Spencer runs after me. "I'll walk you home."

I look back toward Prescott's room. "You should stay with him."

Before I even get to finish, Spencer is already shaking his head. "He'll kill me if he finds out that I let you walk home alone."

"It's just next door. Besides, he needs you more. What if he starts throwing up?"

"Then it's his damn problem for drinking the whole fucking bottle of Jack, isn't it?" Spencer throws his hand around my shoulder as we walk back outside. "He loves you. You know that, right?"

Love was never the issue with Prescott and me.

Some days I thought we felt too much.

It was all the other things that were messed up.

"I wish it was enough." Turning to face Spencer, I give him a sad smile. "Take care of him?"

He nods in understanding. "As much as he'll let me."

Chapter 35

JADE

"Can I get you anything?" Nixon asks as he helps me inside my room and to my bed. It feels like every bone and muscle in my body are protesting the movement, and it takes extreme effort to put one leg in front of the other.

We've just come home from chemo, and so far, Nixon had to stop twice so I could throw up. To say today's not my day would be an understatement.

I give my head a small shake. "I think I'll just try to fall asleep. You go and do your thing."

"I don't have anything better to do." He grabs the blankets, pulling them to my chin before tucking me inside, just like he did when I was a little girl.

"Liar," I croak out, my throat feeling tight.

"I'm not lying." He looks appalled that I'd even suggest it. I would believe him even if I didn't know better.

"I saw your message when you went to the bathroom. That agent's in town, and he wants to talk to you."

Nixon's eyes narrow as he crosses his arms over his chest. "Didn't your parents teach you not to snoop through other people's belongings?"

"Hey, it's not my problem you gave me your phone, and the message just popped up on the screen. I'm serious, Nixon. Go and talk to the guy."

"He shouldn't even be calling."

I roll my eyes. "Because that's how it works."

"That's what the rules say."

"Screw the rules. This is your future we're talking about. Go see what he has to say."

Nixon shifts his weight from one foot to the other, clearly on the fence about it. "Yasmin's out. I think she said she has to do some last-minute Christmas shopping, and she'll also stop to grab groceries."

"Your point?"

"You shouldn't be alone!"

"I'm *fine*, just go and do your thing." I turn to my side, fighting a twitch of pain as I move and pull the blanket closer to me. "I'm going to sleep. Besides, the faster you go, the faster you'll be back."

"Jade," Nixon groans, and it's evident that his need to go is fighting with his need to do right by me.

"Go. I mean it."

"You'll call me if you need anything?"

"I'll call you." My eyes fall shut as I murmur: "Go."

A hand touches my forehead, and he must be satisfied because he pulls back. "Fine. I mean it. Call me."

I murmur something incoherently, my mind already adrift. In the distance, I can hear the door close and soft footsteps walking away, but I'm too tired to pay him any mind.

I just lay there, too weak to move, too weak to even think.

I'm not sure if I fell asleep or not, but the next thing I know, I'm assaulted by the memories.

Mom being sick. Prescott breaking up with me. Doctor's

appointments. Finding the lump on my breast. Dad leaving. Double mastectomy.

Past and present mix together until it all turns into a mess.

Then I'm falling, and no matter how hard I try to hold on, there is nothing to hold onto.

I jolt awake, my stomach grumbling in protest. Shoving the blankets away, I stand upright. Only the sudden change makes me sway on my feet. I try to grab for the nightstand, but instead, I push the lamp. It falls on the ground, the ceramic part shattering into millions of pieces.

"Shit," I mutter, my hand covering my mouth as I hold onto the nightstand, but it's already too late. Before I can stop it or get myself to the bathroom, I bend forward, and throw up.

My whole body is shaking with the movement, my fingers barely holding onto the nightstand for some support.

When I'm finally done, I look down. My hand, my clothes, hell, even my feet are covered in puke. Then the smell hits me, making the bile rise up my throat all over again.

Pushing off the nightstand, I somehow manage to stumble my way into the bathroom. My shoulder collides with the doorway, the pain shooting through me, but I ignore it as I fall onto the tiles just before I start throwing up all over again.

Sweat coats my body, making my clothes stick to my skin as I throw up for what feels like hours. Only when I think I'm done do I press my cheek against the toilet seat, not caring in the least how unhygienic it must be. It feels cool against my flushed cheeks, and I'll take any little reprieve I can get. But it doesn't last long because soon enough, I start to throw up again, or I would if there was anything left in my stomach. This way, I'm only retching to the point my vision turns blurry from the tears.

Why is this so damn hard?

I brush the back of my hand over my tear-stained face, pounding my fist against the toilet seat as more tears come.

Why can't I just get a break?

Leaning against the bathtub, I let out a frustrated scream as my head falls back. I look down at my ruined clothes. I can't stay like this.

Grabbing the zipper, I fight with it as I try to tug it down. Finally, the damn thing gives away, and I shove it off before struggling with the leggings. By the time I'm in my undies and a tank top, I'm breathing so hard you'd think I just ran a marathon.

"I can't do this." I try to clench my fingers into a fist, but even that's too hard. "It's just too much. Too hard."

My eyes fall down on the camera I set on the tripod a few feet away. Although I didn't get the exhibition I wanted, taking photos of shaving my head helped me deal with the pain and loss, so I kept on documenting everything I could.

I scoot closer to it, turning the camera on. I change a few settings, making sure it's all set before I force myself to scramble to my feet.

Although I'd taken my clothes off, I could still smell the stench of the vomit on myself. I should wash up, but I know there is no way I'd be able to get myself into the shower. My gaze goes to the bathtub, throat constricting as the memories slam into me.

Gritting my teeth, I shove them back as I make my way to the bathtub and somehow find enough strength to get myself inside.

I let out a shaky breath as I turn on the faucet, selecting the hottest setting possible, but even that does little to chase away the chills.

I pull my legs to my chest, resting my chin against my knees. Tears fall down my face as I wait for the tub to fill.

"I hate you," Prescott's hand brushes against my cheek. "For making me fall in love with you."

His face is exchanged for Dad's as he walked away. *"I can't do this. It's too hard."*

"J-Jade..." Mom's face flashed in my mind as she was struggling to breathe.

"I can't keep on hurting like this."

I understood where Prescott was coming from.

I didn't want to keep on hurting either.

Not any longer.

I lean my head back, blinking the tears away as I stare at the ceiling.

That other time I stared at the ceiling pops into my head, and this time I don't have it in me to shove the memories away. Instead, I embrace them, letting them fill me, fill this empty hole inside my chest that keeps on getting bigger by the day.

The noises. The need to let out a scream so hard it would shatter glass. The stillness as I did just that, my pain swallowed by the water.

Why am I doing this? Why do I keep fighting?

It would be so easy to just let go.

To sink into that nothingness and let it swallow me whole.

Let it take away all this pain.

My body sinks lower into the tub.

I want it.

I want to not feel pain.

I want to not *feel*.

Sucking in a breath, I dive underneath.

And then I let it all out.

I scream, the bubbles coming out of my mouth and tickling my face as they swallow my anger, my pain, my despair, my loss.

I scream, and I scream until there is no air left in my lungs.

And that's when I see them.

Nixon and Yas are cooking in the kitchen, so damn happy and in love.

My friends huddled around me as we had one of our movie nights, laughing.

Prescott.

His eyes staring into mine as he made love to me.

I can't lose you, Jade. I will lie and cheat and kill. I'll do whatever it takes to keep you alive. To keep you safe. Because the thought of living in a world in which you don't exist is unimaginable for me.

Pushing out of the water, I start coughing as I struggle to breathe the much-needed air into my lungs, my fingers clasping the edge of the bathtub.

What the hell am I doing?

My heart is beating furiously in my ribcage as I take in big gulps of oxygen.

I look around myself, taking in the mess that's my bathroom. Water is spilling over the edge of the tub. There are red smudges on the tiles. I probably cut my feet on the shards of the lamp when I was getting here and hadn't even noticed. There is vomit on the floor, and my clothes are thrown into the corner with my phone next to them.

Gathering all the strength I can muster; I push to my feet and get out of the tub. I'm still in my underwear, which is completely wet, but the towel is too far for me to reach, and I'm too tired to bother.

Sitting down on the floor, I fight the shivers as I pick up my phone, speed dialing the first name on my contact list. It takes a few rings, but my brother picks up. "N-Nixon?"

"Jade?" Nixon asks, the worry clear in his voice. "What's going on?"

"I n-need you," I stutter, fighting the shivers as the cold sets in.

There is a beat of silence before I can hear the chair screech against the floor. "I'm coming home. You just hold on. You hear me? I'm coming home."

"O-okay."

I can hear a loud bang in the background, and the sound of an engine turning on. "Hold on, Smalls."

I nod, although I know he can't see me. He keeps talking to me all the way as he drives back home, and I listen. I focus on his voice, letting it ground me to the present, letting it be my reason to hold on.

The door opens and closes once again, and then I can hear his rushed footsteps as he climbs upstairs. Another door bangs.

"Jade?" Nixon's frantic yell echoes in my ears. "What the—"

He turns around and finds me lying on the bathroom floor, my back pressed against the tub, phone clasped in my hands.

I let it fall down, and for the first time, I say the words that I've been fighting for so long, hoping that if I stay strong, everything will be okay.

But nothing is okay.

It hasn't been in a long time.

"I need help."

Chapter 36

PRESCOTT

"I told you; you should have let go of that silly game and focused on your studies. Now you're behind on your MCATs, and you didn't win the bowl game."

I look at the glass in front of me, wishing that the water magically transforms into something stronger. I wouldn't even be picky about what. But no such luck.

"Not that winning would have made any difference since you had no plans on playing professionally anyway," Dad continues without missing a beat.

He's been criticizing everything since the moment I entered the house, and the only moment of silence I got was when I closed myself in my room in the pretense of needing to study, which I did. The MCATs were just around the corner, and I had to start working on my applications for med school.

I shove the peas from one side of my plate to the other, just like Mom's doing across the table, her gaze fixed on her plate. If I didn't know better, I'd have thought she'd fallen asleep.

She barely looked at me and hadn't spoken to me directly since I entered the house a few days ago. So much for her asking me to be here.

"Not sure why you care one way or the other since you never wanted me to play football, and you never agreed with me going to med school. Besides, I'm not behind on anything. I'll be taking my exams in January just like you asked me to."

"Why do I care? Because I can't have you going around sullying our name, Prescott! That's why I care." Dad downs the rest of his drink, his bloodshot eyes meeting mine. He's been drinking a lot since Gabriel was first diagnosed with cancer, but it seems like he's drinking even more these last few weeks. These days he was drunk more than not. And Benedict Wentworth isn't a fun drunk either.

I watch him as he pours himself another drink, good three fingers filling more than half of the crystal glass as he continues: "If your brother were here, I wouldn't need to be worried. At least I'd have one son to continue our family's legacy. And what am I left with?" He scoffs. "You. A good-for-nothing, lazy waste of space. Gabriel would—"

And it always came down to that—Gabriel would.

He would be better. He would be faster. He would be smarter. He would be more charming. He would, he would, he would.

As if I didn't know that already.

Gritting my teeth, I push away from the table. The legs of the chair scrape against the hardwood floors so loud even Mom looks up from her plate, a look of surprise flashing on her face. "I think I'm done here."

Dad's bushy brows connect as his face turns scarlet. "The dinner's not over yet."

"Well, it seems like I've lost my appetite."

I leave the dining room without a backward glance. Taking two steps at a time, I make my way up the stairs. The house has barely changed since Gabriel died. The photos of the two of us still line the staircase, all the way up to our thirteenth birthday.

Then it all stops.

Like we've been stuck in time.

A prison.

That's what this house is.

A freaking prison.

I go straight to my bedroom, going to the bottom of my closet where there is one loose board underneath. It's where when I was a teen, I usually had a bottle of Jack stashed for emergencies like this one. And sure enough, there is a bottle still hidden inside. It's dusty, a testament to how long it's been since I've last been home.

Home.

What a freaking mockery.

This place hasn't been home since Gabriel died.

I'm not sure if it's been much even before that.

Certainly not for me.

Bottle in hand, I grab my car keys and jacket before I go back down, careful to keep it quiet. I can hear my dad raging as I make my way to the door, but I don't bother stopping.

I have to get the fuck out of here.

Now.

The cold Michigan air slams into me as soon as I slip outside. The snow has been falling heavily, not that it's anything strange for this time of the year. Pulling the zipper of my jacket higher, I go toward the car and slip inside, the engine purring to life.

Then I drive.

Since I have no destination in mind, I just drive on autopilot, looking around as I pass the streets for the little things that have changed since the last time I've been here. Which was over a couple of years ago.

I'm not sure how long I'm on the road, when the headlights illuminate the familiar sign. I step on the brakes with more force than necessary the car swaying a little over the icy ground as it comes to a stop. Letting out a shaky breath, I look up only to realize I haven't imagined it.

Somewhere during my drive, my mind has subconsciously brought me to the cemetery.

For a moment, I just sit in the car and watch the sign. I haven't been here... I'm not even sure in how long. Since the funeral maybe?

Running my hand over my face, I mutter: "What the hell."

Putting the car in park, I get out, and walk inside. The place is eerily quiet, not strange, considering it's after seven at night on Christmas Eve. At least no one can give me judging glances as I make my way to my brother's grave, a bottle in hand.

The knot in my throat grows bigger as I come closer until I'm standing in front of the simple grave.

Gabriel Jonathan Wentworth

A loving son

Taken way too soon

"Hey, Gabby," I croak, the words coming out rough. "Long time no see, brother."

Rubbing my finger under my nose to stop the weird tingling, I move closer and crouch down next to his headstone, staring at the engraved words.

Even in his death, they've taken him away from me. Unclasping the cap, I take a long pull straight from the bottle, the whiskey burning my insides and warming me up.

"I'm sorry, Gabby," I whisper, letting the words I've been holding in for so long finally out. "So fucking sorry. It's all my damn fault. It should have been me. Everybody would have been happier if it were me who got sick and died. Mom wouldn't be so sad all the time, and Dad would have the son he always wanted. And you... You would get the life you deserved.

"I promised you I'd make our dreams come true, but I

messed up. We lost in the playoffs." I let out a scoff, "Although I guess you already know that huh? You were always a better player out of the two of us. Hell, you were always better, full stop. You were my better half, Gabby, and I can't even keep up the promises I made you. How the fuck is that fair?"

My phone vibrates in my pocket. Wiping at my eyes, I pull it out and look at the message.

Doll: Merry Christmas.

Doll: I hope things are going well with your family.

Taking a pull from the bottle, I let out a humorless chuckle, "Wanna know who that was? That was Jade. Just another person I disappointed. I know, Gabby. Shocker, right?" I huff a laugh, taking a swig from the bottle. "She and I used to date. Who'd have thought, huh? But for a moment there, she made me believe I could be different. For her. I wanted to try, anyway." I take another gulp of the drink, letting the silence stretch around us. "But then she told me she has cancer, and I just flipped. I couldn't do it, Gabby. I just couldn't. Watching her go through it reminded me of you too much. And then she ended up in the hospital, and it was all my fault. It was like the past was repeating itself. Dad's right, you know? He might be an asshole, but there is one thing he's right about. I kill everyone I love. And I refuse to be the reason why Jade dies, so I let her go."

My eyes fall down on my phone still clasped in my hand. The screen has long gone dark, but I can still see Jade's words written on there. A beacon in the darkness. That's what she's been for me this whole time.

"I hated every second of it, but I let her go. It's better this way, right? She deserves somebody better than me. Somebody who can give her things I never could. But every time I see her, I want to pull her in my arms and never let go. How fucked up is that?"

I hate you. For making me fall in love with you.

I look down at the bottle, letting out a humorless chuckle. I was judging Dad, when I'm exactly like him.

"I wish you were here. I wish you could tell me what to do. I wish you could meet her." If only wishes came true. "You'd have loved her."

Pushing to my feet, I suck in a sharp breath at the stab of pain that goes through my leg. Although I've stopped taking steroids since there wasn't any point, the pain was even stronger now than it was before.

Sliding my hand into my pocket, I pull out the bottle with pain meds. The bottle is almost full since I met with Manolo to grab a refill before this trip. Shaking two on my palm, I throw them into my mouth and take a pull from the bottle.

"Promise me you'll stop. You can't... Just, promise..."

"Okay, I promise."

Like father, like son.

With one last glance at the grave, I turn around and get the hell out of there.

Slowly I make my way back to my house. I'm not sure who put the decorations up because I'm pretty sure my dad would fall if he even attempted to climb the ladder. It was all for show anyway. To avoid neighbors asking any questions. The inside hasn't been decorated in years.

Pulling the car in the garage, I go inside. The house is blissfully quiet as I make my way up the stairs, only to come to a stop when I see a soft light peeking through the crack in the door of the room next to mine.

Gabriel's room.

I don't think I've even stepped foot once in that room. Not since he died.

My heart is thundering in my chest as I take a step closer, unsure of what to expect. I nudge the door with the tip of my foot. The door softly opens further and I find my mother sitting on the bed, her hands clutched around the stuffed Pikachu Gabriel was obsessed with when we were kids.

I look around, and it's like I've been thrown back in time. Everything was the same. All the things in place like he left them as he went to the hospital that last time.

The time I killed him.

The memories come at me like a tsunami, suffocating me in their intensity.

All the times we spent playing in this room. Doing homework together. Playing video games. Fighting. Lying on the bed late at night and just talking.

Shaking my head, I try to push them back, but it's too hard. Too much. Too soon.

"Your father wanted to throw it all away, but I couldn't let him," Mom whispers, her raspy voice bringing me back to the present.

"What are you doing here, Mom? You should be in bed."

"I can't sleep. The memories..." she shakes her head, tears streaming down her cheeks. "It's too hard. Gabriel loved Christmas."

"I know."

If you would have asked Gabriel, the house would have been decorated on November first and stayed that way well into the new year. He loved everything about the holiday. The music. The lights. The food. The presents.

Moving closer, I crouch in front of her but she looks away instantly, avoiding my gaze. "He's gone, Mom. Has been for years. He wouldn't have liked to see you like this. You have to let him go."

Even before I finish, she's already shaking her head. "I can't," she whispers, clutching that damn toy to her chest. "He was my baby boy. I can't let him go."

I clasp my hands around her wrists, trying to disentangle her fingers from the stuffed animal. "You have to let him go."

"You don't understand. I can't!"

"I don't understand? He was my brother!" I yell right back at her.

Mom's head snaps to me, her tear-stained eyes wide as she stares at me.

"He was my brother, and he's dead. How do you think I feel? How I've felt all these years? All everybody could think about was Gabriel. And I get it. I got it then, and I get it now. I was worried about him too. All the damn time. Every time I left that damn hospital, I worried he wouldn't be there when I came back. *For years.* But now he's gone, has been gone for nine years, and you can't even look at me. Did you know that? Did you know that you haven't looked at me in years, Mom? Not really. My brother died, and then my parents who already didn't think me worthy enough, left me too. Dad thinks I'm a waste of space, and you can't stand to even glance at me for more than a split second. So don't you dare tell me I don't understand." I run my fingers through my hair, messing the strands as the fight slowly leaves me. "You lost your baby boy, but what about me, Mom? Huh? What about me? What about what I need? What I needed all this time?"

"Prescott..."

This time, I'm the one shaking my head. "I needed you too. But you weren't there. You never are."

With that, I turn around and get the hell out.

I need to get out of here.

I need to get away from this toxic environment.

I need to get away from the memories and pain this house holds.

I need...

I need Jade.

Chapter 37

JADE

"How are you doing?" Nixon asks as he sits next to me on the couch.

My initial reaction is to say that I'm fine, like I've done so many times in the past, but I stop myself before voicing the words out loud.

Nixon has been even more worried about me after the incident in the bathroom a couple of weeks ago. And although Christmas has been quiet, he wouldn't leave me for more than ten minutes, if that.

That day, after he helped me clean up and put me back to bed, I called Dr. Hale. She was the therapist I went to just after Mom died, and after explaining the situation, she agreed to meet me. I'm not sure what kind of crazy money Nixon was paying her, but she's been meeting me every other day like clockwork since that call, and for the most part, it's been helping.

I tug the blanket closer around myself, but even that doesn't keep me warm enough. "Still hanging on."

Although barely.

I was two rounds into my second cycle of chemo, and I

swear some days I wish I was dead. Like yesterday. Yesterday I definitely wished I was dead. And today wasn't much better. I'd spent the better part of the morning throwing up until nothing was left in my stomach, and now I was fighting the worst shivers in my life.

"You should be in bed," Nixon chastises.

"I can't lay there any longer. Besides, the TV is bigger here."

Since Nixon didn't have any more football games, we've decided to spend the whole winter break back at the house. This time it was just the three of us. Quiet. It was too damn quiet, and when I had nothing better to do than lay in bed, memories of the past found a way to sneak past my defenses.

"Need more blankets?"

"I'm... f-fine," I stutter, closing my eyes as another shiver runs through my body. "Don't you have better things to do?"

Nixon tugs my beanie back, so it's not falling into my face. "Nothing more important."

"I'd figure you'd be organizing a party for New Year's or something."

"Only if you're planning to come."

I peek one eye open to glare at him. "Do I look like I'm ready to go out and party it up?"

"With you, one can never be sure." He nudges me gently. "But seriously, can I get you anything?"

I let out a soft groan, snuggling deeper into the blankets. "You can stop hovering and let me sleep."

"I thought you were here for the TV."

I glare at my brother, but he only sighs, "Fine. I'll come back in a bit, though."

"Didn't even think otherwise," I whisper dryly.

"Is Prescott coming?"

The question catches me off guard. We haven't talked about

Prescott much. Between the holidays and having to go to the hospital, there just wasn't time.

"He's visiting his family."

At least that's what he said the last time I saw him in Moore's, although I have no idea why he would want to do that after everything that's happened. I tried texting him for Christmas.

Looking back, it was a stupid thing to do. Especially after how things played out that last night and everything that was said, but I was feeling nostalgic, and my fingers were faster than my brain.

It was the first time I felt half-human in days, and I was snuggled in the living room, watching Christmas movies which reminded me of Thanksgiving when we did the very same thing. How is it possible that things have changed so much in a matter of weeks? But he hasn't said anything back, so I didn't try to do it again.

"I figured he'd come by now."

But he won't.

Not now. Not ever.

Because he left.

And left for good this time.

"Nixon, I..."

I have to tell him. The season was over. It was time. I couldn't keep this a secret any longer and expect him not to ask questions.

Before I can get the words out, the doorbell rings. Nixon and I just look at each other. We've been here for over two weeks now, and the doorbell has rung once this whole time. On Christmas Eve morning when Coach and Yasmin's mom joined us for the holiday. That's it. But we knew they were coming.

"You expecting somebody?" I ask, tilting my head back to get a better look at him.

"Not really. I'll go check who it is. You try and rest."

Nodding, I let my eyes close as I doze off. I'm not sure how long I'm out, it could have been minutes or months when I feel a hand gently brush my cheek.

It takes me a moment, but I finally blink my eyes open and then squint, unsure if I see correctly.

Because there is no way that Prescott is standing in my living room when he's supposed to be miles away.

It has to be all in my head.

That's it.

Just a dream.

Or maybe it's a nightmare.

No, I'm pretty sure it is a nightmare since I can feel that familiar ache in my chest at the very sight of him.

"Prescott?" I try to get up, but my muscles protest the movement. My whole body aches. Weak, so freaking weak.

"Shh, I've gotcha."

Soon I'm lifted off the couch, and that familiar scent of pine and citrus, and plain Prescott surrounds me.

Even if it's a nightmare, I don't want to wake up.

The bed creaks in the background, and I feel my body touch a hard surface before the blankets fall over me, warming me up.

Prescott starts to leave, but I grab his hand. "Don't go," I whisper, the desperation clear in my voice. "Don't leave me."

"I'm here." Once again, the bed creaks, and I feel a warm body next to mine. The last thing I hear before sleep claims me is Prescott's soft voice. "I'm sorry, Jade. I'm so fucking sorry."

Groaning softly, I turn around. My muscles still feel tight and achy, but at least I'm not shivering any longer, so that's a win.

Blinking my eyes open, I'm met with the dim light illuminating the room.

And Prescott.

My heart does a little flip as I just stare at him, unsure if this is really happening or if I'm still dreaming.

These days it is hard to differentiate between the two.

I reach forward, my fingers tracing his scruffy jaw.

"You're really here," I whisper, staring at Prescott's familiar face lying on the pillow next to mine.

He's really here.

"I'm here. I'm sorry, Jade. I know I had no right to come, not after everything that has happened, but..."

"What's going on?" Something must have happened to set him off and made him come all this way.

"What didn't happen?" He lets out a humorless chuckle. "I went home, got in another fight with my dad, which led me to visit my brother's grave, and then I found Mom sitting in Gabriel's room only to get into a fight with her, and the only thing that was on my mind was to come back home. To come back to you."

"Prescott..." I shake my head, my throat feeling tight.

"I was surprised when Nixon didn't punch me in the face the moment he opened the door, so I figured you didn't tell him."

"No, there wasn't time."

Prescott gives me a pointed look which clearly states that he knows I'm full of crap, which I am. We'd been in this house for weeks, there was plenty of time to tell him what happened, but I didn't want to. Saying it would mean admitting the truth, and I wasn't ready to do that. It meant that this thing between Prescott and me was actually over, and I didn't want that to be true.

Prescott extends his hand, his fingers sliding through mine.

"When everything else goes to shit, I always come back to one person. You. You're my person, Jade. You're my everything, and I hate myself for pushing you away when all I want to do is hold you close."

"I hate you for making me fall in love with you." I start to pull my hand out of his, but he doesn't let me budge. "That's what you said the last time we talked. I can't keep doing this, Prescott. I can't keep playing your games. I can't keep watching you walk away, I..."

"I'm not going anywhere, Jade. I need you like I need the fucking air to breathe."

"Then why do you keep pushing me away?!" I ask, my voice breaking. I bite the inside of my cheek to stop the tears from forming. God, I hate myself when I'm like this.

So weak. So needy.

"Because I'm scared, okay? I'm so fucking scared of losing you. I'm so fucking scared of being the reason you die."

The reason you...

"What are you talking about? I have cancer, Prescott. That's not your fault. None of it is. If I die, it'll be because of the cancer and not something any of us did."

"But it would have been. If something had happened that day after the game, it would have been my fault. Just like Gabriel's death is my fault."

"Prescott, no..."

He shakes his head even before I can finish. "It's true. I killed him. I let him convince me that going out would be a good idea. He was so miserable being stuck in the hospital, and he just wanted to get out. You should have seen his face—the relief when he breathed in some fresh air. We were thirteen-year-old boys, and he was happy to *breathe*. How fucked up is that? And then, instead of going straight inside after we got the ball, we started to play catch right there in the open. He was so happy, and after months I finally had my brother back, so the time got away from us. When we got back inside, it was too late. Gabriel had already been fighting an infection, and being outside in the freezing night in the middle of November was the stupidest thing we could have done. His fever spiked, and the infection spread. He died shortly after."

I press my hand against my mouth, trying to fight tears.

Now it all made sense.

Fever, fainting, hospital.

It all brought back memories of what happened to his brother.

"It wasn't your fault."

He shakes his head, a tear falling down his cheek.

"It wasn't. He wanted to go out, and you just went with it because you wanted to see your brother happy. If you want to blame somebody, blame cancer. You didn't know, and the only mistake you made was wanting to see your brother happy. There is no shame in that."

"I should have done better."

"You were just a *boy*, Prescott. And I'm sorry, I'm sorry that you had to go through something so horrendous at such a young age. I'm sorry that you have to go through this now. I wish... I wish I had walked away that day in the woods. That way, none of this would have happened. I never wanted to hurt you. I never..."

"You're not hurting me." Prescott grabs my hand, squeezing it tightly. "I knew saying that would be the safest way to get you to leave me, and I was right."

"I never wanted this for you." I shake my head, the tears burning my eyelids. "Any of you."

"I know, doll." He leans closer, pressing his mouth against the top of my head. "I know."

"Where do we go from here?"

Everything about us was so messed up. I didn't want to keep hurting him, and I knew if we stayed together, no matter what he said, I'll end up doing just that. But I also couldn't push him away, not now that he was finally starting to open up. I just couldn't do that to him.

No matter what road we chose, heartbreak seemed inevitable.

"How about we take it one day at a time?"

"One day at a time," I whisper, testing the words on my tongue. "I think I could get behind that."

Chapter 38

PRESCOTT

"Why is there no food in here?" Jade asks as she closes the fridge and glares at her brother.

Today she's feeling more like herself, so she decided to get out of bed and grab something to eat. She was still too pale for my liking, but I knew we were still on thin ice, so I decided to keep my mouth shut.

"I was planning to go yesterday, but somebody," Yasmin looks pointedly at Nixon, "kept me distracted."

Jade groans, "I don't need to listen to this. Can you just make me a list? Prescott and I can grab it on our way."

"We can?" I ask, raising my brow. I wasn't sure where she was going with this, but you won't hear me say no to more alone time with Jade.

"Yes, we can. On our way home from the diner."

"You want to go to the diner?"

"I want coffee. And food." Her whole face lights up. "They have these pancakes that are so good here. You have to try them."

"Hey, what about us?" Nixon protests. "Maybe we want pancakes too."

Yasmin gives him a side glance. "Didn't you just eat cereal?"

"Your point being? You should know better than anybody how much I can eat." He pats his flat stomach. "This is a growing body."

Jade rolls her eyes. "You know you can't keep using that excuse forever, right? It's all good now that you're still in the game, but one day you'll retire, and before you know it," she snaps her fingers, "you'll have a dad bod."

Nixon glares at her. "You did not just say that."

"Oh yes, she did, and she's totally right, too." Yasmin grins, lifting her hand for a high five.

Nixon gets up and slips his arms around his wife's waist. "Well, you'll still love me even when I have a dad bod, right?"

"She has to suffer through your personality. I think the dad bod is the least of her worries."

Nixon's mouth falls open at Jade's taunt. "Oh, now you went and done it." He tries to walk around Yasmin, but she doesn't let him pass, giving Jade enough time to slip away.

"You left yourself wide open for that one. Don't blame me!" Her blue eyes shine with mischief when they meet mine. "I'm going to grab a sweater, and we can get going."

With that, she leaves the kitchen. Nixon watches her go, a small smile on his lips. "She seems to be doing better today."

"She is," I agree.

"It's just so hard for me to wrap my head around it. Two days ago, I was helping her as she was throwing up in the bathroom, her body so weak she couldn't get to her feet and into the bed on her own, and today she's... fine."

Yasmin grabs his hand, giving it a firm squeeze. "This is a rough patch, but she's going to get better."

"I hope you're right. I can't lose her, Yas."

My throat tightens at his words.

He isn't the only one.

"You were right. Those are the best pancakes I've ever tried."

Jade looks over her shoulder, a smile on her lips. "I told you so."

The need to lean down and kiss her is so strong it's almost overwhelming. I must have it written on my face because Jade's blue eyes turn dark, as her gaze drops to my lips.

Unfortunately, our moment is broken when somebody clears their throat. *Loudly*.

"You planning to get out anytime soon?" Nixon asks, his narrowed gaze meeting mine.

"Cockblocker," Jade mutters, pushing the door open.

"Did she just..."

"Call you a cockblocker? Yes, I did," Jade says just as an older couple exits their car, wide eyes and horrified looks on their faces.

"You're crazy!"

"What? I'm dying; if I'm not going to be unapologetic about what I say now, when will I be?"

"You're not—" I don't get to finish because Jade comes to a sudden stop.

An older guy is staring at her a few yards away. There is something familiar about him, but I'm not sure where to place him. His mostly gray hair is a mess, and the lines on his face are hardened. His dark eyes are bloodshot, and heavy stubble covers his jaw. He looks like somebody who has had a few rough weeks and decided to drink his weight in alcohol to solve it.

"Jade, what..." He takes her in from head to toe, his eyes finally settling on the beanie covering her head.

I close the distance between us, my hand going protectively to the small of her back just as Nixon moves in front of her and throws a menacing glare at the man.

"What are you doing here?"

"I live here." The guy takes a step closer, his eyes still on Jade. "What happened to you?"

Jade's body goes stiff under my touch, but she doesn't cower. Instead, she lifts her chin, meeting the guy head-on. "Cancer. Which you'd know if you were ever around. Oh, that's right. You don't do well when your family members are sick, right, Dad? You walk away because it's *too hard*."

The guy staggers back, his mouth falling open. "You have cancer?"

"I'm just about to finish my second round of chemo."

"Cancer," he shakes his head. "That's not possible. That..."

"Well, it's true. I have cancer."

"No, no, no. You're lying."

"Do you even hear yourself?" Nixon asks. "Why would she lie about something like that?"

Mr. Cole turns to Nixon and points his finger at him. "Because of you! You want to punish me. For walking away. For leaving."

"Nobody's lying to you. I have cancer." Jade shakes her head. "Go away, Dad. Just go."

He stares at her for a while before his gaze darts to Nixon. For a moment, I think he might change his mind. For a moment, I think he might stay. But without another word, he turns around and walks away.

"Fucking coward," Nixon yells after him, but thankfully Yasmin's holding onto him, preventing him from going after his dad.

If I want to go and punch some sense into him, I can only imagine how Nixon's feeling.

But the reality is, he doesn't matter.

I walk around Jade, my hands cupping her cheeks as I lift her face to me. Her eyes shimmer with unshed tears.

"Are you okay?"

She forces out a smile. "I'm fine."

Pressing her mouth against my palm, she takes a step back. I let my hands fall as I watch her go to Nixon, her hand slipping around his waist. They whisper for a moment, and then I hear Jade say: "Let's go home."

He nods his head, his mouth brushing against the top of her head. We all huddle into the car, Jade slips into the back seat next to me. Her hand meets mine in the middle, her fingers intertwining with mine as we quietly drive home, only stopping at the supermarket so they can stock up.

We're just pulling into the driveway when Maddox calls, letting us know they've arrived a bit early. And sure enough, his Tesla is there, along with the familiar black Escalade.

Yasmin and Nixon exit the car, but Jade doesn't move a muscle, just gazes out the windshield as Yasmin goes straight for Edie, pulling her out of Maddox's arms and into hers.

"You okay?" I whisper, giving her hand a squeeze.

I know what happened earlier must have upset her. To know your parent is out there, but he keeps walking out on you when you need him the most?

"I'm fine. It's not like I expected anything better from him."

"Jade, he's your father—"

"He left me, Prescott." She turns to me, those blue eyes blazing with anger. "He left Mom and me to deal with her cancer all alone. He only came back when it suited him, and even then, the moment things got tough, he walked away. Because that's what he does, he walks away. Besides, I don't need him."

"It's clear that seeing you like this was a shock for him." I'm not sure why I'm insisting on this so much, but something about it doesn't sit right with me. "You never know, maybe he..."

"He won't come. I don't want him to come. I meant what I

said. I don't want him in my life. We might share DNA, but it takes more than blood to make a family. These people here?" She points out the window. "Despite everything that I did, all the lies and secrets I kept, they're still here. They are my family. I don't need Kevin Cole to be whole, Prescott." She looks out the window, a smile forming on her lips. "They're my family, and I wouldn't have it any other way."

JADE

"So, Prescott is here," Grace says quietly as she sits next to me and hands me a cup of hot chocolate.

I look toward the table where all the boys sit and play poker. Prescott's brows are pulled together in a scowl as he glowers at his cards.

"He's here," I say, shifting my attention back to the TV where some Hallmark movie is playing in the background. It would be so much easier if my life were anything like those movies.

"Didn't we want to kick him in the balls last I saw you?"

"Maybe." I take a sip of my drink, enjoying the sweet taste on my tongue.

"What changed?"

Yasmin sits on my other side. "That's what I want to know too."

I roll my eyes at my friends, letting out a long sigh. "Do we really have to discuss this? Now?"

"Yes!" the two of them say in unison.

"What are we talking about?" Aly asks as she enters the room and plops down in the armchair across from us.

"Prescott and Jade," Yasmin mock whispers as she grabs a

bottle of red and starts pouring it into the glasses. She looks at me, but I just shake my head. "Spill."

"There is nothing to spill."

Yasmin quirks her brow at me, clearly calling my bullshit. "He came here when you told us you all were broken up!"

Aly's eyes widen as she looks from me to Prescott and back. "You two are not together?"

"We are... I'm not even sure what we are," I say honestly. "His family is a piece of work, and that's saying something when it comes from me."

"So what? He just decided to come here instead?"

When everything else goes to shit, I always come back to one person. You. You're my person, Jade.

A shiver runs through me as his words ring in my mind. I couldn't get them out of my head, just like I couldn't forget what he told me.

He thinks he is the one responsible for his brother's death.

"There is a reason why he reacted the way he did." Grace opens her mouth to protest, but I stop her before she can utter a word. "I mean it, Grace. It was a damn good reason too."

"I'll believe it when I hear it."

"Well, you're not going to hear it because it's not my story to tell." I grab one of the cushions and throw it at her. "Now, enough. I don't want to talk about it any longer."

"What don't you want to talk about?"

A hand touches my shoulder, making tingles go down my spine. I tilt my head back to find Prescott standing behind me, his gaze on me.

"You guys done?"

"He wiped the table," Mason yells.

The corner of my mouth tilts upward. "Did you now?"

"Maybe."

"Then why not keep playing?"

Prescott smirks. "I have to leave them with some dignity, at least."

I let out an exaggerated sigh, "I guess there is that."

"So what you wanna do, doll?"

I take a deep breath, giving myself a moment to think. I've never really thought much about what I want to do. Not lately. It was all about things I *had* to do in order to get past this. There wasn't any room for my wishes and wants.

Not tonight, though.

"I want to snuggle on the couch and drink hot chocolate as I watch silly, unrealistic movies with my friends. And then, at midnight, I want to go out and watch the fireworks."

"Sounds like a plan to me."

He walks around the couch and picks me up before he sits down and places me in his lap. "How is this?" Prescott asks, pulling a blanket around me tighter.

I lean my head against his chest, inhaling his familiar scent. "Perfect. This is perfect."

Soon, the rest of the guys join us, and we all laugh at the absurdity of the movies. In the end, we make a unanimous decision to watch Avengers instead.

We're halfway through the *Age of Ultron* when midnight sneaks around. Putting on the winter gear, we go outside. Some people are already firing fireworks, so I tilt my head back and watch the color splash over the dark sky as I inhale the icy night air.

Hands sneak around me, and Prescott leans his chin against my shoulder as he pulls me into his body.

"You don't want to play with fireworks?" I ask, tilting my chin to Nixon, Mason, and the girls, who are all out in the yard setting up.

"I'm perfect where I am."

"Okay," I whisper, placing my hands over his.

From the corner of my eye, I can see Aly wrapping another blanket around Edie as she pulls her closer and points at the sky. Maddox's arms are wrapped around his two girls.

Our friends start the countdown, so we join in. Nixon crouches down to light up one of the fireworks, which blasts into the sky just as we get to zero.

This time I don't get to see it because Prescott turns me in his arms, his hand going to my nape as he pulls me in for a soft kiss.

My entire body melts in his arms as he kisses me for what feels like forever. Pulling away, he presses his forehead against mine.

I let out a soft chuckle. "Happy worst year of my life."

Prescott shakes his head. "Happy *best* year of your life."

"Hardly. I still have months of chemo in front of me."

His thumbs skim over my cheeks. "But you'll beat this thing, and once you do, you can go back to your life. I believe in you."

"Well, at least one of us does," I scoff.

"I do." Leaning in, he presses his mouth against mine once more. "Happy New Year, Doll."

I wrap my fingers around his jacket, not letting him pull away. "Happy New Year, Hotshot," I whisper, and this time as our mouths meet, there is nothing gentle about our kiss.

Chapter 39

PRESCOTT

"You going to grab lunch?" Spencer asks, looking over his shoulder.

"Yes, I have to eat something before I get back to studying." Pulling my hoodie over my head, I grab my phone but don't find any messages waiting for me.

"I'll go with you. Just let me wash up quickly."

Spencer disappears into the bathroom. So I hastily slip my hand into my pocket and pull out some pain pills, tossing them down as I take a seat.

I should have probably used all the time I had studying, but after staring at books for the past six hours straight, I needed a break, an outlet for all this nervous energy coursing through me, but I might have overdone it.

I'm about to pull out my book to get some reading in while I wait for Spencer when my phone rings.

"Are you ready for your MCATs?"

My fingers tighten around the book at the sound of my father's voice. We haven't talked since I left my childhood home. Not that that actually surprises me. "Hello to you, too, Dad. It's nice to talk to you."

Not.

"What would be nice is to know my son is taking his responsibilities seriously. You have your test in two days. Are you ready?"

I grit my teeth, irritated with this conversation. "I told you I should have taken the later exam, but you were the one who insisted I take the first available date."

"As if the results would be any different at a later date. You're just looking for excuses to be lazy. Get your ass to work and pass the damn exam!" he bellows.

Because, of course, it was that easy in his mind. You sit down, and the knowledge will magically transfer into your head.

Let's ignore the fact that it takes a good fourteen years to become a doctor while it only takes you seven to become a lawyer.

"I don't have time for this, Dad. I have studying to get back to."

"You listen to m—"

I hang up before he can finish, tossing the phone back into the bag just as Spencer gets out of the bathroom.

"Did you say something?"

"Nope," I shake my head. "Nothing. Maybe I should just go to the lib—"

"You won't get any studying done on an empty stomach."

As if he called it, my stomach chooses this exact moment to rumble loudly.

"See? Let me throw on some clothes, and we'll be out of here."

True to his words, in less than fifteen minutes, we're in the cafeteria, and the line isn't even that long. Grabbing our food, I'm about to take the first open table when Spencer shoves me in the opposite direction.

"What the..." I look up, my eyes locking on Jade's. She smiles, and I feel that grip tighten around my stomach.

"Maybe she'll help you chill for a moment. You should probably have sex. It helps me when I'm on edge."

"Of course it does."

"Hey, it's true. Don't tell me you haven't tried it."

"I'm not talking about my sex life with you," I say as I walk over to Jade.

Slipping into the open seat next to hers, I brush my lips against the top of her beanie-clad head. "Hey you, I didn't realize you were on campus today."

Jade decided to cut out most of her classes and only has one class this semester, which is on Tuesdays and Thursdays.

"I have to eat something, don't I?"

"I guess there is that. You won't hear me complain about it."

"Where are you guys coming from?" Grace asks as Spencer takes the seat next to hers.

"Gym. I found this asshole lifting so much the damn thing fell on his head."

"I had it under control until you came and decided to meddle," I mutter, pulling out my book.

"I'd see if you broke your nose when all that weight fell on you."

I roll my eyes at him. "Whatever you need to tell yourself to sleep at night, dude."

I tune them out, focusing my attention on the book in front of me as I go over the prep questions. At this point, I've gone over them countless times, but it never felt like enough.

Because that's what you do, you fail, Prescott. You fail people around you. You fail at football. You fail.

I'm not going to fail.

Not this time.

"Prescott?" A hand touches my arm, making my head snap in surprise. "What?"

Jade's watching me, worry in her eyes. "Are you listening to me?"

I lift my MCATs prep book up. "I kind of have my hands full right now," I snap.

The table falls silent as all eyes turn to me. Jade just gawks at me for a moment, unblinking. I expect her to fire something back at me, but in the end, she just nods. "Well, we're leaving so you can get to it."

Pushing her chair back, she grabs her tray and walks away without a backward glance.

Shit.

"Jade..." I try to call after her, but she's already out of earshot.

"You're an asshole, and I don't know why she puts up with you." Grace, on the other hand, glares at me before rushing after her friend.

Running my hand over my face, I turn back to the table only to find Spencer watching me.

"She's right, you know. You are an asshole."

I glare at him. "As if you'd side with me even if I was right."

"You need to get your head out of your ass. I know you have your hands full, but damn, there was no reason for you to snarl at her like that."

I let out a sigh. I know he's right, but the whole conversation with my dad had me on edge. As if I didn't put enough pressure on myself as it is, I didn't need him to do it too.

Spencer checks his phone. "Shit, I have a class to get to. I'll see you later."

Before I can say anything, he walks away.

"And then there was one," I mutter, sliding my phone out.

I pull up Jade's contact and just stare at it for a moment.

Me: I'm sorry I was an asshole. This damn test has me on edge but give me two more days, and I'll make it up to you, doll. Please?

Thankfully I don't have to wait long for a response.

Doll: I know. Kick that test's ass, and you know where to find me.

Picking a pebble from the ground, I toss it at the closed window on the first floor. I wait for a little bit, but when I don't see any movement behind the curtains, I do it again as a couple of girls exit the building. They give me wary looks as they walk around me like they expect me to jump at them or something.

Great, just what I needed.

One more.

Picking one of the bigger pebbles, I toss it at the window just as the curtain is pulled open, and Jade's face peeks at me.

She shakes her head but lifts the window open, leaning against it just like she did a few months ago. "Seriously? Are we back to this again?"

I grin up at her. "It seemed more fitting."

"More fitting for what?"

I grab the ladder by the side of her wall and start to climb up. "For the surprise I have in store for you."

"It seemed more fitting to steal me through my window?"

She moves so I can hoist myself up. "To pick you up." I brush my hands against the sides of my legs. "Just like the good ol' times."

"You're weird, Wentworth."

Jade starts to walk away, but I slide my hand around her waist, pulling her to me. "Yeah, but you still love me."

Her fingers press against my chest as she looks up at me. She's lost more weight in recent weeks, but that smile is still on her face as she watches me.

She jabs her finger into my chest. "You should consider yourself lucky."

"I do." Leaning down, I press my mouth against hers.

What started off as a slow kiss soon turned frantic. Jade tugs me closer, her body brushing against mine as I lower my hand to the small of her back, my tongue slipping into her mouth.

She moans softly, snapping me out of my head. With one final swipe of my mouth against hers, I reluctantly pull back. "Surprise first."

Jade lets out a frustrated huff. "Can't it wait? We were just in the middle of something here."

Her cheeks are flushed, lips pursed in displeasure. I would find it cute if my cock wasn't throbbing in protest. We haven't had sex in weeks, not since that time, just after she took her drains out; between everything that was going on, there just wasn't time. Plus, I meant what I said. She needed time to heal properly. What she was going through wasn't easy by any means. And then we broke up.

"Is it me? I mean, I know I'm not what I—"

I press my finger against her lips, stopping her from finishing that sentence. "You're perfect, Jade. So fucking perfect, and I can show you just how much later on, but we really need to leave now." I push her toward the door. "C'mon, let's grab your jacket."

She looks over her shoulder. "We're going out? I should put on some—"

"Jacket," I finish for her. "You really need to put on a jacket."

She crosses her arms over her chest and huffs as I continue

pushing her down the hallway. "Some makeup would be nice too. I look like a ghost."

"One sexy ass ghost."

Grabbing her jacket from the hook, I hold it open for her as she slides her hands inside, and I zip her all the way up, taking her hand in mine as I open the front door. "Let's go."

We descend the stairs and get out before I cover her eyes with my hands.

"What are you doing?" Jade's hands cover mine, but I don't let her push me away.

"Surprising you."

"Really? You know, I'm not a fan of surprises."

"You're not?" I ask, not making any attempt to move my hands from her face as I guide her.

"I'm not. I'm really, really not."

"Well, you'll have to deal with it for a little while longer."

"Your surprise is in walking distance?"

"Something like that," I say, shifting my hands so I cover her eyes with one palm while I open the door with the other one.

"It is! I heard the door creak."

"Watch the steps."

"I knew it."

"Next time, I'll put a scarf around your mouth."

"You wouldn't dare."

"Try me, doll."

"You could have just surprised me without all the secrecy, you know. I'm sure whatever it is you did is going to be amazing anyway."

"Amazing, huh?" I ask, unlocking the door to my place. Thankfully she's talking, so she pays zero attention to what I'm doing. "I thought you just said you don't like surprises."

"I don't, but that doesn't mean I won't like it. And even if I don't, I can..."

I let my hands drop as we stop in the doorway of my living room. I watch as Jade blinks her eyes open and stares at the room in front of her, her mouth wide open.

"You were saying?"

Jade just shakes her head as she moves further into the room, her eyes scanning the space as she takes everything in.

It looked nice; even I had to admit it. I lit a few candles, scattering them around the room. I made sure they were one of those vanilla kinds that didn't make her nauseous. A few blankets and pillows are placed around the room, and there is a jumbo pizza on the coffee table along with some ginger ale that she's been drinking lately to help her deal with the chemo side effects. Okay, and I might have gotten a bouquet of flowers.

Jade looks over her shoulder at me, a smile playing on her lips. "Deep down, you're a romantic, aren't you?"

A romantic? Yeah, right.

Just because I did something nice for my girlfriend—as an apology for being an ass, no less—doesn't make me a romantic.

"I don't know what you're talking about."

"It's okay. I won't tell anyone."

"Good because there is nothing to tell."

"Mhmm... Whatever you say."

"It's the flowers, isn't it?"

I knew I shouldn't have gotten them, but the lady at the store insisted I should, and I didn't want to disappoint her. Besides, I don't think I've ever gotten flowers for anybody before.

"Not just any flowers." She goes to the bouquet I put in one big cup I found in the kitchen and takes a sniff of the red buds. "Roses, too. I told you. Romantic."

Joining her on the blankets, I point at the box. "I got you pizza. If I were a romantic, I would have gotten you something better."

"Is it a cheese pizza?"

I roll my eyes. "Is there any other kind?" She starts to open her mouth, but I point my finger at her. "And if you say I'm a romantic one more time, I'll..."

"You'll what?" she asks, moving closer, so our knees are touching. Her teeth sink into her lower lip as her eyes fall on my mouth.

"Screw pizza." Getting to my knees, I push Jade into the pillows as I tug my shirt over my head. "I want to have you first."

Chapter 40

PRESCOTT

February

Doll: Any news?

Me: Not yet.

Doll: Well, it shouldn't take long. Besides, I don't need the scores to know you've passed.

Me: You don't know that.

Doll: I know everything!

Doll: Are we still on for tomorrow? You sure you have time to drive me to the hospital?

Me: Yes, I'm going with you to the hospital.

Doll: Okay, I'm off to my class. Text me when you know something more!

Shaking my head, I turn my attention back to my homework. I try to concentrate, but after I stop for the third time in the middle of an equation, I let out a frustrated groan.

I drop the book on the desk and stretch my sore muscles, my gaze falling on my phone.

"Still nothing?"

I turn around to find Spencer leaning against my doorway.

"Nope. Still nothing."

January has passed in a heartbeat. Between classes starting once again, spending as much time with Jade as possible, and the final preparations before taking the MCATs, I've hardly had any time to breathe. But today was the moment of truth. The MCAT results were supposed to be posted sometime today, but it was late afternoon, and so far, there was only silence.

"Well, I know one way how to distract you. Get dressed."

My brow quirks up. "Where are we going?"

"We just smashed our opponents, so the guys are throwing a party before we leave for a few away games tomorrow morning."

A pang of jealousy hits me at his words. That was supposed to be the football team. Instead, we lost, and the hockey players were still cleaning the ice with their opponent's asses. If they continue this way, they could go all the way to the Frozen Four without any issues.

"Like there wouldn't be a party if you guys lost."

"Win, lose, is there even a difference any longer?" Spencer shrugs, tapping his fingers against the doorway. "Meet me out in twenty?"

"What are you? A girl?"

"Nah, I figured that'll give you enough time to take care of that bush that's grown on your jaw."

"Fuck off," I mutter, rubbing at my jaw defensively. "That bush, as you call it, is a beard. Not that your thirteen-year-old self can recognize it."

Spencer covers his chest dramatically. "Now you wound me. I'm at least sixteen."

"Get the hell out of here."

"I'll see you in twenty, old man."

"Old man," I scoff and shake my head. I'm about to go to the bathroom when my phone lights up.

I suck in a breath, my stomach clenching as I slowly pick it up and unlock the screen.

The results are in.

Holding my breath, I open the e-mail and click on the link.

It feels like forever as the page uploads.

"Fucking final—"

My heart starts beating faster as I look at the score on the screen. I blink, hoping I have it wrong, but it's still the same.

A vice grip clenches my stomach, the bile rising in my throat as my mind processes what I'm seeing.

I didn't pass the MCATs.

An incoming call flashes on my screen, Dad's name written in bold letters. My gut twists. I could let the call go to voicemail, but he wouldn't stop at that one call, so it would only be putting off the inevitable.

"What?!" I ask, not in the mood for chitchat.

There is a beat of silence on the other line before, "I was right, wasn't I? You failed, just like you failed everything and everybody else in your life."

My fingers grip the phone as I grit my teeth. "I wouldn't have failed if I didn't let you talk me into applying for the date that was too early, and I knew it. I knew I wouldn't have enough time to prepare for it properly."

"Tell those excuses to somebody who wants to listen to them, Prescott. Maybe they won't give a crap that you're a failure, but we both know the truth."

"Screw you. I'm so done with this, Dad. I'm a failure? Great, now you won't have to deal with me any longer."

"Prescott..."

I cut him off before he could say anything else. My heart is thundering in my ribcage, the weight of his words suffocating me and making the bile rise up my throat.

You're a failure.

Throwing my phone at the wall, I watch it shatter to the ground.

Spencer appears in my doorway, a worried look on his face. "Are you... *Shit.*"

See? Even he isn't surprised you failed.

"You mentioned drinks? Then let's go drink."

JADE

"Thanks for picking me up," I say as I slide into Nixon's car. Turning the phone in my hand, I check for the hundredth time if I have any messages or calls, but still nothing.

Where the hell is he?

I tried texting Prescott numerous times after my class yesterday and this morning, but he hasn't picked up, and he hasn't texted me back, so I had to call Nixon instead.

"No problem. What happened to Prescott?"

"I..." The lie is on the tip of my tongue, but I bite it back. "I have no idea. We texted before I went to class yesterday, but he's been MIA ever since. Have you talked to or seen him? I'm kind of starting to get worried."

Nixon presses his lips in a tight line, clearly not happy with the revelation. "No, I haven't talked to him."

Damn. Where are you, Prescott?

I unlock my phone and start typing again.

Me: Nixon picked me up. Can you just text me so I know you're okay?!

Nixon places his hand over my knee, giving it a firm squeeze. "It's going to be okay."

I'm not so sure.

The rest of the drive is quiet. I'm too lost in my own head, and I can't stop worrying about Prescott. Thankfully there isn't much you have to do when you have chemo dripping into your veins. Still, it feels like forever before I'm done and we can go home.

Just as I'm getting out of Nixon's car, I see him pull out his phone and frown at whatever message he got.

"Do you have a key?"

I pull my brows together, unsure of where he's going with this. "A key?"

"Yes, a key. To Prescott's place."

Prescott's place? Why would he need a key to Prescott's place?

"No, but..." I wrap my arms around myself tighter, unease creeping up my spine. "What's going on? Where is Prescott?" I glance over his shoulder as if the man in question will suddenly appear behind him.

"Spencer texted me and asked me to check in on Prescott, but he forgot to tell me how I should do that if the dumbass doesn't actually open the door. So, the key?"

Spencer texted Nixon and not me? Why? What the hell's going on here?

I nibble at my lower lip, my stomach twisting into knots with every word he says. Or maybe the chemo is starting to do its thing.

"I don't have it, but..." I weigh my options. I don't want to betray Prescott's trust, but then again, Spencer asked Nixon to check in on him, and Prescott's not answering. What if something's wrong? "I know where they keep the spare one. In case they forget it or something."

Nixon runs his fingers through his hair. "Yeah, sure."

We walk in silence all the way to the building next door and climb to the third floor where Prescott's apartment is. My muscles are quivering from the climb, a wave of heat going through me, but I force myself to push through. It's definitely the chemo.

Rising on the tips of my toes, I slide my hand over the edge of the doorway until I find the small indent and slip my finger inside to get out the key. My throat bobs as I slide it into the lock and turn it, unsure of what I'll find inside.

Nixon places his hands on my shoulders, giving them a firm squeeze. "Maybe you should go back home. You don't look so good."

And wonder what the hell's going on? Screw that.

"I'm fine," I say, pushing open the door.

The place is dark when we step inside. The smell of stale food and something else, something familiar, makes my stomach roll. My hand flies to my face, covering my mouth and nose, willing my stomach to calm down. That's when I see him.

"No." I shake my head. "No, no, no."

My heart stops when I get to the middle of the room just enough to find Prescott lying on the floor, unconscious.

Nixon swears and pushes me away as he turns Prescott onto his back, leaning down so he can check if he's breathing.

What if he's not breathing?

"The asshole is still alive," Nixon mutters. "Just unconscious in his own vomit."

With that, he slaps him on the cheek. Hard.

The sound of skin connecting to skin snaps me out of the daze. "What are you doing?"

"Trying to wake him up. What does it look like I'm doing?" He slaps him again. "Wake up, you idiot." He glances at me. "Sit down, Jade. I can't have you passing out, too."

Nixon grunts as he slips his arm around Prescott's waist and helps raise him off the floor. Prescott groans, and relief slams into me, almost bringing me to my knees.

He's okay. He's okay. He's okay.

I chant those words as I watch Nixon carry him into the bathroom before following after them. He goes straight into the small shower. After a few silent curses, the water turns on, and Prescott bellows at the cold water hitting him out of nowhere.

"What the fuck?"

"Since the nice way didn't work, I figured this would have to do. You can thank me later for not leaving you to suffocate in your own puke."

Nixon's words are hard and unyielding.

I can still see it, *see him* lying down on that floor. Utterly unaware of what was going on. Would he be okay if Nixon hadn't decided to check in on him? Would he still be alive?

Wrapping my arms around myself, I take a step back.

I have to get out of here.

Out, out, out.

The moment I'm in the living room, that horrible smell hits me once again. I barely make it to the sink before I start throwing up. My fingers grip the counter, knuckles white as I get everything out of me, a cold sweat coating my skin.

Only when I'm sure I'm done, do I turn on the faucet, letting the water wash away the puke, and splash some water on my face before I get down on the floor, pulling my knees to my chest. I'm about to place my head on my knees when something white catches my attention.

Bracing myself, I push upright and make my way to the middle of the room, sliding my hand under the coffee table and pulling it out. I know what it is even before I turn it to see the label.

"I'm going to find some dry clothes to change into," Nixon says, startling me.

I grip the bottle tighter, looking up at him. "Sure thing."

Nixon stops, those wary eyes of his that see more than they should, narrowing slightly. "Are you okay? No side effects? You look like you've seen a ghost."

"Yeah, it's just..." I inhale deeply. "I'm fine. Go change."

"Okay, I'll be back in a few." He looks over his shoulder again before finally disappearing out into the hallway.

I unclasp my fingers, looking at the label on the bottle. It's worn like the bottle has been used regularly for months.

Dammit, Prescott! You promised.

I flip the lid open, noticing only a few pills left, and the half-empty bottle of Jack is on the table.

I press my lips together to stop them from wobbling. Spiraling. He's spiraling. I know because I've been there. I've been swallowed by my darkness. I've been fighting it for months now. Resisting the pull as I toe the line so very carefully.

Curling my fingers around the bottle, I watch the color drain from my knuckles. I rub my free hand over my face.

Tired.

I'm so damn tired.

"Jade..."

His soft words make tingles run down my spine. I let my hand drop down and wrap my arms around myself as I slowly turn around to face him.

Prescott is standing in the doorway, a loose pair of sweats hanging on his hips, his chest bare. His hair is wet, and the circles under his eyes are so dark they're almost black. He rubs his jaw, the stubble on his chin so long, it's a full-on beard.

"You promised," I say softly, but the accusation is clear in my voice.

He takes a step toward me. "Jade..."

"You promised!" I yell, throwing the bottle at him.

Of course, he's faster, catching the damn thing before it knocks him in the head. He looks down at the bottle, guilt flashing in his eyes. "You don't unde—"

"Oh, I understand it perfectly," I interrupt him, not in the mood to deal with his bullshit. "I understand that you ask one thing of me when you do the exact opposite. You ask me to fight when you've given up."

"Jade, I'm..."

"Save it." A tear starts to slide down, but I wipe it away quickly. "I can't keep doing this, Prescott," I whisper, knowing there will be no going back once the words are out.

He blinks a few times, the realization flashing in his eyes. "W-what..."

"I can't keep on doing this... this *thing* between us. It's toxic. *We are toxic.*" I shake my head. "And I can't keep on watching you throw away your life for the demons haunting you."

"No, Jade," he takes a step closer. "I'm sorry, I—"

"I just can't." I shake my head once again as I take a step back. "You were lying on that floor, Prescott!" I point at the place where we found him. Traces of puke and God knows what else still spilled on the hardwood. "You were lying there, and I thought..." I clench my fingers into fists by my sides, the words coming out so fast they're a blur. "I thought you were gone. For a split second, I thought you were dead, and the only thing I could think about was that it was my fault. That I..."

"No, Jade, that's not tru—"

"That I did this to you," I finish, needing to say it. Needing to voice the words out loud. My guilt. So much guilt. "Because I selfishly wanted to keep you by my side, although I knew, *I knew* I should let you go."

"This isn't your fault."

"It is. I should have never dragged you into this when I

knew I was sick. When I knew what you've been through. You and me, Prescott? We're broken."

"You're not broken."

"I am. I'm so broken that I don't know how to put the pieces back together. But I have to. I have to because I have people counting on me. Nixon and Yasmin, Grace, Rei, Penelope, *you*... Everybody is counting on me to be strong and to beat this thing, and I can't do that if your broken pieces are mixed with mine."

"W-what..." Prescott's throat bobs as he swallows. "What are you saying?"

"I'm saying that I'm going home because I can't keep on seeing you like this. It hurts too much. I'm going home so I can heal, and for your sake, I pray that you can do the same."

"Don't do that, Jade." He closes the distance between us, pulling me into his arms, and I let him. Because for all that I said, deep down, I'm weak. I'm weak, and I crave him. I crave his strength, his love. So I let him hold me. One last time, just for a few heartbeats longer. "I'm sorry. I'll do better. I'll— Just don't leave."

Another shake of my head. Another tear falls down as I gently disentangle his arms from around me and take a step back. "I have to."

For him and for me, and for any hope of the future either of us has, I have to walk away.

So that's exactly what I do.

"Jade!"

His voice breaks, as does my heart, but it doesn't slow me down.

Broken.

We're both too broken to be together.

To even be around one another.

Maybe in another lifetime.

But not now.

My eyes are blurry as I get out in the hallway. I bite the inside of my cheek to stop it from wobbling as I reach for the door handle.

"Jade, what are you..." the words die on Nixon's lips as he sees me standing in the doorway, tears falling down my cheeks. "What happened?"

"It's over. I'm going home."

His jaw clenches. "I'm coming with you."

I shake my head. "Stay. He'll need somebody, and I... I can't be that somebody, Nixon. Not any longer."

My brother grits his teeth. "He made you cry."

"I made myself cry," I whisper. "Stay. Please."

There is a beat of silence, and for a moment, I think he'll refuse me.

"Fine," Nixon agrees reluctantly. "I'll come by before I go home, okay?"

Wiping away the tears, I just nod.

Nixon comes to me, cupping my cheeks and swiping away the wetness. "It's going to be okay, Smalls."

I'm not so sure about that.

Chapter 41

PRESCOTT

"What have you done to Jade?" Nixon asks as he barges into the living room dressed in a pair of my sweats and a tee.

I chug down the Jack, but the asshole whips the bottle away, spilling some of the amber liquid onto me in the process. "Why don't you figure it out yourself?"

"You've had enough of that, don't you think?"

Don't I think?

"I'm still coherent, so I'd think not." I try to reach for the bottle, but he pulls it out of my reach.

"Gimmie that."

"No, and if you don't stop with this nonsense, I'm going to spill it all down the drain. Hell, I might do that anyway. What. The. Hell. Happened?"

I glare at him for a moment, but the asshole is unwavering.

"Fine," I push to my feet abruptly. "I'll just get another one."

I start for the kitchen, tugging the door open so hard it bangs against the cabinet. Without even looking, I pull out the first bottle I come across.

Vodka.

Not even the good kind, but oh well, it'll have to do.

There is a soft ping behind me.

"What the—" Taking off the lid, I take a swig from the bottle and turn around. Nixon is crouching down. I watch in slow motion as he picks up the pill bottle Jade threw at me mere minutes ago and looks over it. He slowly lifts his gaze, those hard eyes meeting mine. "Pain meds? Why the fuck are you taking pain meds? And mixing them with alcohol? Are you fucking insane?"

My fingers tighten around the bottle as the anger boils inside me. "What I am, is in *pain.* I've been in fucking pain ever since the first injury," I yell, smashing the bottle against the counter. Nixon's eyes widen, surprise written all over his face. "Not like anybody else noticed," I laugh humorlessly.

"Prescott, I—"

"Save it," I snap, not in the mood to listen to his excuses or apologies. "I didn't do it for you. I didn't do it for the team. I did it for me." *I did it for Gabriel.* Just another secret. Just another lie. "I did it for me, so I could play this one last year." *So I could keep the promise I made to my brother*. But even that, I couldn't do right. "A lot of good that did us." I shake my head. I'm done with this, so fucking done. "So yeah, I might be insane, but I'm dealing in the best way I can. The only thing that kept me relatively sane just walked out that door, and she's not coming back."

You and me, Prescott? We're broken. Everybody is counting on me to be strong and to beat this thing, and I can't do that if your broken pieces are mixed with mine.

Tightening my grip on the bottle, I tilt my head back and pull a long swig. My eyes fall shut as the vodka burns its way down my throat.

She's not coming back.

"What happened, Prescott?" Nixon asks, his voice softer.

"She left, but maybe it's better that way."

You kill everyone you love.

I try to take another pull, but once again, Nixon grabs the bottle from me.

I lunge for the bottle, kicking it out of Nixon's hand. It shatters on the floor, the alcohol splattering everywhere.

"You can't drink anymore."

"Try and fucking stop me."

"You're insane."

"We've already established that. Go back to your perfect little wife and your perfect little world, Cole."

"Perfect?" Nixon hisses. "Nothing about my life is perfect."

"Try dealing with my demons for a day, and we'll see what you think." Grabbing a new bottle, I shove him out of my way. "You know where the door is. See yourself out."

With that, I go to my room, shutting the door firmly behind me.

JADE

"Jade, what are you doing?"

Brushing away the tears, I look up to find Nixon marching toward me.

"Is he okay?" I ask, wrapping my arms around myself as another shiver runs through me.

Nixon stops in his tracks and just stares at me like I grew another head. Maybe I have. "You're asking about him? After everything that has just happened?"

"Yes! Is he okay?"

I needed to know that he was fine. Or at least that he's going to be eventually.

This was the right thing to do.

It might not feel like it right now, but it will someday. I know it will.

I meant everything that I said to him. I knew it for a while now. We've been going back and forth ever since we met. And there were days when things between us were good, so damn good, but then something would happen that would trigger us, and things would turn bad really fast. It wasn't healthy, this thing between us.

Too broken.

That's what we are.

Too damn broken to be together.

To have any future.

"He was drinking when I left him. I tried stopping him, but..."

I close my eyes as more tears threaten to fall.

Dammit, Prescott.

"Did you know that he was using? I saw the pain meds in his living room."

My throat bobs as I swallow, but I force myself to nod. "I did." I brush the back of my hand over my cheek. "I saw him a few weeks back. It wasn't just pain meds, Nixon. He was using steroids too."

"Fuck, Jade! Why didn't you say something?"

"Because he promised! He promised he would stop."

And then he broke his promise.

"And look how good that turned out."

"Do you think I don't know that? Why do you think I left?"

I grab my suitcase, but the damn thing is too heavy. Or maybe I'm just too weak because I sway on my feet. I'd probably face plant if Nixon didn't put his hands on me to steady me.

"You're not okay. Sit down."

I don't try to fight him as he moves the suitcase to the floor, and I sit down, pulling the blanket around me.

"What are you doing, Jade? You should be in bed, resting. You just had chemo."

"I can't be here. I just..." I shake my head. "I can't be here. If I stay, I'll waver, and I can't do that. I can't be with Prescott when he's like this and, at the same time, fight my own battle, Nixon. I've been drowning for months now, and I fear that if I'm Prescott's lifeline, we'll both end up drowning instead. I have to go."

"Okay," Nixon nods. "Just let me get home and pack some shit, and we can..."

"No." I place my hand over his, stopping him. "You can't leave. You have classes. You have to keep up with conditioning, and you have all the pre-draft stuff to deal with. You have to be here."

"Jade. I'm not letting you..."

"I'm not letting *you*, Nixon," I snap, not in the mood to deal with this, too, on top of everything else. "I'm not letting you mess your life up now that you're so close to fulfilling your dreams. You have to stay here. I'll be fine back home."

"You're going through chemo; you can't be alone!"

"You can still drive me."

"So freaking generous of you. I mean it, Jade, you know how things get..."

"I know, Nix. I freaking know. It's my life! But I can't be here, and you have to stay here. We'll figure it out, find a schedule, just... Stay."

Nixon lets out a shaky breath, running his hand over his face. The bags under his eyes are deep, and some days, it feels like he has aged ten years in the last few months. "Okay. We'll figure it out."

Nixon starts to pull my suitcase toward the door, but I grab his hand and stop him.

"Nixon."

He looks over his shoulder, and he must see something on my face because he's already shaking his head. "Don't ask that of me."

"You're angry, and you have every right to be..."

"Damn right, I do! All Prescott's done this year is lie to me. Makes me wonder if anything he ever said was the truth."

"He's your friend."

"Friends don't lie to friends, Smalls."

"Neither does family, and yet I lied to you. I need you to do this for me. I need you to take care of him."

"Jade..." Nixon lets out a frustrated groan, but I can see him wavering.

"I love him, Nixon. I'm in *love* with him, and the thought of losing him..." I press my lips together to stop them from trembling. "I can't be here, but I can't leave him to fight his demons on his own, either. Help him."

My brother is quiet for what seems like forever. For a moment, I think he'll refuse me. I'm sure of it, really. We've both hurt Nixon so much in this past year.

"Fine. I'll do it. For you. I'll do anything for you, Smalls."

"Just..."

Nixon points his finger at me. "I will not promise *not* to punch him. That's where I draw the line. Take it or leave it."

"Fine."

I could take him broken and bruised, but I needed him to be alive.

Chapter 42

PRESCOTT

A loud *bang* startles me out of sleep. At first, I thought it was all in my head, a part of my dreams, my nightmares. Or maybe it's just the consequence of drinking after Jade left. Hell if I know. But then the curtains are pulled apart, and the bright light blinds me.

"What the—"

"Get your ass off the couch," Nixon growls.

"I'm not going anywhere."

"You either get your ass up, or I'll make you get it up. The choice is yours."

"You can sure as hell try." I start to turn around, but fingers dig into my shoulders, and I'm tugged back. The force of the pull has me falling over the edge of the couch and on the floor, pain shooting through my leg.

"*Fuck,*" I hiss, my hands going to my leg instantly.

"I warned you."

"Are you trying to fuck up my leg?"

"You did that all on your own. Now get your ass up and get to the shower. You reek of alcohol, and Dr. Snow will not appreciate it."

"I don't care if she'll appreciate it or not because I'm not going."

Nixon makes the sound of the buzzer going off. "Wrong again. She's expecting us in..." he glances down to his wrist, "forty minutes. She cleared her schedule because I took my sweet time in charming her, so you'll get up, shower, drink some goddammed coffee, and then we're going to see her so she can tell us how the fuck we can fix your leg so I can kick your ass for making my little sister cry. *Again.*"

You and me, Prescott? We're broken. Everybody is counting on me to be strong and to beat this thing, and I can't do that if your broken pieces are mixed with mine.

"There is no fixing it."

Not my leg.

Not my future.

And certainly not Jade and me.

I'm saying that I'm going home. I'm going home so I can heal, and for your sake, I pray that you can do the same.

There is no healing for me.

No forgiveness.

"We'll see about that." Nixon crosses his arms over his chest. "Are you getting up, or am I doing it for you?"

"It's useless."

"So is fighting it. Because I'm not giving up."

I hear the words he leaves unsaid. I'm not giving up. Not on your leg. Not on you.

"Fine." Groaning, I push to my feet. "Suit yourself."

If he doesn't want to give up, I'll show him just how hopeless it is so he can finally get the hell out of here and find somebody else who needs saving.

"Why the hell didn't you come here as soon as this happened?" Dr. Snow grumbles as she looks over the x-ray of my knee.

Nixon's eyes narrow in that annoying I-told-you-so way, but I just shrug. He was the one who wanted to come here, so he might as well deal with her.

But before he can say anything else, Snow waves her hand in dismissal. "Football players, of course, because you dumbasses think you're badass and can play through the pain as if injuries heal themselves." She shakes her head as if she wants to throw a few more choice words but is biting her tongue. "At least the season is over, but playing pro..."

"I'm not planning to enter the draft," I say, my voice hoarse from lack of use. "I'm going to me—"

My words trail off as I realize that, no, I'm not going to med school because I failed my MCATs—just another failure in a row. What's one more, right? I guess I should be used to it by now. I'm used to being the disappointment.

"Good, because looking at the x-ray and from what I've seen you've been using to deal with it," the note of disapproval is clear in her voice. "I really don't think you could play pro even if you wanted to."

"Well, I'm not playing pro, so can we go?"

"Not if you want to use that leg without a limp."

I open my mouth, but Dr. Snow raises her brows as if silently daring me to protest. I shut my mouth.

"Good. Let's get to work, shall we?"

"I don't need babysitting," I grumble an hour later as we get out of Dr. Snow's office. A shiver runs through me as the cold air slams into me. My clothes are damp with sweat and clinging to my skin.

"I drove you here."

"I can walk home," I grit, tugging the zipper of my jacket higher.

"After what Snow put you through, *I* can't walk home, and I'm not even the one who was on that table." The lights of his BMW flash as he unlocks the door. For a second, I weigh my options but then decide he's right. Might as well get home fast and avoid this fucking cold. I follow after him, sliding into the car, unable to hold a wince.

"Besides, I'm not taking you home."

"What?" I look at Nixon just as he turns on the car and pulls out of the parking lot. "Where the fuck are we going?"

My leg is aching from all the work Snow put me through, and I'm ready to get back to my place. Find something to dull the throbbing.

"You'll have to wait and see."

"I'm done playing your games, Nixon. Take me home."

"Nope." His fingers tighten around the steering wheel. The street lamp's light illuminates his stony face as he stares at the road ahead. "Jade loves you," he says softly, eyes firmly on the road. "God knows why she does, but she loves you."

"She was the one who walked away," I say, my fingers curling around the door handle. I'm half tempted to open the door and jump out the first chance I get. Anything to avoid this conversation.

What's the point, really?

"Because she can't deal with your self-destruction, not when she's fighting cancer. Not when she herself is toeing the line."

The haunted look I've seen in those blue eyes so many times in the last few weeks flashes in my mind. Nixon runs his fingers through his hair.

"You don't know this, but she was so close to breaking over winter break. We came home from the chemo, and she insisted

I should go to a meeting with some agent that was in town, so I went. I was away for one hour, just one hour before my phone rang, and I knew immediately something was wrong. She was broken, Prescott. Completely and utterly broken. I could hear it in her voice, so I made her stay on the line while I rushed back home. It was only a few minutes, but to me, it felt like hours, and when I got there..." He shakes his head as if he can still see the images in his head. "The lamp was broken, shattered pieces scattered on the floor, and she must have stepped on them as she was going to the bathroom because there was blood on the floor. And once I stepped into the bathroom, it was like being thrown back in time. She was sitting on the floor, her legs pulled to her chest, completely wet, and water spilled on the tiles around her. She never told me what exactly happened in that room while I was gone, but I could piece it together because this wasn't the first time she's done something similar, and I almost missed it. *Twice* now. First after Mom's funeral, and now again." His voice is stony as he tells me, each word landing like a blow. "I'll never forget the fear of seeing her in there, the fear of seeing her struggle for breath once I pulled her out. That's when I finally looked at her and saw it—the darkness. I never knew how long I was blind to it, blind to her silent suffering, and I swore I'll never do it again. And once again, I almost missed it. Once again, I almost failed her. Thankfully, this time she was stronger, and she reached out to me for help." He glances at me for a split second, jaw-hardening. "And she's not the only person I failed. I've been so focused on Yasmin, Jade and the cancer, and football, that I haven't seen you struggling."

I close my eyes, my chest feeling tight at the revelation.

Jade in the bathroom.

Jade trying...

I shake my head, pushing the thoughts away.

She didn't go through with it. She was alive and well, and that was the only thing that mattered.

"I didn't want you to see the signs. I didn't want anybody to see them."

"Neither does she. But I know her, and I know *you* better. I should have seen them anyway. I should have done something to help, and for that, I'm sorry."

"There was nothing that you could have done. The only other option was for me not to play, and I couldn't risk it. Not when I had a pro—" I bite the inside of my cheek, stopping the words from coming out.

"A what?"

I shake my head. "It doesn't matter. What's done is done."

It's true. Gabriel is gone, has been gone for years, and the only thing I promised him I'd do, I messed up in the end.

"But it's not done, is it? Your leg's hurt. You're drinking, and not even just that, you're mixing it with pain pills. You and Jade are broken up... You need *help*, Prescott. And I want to help you."

I frown at the building as he pulls into the parking lot, unease creeping up my spine. "What the hell's this? Why are we at church?"

Neither of us was religious, and I didn't see how talking to a priest would help with any of my problems.

"Because you need help, and I don't know how to help you besides bringing you here. I asked around, and they have a NA meeting, I fi—"

I turn toward him, the belt digging into my chest. "You did *what*? I'm not a fucking junkie."

"I didn't say you were, but I've seen the pills, Prescott. The drinking and Jade told me about the steroids too. Looking back, I don't know how I missed it for the whole season."

"So what? A guy uses some pain pills to manage the pain,

and he's instantly a junkie?! What the fuck, dude?" I yell, my brain reeling. "Did you tell anybody else? Does the team know? Coach?"

Nixon just watches me quietly, and I want to put my hands on his shoulder and shake some sense into him.

"Nobody knows. And even if they did, you think you're the only guy with the same problem? We've all tried to manage the pain at one point or another."

"Like you know anything about managing the pain. The golden boy, with the golden hand, destined for greatness," I mock. "Not all of us are like you, Nixon. Not all of us are perfect like you."

Unbuckling the seatbelt, I shove open the door and scramble out. "I don't want or need your fucking help. I'm fine."

"Prescott..."

Not in the mood to listen any longer, I shut the door and storm off. My fingers are clenched by my sides. I don't know where I'm going. I just need to get out of there as far and as fast as I can.

"Son?" I turn around to find an older guy watching me from the bench outside. Why anybody would be sitting out in this cold, I have no idea. His dark eyes assess me silently. "Are you alright?"

I let out a strangled laugh, "Great. I'm just great."

He opens his mouth, but before he can say another word, I turn around and walk away.

Chapter 43

JADE

"How have you been doing, Jade?"

I look up at the ceiling, tugging my sweater over my icy fingers as I inhale the sweet rose scent that's always present in the room. Probably from the candle burning in the corner of Dr. Hale's desk.

"Sometimes you sound like a broken record, you know?" I glance at the young woman. Dr. Hale is in her early thirties; her blonde hair is pulled into a braid that falls over one of her shoulders as she observes me from her desk. She was the psychiatrist I went to after Mom died. I was going for about a year after my "incident," but then I stopped, until now.

"You know you don't have to lay there, right? The couch is more for show than anything else."

"A broken record." This isn't the first time we've had this very same conversation, nor will it be the last, I'm afraid. "I like the couch. It's really cushy."

"You need me to bring you a blanket?" Dr. Hale asks, those astute eyes glancing at my fingers before they return back to me. No pity there, just straight facts.

"Nah, I'm good. On the other hand, my circulation is for shit, and I'm constantly cold."

Dr. Hale nods her head, scribbling something into her notebook. "So, how is chemo going? You're what, halfway through?"

"Yeah." It was still hard to grasp that I'd already done three cycles. "The last time I was in the hospital, they did some scans."

"What did your doctor say?"

"The tumor is shrinking, but it's still there."

"That's a good thing."

"I guess so."

I would have much preferred that it was already gone, but I'll take any small victory that I can get.

"You should celebrate thi—"

"Prescott and I broke up," I blurt out before she can give me more of her positive mumbo-jumbo.

Dr. Hale quirks her brow at me. "Oh?"

"For good this time," I whisper. Saying the words out loud breaks something inside me even further, and that's saying something considering I didn't think there were any more pieces left of me to break.

"What happened?"

I bite my lower lip, chewing on the plump flesh as I think over my words. "I'm not the only one who's been dealing with a lot."

Then I tell her everything that has happened since the school year started. I tell her about hooking up and our crazy connection, but also about Prescott's and my demons. We barely start dissecting pieces of it when my hour is up, and we agree to pick this conversation up in a couple of days during my next appointment.

I figured I might as well focus on therapy since I didn't have much else to do except go to that one class a week. And chemo. Can't forget about that one.

My phone vibrates just as I start my SUV and pull out of the parking lot. A small smile appears on my lips when I see the name on the screen, and I press the answer button.

"Hey, Gracie."

"Hey, how are you doing?"

I let out a soft chuckle. "You know you sound just like my shrink, right?"

There is a moment of silence as my friend mulls over my words. "That doesn't sound like a compliment."

"Good, 'cause it's not."

"So the whole shrink thing isn't going well, I take it?"

"It's going." I let out a sigh. "I can't say I'm a fan, but I know I need this. Plus, Dr. Hale is nice enough when she's not busting my balls, so there is that. What's up with you?"

"Just going to grab coffee between classes, and I missed you, so I decided to check in. I hate that you're all alone out there."

"Nixon is here every day, so I'm hardly alone."

No matter how many times I told my brother that he didn't need to worry about me, he didn't want to listen. He was here most days, and if he wasn't, Yasmin, or hell, even Callie, came to check in on me. Make sure I'm still alive.

"I know, but still, your place is here."

"You know I can't be there, not when..."

Not when I'd be so tempted to give in to Prescott. One glance at him. One pleading look. One touch. And my resolve would fall down like a tower of cards.

I had to do this.

I had to be strong.

For both of us.

"I know. Doesn't mean I miss you any less."

"I miss you too. Maybe you should come here one day, and we can have a sleepover or something."

"Sounds like a plan. Are you still coming to watch Rei compete at the Winter Games? Everybody will be here."

The hairs at the back of my neck rise. "Everybody?"

"Well, everybody but *him*. Please say you'll at least think about it."

"I'm going to think about it," I say, pulling into the driveway just as there is a familiar *chime* in the background. "Say hi to Yas for me and have one of those delicious coffees of hers."

"I feel like you're more upset about not having coffee than about not seeing your friends."

"Of course not."

"Mhmm... Talk to you later?"

"Sure."

"Think about what I said."

I roll my eyes. "I already said I will."

So far, I've been good at avoiding Prescott. It helped that I wasn't on campus often and that the only class I took was on the other side, where I could never stumble upon him by accident.

I didn't even ask Nixon what was going on with him.

Not knowing was killing me, but I didn't ask.

Going back to the apartment?

It felt too much like playing with fire, and I wasn't sure if I was ready to take the burn.

Chapter 44

PRESCOTT

"Dude, what the hell is this?" Spencer is panting as he leans his palms against the counter, glaring at me.

He'd been out of town the last few days for an away game, but I guess he came back home.

"A party!" I yell back. Lifting my hand in the air, I bring the bottle I've been holding to my mouth and take a long gulp.

"I can see that. Why is there a Wednesday night party with half the campus at our place? The old lady who lives on the first floor glared at me so hard I thought she'd kill me."

"She needs to chill. It's fun."

"Apparently, she isn't having fun because she threatened to call the cops if we don't stop this."

"She can damn well try."

With another pull from the bottle, I move through the crowd to the living room. The alcohol dulled some of the pain Dr. Snow put me through earlier, but not nearly enough.

When will the fucking pain finally stop?

"Hey, handsome," a redhead smiles at me as she moves closer. She's wearing a skin-tight dress, her hair is messy, and her makeup is slightly smudged, but it doesn't make her look any less hot. On the contrary, "Mind sharing that with me?" she tips her chin at the bottle in my hand. "The only thing I managed to find is a beer keg."

"What's wrong with beer?"

"Except that it tastes like piss?"

I guess there is that.

Silently, I offer her a bottle. Her fingers brush against mine as she takes it from me, those dark eyes holding mine as she brings it to her lips and downs a healthy swig.

"Much be—"

Her words are cut off when somebody pushes her from the back, making her stumble into me. Her body crashes into mine, and I grab her arms to steady her.

"Oops." She lets out a chuckle and looks up at me. Her eyes turn dark as her teeth graze over her lower lip. "I think I spilled some on you. Sorry about that."

"It's fine," I rasp, my fingers tightening around her.

We just continue staring at one another. My heart starts thumping faster, the furious beat echoing in my eardrums and making all the other noises disappear.

It would be so easy.

So easy to lean in and kiss her.

So easy to lose myself in her and forget, even if for just a moment, about the shitty day—*shitty few months*—I've had.

She wants it, too.

It's written all over her face.

But just as she leans in, my body revolts.

Wrong, wrong, wrong.

Wrong hair color.

Wrong eyes.

Wrong smell.

Wrong woman.

All the alcohol that I've put in myself today rolls in my stomach, threatening to make a reappearance.

"Shit."

Shoving her out of my way, I start for the bathroom, but I trip over something, and my leg twists slightly. The pain shoots through my knee as I fall to the ground.

Fuck.

Fuck, fuck, fuck.

The pain is unbearable, to the point that it takes me a moment to realize somebody cut off the music.

"The party is done." Spencer's loud shout is accompanied by groans in protest from the partygoers. "I know, boo-hoo. You know where the door is, don't let it kick you in the ass on your way out."

People start shuffling around me to the door. Some give me curious glances, but I ignore them as I push to my feet. My leg is useless, so I hold onto the wall as I limp my way into the bathroom.

Sweat coats my body as I get there, the bright light blinding me as I search the cabinets for any kind of pain relief.

"Where the fuck are the stupid pain meds?" I mutter, pulling open one of the cabinets, my eyes landing on a bottle. It's not the good stuff, but it'll have to do.

Anything will do at this point.

My hands are shaking as I try to open the pill bottle. It falls from my hand, a few pills scattering into the sink.

"*Fuck,*" I mutter as my vision turns spotty.

I grip the edge of the sink, trying to steady my hands, trying to steady myself. I gulp in a few breaths, willing my heart to slow down.

What the fuck am I doing?

My knuckles are white as I squeeze the sink, trying to stay upright as my body sways on the balls of my feet.

Just what the fuck am I doing?

I look up, forcing myself to face my reflection in the mirror. I'm a sweaty mess. My hair is disheveled, my beard long and unkept, my pupils dilated, and my eyes are bloodshot with dark circles so big they almost look like bruises under my eyes.

Jade's face flashes in my mind. The pain in her eyes as she found the pills. No disappointment. No anger or outrage. Just pure pain.

I'd done that.

The door creaks open, the sound piercing now that the music is turned off. I look up to find Nixon and Spencer slipping inside. I'm not sure when Nixon got here or who called him because I sure as hell hadn't, but he's here.

I expect him to lunge at me. To punch me for hurting his sister. I'd welcome it even, but he just stands there, watching, waiting.

I lift my shaky hand and rub at my face.

She was right.

I'm broken.

No, not just broken.

A freaking addict.

That's what I am.

An addict.

It's not even strange she left.

Swallowing the lump in my throat, I force myself to look at my best friend. Really look at him. And that's when I see it.

He's pissed at me, all right, but he's still here. Despite everything I've done, he's still here. And so is Spencer.

Letting go, I slump onto the closed toilet seat. I bury my head into my palms as the weight of realization settles on me.

Then I croak out the words I never thought I'd have to say: "I need help."

Chapter 45

PRESCOTT

"We're here," Nixon's quiet voice breaks me out of my thoughts. I blink and look up, realizing that he's right. We're here. Back at that church he took me to a few weeks ago—a meeting place for narcotics anonymous.

I wanted to go that same day, but the meeting wasn't for two more days. A part of me wondered if I'd make it that long. If I wouldn't change my mind.

Nixon and Spencer didn't let me, though. They took me to the ER, where they did an x-ray of my leg and put me back in a brace until an orthopedic surgeon could look at it because my ACL tore once again. Then they stood by as I came home, still half-drunk, and watched me toss every single pill in our apartment down the drain before the alcohol followed. Bottle after bottle, until there was nothing left.

The next morning, sober and hungover, I was cursing at myself.

In the last couple of days, I've come to realize sobriety is a weird thing. I didn't even realize how bad things had become. My hands were shaking, my feet were constantly bouncing, and

I was sweating even while doing small things. The pain feels more intense too.

"If that isn't some poetic bullshit, I don't know what is," I scoff, running my fingers through my hair. "I'm not even religious."

From the corner of my eye, I can see Nixon turn to face me. "I thought you wanted to come here."

"I did," I say, running my fingers through my hair and correcting: "I do. Doesn't mean God doesn't have a wicked sense of humor."

Nixon is quiet for a moment. "You don't have to do this, you know."

I chuckle, but the sound is bitter. "I have to do this."

Of course, I have to do this.

"For her."

Nixon nods absentmindedly. "But not before you're ready. First and foremost, you have to do this for yourself. That's the only way it'll work."

I give him a side glance. "Did you read some motivational bullshit, Nix?"

Nixon glares at me. "I just want what's best for you."

"I know."

And I do. That's the only thing my friends have ever wanted for me.

The silence stretches between us as we just stare out the windshield.

"I'll go out," I clear my throat. "In a little bit."

Nixon shrugs. "I don't have anywhere better to be."

It's bullshit, and we both know it. He has a wife waiting for him at home. He has a future he has to prepare for—a sick sister.

I shake my head, not allowing myself to go down that road.

"I have a brother." The words are out before I can second-guess them. "I *had* a brother. He died when we were thirteen." My throat bobs as I swallow, my palms turning sweaty. "Leukemia."

"Shit, Prescott, why didn't you say something?"

"I didn't want you to know. Nobody knows," I whisper, my eyes still glued to the church. "Well, except Jade. Talking about Gabriel, about what we'd gone through, has never come easy. The first time he got sick, we were nine. He beat it, but on his three-year check-up, we found out the cancer was back, and it had metastasized. There was nothing they could have done for him. Back home, it was the only thing people talked about. I was the guy whose brother had cancer. The guy whose brother died. I didn't want to be that guy here too, so I kept quiet."

"That's why Jade..." He shakes his head. "I guess some things now make more sense."

"It's not an excuse by any means. It's just... What happened to Gabriel shaped me. We had so many plans, and when he died... I couldn't let it all disappear. He died, but I could still make those things happen. For him."

"So..."

"The football. Gabriel loved football. He lived for it. And he was good. So damn good. It was always his dream to play pro, and I'm sure he'd have succeeded if only he had more time. He wanted us to play together, win it all."

"That's why you worked so hard after the injury?"

I nod my head. "Going pro was never my thing. Since the moment he got sick, I knew I wanted to help kids like him one day, but I could help the Ravens go all the way. That was my promise to him. And I broke it."

"You didn't break anything. You worked your ass off, but it wasn't enough. That's plain football for you. Sometimes no matter how much you work, luck's just not on your side."

"Rationally, I know that, but..."

"There are no buts, Prescott. It's just the way it is. Besides, would he want that, though? I'm not saying to forget him, but would he really want you to live your life for him?"

"If he knew what happened, he would have kicked my ass," I let out a soft chuckle. "I think I'm ready to go inside now."

"Do you want me to go in with you?"

Like I'm a fucking baby? Yeah, right.

"I'm sure you have better things to do. Yasmin is probably waiting for you and Jade..."

Just saying her name has a pang of guilt stabbing me in the chest. God, I missed her. I missed her so damn much, and I hated myself for putting us in this position in the first place.

"You're my best friend, Prescott. Besides, Yasmin and Jade are fine on their own for a little while. They're probably throwing a party right about now to celebrate that I left them in peace for longer than five minutes."

My throat bobs as I swallow. "How's she doing?" I finally ask the question that I've been dying to ask since I saw him.

"She's doing better. Going to therapy and chemo. She's still in pain, not that she's showing it. Stubborn woman. I seriously don't know how I ended up surrounded by them."

I chuckle because I can see Jade giving Nixon shit for fussing over her.

"That's good. She's halfway through."

Although I say it as a statement, Nixon nods his head.

"Three more to go." He glances at me. "The scan isn't completely clean, but she's getting there."

Which means the tumor is shrinking.

Good. I close my eyes, letting out a shaky breath. *That's good.*

I wrap my fingers around the door handle. "If something were to happen to her..."

"I know." Nixon tilts his chin toward the church. "Go inside. I'll wait here until you're done."

I push open the door and grab my crutches, but I don't get out. "Or you could come with me?"

The corner of Nixon's lips tilts upward. "You know it."

Chapter 46

JADE

"I'll see you all in a week."

Grabbing my things, I slide them into my bag and throw it over my shoulder. I pull out my phone as I make my way out of the classroom, ready to text Grace to let her know I'm done.

I've postponed coming back for as long as I could. Grace and Penny came to my house, where the three of us watched the team part of the figure skating competition, which Rei smashed, and then I watched the short program on my own. But Grace was not budging when it came to the long program, so here I was.

Me: Done with class. Meet in CIU?

"Jade?" I turn around to look at Professor Reyes watching me. "Can I talk to you for a moment?"

I look around, noticing the classroom has mostly emptied out already.

"Sure, is everything okay?"

"Do you mind coming to my office?"

Office? Why would she need me to go to her office?

"Yeah, sure."

Is this about missing classes? The last couple of sessions have been really hard, and it has taken me days to even get out of bed to the point Nixon stayed with me and drove to classes from our childhood home. I felt bad for him, but he reassured me it wasn't an issue.

But she knows about my chemo, and I've made sure she understood I might be missing some classes because of it.

Mind still reeling from all the possibilities, I follow her as she makes her way into her office. The room is small, with a desk dominating the space for the most part. And photos. Her walls are filled with different photos, most of them black and white, striking in their simplicity.

She goes behind her desk and signals toward the chair. "Take your seat. I wanted to talk to you, but you're a hard woman to find."

"Is this about the classes?" My brows pull together as I hurry up to add: "I know I haven't really been present, but you know..."

"Relax, this isn't about the classes."

"Oh..." I let out a breath I hadn't even realized I'd been holding. "Then what's going on?"

A small smile tugs at the corner of her mouth. "Do you remember the photos you submitted last semester?"

How could I forget? It was the most difficult thing I've ever done. The most vulnerable I've ever felt.

"Yes. Vicky won the competition, right?"

I was happy for her. Vicky was a talented photographer, and her stuff was good. She deserved it.

"Yes, she did. Her work fit the exhibition the best. But I recently had lunch with Angie, my gallery owner friend, and she brought up your photos."

My throat tightens at her words. "Oh?"

"I think the words *stunning* and *couldn't get them out of her mind* were the ones she used when we talked about them." Professor Reyes places her hands on the table and clasps them together. "She wants them."

"What?" I shake my head, unsure if I heard her correctly. She wants them? As in... buy them? "I'm not sure I'm following."

Professor Reyes smiles at me. "She wants to do an exhibition of your work. Just your work, Jade."

"Sorry," I say as I slide into the seat opposite Grace's. "Professor Reyes wanted to talk to me after class."

Grace's eyes narrow in suspicion. "She didn't bitch about you missing classes because if she did, I'll go right there and show he—"

"No, she didn't," I say quickly before Grace really gets into it. "She wants my photos. Well, her friend, the gallery owner, wants my photos."

I still couldn't believe it.

My photos.

In a gallery.

"Of course they want your photos." Grace waves me off like it's a given. She grabs her cup, but her hand stops halfway to her mouth. "Wait, what photos?"

"The self-portrait."

Her eyes turn into saucers, her mouth falling open. "*Those* photos?"

"I know."

"Even I haven't seen them, and they want to put them in the gallery?"

"*I know.*"

Nobody has seen the photos. Well, except Professor Reyes and her friend. Those photos weren't for anybody else but me.

Or so I thought, but now...

"Did you agree?"

I bite my lip and shake my head no.

"What? Are you crazy? This is an opportunity of a lifetime!"

"I know," I repeat, letting out a sigh.

It was crazy. This kind of opportunity didn't present itself on any given day. Photographers had to work for years, and even then, some of them never saw their photos hanging on the gallery walls. Not to accept this would be career suicide, but accepting it...

"If it were any other work, I wouldn't think twice about it, but it's me, Grace. It's me at my most vulnerable. To see those photos exposed like that, let people see them. See *me*." I shake my head. "I don't think I can do it."

Grace's hand covers mine. "I know. It's okay if you don't want to do it. If it's too soon. Too raw."

"Professor Reyes told me I could think about it, but I have to let her know soon. The current exhibition is coming to an end, and she wants to place my photos next."

"So you didn't tell her no," Grace states.

"I didn't tell her no."

Pulling my hand back, I grab my cup and take a sip of the coffee.

Saying no was a gut reaction. Professor Reyes knew it too, so she stopped me before I could even open my mouth, telling me I should take some time, and then she proceeded to persuade me, pointing out how my photos could be useful to other people going through something similar.

I knew she was right.

But that didn't mean I was ready.

Thankfully Grace lets the topic drop and changes the subject. "You look better."

"It's the wig. I guess it makes me seem... normal?"

"Nah, that's not it." She leans in her chair, her eyes taking me in. "You seem more relaxed, I guess. More like you."

I twist the strand of my hair around my finger. Today I've settled on a shoulder-length, dark purple wig. It's cute. I could see the point in what Grace told me a few weeks back, although I don't think I'd ever consider coloring it that way. Too much work.

"My next session isn't until tomorrow afternoon, so I finally feel half-human."

The last round of chemo was harsh. I was in bed for close to a week, and those first few days were so bad that I had to throw up in a bucket. My body was so weak I could barely stand on my feet, and being cold constantly didn't help. I tug the sleeves of my sweater over my fingers. Even now, my hands were still cold. I've read somewhere that, for some people, it never goes away, and just the idea of it had a shudder running through me. So like all the other things I didn't want to deal with, I pushed it to the back of my mind.

"Right," Grace nods, her fingers curling around the cup. "How much longer?"

"Two more rounds."

Her eyes widen in surprise. "And that's it?"

"Then that's it," I whisper.

"It feels so... *fast*."

It was hard to believe. When this whole thing started a few months back, it felt never-ending. It still does. The first few days after the chemo, when the pain is so strong, I'd rather die than deal with any of it for a second longer. But I push through. One foot in front of the other. One second, minute, hour, and day at a time.

Her eyes meet mine, and she gives me an apologetic smile. "I'm sorry. I know for you it certainly wasn't fast, but..."

"Some days, it feels fast, others slow," I shrug. "It's just different now, that's it."

"Then what? When will you know if it worked?"

"After the last round, we'll do some tests. If they're good, I'll go back every six months for check-ups, if not, we'll have to continue with the treatment."

Grace's hand covers mine over the table. "It's going to be okay."

"Well, let's hope so. Anyhow..." I smile, changing the subject. "I'm excited for Rei. Did you get a chance to chat with her?"

It was mind-blowing thinking how much Rei's accomplished in the last few years and now the Winter Games. The crown of her career. The team won a silver medal, and she smashed her short program, and now it was the hardest part, the long program and landing the quad Axel. The jump that was never performed in a competition before and never successfully landed, and she's been working on it for the past year. 'Cause, of course, she couldn't settle for simply winning.

"We have to throw her a party when she returns."

"Zane and I are already on it. He mentioned he wanted to do something special but was worried since he's over there with her, so I suggested I'd deal with the logistics as long as he takes care of her."

I snort. "As if that was ever in question."

The guy was so hopelessly in love with her it was hard to watch. But Rei definitely couldn't have picked a better guy for herself. Zane was strong and reliable, and he had zero issues standing behind her and letting her do her thing as he cheered her on from the sidelines.

An image of Prescott doing just that as I was going through chemo flashes in my mind.

You're not going there, I chastise myself. I was doing better, but being back on campus is messing with my head. The notion that I could see him walking around both thrilled and terrified me.

I haven't seen or heard from Prescott in weeks. Not since the incident in his apartment. Not since I walked out on him. Sometimes I still woke up to him begging me to stay. But I couldn't. I just couldn't.

"True. He's just—"

"Ladies."

The skin at the nape of my neck prickles at the sound of the familiar voice, my heart stopping in dread, or maybe anticipation? Hell if I know.

Grace looks over my shoulder and smiles softly. "Spencer. How are you doing?"

Tentatively, I glance over my shoulder, and sure enough, Spencer is standing there. Alone.

My heart plummets down in disappointment.

There is nothing to be disappointed about, I remind myself. *You don't want to see him.*

"Good. Busy. The team has to pick up the slack since Zane decided to ditch us at the very last minute."

"I mean, would you decline the opportunity to watch the Winter Games live?"

"Hell no. That's why I'm pissed." He shakes his head. "Lucky bastard."

Then his eyes drop to me, surprise flashing in his irises. "Hey there, gorgeous." He flashes me that panty-melting smile of his as he runs his fingers through his hair. "I almost didn't recognize you with that hair."

"Now I know you're lying."

"Me?" He places his hand over his chest dramatically. "Never."

"Yeah, right."

He tips his chin at me. "I didn't realize you were back on campus."

"Just for a few days."

I couldn't stay here. Not knowing *he* could be just around the corner. I couldn't deal with it. Always wondering when the next time I would see him would be.

The next time I'll give in.

"I managed to convince her we should watch Rei compete together," Grace chimes in. "But I'm working on getting her to stay. I worry about her when she's all alone back home."

"*She* is here," I say, giving Grace a pointed look. "And I'm not alone. There is always somebody with me just after the chemo."

"How is that going?" Spencer asks, his voice turning gentler. As if I might break if he probes too much. I hate it. I hate feeling like people have to walk on eggshells around me.

"Good," I force out a smile. "Just a little bit more."

Just a little bit more, and things will go back to normal.

Although what is normal these days?

"That's good to hear, Jade." Spencer gives my shoulder a squeeze just as somebody calls out his name.

My body freezes for a moment until I see that, by the looks of it, it's just some guys from the hockey team.

"In a minute," he yells, returning his attention to us. "When's the game starting?"

"It's a competition, and three in the morning."

"Okay, thanks. I'll try to catch it if I can. I'll see you ladies around?"

"Sure thing."

His gaze lingers on me for a moment longer. "It was good seeing you."

With that, he's gone, and I finally let out a shaky breath.

"You okay?" Grace asks softly.

"Yeah. I'm fine."

She opens her mouth to protest, most likely, but I stop her. "So, what's the plan for tonight?"

Chapter 47

JADE

Waking up just shy of three in the morning? Not my best decision. We didn't plan to fall asleep, but at some point during the Twilight marathon, we did just that. Well, *I* fell asleep, but apparently, Penelope and Grace didn't have a problem staying awake. But I guess, whether I want to admit it or not, my body is still healing.

I bury my face in the mug of freshly brewed coffee, willing the smell of caffeine to wake me up when there is a knock on the door.

"Who else is coming?" I call out to Grace, who went to get something in her room.

"Probably Mason. Can you open it?"

"Sure thing."

Mug still clutched in my hand, I make my way to the front door and pull it open, only to come to a stop.

"Spence—" my words die down when I look over his shoulder, and my eyes meet that familiar dark gaze. It's like all the air has been sucked out of my lungs.

A month.

It's been almost a month since I've last laid eyes on Prescott.

He's here.

At my front door.

He's here. He's here. He's here.

My fingers clench around the doorknob to the point of pain as I just stare at him. I'm not sure who's more surprised, him or me. Because the look of shock on his face? It's the real deal.

"W-what..." My voice breaks, so I clear my throat before trying again. "What are you doing here?"

"Well..." Spencer scratches the back of his head uncomfortably. "I got up to watch Rei, but you know how our TV can get. Of course, today the signal decided to be shitty as fuck, so I figured I might come here since I'm up and all."

"Right." I bite the inside of my cheek, my eyes glancing toward Prescott, who's still watching me, before I quickly look away.

His eyes give the impression they see everything, too unyielding, too intense... Just too much.

"He was up, so..." Spencer explains.

At three in the morning?

My gaze snaps up to his, and I give myself time to actually take him in. He seems to be doing better. His beard is trimmed to a scruff, and he must have had a haircut recently because his hair isn't all over the place like it used to be. The circles are still under his eyes, but they're no longer deep, dark smudges, and his cheeks aren't as hollow as they were the last time I saw him. But maybe the biggest difference is in his eyes. That glazed, haunted expression? It's gone. Not completely, I don't think people like us can ever completely chase away the demons haunting us, but they're dancing around the edges, present but under control.

I'm about to look away when I see them—the crutches. I suck in a sharp breath, meeting his gaze. "What happened?"

"An accident. I tore my ACL again, but it's healing." He

shifts his weight as if he's uncomfortable under my gaze. "If you want me to leave..."

"I... No." I shake my head. "Of course not."

Of course not? What the hell, Jade?

You need him to go. You need him...

As if he can read the panic on my face, Prescott looks at me. "It's okay if you want me to leave."

"No," I repeat, this time slower. "Really. It's fine. We have the same friends." *Same friends, right*? I nod. "Besides, this isn't about you or me. It's about Rei."

"It's starting!" Penny yells from the living room.

I move to the side, letting them pass. Spencer makes another attempt at an apologetic smile, but I'm not buying it. He knew I'd be here. He knew Prescott and I had broken up. Yet still, he invited him here?

Prescott steps closer, close enough that his tall frame enters my personal space, a wisp of shampoo, cologne, and something that's just plain Prescott washes over me. Keeping my eyes level with his chest, I inhale deeply, memorizing that fragrance, that familiar ache squeezing my heart.

Damn, I missed it.

I missed *him*.

"I mean it, Jade, if you'd rather..."

"Just get inside, Wentworth," I say, my fingers digging into the doorknob to stop myself from doing something stupid. Something like reaching for him, burying myself into his side, and never letting go. "I'm not missing Rei's performance, so either you get in, or you go home."

"We're back to Wentworth, huh?"

A few heartbeats pass as we just stare at one another. Half of me wants him to go so I can finally breathe easier, but the other half? It wants to dig my fingers into him and never let him walk away.

Will this ever get easier? Being around him? Will it ever feel like I'm not drowning in him?

"I'm here. I was just—" Grace's words die when she steps into the hallway and notices Prescott and me standing together. "What's going on here?" Her gaze shifts to Prescott, eyes narrowing. "What are *you* doing here?"

"I'll just..."

"He came with Spencer. Their TV isn't working," I explain. "I told him to stay. Now, *if* he would get his ass inside, I can finally watch Rei skate." I quirk my brow at him, putting all I have left of the bravado into that one movement.

I gave him an in—God knows why, but I did—now it was up to him to take it.

Finally, after what feels like forever, Prescott nods. He steps the rest of the way inside, and I close the door. My eyes fall shut as I take a moment to collect myself. When I turn around, I find Grace watching me with worried eyes, but I look away, my fingers curling around the cup in my hand. Coffee, right.

"I'm going to grab a fresh mug," I say to no one in particular as I walk back into the main area, going straight for the sink and spilling cold coffee down the drain before putting my mug under the machine for a fresh cup.

Penny and Spencer are chatting as the skaters warm up on the ice. Prescott appears in the doorway, looking around as if he's expecting to be thrown out any second now, and behind him are Grace and Mason.

"You guys want anything to drink?" I ask, needing to do something before I go crazy.

"You have Coke?" Spencer asks, and others throw in their drink orders. Grace grabs them as I pull them out and distributes them. Until there's only one person left.

He's sitting on the couch talking with Mason. He must feel my gaze because he looks up, those dark eyes meeting mine.

"What about you?"

"Coffee's fine."

The coffee machine beeps. "Okay. Coffee."

I can do coffee.

Coffee is easy.

I turn my back to them, pulling out my mug and placing a fresh one. *You can do this. He's just sitting here. It's not like it's a big deal. You've done this a thousand times before and today isn't any different.*

Grabbing two mugs, I turn around. Everybody has already taken a seat, leaving only one place open, the armchair, which is seated right next to...

"Of course," I mutter to myself as I make my way to the chair.

"Here you go," I say, handing Prescott his coffee before curling into my seat. The first girl is already out on the ice.

"What are they doing again?" Mason asks. His arm is thrown over the back of the couch, fingers skimming absent-mindedly over Grace's naked shoulder.

"This is the long program," Grace explains, her eyes still on the screen. "Basically, every girl will get out on the ice and has a little over four minutes to perform her program in front of the judges."

"That's it?" Prescott asks. "How do you know who wins then?"

Tingles run down my neck at the sound of his soft, gravelly voice.

I turn to him, only to find him already watching me. My heart does a little leap, and my tummy clenches at the heat in his gaze. "There is a point system." My words come out tight, so I clear my throat before continuing. "Each element wins her points, and based on the execution, the judges will give her a certain number of them. The points from the short program and long program will give her a total score that will determine her overall ranking."

The understanding flashes in his eyes like I knew it would. I shift in my seat, my hand bumping against his, and even that small touch feels like I've been burned.

"Sorry," he whispers.

"It's fine."

"It's crazy when you think about it," Spencer leans forward, rubbing at Henry's fur. "We're sitting here, and she's out there competing in the most prestigious sporting event there is."

"Maybe you'll be there one day," Grace says. "They do have hockey, you know."

"Yeah, maybe."

We continue chatting as the girls perform their programs one by one until there is only Rei left.

I tug my sweater over my palms, too nervous to stop fidgeting. "C'mon, Rei," I whisper as I watch her skate over the ice, shaking her limbs to warm up.

"What did she say? Is she doing a quad Axel?" Spencer asks, leaning his elbows against his knees.

"She damn well is going to try it," Grace whispers.

"Quad Axel?"

"It's one of the most difficult jumps, right?" Penny asks. "I remember Rei talking about practicing it."

"It is. She's been working on it for over a year now. Four and a half rotations in the air." I shake my head. I've seen Rei attempt it a few times. I've seen her fall time and time again. I've seen the beating her body took, the bruises. "It's a jump that has never been landed in a competition. Hell, I'm not even sure if any of the girls have ever even attempted it."

Mason's brows raise. "It's that hard?"

"It's that hard," I whisper just as the camera lands on Rei's serious face. Sometimes it is hard to connect the person we see on TV with our friend.

"She landed it a few times in practice, but she herself admitted it was a frivolous jump. Too hard to control."

"And yet she's trying it? What if she gets hurt?" Mason asks.

The familiar music starts, so I keep my eyes on the screen. "But what if she lands it? We can avoid being hurt all we want, but there are no guarantees in life. The only thing you'll miss out on is life and all the great things that could happen."

We watch Rei skate the beginning of her routine, her body one with the beat of the song.

"Here it goes," the commentator says just as Rei leaps off the ice.

All the air is sucked from the room as we silently watch her spin in the air. She's so fast I don't know how anybody can count the rotations.

C'mon, Rei. You can do it.

Fingers wrap around mine. Startled, I look down only to realize my hand is clasped in Prescott's. Or is his in mine? My head snaps up to find him watching me, our fingers still interlocked. His hand is warm, reassuring, and so damn familiar.

The TV and room erupt into cheers. I shift my attention back at the screen just as the camera continues following Rei's skate across the ice. You can see the tears shining in her eyes, but she flashes a blinding smile as she continues her program.

"She did it!" Grace yells, throwing her arms around me.

Prescott's hand slips from mine as I hug Grace back. "She did."

"You've just witnessed history, people. Rei Mitchell-Nagasaki has just landed a beautiful quad Axel right here at the Winter Games," the commentator says, returning my attention to the screen.

Rei lands every single jump after that, finishing the program with a standing ovation from the fans and skaters alike. For a split second, we even get to see Zane and that asshole of her coach waiting for her at the door as she exits the rink, only to jump right into Zane's arms. Their mouths move as they talk, and just when I think they'll cut to the commercials, the camera returns to Rei and Zane kneeling in front of her.

"Oh my God," I breathe, my hands covering my mouth as I just stare at the screen.

Grace's wide eyes meet mine. "Is he..."

"What?" Penny looks around. "A blind girl here. Can somebody tell me what the hell's going on?"

"He's proposing," I whisper, just as Rei nods her head and jumps onto Zane right there, in front of the whole world to see.

"Did she say yes?" Penny asks, her hand sinking into Henry's fur.

"Oh, she said yes," Spencer mutters, but there's a smile on his face. "Lucky bastard."

The moment the results are announced, I jump to my feet. "I need to go to the bathroom," I say out loud, and not waiting for an answer, I dash out of the room.

Chapter 48

PRESCOTT

I look over my shoulder just to catch Jade's back before she disappears into the hallway, the absence of her small, cold hand in mine almost like a phantom touch.

Spencer gives me a 'what the fuck look' while Grace glares at me from her seat.

Great.

I want to scream that I didn't do shit. Except touch her when I had no right to do so. None whatsoever.

You're an idiot, Wentworth.

I rub my palm over my face, the stubble scratching my jaw.

Maybe I should have left when I saw where Spencer was going, but I didn't expect to find Jade here. Not when I knew she had gone back home. Went back home so she could stay away from me.

I couldn't blame her. Not really. Only now, after being off the pain meds, steroids, and alcohol—hell, even Jade—did I realize how off I've been this entire time. How messed up the whole situation was. Jade was right. She and I, we are broken, and our pieces have started to mend together, but none of the parts fell right, and we ended up hurting each other more than we were healing.

We needed to heal.

Both of us, in our own way.

We can avoid being hurt all we want, but there are no guarantees in life. The only thing you'll miss out on is living and all the great things that could happen.

I hear her footsteps coming back and see her slipping into the kitchenette. Before I can question myself, I get to my feet and hop after her, thankful that our friends have turned their attention to the screen once again.

She's standing at the counter, her fingers gripping the countertop, head bent down. Seeing her is like a punch to my gut. She really looks better. Not healthy, but like she might get there, and a part of me hates myself for not being there for her when she needed me.

"Jade?"

Her head snaps up. Those blue eyes widen when she sees me standing so close.

She lifts her hand as if she wants to brush away a strand of her hair, only to remember that she doesn't have any.

"I just wanted to get some water," she says, fidgeting. As if she needs to explain herself to me in her own home. I should count myself lucky that she even allowed me in. I do consider myself lucky because I got to spend this time with her, no matter how short.

Slowly, I move closer. Half of me expects her to bolt. I don't know why since Jade's never been a coward. Not even close.

"I seriously didn't know that he was coming here. If I did..."

She shakes her head. "I told you, it's not a problem. We have the same friends. I'm not going to..."

I place my hand on the counter, our fingers so close they're almost brushing. Almost but not quite. My fingers twitch, the need to cross that tiny distance so I can touch her so strong I can barely hold back.

Take a step back, Wentworth. You don't want to scare her.

"I know. I just didn't want you to think that this was some master plan or something."

She looks up, letting out a small chuckle, "A master plan?"

The corner of my mouth jumps upward. "Hey, you never know."

"I guess you never do," she whispers, biting the inside of her cheek.

Color spreads over her pale skin, and my heart starts to beat faster. My gaze falls to her lips, lingering there longer than necessary. The need to press my mouth against hers, taste her so I can remind myself what she feels like, how she tastes, is almost overwhelming.

Seriously, Wentworth? The girl ran away from you when you held her hand! If that's not a sign to stay the fuck away, I don't know what is.

Clearing my throat, I force myself to move my eyes from her kissable lips. "How are you doing?"

"Good."

Those blue eyes gaze into mine, tracing every line of my face as if she wants to commit it to memory. As if she can't believe we're here. That this is real, I can feel it. I swear it feels like she's touching me.

"You look better," I say, my voice coming out rough.

"My chemo is tomorrow."

I nod my head in understanding. She doesn't have to explain it to me. I know all about chemo. How a person can almost seem normal, like nothing is wrong with them—the calm before the storm.

My pinky brushes against hers, and I swear I can feel it

down to my toes. The smallest of touches, and she brings me to my knees.

"Two more rounds," I whisper.

Something that looks a lot like surprise flashes in her eyes. Her teeth scrape over her lower lip. "Two more rounds."

No, Jade. I haven't stopped counting. I haven't stopped hoping. I never will.

Two more rounds, and then it'll be over, at least until she gets back her scans.

I want to say those words out loud, but I bite my tongue since I know they won't do us any good. Not that there is an us. But she knows. I can see it in her eyes. *She knows.*

She has to be okay. Destiny wouldn't be so cruel to take her away from me, too, not after robbing me of Gabriel. Even though she isn't technically mine, she probably never will be again. But just knowing she's out there, healthy and happy, will be enough.

Will it really?

It has to be enough.

I move closer to her, my lips parting, but before I can say anything, Spencer yells: "Wentworth, you going? The guys are already at the gym."

I close my eyes, letting out a shaky breath.

"Coming," I say, opening my eyes to find Jade watching me, a worried expression on her face.

"You're going to the gym? What about your—"

"My leg's fine." That familiar pressure in my knee mocks me. "Well, not fine, *fine*, but better. The doctor told me I can still exercise as long as I don't overwork myself, and trust me, the guys don't let me overwork myself."

"I know, but..." Her teeth sink into her lower lip, and she shakes her head. "Forget it."

"But what?" I ask, genuinely wanting to know. Or maybe I

just want to prolong this as much as possible. Because if she's talking to me, I don't have to look for a reason to stay.

"But why the gym? Working out and pushing yourself were the reasons why you ended up like this in the first place."

"I guess there is that..." I rub the back of my neck. "But it's also the only reason why I stay sane these days. The only thing that keeps my demons at bay."

Jade's eyes widen in understanding.

A small smile works its way to my lips. "I want to get better, Jade."

I want to get better for you. But also for me too.

I don't say those words because I know they won't bring anything good to either of us, so instead, I take a step back. "I should go."

"Okay."

With a nod, I turn and go for the door, but at the last second, I stop in the doorway. "Jade?"

"Yes?"

I place my hand against the wood. "You don't have to leave again," I say slowly, weighing my words. "I won't be in your way if you don't want me to. I promise."

It might kill me, but I'm going to stay true to my words.

Because the idea of her going back home, so far away from everything and everyone, scares me shitless. At least this way, she's going to be safe and surrounded by people who love her, even if that can't be me.

Not giving her a chance to answer me, I push from the doorway. Spencer is talking with Grace in the hallway. They both turn toward me when they hear me come.

"Let's go," I mutter as I head toward the door. My gaze meets Grace's, and I give her a curt nod. "Grace."

With that, I leave before I do something stupid.

Like march back into that apartment, grab Jade, kiss her senselessly, and beg her to take me back.

"What has your panties in a twist?" Nixon asks, eyeing me from above. I push the bar in my hand, too focused on breathing through the set to answer him. Not that I'd answer him anyway. What was there to say? I was inches away from your sister, and now I have to beat this need coursing through me to go back to her into submission?

Yeah, right. Like that'll go over well.

"Your sister has," Spencer smirks.

"What?" Nixon bellows just as my arms give out on me mid-set. Thankfully, he catches it just in time before it crushes me. "Where the fuck did you see Jade?" he asks, holding the bar just above me. A part of me wonders if he's playing with the idea of "accidentally" letting it drop. With him, you can never be too sure. Not when Jade's in question.

"Yeah, Spencer. Tell him where we saw Jade," I coax. After all, the dude just threw me under the bus, and it's not like he's clean in all of this.

"Hey, now, don't blame me. You looked like a sad puppy. I couldn't leave you all alone."

"Yeah, blame it on me. Why dontcha?"

"Well, I really thi—" he starts, but before he can finish, Nixon explodes: "Will somebody answer me?"

"We went to watch figure skating at their apartment since the signal is shitty at our place," I look up at him. "Now, can you put that back in place before you drop it on me?"

Nixon just glares at me before doing as I ask, a loud *clank* joining all the other noises in the gym.

Sitting upright, I wipe the sweat off my face with the back of my hand.

"You seriously think that's smart?"

No.

There is nothing smart about being so close to Jade. I can see her, smell her, and *touch* her when I have no right whatsoever to do any of those things.

"I didn't know we were going there. Hell, I didn't even know she was here."

My best friend watches me for a moment as if he's trying to decide if he believes me or not.

"I wouldn't have gone if I knew," I say, watching him carefully.

It would have cost me everything, but I meant what I told her. I wouldn't go seeking her out.

I was a bastard, but I would never do that to her.

Not to her.

"Okay. I know you..." There is a slight pause as he chooses his words carefully. "I know how you feel about her, but you can't mess this up for her, Prescott. She is finally doing better. She restarted her therapy and is dealing with cancer. She's so close to being done with chemo. Just... give her time. Give you both time."

"Don't you think I know that?" I snap, running my fingers through my hair. "I *know* that. Why do you think I'm here? Now, will you spot me, or do I have to find somebody else to do the job?"

Thankfully, he steps back to the bench. "What do you need?"

"Add another set of weights."

He doesn't protest as he adds the weight, helping me lift the bar off the rack, and watches as I push through the reps. An hour later, my body is spent, every muscle in my arms quivering from the exertion as we get back into the locker room and shower.

"Where are you going?"

Rubbing at my thigh, I shove my stuff into the duffle bag, my hand reaching inside for— *shit*. "I have studying to do if I want to go to the meeting tonight."

"Didn't you go yesterday?"

My fingers curl and uncurl by my side. "I need one tonight too."

Understanding flashes in his eyes. Bright blue. A perfect match for his sister's. "Need me to go with you?"

I shake my head. "I'm good, but thanks."

"Okay, but if you need me..."

"I know, I know," I roll my eyes at him, going for the door and throwing over my shoulder, "You're getting soft in your old age, Cole."

The only answer is a soft *thud* as something hits the door just as it closes behind me, making me chuckle.

Chapter 49

JADE

March

"Are you sure?"

Unbuckling my seatbelt, I look up to find Grace watching me with worry in her eyes.

"Yes, I'm sure," I curl my fingers around the door handle and push it. My whole body feels heavy, but I force one leg out, followed by the other. "You have a class to get to, and I need to buy a few things."

"I feel shitty for just leaving you here. You just had chemo! Are you sure you're feeling well? No side effe—"

"I'm fine."

For now.

Grace offered to drive me to the hospital for chemo today since Nixon had to discuss something about the upcoming draft with Coach, and Yasmin had work. Yas wanted to exchange her shift, but Grace had the morning free, so I asked if she could do it instead. I would drive myself, but each treatment was so unpredictable. Once I started to throw up in the hospital, sometimes I'd be a shaky mess in the car on the way home. Others, I was completely fine until hours after the treatment. It sucked to have to depend on others, but I'd do it rather than risk getting people hurt because I insisted on an independence I didn't really need.

"Besides, it's just a five-minute walk. I'll be fine."

"Call me if you need help. Please?"

"Okay. Now go to class. I don't want you to be late because of me."

Just as I shut the door, she yells: "Text me when you get home."

"Fine, just go already!"

Pulling the strap of the backpack higher on my shoulder, I force myself to put one leg in front of the other as I make my way inside. First, I stop at the pharmacy to refill the medication I'll need in the next few days. The lady eyes me warily, but I don't have it in me enough to care.

Grabbing the medicine, I go toward the exit. I can feel the headache looming just behind my temples, and my mouth feels dry, a bitter taste lingering on my tongue.

Maybe I should grab a water?

Walking down the aisle, I narrow my eyes, trying to see what's inside, but my vision is blurry. Is it? It looks like drinks.

I'll just grab a bottle, and then I'm out.

I inhale deeply, trying to calm my breathing.

"Jade?"

I turn around, but the fast movement makes me dizzy. Black spots cloud my vision, as my legs wobble underneath me.

Shit. I extend my hand, trying to find something, anything to hold onto, as my body sways, but there is nothing. Strong arms wrap around me just when I think I'll fall on my ass. My body tenses for a moment until the familiar scent reaches my nostrils.

Prescott.

"I'm here," he whispers as he pulls me to his chest. "I've gotcha."

I let my body sink against him, knowing he won't let me fall. A shudder runs through me. I clench my fingers around his shirt, trying to hold on to some of his warmth.

"Are you okay? What's wro—" He moves me at arms' length, and even with blurry vision, I can see the frown between his brows, the worry in his eyes. He lifts his arm and presses his palm against my forehead, which earns him another shudder. "You're burning up."

I guess I should have expected it. Fever wasn't one of the symptoms in those early few rounds, but the last couple of times, I've had it.

"What are you doing here with a fever?"

"I had to pick up some medicine, and then I figured I might grab a few things for the house."

"And you've figured doing it with a fever is a good thing?" he snaps.

"Well, I didn't have a fever when Grace dropped me off after chemo. It's fine. I'll just grab what I have and go home," I try to push him back, but the only thing it does is make me sway harder.

"You're not going anywhere on your own. You can barely walk as it is." His hand slides around my waist, and he pulls me to him. "Let's get you home."

This time, I don't even try to protest. I let him drag me out of the store and help me into his car and buckle me in.

The moment the door is closed, I lean my head against the window, enjoying the coolness of the glass on my skin even as a shudder runs down my spine. I'm so focused on it that I barely notice the drive, or maybe I just dozed off because the next thing I know, the cool air is hitting my face, and then Prescott's arms are around me as he pulls me to his chest.

I blink a few times, trying to bring him into focus.

"You shouldn't carry me," I mumble as my head leans against his shoulder. "Your leg..."

"My leg is fine. Where's the key?"

"Bag."

There's a *bang* as the front door closes behind us.

"Can you get it out for me?"

He isn't even winded as he walks us up the stairs. With trembling fingers, I work the bag's zipper and slide the keys out just as we stop in front of my apartment. He crouches down, and it takes me a few tries since my fingers are shaky, but finally, I manage to slide the key in place and unlock the door.

The apartment is quiet when we get inside, and Prescott takes me straight to my room.

"You're shivering," Prescott murmurs, his face serious as he tucks me in.

"It's been happening more lately. It's like my body is fighting it."

Prescott presses his lips in a tight line. His brows are pulled together, creases marring the skin.

"I'm fine," I whisper. "Really. You should g-go."

"You're in bed, shivering with a fever. You're anything but fine. I'll call Nix—"

"No," I grab his hand before he can pull away.

"What? You can't be alone when you're sick."

"You can't call Nixon. He has some draft stuff he's dealing with. I can't..." I shake my head. "I'm not going to mess this thing up for him with my disease too. I'll be fine on my own. It's not like this is the first time—"

"Jade..."

"—I've dealt with it," I finish, ignoring his protest. "It'll be fine."

"Stop saying it'll be fine," Prescott yells. "It's not fine, and you shouldn't be alone!"

"Then what do you want me to do?" I shout back, panting.

"I don't want you to be alone. I can't..."

"Then you stay with me." The words are out before I can think them over and realize the implication. His eyes widen at the invitation, so I rush out to say. "Until somebody comes home, that is."

The uncertainty is clear on Prescott's face. "Until somebody comes home?"

Because he can't be here? Or he doesn't want to be here? Maybe he's moved on. It's been weeks since we broke up. Maybe he found somebody else. Somebody who doesn't have cancer. Unlike me.

"Yeah," I look away. "Although I'm sure you have better things..."

Fingers skim my jaw, the touch almost feather-like, coaxing me to turn around and look at him. My throat bobs as I swallow.

This is bad. I should have never suggested it. I should never have...

"Nothing," he whispers, his voice unyielding. "Nothing will ever be more important than you, Jade."

"Prescott..."

He shakes his head. "I know I messed up. I know it, okay? I should have done better by you. I should have been stronger."

"No—"

"Yes. I should have." He cups my face, his fingers gently stroking my cheek. "I should have been stronger. I should have just been there. I get why you did what you did. I really do, but that doesn't mean I don't..."

My heart speeds up at his words, fingers clinging to the covers as I wait for him to finish the sentence, but he just closes his lips and looks away.

It shouldn't hurt.

But it does.

"People, I lo—" He clears his throat. "People I care about die, Jade. I couldn't do the same to you. I couldn't be the reason—"

I nudge his hand with mine. The darkness is pulling me in, promising temporary oblivion, but I fight it the best I can. "It's not your fault. Not Gabriel. Or me. It's just life. Never you."

"It's me. I took Gabriel out that day, which caused the infection that killed him. Not cancer, but something that I did. The day you ended up in the hospital? We had a fight, and that's why you'd been walking around instead of being home and safe. And rather than staying by your side, I walked away. I'll never be able to tell you how fucking sorry I am, Jade. Nothing I do will ever be able to justify what I did."

"Not your fault," I shake my head, my eyelids too heavy to hold them open. "I forgive you. Not because I think you're guilty but because you need to hear it. I forgive you, Prescott. And I'm pretty sure Gabriel feels the same way. It's not your fault. Never..."

PRESCOTT

I forgive you.

Jade's words still ring in my head as I watch her sleep, her body visibly shivering under the covers.

I didn't even realize how much I blamed myself and needed to hear those words until she said them out loud. It's like a weight has been lifted off my shoulders.

For the better part of my life, my parents blamed me for everything that had happened to Gabriel. And while there were things I could have probably changed, ultimately, it wasn't me. It was the cancer. And even if I didn't let Gabriel convince me to take him out, he wouldn't have recovered. He would have had a little bit more time, but he would have never recovered.

And Jade...

"Hey, I got here as soon as I could," Nixon whispers as he enters Jade's room, his eyes moving from me to his sleeping sister. "How is she doing?"

"Still feverish, although I think it went down a little. She stopped throwing up about fifteen minutes ago and crashed almost instantly. I tried giving her some water, but she didn't want any."

"Damn," Nixon goes to the other side of the bed, gently laying his fingers over her forehead. "I wanted to take her to chemo today, but my agent wanted to go over some things for the draft. Jade convinced me she was fine, and Grace was supposed to drive her. Thanks for getting her home, man. I don't even want to..."

"That's not something you need to thank me for." I look up at my best friend. "Ever."

Nixon nods his head, understanding flashing in his eyes.

Looking away, I allow myself one last glance at Jade. My fingers itch to touch her, so I curl them into fists, pushing to my feet.

"Take care of her, will you?"

"Always."

Pressing my lips together, I nod and get out of there without a backward glance. But instead of going to my apartment, I go straight back to my car.

In hindsight, I'm not sure that was the best idea considering Jade's scent still fills the small space.

Lowering the windows, I turn the ignition and start to drive. I have no destination in my mind, just the road. For a moment, I contemplate going to the clearing, but even that doesn't have any appeal. What used to be my safe space turned into another memory connected to Jade, and going there would just hurt too much. So instead, I drive until the sun starts to set over the horizon, coloring the sky in oranges and pinks.

Checking the time on my console, I let out a shaky breath before turning around and going back to Blairwood.

I pull into the parking lot of the church with just enough time to get my ass to the basement before the meeting starts.

I never thought about these meetings in the past. It seemed like something abstract. Something that exists in another world, something that can't happen to me. Until it did, and then I came here and looking at these people, all so different in their own way, I realized that there aren't rules to addiction.

Anyone can become an addict.

It doesn't choose you based on your gender or age or where you come from.

You're the one who makes the choice. You can say yes, or you can say no.

For a while, my answer was yes.

Not any longer.

I scan the group as I go to my seat, nodding at the few familiar faces just as Richard, our group leader, steps into the circle and offers us a kind smile. I listen as he greets everyone, and a few new people stand up to introduce themselves.

Some people share their experiences, while some just say their name. Either way, it was fine. That was what I loved about these groups. There was no judgment whatsoever. We've all done things we aren't proud of, but we've made the first step toward getting better.

"Is there anybody who'd like to share something today?"

I lift my hand, and Richard's eyes meet mine. As it turns out, he was the same guy that was sitting outside when Nixon brought me here that very first time. Later on, when I asked him why he didn't try to stop me from leaving, he told me that he couldn't help me if I didn't want to help myself, so he let me go hoping I'd come back.

He nods at me, so I stand up and clear my throat.

Saying these words never got easier, but still, I pushed myself to say them out loud.

A reminder of what I've done.

How much I've fallen and all the things I've lost because of it.

"My name is Prescott, and I'm an addict."

Chapter 50

JADE

"I'm so, so sorry, Jade. I should have never left you alone."

I push upright, my back muscles stiff from lying in bed for so long. It's been two days since my last chemo session, but I was finally starting to feel more human. "You didn't leave me alone. I told you to go. You had a class to get to."

Grace shakes her head. "I shouldn't have listened. God knows I know better than to listen to you."

"She has you there," Rei chimes in from the spot next to me.

"Gee, thanks, you two."

"I'm serious! Anything could have happened to you."

"But it didn't," I insist, relaxing against the pillows behind me.

"Because Prescott was there," Rei gives me a pointed look that has the color rising in my cheeks.

"Right," Grace drawls slowly.

I look away, rubbing the back of my neck as I weigh how hard it would be to get out of this bed, so I don't have to face this conversation.

"First, he was here to watch figure skating with us, and now this?" Grace continues. "What's with that anyway?"

"He didn't know about the skating. It was all Spencer's fault," I point out.

In all honesty, I don't know what else to tell her. There was nothing going on, not really. I returned to campus after the Winter Games, but for the better part, I didn't get to see Prescott. God knows I haven't been actively looking for him. But still, our paths would cross occasionally. There was no escaping that.

"Does it ever go away?" I ask softly, looking at Grace.

"What?"

"This feeling." I rub at my chest, right where that ache is always present, like a phantom limb. "Like half of your heart is missing when he's gone? Like all the air is sucked out of your lungs when he's not around, and you're drowning on dry land?"

Those green eyes soften in understanding as she shakes her head. "No. At least it didn't go away for me. Not in all the time Mason was missing."

"Yeah, I didn't think so."

Rei places her hand over mine. "You still love him."

"I still love him," I confess.

It's like our lives have been intertwined together from the very first moment our paths crossed. Like he was my destiny, and I was his. Like we had to fall together into the dark, so we could find our way back.

What we had wasn't easy or good. It was dark and twisted, but in a weird way, it was true. We were broken and bruised, but we were us.

And we survived.

We found our way back.

"Some days, I fear I always will."

And if those aren't the truest words I've ever spoken, I don't know what is.

"How are you doing?" Yasmin looks at me as she hands me my coffee. "Nixon almost got a coronary when Prescott called him to say that he found you all but passed out in the supermarket."

I tear a small piece of chocolate muffin and tentatively bring it to my mouth. "Nixon worries too much."

"You almost fainted in the store! If that doesn't require him to worry, I don't know what does."

"I know." I let out a sigh. "I thought I had more time. But I'm fine now. Just one more round, and then it's over. I'm done."

"Hell, yes. We're throwing a party once you're done."

"Shouldn't you be preparing Nixon's draft party?"

"Oh please," Yasmin waves her hand. "That's already all organized."

I let out a chuckle. "I don't know why I ever doubted you. How do you feel about all of that?"

"You know," she shrugs, taking a rag and cleaning the counter. "Nervous. I want what's best for him, but I also want him close."

"It's just one year."

"I know, but it's going to be the second hardest year of our lives." She drops the rag into the sink and faces me. "But as long as you're healthy, everything will be fine."

"I know."

Neither of us had to voice it out loud, but we both knew there was no way Nixon would ever agree to move away if my tests didn't come back clean, and I had to continue with the treatments. I didn't allow myself to think about it because just the idea of having to continue with all of these for another six months was excruciating. I wasn't sure I would be able to do it.

The bell chimes and Yasmin looks up, her eyes widening

slightly. "Don't turn around," she mouths, her words so quiet they're barely audible.

I pull my brows together. "What..."

"Hey."

Goosebumps spread over my skin at the sound of his voice, the warmth of his body as he pulled me into his arms still alive in my mind.

"Hey, what are you doing here?" The words are out before I can think them through, and I want to slap myself over the head.

"I'm here to grab a coffee," he lets out a soft chuckle, his eyes taking me in. "I have labs in thirty. You look better than the last time I saw you."

"I'm not about to faint if that's what worries you."

I'm not about to faint? What the hell, Jade?

The color rises up my cheeks, so I duck my head, letting the hair fall in my face and cover my burning cheeks.

"I don't really mind you fainting."

And if I thought things couldn't get more awkward.

There's a beat of silence, neither of us knowing what to say to make this less weird. Finally, Prescott clears his throat and turns to Yasmin. "Can I have that coffee? Black, please."

I peek up to find Yasmin looking between us, clearly amused. "One black coffee coming right up."

I give Prescott a side glance to find him already watching me. We both look away at the same time as Yasmin places a tall cup on the counter. "Here you go. Anything else?"

"No, this is fine." Prescott places a bill on the counter and turns to me. "I'm glad to see you're doing better, Jade."

I sink my teeth into my lower lip, my heart beating so wildly in my chest that I'm surprised it doesn't burst out.

Before I can say anything, he turns around and walks away. I keep staring after him even once the door is closed.

Sighing, I turn around only to find Yasmin laughing her ass off, her palm covering her mouth to stifle the noise.

I glare at her. "Don't you dare say anything."

"Oh, please! You have to admit that was hilarious."

"It was painful. That's what it was." I press my hands against my cheeks, still feeling their warmth.

"*I don't really mind you fainting,*" Yasmin says, trying to emanate Prescott's deep voice. "Not that you were any better, mind you."

"Yasmin!" I yell.

How bad would it be if I launched across the counter and strangled her? Maybe Nixon wouldn't mind if I told him what happened. No, there is no way I'm telling anyone what just happened, least of all my brother. I won't hear the end of it.

"You're really being mean. To a girl with cancer, no less."

Yasmin gives me her who're-you-trying-to-shit look. "Does that work?"

"Sometimes," I shrug.

"Try again, missy. But seriously, you two are totally pining over one another."

"We're not. We broke up."

"A few times so far, if I'm not mistaken, and we all know how that turned out."

I shake my head. "This time was for good. He's been doing better since we broke up."

If that wasn't a sign that we were better off without each other, I don't know what is.

"He is. He's been going to NA meetings."

My mouth falls open. "He is?"

Yasmin nods her head, her face serious. "Sometimes Nixon goes with him. That's the only reason I know. He doesn't talk much about it, and I don't ask."

No, I would guess not.

"That's good. I'm happy for him." A small smile spreads over my lips. "That's the only thing I ever wanted for him. To be happy."

Understanding flashes on Yasmin's face. "I know exactly what you mean."

I stay there for a little while longer, finishing my muffin and talking to Yasmin between a few other customers until a whole bunch of people enters the café.

Waving at Yasmin, I grab my cup as I make my way across campus toward Professor Reyes' office.

I knock on her open door, waiting until she looks up. "Do you have a moment?"

Chapter 51

PRESCOTT

"How about this one?" Nixon leans against the table. "What's the—"

"No," I shake my head. "I'm done. I can't take it any longer. If I hear one more question, my head will explode."

"Dude, your MCAT is tomorrow!" Spencer protests. "C'mon, just a few more and the—"

"No way. I'm done. If I didn't learn it all by now, I wouldn't do it in the next few hours either."

My friends have taken it upon themselves to quiz me for my MCATs any chance they got, and the more the exam neared, the more they bugged me about it. I'm grateful for their help. I really am, but damn, I'll strangle them if I don't get some breathing room.

"It's just..."

"No." I push to my feet. "You know what I need?"

Two skeptical pairs of eyes look at me. "What?" Nixon asks.

"Not to think. That's what." I grab his jacket and toss it at him. "Go home to your wife, and you..." I turn to my roommate. "Go and hook up with somebody."

"And what are you going to do?"

"I'm going for a run to clear my head. I better not find you here when I get home."

Before either of them can protest, I grab my earbuds and leave my room, slipping on my sneakers before I take two steps at a time and go outside.

My leg has healed nicely, and I started going back to PT. I was still a far cry from my usual strength, but I was slowly getting there.

Almost automatically, my eyes dart toward Jade's window. It's cracked open, and I feel a pang of longing at the sight.

If it was any other time, if we were the people we used to be, I'd say fuck it to running and climb inside.

But we weren't those people.

And honestly? I didn't want to be that person any longer.

Turning my back on the building, I slip the buds into my ears and start with a slow jog. These days I try not to push myself too hard and give my leg time to heal on its own.

Slowly, I pick up my pace. Pushing back all the thoughts, I focus on the music instead and let my legs decide on the route I want to take.

The sweat slowly coats my skin, my heart thumping furiously in my chest as I try to keep my breathing steady, which is harder with every mile behind me.

Some twenty minutes later, I see the familiar fence in front of me. Slowing down, I come to a stop right in front of it. I expect to find the practice field empty, but I'm surprised when I see one lone figure running the drills, a football tucked in the crook of his arm.

His head is ducked low as he runs over the field. Each time he reaches a yard line, he goes back to the beginning before running one more—again and again.

I cross my arms over my chest, watching his body work. He's twenty yards away when he finally looks up and sees me.

Surprise flashes on his face, and he trips over his own feet and almost faceplants on the grass but catches himself at the last second.

"You need to keep your eyes on your opponent," I yell, going to the door and slipping inside.

"How long have you been here?" Sullivan asks, wiping the sweat off his forehead with the back of his hand.

"Enough to see that your visibility will be shit if you crouch too low. You need to have your eyes on your opponent at all times. Look for the openings."

"I got faster," he says defensively.

"Which is great, but it'll only take you so far. You need to learn how to read the defensive line. See where they'll move even before they know it themselves. Ever played chess?"

"Chess?" Sullivan pulls his brows together. "Like a board game?"

"Know of any other chess?"

"Not really, no."

"Maybe you should. It'll help you learn how to read your opponents better."

I grab the ball out of his hand, my fingers wrapping around the leather. It feels weird. I haven't touched a ball in months, ever since we lost in the playoffs.

"Hey, give that back. I have more work to do." Sullivan tries to reach for it, but I pull back.

"Of course you do."

I rattle off a play, one I've heard Nixon call out countless times, only this time, I'm the one holding the ball. I'm nowhere near as good as Nixon, and it feels weird to be the one throwing the ball, but I force my body to make the right motions before letting it fly.

Sullivan is completely thrown off guard, so it takes him a

moment to snap into action, but in the end, he manages to catch the ball.

"What are you doing?"

"Helping you?"

He frowns at me, the distrust evident on his face. "Why?"

"Because you need help?"

The guy just glares at me. "I don't need your help."

He turns around and starts to jog away. Cursing silently, I follow after him.

"Sullivan, wait."

"I'm serious. I've had enough—"

"I'm sorry, okay?"

Sullivan turns around, surprise flashing on his face before he can school his features.

I run my hand over my face, letting it drop by my side. "I was an asshole this year. It wasn't easy for me to watch you take my spot after I was injured, and I knew I'd have to work my ass off if I wanted to get it back, which again wasn't easy. Seeing you around was a reminder of all I had to lose if I messed up, so I lashed out."

"You mean you acted like a complete dickhead."

"As if you were much better."

He silently raises his brows but doesn't try to contradict me.

"You've gotten better this year, and if you keep it up, you'll make a good player. I was just trying to help."

"Why?"

"Because I can?" I shrug. "Okay, there is also the fact that I'm pretty sure Nixon and Spencer are still at my place waiting to ambush me with another round of MCAT prep tests, and if I go back home, I'll kill them."

"So basically, I'm helping you. That's what you want to say."

I arrow my gaze on him. "Do you want that help or not?

Chapter 52

JADE

May

My phone buzzes in my pocket just as Professor Reyes finishes her presentation. I pull it out, my stomach twisting as I look at the number on the screen before I silence it and shove it back in place, turning my focus back front.

"For our next class, I want you all to bring one photo for each technique we discussed today. I look forward to seeing them next week."

My mind goes straight to possibilities. The day was nice, and I had some time, so I might as well go back to my apartment to grab my camera. It definitely beats sitting home and watching Netflix. If I watched another episode in the near future, I swear I might puke, which is saying something.

"Jade?"

I look up to find Professor Reyes watching me. "Can you wait a minute?"

"Sure."

I shift my weight from one foot to the other as she finishes the conversation with one of the students before turning her attention to me.

"I got the tickets for you."

"Tickets?" On autopilot, I take the paper from her hand, scanning the front.

"For your exhibition. The opening day is this Saturday, and Angie, the owner, would love it if you'd be there."

"*This* Saturday? As in two days from now, Saturday?" My heart does a little flip as I read the info on the ticket, and sure enough, it says right there: May 7th.

Holy shit, this is happening.

It's really happening.

"Yes, this Saturday," Professor Reyes chuckles, clearly amused by my reaction. At least one of us is. "Although she's aware of your disease, so if you're not feeling up to it..."

"No, of course."

My exhibition.

In a freaking gallery.

"Anyhow, she gave me a few extra tickets so you can invite your friends. And she's very excited to meet the artist behind the photos."

I let out a self-conscious chuckle. "More like the basket case in the photos."

"I'll have to disagree on that one. What we see is a fighter, a survivor."

The pressure rises in my chest, making it hard to breathe, but I force the words out: "Thank you."

"I hope to see you at the exhibition."

As if I'd miss it.

I'm still in a daze when I leave the classroom. As I'm putting the tickets safely in my bag, so I don't lose them, I almost run into somebody.

"I'm so sorry, I wasn't—" I look up, only to find Sullivan smiling at me.

"Hey, Jade."

"Hey. Sorry I didn't see you there."

"It's fine. No damage done." He looks behind me. "Done with your class?"

"Yeah, I was going to grab a coffee before I take a walk around the campus. I want to use the light to shoot for a little bit. Where are you going?"

"Meeting a few friends for lunch. Wanna walk together?"

I start toward the exit. "Yeah, sure."

PRESCOTT

Scanning the page, I turn back to the laptop and finish the paragraph I've been working on for my chem class, reaching for the cup of coffee by my side only to find it empty.

Because why not.

Saving the essay, I look up, ready to get up and grab a refill when I see her.

Jade.

It's been a few weeks since I last saw her.

The encounter at the café was awkward AF. I didn't know how to act around her. Not when I wanted so much more than she was willing to give, and rightfully so.

I still remember that day I had to walk away when she was lying helpless in bed. If I thought that throwing down all those pills and booze was hard, it was nothing compared to turning around that day and leaving Nixon to help her when all I wanted to do was stay.

Then I see Sullivan standing next to her.

My jaw clenches instinctively as I watch them exchange a few words. Jade laughs at whatever he said before he finally walks away.

I expect her to leave too, but something catches her attention. She turns her bag to her front and pulls her camera out. I watch her lift it to her face, taking a few quick shots of whatever's got her attention.

She pulls the camera down, presses a few buttons, and checks the screen before letting it nestle against her chest. Her hand slides into her pocket and pulls out her phone. Jade studies the device before sliding it back inside and picking up her camera once again.

I watch her as she looks around, raising the camera back to her face. She turns around until... The corner of my mouth lifts as the camera stops on me, and she lowers it.

I stay in my seat and watch her debate if she should come or walk away, but finally, she starts moving.

Not away, but toward me, and my heart does a little leap.

Calm the fuck down.

But I can't.

Because this is Jade, the girl I've been helplessly falling in love with for the last year. The girl that changed me in ways I never thought possible—the girl who made me want to do better. Be better.

"I was half tempted to text you to see if you'd brush me off," I say in way of greeting as she stops by my table.

Since the weather is nicer, Cup It Up put the tables out on the terrace, but most people preferred to sit inside, so we were alone out here.

"Have you been watching me?"

"Maybe a little bit," I shrug. I promised not to seek her out. I didn't say anything about not watching when she's around. God, I missed her. I miss her something fiercely. "So?"

"So what?"

"Would you brush me off if I texted you?"

"I—"

Just then, the familiar buzzing sound comes from her pocket. She presses her lips in a tight line.

I raise my brows. Case in point. "Somebody obviously wants to talk to you."

"And I'm talking to you."

What she's doing is avoiding. The question is, what exactly?

"So if I texted you, you wouldn't have ignored me?"

She blinks, those eyes of hers seeming bluer somehow today. "I could never ignore you."

And that was always the problem with the two of us. No matter how far away we were, that pull between us was always present. Somehow, someway, we always found our way back to each other, even if it destroyed us in the process.

"How have you been?" I ask, drinking her in.

Jade looks down, her fingers tucking a strand of her hair behind her ear. Once again, she has that long dark brown wig close to what her natural hair used to be, only with the front two strands white. It looks good on her.

She looks good.

Healthier.

"I've been good. Trying to get back to work. Photography is my happy place, but I've been pushing it back because I haven't been feeling well. It feels good to be back." She shifts her weight from one foot to the other. "What about you? Studying here?"

"I should be." I rub the back of my neck, my gaze falling down to the envelope sitting in front of me. "I'm just pushing off the inevitable at this point."

"I know something about that."

My head snaps up, and I don't miss the distant look in her

eyes—the flash of fear. My throat tightens, fingers curling to stop myself from physically reaching out to her.

"I got my MCAT results, but I'm too scared to open them. Hell, I even asked Spencer to do it for me, but the asshole printed the results out and gave them to me sealed in an envelope." I tilt my chin at her. "What about you?"

"I..." She glances over her shoulder. She's ready to bolt. Not yet. I'm not yet ready to lose this.

"C'mon, doll," I whisper, trying to keep my voice light, teasing. "I'll show you mine if you show me yours."

It works because a small smile flashes on her lips before she schools her expression, and that familiar glare—the one from the beginning—is back in place. "That's so lame. What are you? Five?"

"Maybe," I shrug. "But it worked, didn't it?"

There is a beat of silence. Jade nibbles at her lower lip, thinking. I let her have this moment to decide. So many things have been out of her power lately, and I'll be damned if I'll be one of them. Besides, she's here. I'll take any small win I can.

Just then, her phone lights up, and an unfamiliar number shows on her screen. She just looks at it for what feels like forever before her throat bobs. "It's... it's the hospital. They've been trying to call me."

My body freezes at the mention of the hospital. Although we haven't been talking, I've been following the days and weeks. She was done with her chemo by now. Which could only mean one thing, they had her final scans.

Schooling myself, I ask slowly: "Have they?"

"Yeah. They probably have the results back by now."

"And you haven't been answering?"

She shakes her head. "I'm not sure I want to know."

The tremble in her voice, the fear shining in her eyes, they're my undoing. I reach across the table, placing my hand over hers. "Jade..." That familiar jolt courses through me at the touch, and I relish in the familiarity of it. In how good it feels to have her in my arms, even if it's just my hand covering hers.

Mine.

Mine. Mine. Mine.

"As long as I don't pick up that call, I can live in denial, you know?" she chuckles nervously, her eyes glued to our joined hands. But she doesn't pull away. Maybe it's the shock of the touch. Maybe she misses me as much as I miss her. Either way, I'll take it. "As long as I don't pick up that call, I'm in between. I can pretend that I'll be okay. That this nightmare will soon be over and everything will be fine, but if I answer..."

"If you answer, you could be healed," I tell her gently, my thumb stroking over her slender knuckles. She's lost so much weight in the last few months. Just a shadow of the woman she used to be. But that fire, it's still burning inside her.

"Or I could still have cancer," she fires right back, her gaze meeting mine. "And then I'm back at square one." She presses her lips together. "I'm tired, Prescott." The admission is so soft I have to lean closer to hear it. "I'm so damn tired, and the idea... The idea that this might not be over, that I'll have to go through it all over again. It scares me shitless."

Her words are my undoing.

I can feel it.

I can feel how drained she is from the last few months. Any sane person would be. What she's been through... nobody should ever be forced to go through it.

"I know, baby," I say, the words coming out rough. "But you can't live in this limbo forever. Eventually, you'll have to pick up that phone."

"Just like you'll eventually have to open that damn letter." She gives me a pointed look.

"Touché," I smirk, my hand still holding onto hers. "How about I make you a deal?"

There is a beat of silence before… "What kind of deal?" she asks tentatively.

I start to sweat just at the thought of it. I've had the letter with me for the last week, and I've pushed off opening it. What if I failed again? What if I failed, not just Gabriel but myself too? Because while a part of me was doing this to honor him, being a doctor was what I wanted to do. I wanted to help kids, both the sick ones and the ones who were standing by that bed, watching their loved ones die. But I couldn't ask her to face her fears while at the same time refusing to face my own.

"I'll open the letter if you answer that call. We'll do it together."

Whatever it is, I know I can deal with it if we're together.

But you're not together, are you?

But what if there could be an us again?

Now, with a clear mind, I understood why Jade did what she did. I understood what she meant when she said we were broken. She was right. Of course, she was. We've both come with so much of our baggage, and we started to drown as we were trying to help each other heal instead of helping ourselves heal first.

But maybe, just maybe…

"You'll open it?"

I nod. "If you pick up that call."

"What if they say the cancer is still here?"

No. Just the idea of it had the anxiety rising inside of me, suffocating me. *This isn't about you*, I remind myself.

"Then we'll figure it out."

Her throat bobs as she swallows. I hold her gaze, trying to silently tell her that I'm here and that she can do this, that I believe in her.

"O-okay," she whispers, her voice coming out shaky. "Okay."

I watch as she answers the call and slowly lifts the phone to her ear. She turns her hand under mine, and I let her link our fingers together as she squeezes my hand tightly. All the color has drained from her face, but her voice is steady as she answers.

"I'm Jade Cole."

I suck in a breath, my heart beating so wildly as I try to listen carefully in case I'll hear whoever's on the other side of that line because her face is completely void of any emotions. The time seems to slow down as she listens.

Why the fuck is it taking so long?

I'm half tempted to grab her phone and ask what the hell's going on when she says: "O-okay, thank you."

With my heart in my throat, I watch her hang up and put the phone back down. She slowly looks up at me, that mask firmly in its place.

It has to be bad. She's in shock. Dammit, this can't be happening. It just ca—

"The results came back clean."

Her words are so soft I don't register them at first.

I blink, pushing my thoughts to the back of my mind. "What?"

"The results," her fingers grip mine tighter, her short nails digging into my skin, but I welcome the pain. It means this is real. It's actually happening. "They came back clean. The cancer is... gone."

"Fuck yeah."

Before I know what I'm doing, I'm pushing back my chair and going toward her, lifting her into my arms and squeezing tightly.

Jade wraps her arms and legs around me, burrowing her head in the crook of my neck as she lets out a sob.

"It's okay," I whisper, my hand rubbing up and down her back as she shakes in my arms. My eyes burn with unshed tears as I hold her closer, cherishing every second I have her in my arms.

It's done.

It's actually done.

I brush her hair away so I can look at her face. See her eyes. "You're okay. You're alive. You *survived.*"

Tears keep streaming down her cheeks, the disbelief evident on her face. I remember it clearly from when Gabriel was sick too. For months you're in survival mode, doing everything you can to get better, and then suddenly, you're fine again, and you can continue with your life as if nothing happened. Only you can't, not really. Because no matter how much you've fought for survival, a part of you was prepared to die, and you'll never, *ever* look at anything the same way again.

I skim my thumb over her cheekbone. "You're going to be oka—"

"What the hell's going on here?" Nixon growls, his hand gripping my shoulder as if he wants to rip it out of me. "Why is she crying? What did you do?"

"I-I..." Jade tries, but she starts to cry harder.

"Fuck it, Wentworth. I'm seriously going to kick you—"

"It's g-gone."

Nixon's brows furrow. "Gone?" He looks from her to me and back. "I don't think I follow."

"C-cancer." She wipes the tears with the back of her hand. "It's gone."

Nixon just blinks, dumbfounded. "Gone? As in, *gone* gone?"

Jade nods. "Dr. Hendriks just called. The results have come back clean. I'm... I'm cancer free."

"Dammit, Jade," Nixon croaks, going for her, but since she's still clinging to me, it ends up being a weird three-way hug of sorts. "I knew you'd do it." His eyes meet mine over her shoulder, and I can see tears shining in them.

The disbelief.

The hope.

The *relief*.

They're written all over his face, and they're like a punch to my gut. Too much. All of this is too much. Too similar to my own feelings the first time we found out Gabriel's leukemia was gone.

"I don't know why I'm crying. I shouldn't be crying. I should be celebrating."

"You should feel whatever you want to feel." I brushed the strand of hair that got stuck to her cheek from tears. "There is no right or wrong way to feel after hearing this news."

"It just..." She sniffs. "It feels surreal."

Her fingers slide over my shoulder where her head was only minutes earlier. "I messed up your shirt."

"It's just a shirt."

Nixon clears his throat as he pulls back, effectively bursting our bubble. Slowly, I let out a shaky breath. "I think I should get going."

Jade blinks as if she just now realized where we're at, that she's still in my arms, clinging to me.

"Right, sorry." She jumps to her feet, turning her back to me as she rubs the back of her neck. "I'm sure you have other things to do."

Fuck other things. I want to stay. Ask me to stay.

But she doesn't.

Of course, she doesn't.

I've messed up. Time and again, I messed up.

And after everything we've been through, everything *she's*

been through, getting back together is the last thing she probably wants.

I give her a small smile, struggling to keep my arms firmly by my sides when all I want to do is reach for her and never let her go. "I'm sure you want to go and tell your friends the good news."

"Yeah, of course."

Unable to resist it, I move closer. Lifting my hand, I cup her cheek, brushing away the last of the tears still clinging to her skin. "I'm so happy for you, Jade."

Letting my hand drop, I grab my things and walk away.

Chapter 53

JADE

My heart thunders in my chest as I watch Prescott walk away.

Again.

It shouldn't hurt.

Dammit, it shouldn't hurt.

It's not like we're together.

So what if all I want is to bury myself in him and forget the last few months ever happened?

Okay, that's a lie. Because if it weren't for the last year, Prescott and I never would have been together. And I would go through this hell as many times as necessary if it meant I got to be with Prescott Wentworth. No matter how short that time is.

"Are you just going to let him walk away?"

My brother's soft words snap me out of my thoughts.

"I thought you didn't approve of us being together."

"I didn't approve of you being hurt."

I give him a pointed look.

"Or you two sneaking behind my back and lying to me. But the point is..." Nixon glances toward Prescott's retreating back. "That man loves you, Jade. I've known him for four years now, and I've never seen him love anybody the way he does you."

"He walked away."

"And so did you." Nixon's finger slips under my chin, tilting my head up. "You both did what you had to do to survive, but now it's over. Knowing him, he won't make the first move, you'll have to be the one to do it. So I ask you again, Smalls. Are you just going to let him walk away?"

I turn my head toward Prescott's rigid back. He hasn't gotten that far away yet. If I want to stop him, I have to do it now.

Could I do it? Could I just let him walk away? Let us both move on with our lives. Wouldn't that be for the best? We've been down this road, and it didn't work. Repeatedly. There was always something standing in our way. Is this what our life will be? An obstacle after obstacle? What if, down the road, the cancer comes back? It's possible. Yes, he's going to be an oncology doctor and...

"Son of a bitch!"

Nixon startles back at my outburst. "What now?"

"He didn't open the damn letter!"

And then it hits me. Grabbing my backpack, I pull out one of the tickets and shove it into my back pocket before tossing the bag at Nixon. "Wait here."

Then I run.

My legs feel heavy, and my breathing turns ragged after merely a few steps, but I push through the pain as I hurry to catch up to him.

"Prescott!" I yell.

Heads turn in my direction. People probably wonder who's the lunatic who's running like crazy holding the top of her head, but ask me if I care.

Prescott turns around, his eyes wide when he sees me. I come to a stop, bending forward, my hands gripping my knees so I can catch my breath.

"Your l-letter," I pant, pushing upright so I can face him.

His brows pull together. "What?"

"Your letter," I repeat. "You didn't open your letter."

I watch as the realization dawns on him.

"MCATs, right." He rubs his hand over his jaw.

"I answered the phone. You have to open it."

I wasn't about to let him get out of this. He wanted to make a deal. Well, now it was his time to pay up.

But more than that, I didn't want him to walk around not knowing the answer. I've been doing that for the last few days, and I knew just how excruciating not knowing was.

Prescott opens one of the books in his hands and pulls out the envelope. He flips it from one hand to the other and just stares at it. The paper is worn from the many times he probably took it in his hands and did the very same thing before he put it back down. Unopened.

"I can't." His Adam's apple bobs as he gives me the letter. "You do it."

"You want me to open it?"

"Yeah, and then you can tell me the results. Or not tell me." He shoves the letter at me. "No, tell me. One way or the other, just tell me."

"Are you sure?" I ask, gently taking the letter.

"Yeah. Just do it."

"Okay."

My gaze is locked on his as I slide my finger under the seal and rip it open. Prescott closes his eyes. Sweat has gathered over his forehead and upper lip.

He's nervous.

Not just that, he's petrified of seeing those results.

Sinking my teeth into my lower lip, I pull out the letter, but instead of opening it, I grab the ticket from my pocket. Not letting myself think too much about what I'm about to do, I slide the ticket along with the letter and place it back into the envelope.

"So?" Prescott asks, his eyes still firmly shut as he shifts from one leg to the other. "It's bad, right? I didn't pass. Shit, I knew—"

Lifting on the tips of my toes, I press my mouth against the corner of his as I place the envelope into his hand.

"You have to be the one to open it, Prescott."

He blinks his eyes open. "You didn't read it?"

I shake my head. "I don't need to open it. I believe in you. And you need to believe more in yourself too." Clasping my hands over his and the letter, I smile at him. "Face your demons, Prescott."

"What if I lose?"

"But what if you win?"

My eyes are still on his. I take a step back and another one. With the third step, I turn around and walk away, hoping this time he will follow.

Nixon is still waiting for me as I make my way to Cup It Up, my backpack in hand.

"So? How did it go?"

"I told him it was time to face his demons." Nixon opens his mouth to protest. "All his demons. He has to open that letter himself, and when he does, I hope he'll come and find me."

Nixon runs his hand over his face. "Jade..."

I take my backpack from my brother's hands and grab two more tickets, handing them silently to him.

Nixon looks at them, reading over the label before his head snaps up, his blue eyes huge as a smile slowly makes its way to his lips. "Is this..."

"A few weeks back, Professor Reyes asked me to do the exhibition."

"But you didn't win."

"I didn't. But the gallery owner loved my work so much she wanted to do an exhibition with just my work."

"Jade, that's amazing!"

Nixon pushes to his feet and grabs me, picking me up and spinning me around like crazy.

"Nixon!" I protest, laughing. "Put me down, or I'll puke on you."

"I don't care."

"But I care! Put me down. Now."

Finally, this time he listens. He puts me down on the ground, his hands landing on my shoulders to help steady me after all the spinning.

Making sure my wig's in place, I look up only to find Nixon watching me, a soft smile on his mouth.

"What?"

"You're laughing."

I pull my brows together. "Yeah, so?"

By the way he says it, you'd think I'm some kind of grinch or something.

"Nothing. It's good to see you laugh. I haven't seen you so happy since..."

Since cancer.

Before really.

There weren't many reasons to laugh when you were fearing if you were going to make it to the next day.

"Nixon..."

He shakes his head and throws his hand over my shoulder, pulling me closer. "That's good, Smalls. It feels good to see you happy. *Healthy.*"

I slip my hand around my big brother's waist and lean my head against his chest. "I think I'm far from healthy, but I'm getting there. One day at a time, right?"

"One day at a time," he agrees as we start walking. "So this gallery thing...You gave Prescott an invite?"

"I left it in his letter."

"I thought you didn't open the letter."

"I opened it, but in the end, I decided against reading it. When he's ready, he'll find it."

"But the exhibition is this weekend."

We come to a stop in front of Nixon's car, so I let go of him. "Then he better be ready fast." I turn to Nixon and give him a warning glare. "And do not tell him. He has to do this on his own, Nix."

"Fine," he lets out a sigh. "Where are you going? Want me to give you a ride?"

"Actually, yes. I want to stop by the store and surprise the girls with the good news. Hell, why don't you call Yas and tell her to come too? We can make a party out of it."

I might not know what's in store for me down the road, but today was a good day, and I damn sure planned to make the most of it.

Chapter 54

PRESCOTT

"Are you ever planning to actually open this thing, or are you just going to stare at it?" Spencer asks as he makes his way to the fridge. He pulls out a carton of orange juice, leans against the counter, and drinks straight from it.

Face your demons, Prescott.

I flip the letter, willing it to reveal its secrets to me, but the damn thing is quiet.

"Seriously, how can you not know? It would drive me insane by now."

"It's better than knowing you failed," I mutter, my head still on that conversation with Jade. On her words. "Besides, I gave you a chance to do it, but you didn't look at the results either."

"Because it should be you who opens the damn thing!"

What if I lose?

But what if you win?

I could still feel the taste of her soft lips against mine. Smell that sweet scent that's just her.

I wanted to do it. I wanted to know, dammit, but... There was always a but of some sort.

"Just open it and be done with it. You've either passed or

failed and have to get your ass to work once again if you want to go to med school, like you've been talking about from the first day I met you. Seriously, Wentworth, I didn't take you for a wuss." With a shake of his head, he goes toward the door.

Grateful that he's finally leaving me alone, I turn the letter over, my eyes fixing on the broken seal.

Face your demons, Prescott.

"See, even Jade's doing better than you. Going out on dates and—"

"What?" I sit upright, the letter falling to my lap as I stare at Spencer. "Jade's going on a date?"

My heart bangs against my chest as Spencer's words ring in my mind, mixing with the vision of Jade going out, sitting across from another man holding hands, kissing, and more, so much more. A man that's not me.

Spencer turns his attention from the window to me. "She's all dressed up, so I guess she is. Why would she wear a dress otherwise?"

A hundred different reasons.

I push to my feet, going to the window, just to catch a glimpse of a dark SUV pulling out of the parking lot.

Where the hell is she going?

What if I lose?

But what if you win?

With my heart in my throat, I go back to the couch where I dropped the envelope when I got up. The damn thing almost falls in a hurry, but I manage to catch it at the last second. Sliding my fingers through the open seal, I pull the letter out and let the envelope drop to the ground as I start to read.

Dear Mr. Wentworth,

We're happy to congratulate you...

I reread the letter three times, just to make sure that I have it right before my legs give out on me and I fall down on the couch.

From the corner of my eye, I can see Spencer move closer. "That bad? It's not the end of the world. You can alwa—"

"I passed," I say, turning my attention to Spencer, who slowly grins.

"Hell yeah, you did! I knew you could do it." He slaps me over the shoulder. "Congrats, man!"

I give him a side glance. "Weren't you just about to tell me I can retake it?"

"I was trying to be supportive. Not that you know how to appreciate it, asshole."

I lean against the couch, running my hands over my face.

I passed.

I'm going to med school.

I'm going to freaking med school next year.

"Hey, what's this?"

I let my hands drop and look at Spencer just as he picks up the envelope I dropped earlier.

"Oh, I don't nee—"

He flips the paper over, that frown between his brows deepening. "Since when are you interested in exhibitions?"

Exhibitions?

"Give me that," I mutter, pulling the paper out of his hands as I scan the ticket. "This has to be a mi—"

Then I see it.

The name.

From the Ashes, *an utterly devastating and yet beautiful collection of photos by up-and-coming photographer Jade Cole will be displayed...*

I go back to that day.

"You didn't read it."

Jade shakes her head. "I don't need to open it. I believe in you. And you need to believe more in yourself too." She places the letter in my hands, giving them one final squeeze as she smiles at me. "Face your demons, Prescott."

"What if I lose?"

"But what if you win?"

"She gave it to me," I breathe, still staring at the ticket. She did it. Her photos are actually going to be displayed in a gallery. She did it.

"Who did?"

"Jade." A smile slowly makes its way to my lips. "It's Jade's exhibition."

I look down at the ticket.

"Fuck. And it's today." Pushing to my feet, I rush to my room. "I have to go."

Chapter 55

JADE

"Jade, these are..." Grace shakes her head, tears glistening in her eyes.

"Disturbing?"

"Beautiful!" She rushes to me, her hands wrapping around me as she pulls me in for a hug. "They are beautiful. Just like you are."

"I wish I could see them," Penny says as Grace finally lets go. "The girls described them to me, but I'm sure it didn't do them justice. No offense."

"None taken." Rei gives Penny's arm a little squeeze before she turns to me, a sad look in her eyes. "Grace's right; they're beautiful, Jade. And I'm sorry."

"What? There is nothing you have to be sorry about!"

"There is. I was barely present for the better part of the year. I should have done more. Been there more."

"Don't be ridiculous. You all have been doing more than enough. I didn't expect you all to give up your lives because I had to put mine on pause."

"I know, but to see it all like this... you've been through so much."

I take her hand in mine and give her a firm squeeze. "And I survived."

My gaze goes to the photo that's just behind her shoulder. It's a black and white photo of me sitting on a bathroom floor in just a plain tee and panties, leaning against the bathtub, crying. I knew exactly the day I took it. It was my second cycle of chemo, just after my second round. I felt like shit. I was so weak I could barely get to the bathroom. It was the day I wanted to give up. You can see it in my eyes. The defeat and the demons ready to pounce.

But I didn't give up.

"I survived," I repeat, feeling the tears prickle my eyes.

It felt good to say it out loud.

To look at the photos, *my photos,* plastered all over these walls, see the hell I've been through and say I've made it to the other side.

Broken and bruised, but alive.

"You did. And you turned your pain into something beautiful."

"Stop it," I protest, sniffling. "You guys are really going to make me cry!"

The girls huddle around me, pulling me into a group hug.

"Jade?" I look up to find the gallery owner waiting for me with a woman by her side. "Do you have a minute?"

"Yeah, sure, just a second." I turn back to the girls. "Before I forget." I open my bag and pull out an envelope. "I really hope you packed your bags like I told you because we're staying the night here." Taking Penny's hand in mine, I place the envelope into her hand. "Happy birthday, Penelope."

"What?" Her fingers tighten around the envelope. "But my birthday isn't for another month!"

"Exactly! When you're back in Bluebonnet. So, this is an early present from me. Open it."

It takes her a minute to find the seal and open the envelope. She pulls out the paper, her eyes widening when she finds it's written in braille. It took me some sweet time to get it, but these past few months, I didn't have anything but time. And the hassle was totally worth it for the look on her face.

"You did not!" Her mouth falls open as she goes back to reread it.

"What?" Grace asks, looking from Penny to me and back.

"Tell us already. The suspense is killing me," Rei agrees.

"She got me tickets. For Sebastian Black's concert tomorrow. How did you get those? They were sold out in like two minutes tops."

"Technically, I got *us* tickets to his concert. And let me tell you, it wasn't easy at all."

Penny returns the ticket back into the envelope. "I can't, It's too much."

"Oh, shush. It was the only fun I had when I was lying in bed. I know how much you love that guy."

"I love his music," Penny says, the color creeping up her cheeks.

"Are you blushing?" Grace teases.

"Am not," Penny protests. It would be more convincing if her cheeks didn't turn even redder.

"I'll see you guys in a little bit," I say, going to meet Angie and the woman next to her.

"Regina, this is Jade. She's the woman behind the camera."

"And the one in front of it," I say jokingly.

"Indeed." The woman, Regina, offers me her hand. "It's so nice to meet you, Jade. I have to tell you. The photographs are simply stunning. It's not just the feelings they portray but also the story they tell. Well done."

"Thank you. I—"

The words die on my lips when I hear a commotion behind me. Both women look over my shoulder in surprise.

The hairs at the back of my neck prickle, and even before I turn around, I already know who I'll find behind me.

I didn't dare think about the what-ifs.

If he'll find the ticket and what would be the outcome.

But now…

Slowly, so painfully slowly, I turn around in my heels.

And there he is.

Prescott.

Chapter 56

PRESCOTT

There she is.

I'm still panting hard from running. The parking lot was full, and I couldn't find a single spot in a five-block radius. I was half tempted to just leave my car by the curb and call it a day when I spotted somebody pulling out. I snatched that spot faster than you can blink, and then I started to run.

Now my knee is killing me, and I'm a sweaty mess in a monkey suit, but it's so damn worth it because I've made it.

With my eyes glued on Jade's, I smooth my shaky hand over my jacket as I make my way to her.

God, she looks stunning.

She has on a tight black dress that falls to her mid-thigh and a killer pair of heels that give her a few extra inches. Today she forwent the wig and settled on a delicate black scarf with some flower pattern on it instead. Her makeup was minimal, but it made her look healthier.

I drink her in, my heart aching at her beauty, at the peace that seems to surround her as I finally come to a stop not even a foot away.

"You came," she whispers.

As if that was ever a question.

"I'll always come for you."

Her lips part almost as if in surprise. I take a step forward, my hand itching to reach for hers, and it takes everything in me not to do it.

"I mean it, Jade. You call, and I'll answer. Any time, any place. It doesn't matter what we are or how we left things before. I *will* come for you."

"Prescott, I..."

But before she can say whatever she wants to, Nixon and Yasmin come to us, Jade's friends behind them. "Hey, Smalls. The crowd is slowly clearing, so we'll head out too." He looks from Jade to me and back. "Need something before we leave?"

Jade shakes her head. "I'm good. I'll see you at the hotel later."

Nixon pulls her into a hug. "Brunch tomorrow morning to celebrate before we leave for campus?"

"You know it. Thanks for being here tonight."

"Always." Nixon lets go of her and turns to me. I expect him to give me some kind of warning, but instead, he pulls me into a side hug and slaps my shoulders. "Congrats, man."

"What?"

I look from him to Jade. "You read the letter?"

She said she didn't but maybe...

"She didn't read it," Nixon says quickly. "You either passed or failed, but instead of reaching for alcohol and drugs like you would have done just a few months ago, you came here instead. Either way, congrats."

With a smile aimed at me, he pulls Yasmin into his side as they all start to make their way out of the gallery.

"Nixon?"

My best friend glances over his shoulder. "I passed."

He just watches me for a moment before nodding. "I didn't expect anything less. Congrats."

With that, he closes the door, and it's just the two of us. Quite literally.

"I guess I came in too late," I say, just as Jade asks: "You passed?"

"I did, I..."

Before I can finish, Jade rushes toward me, her arms wrapping around my middle. All the air leaves my lungs as her body connects with mine. Energy sizzles between us as I slowly lift my arms and pull her closer to me, burrowing my head in the crook of her neck and breathe.

"I'm so proud of you, Prescott. I know how much this means to you."

Not as much as she does.

Nothing will ever be able to compare to her.

I wasn't joking when I said I'd come whenever she needed me.

There wasn't another person who was more important in my life than she was. No, our story wasn't pretty or easy by any means, but we made it. And no other woman, hell, no other person, will ever mean to me as much as Jade does. I'll never love another woman as I do her.

The only question is, does she still love me?

"I always knew you would." Jade pulls back, a big smile on her face. "You'll be a great doctor, Prescott. And one day, you'll change people's lives for good. You've already changed mine."

"Jade, I..."

"You guys wanna stay a little longer?" A dark-skinned woman Jade talked to earlier, smiles at us.

Jade shifts her attention between the two of us. "Angie, I'm not..."

"Can we?" I ask the woman. "The traffic was insane, so I couldn't get here sooner."

Angie winks at me. "Sure thing, sugar. We can't have you leave without getting a glimpse at these. They're really breathtaking." She turns to Jade. "You can stay for a little while longer while I finish some stuff in the back. Let me know before you leave?"

"Thank you, Angie." Jade smiles at her. "For everything."

"Thank *you*. I've already had people asking if they can buy certain pieces."

Jade's eyes widen in surprise. "You did?"

"I'll call you next week, and we can discuss it. How does that sound?"

Jade nods her head silently, clearly at a loss for words. With one final smile, Angie disappears behind a door, leaving Jade and me in the gallery. All alone.

"A private tour by the photographer herself. What did I do to deserve this honor?"

Jade shoves me away gently. "Don't make fun of me, Wentworth."

"I'm not making fun of you, Jade. This whole thing..." I take in the photos displayed on the walls before my gaze settles on her. "It's amazing. You're amazing. Your mom would be so proud."

"She would, wouldn't she?" Wiping the corner of her eye, Jade tilts her head to the side. "Wanna see it?"

"Yes."

Wiping my hands against the side of my legs, I follow after her as she leads me to the first photo, and I just stare.

Jade is holding scissors to her hair.

I move past her, following the images as they're displayed on the wall—telling a story of Jade's battle photo by photo, piece by piece—my throat tightening as the onslaught of emotions assaults me.

Seeing her like this, out in the open, unafraid to show herself to the world, her emotions, her battle, her truth, even after everything that she's been through, humbles me.

The next one is an up-close photo of her. The shadows play over her face, the clippers pressed against the top of her head, one lone tear sliding down her cheek as she stares at her reflection.

"I'm so sorry, Jade." I turn toward her. "I should have been the—"

"There is nothing to be sorry for, Prescott. You were there."

She takes my hand in hers. I suck in a breath as her icy fingers clasp around mine, but before I can react, she stops in front of another photo.

Of us.

I'm holding her in my bed, both of us fighting our own demons.

"You were there when it mattered. When I was at my lowest, you were there, and you helped me cling to reality. Cling to life. But that's as much as you could do. I know that now. I knew that when I saw you lying passed out on your living room floor. I knew it before, but that was when it hit me. Really hit me."

I turn to her to find her eyes glistening with unshed tears.

"We were each other's life jackets. But a life jacket can only help you so much. After a while, you'll either have to learn how to swim or drown trying. I picked swimming, and I was praying you'd do the same."

"I was drowning." My throat bobs as I swallow, but I force myself to say the words out loud. "You left, just like Gabriel left. I lost football. I failed MCATs. I *failed*, Jade. And I was drowning. It wasn't until I almost made the stupidest mistake of my life that I realized how far I'd sunk and that if I wanted to make things right, I'd have to fight."

"Prescott..."

She tries to take my hand, but I step back, needing to say the words.

"I did a lot of stupid shit this last year, Jade. I put it all on the line, and I still lost. I lost it all. But I'll never regret anything as much as I regret losing you. There are a lot of things I'd do differently if I could, but not our story. Not you. We went through hell, and we've made it out, and I'd do it as many times as I'd need to if it would mean I got to have you for only a second longer."

"Prescott, you..."

I shake my head. "Let me finish. I'll never regret falling for you. I'll never regret loving you because I *do* love you, Jade. I'm not sure when it exactly happened, but somewhere on the way, somewhere in this hell, I've fallen in love with you. You were my light, my saving grace. You, Jade, you're what saved me. When you walked away, you saved me. I didn't know it at the time, but you were right. I'm not going to lie and say things have been easy these last few months. They haven't. My leg will never be the same, and some days when it hurts, my first reaction is to reach for that bottle and relieve the pain, but I haven't done it. I've been clean for three months now, and the only reason that's possible is because of you."

Jade shakes her head, her blue eyes shimmering with tears. "It's because of you. You put in the hard work. You say no when the temptation is there. Not me, *you*."

"Because you showed me I can. You make me want to be a better man, always have. I just hope..."

"What?"

"I hope that you can give me a second chance. Or maybe it's a third chance?" I run my fingers through my hair. "The fuck if I know. It doesn't even matter. The point is... I want us to try again, Jade. For real, this time. No sneaking around. No lies. No pretending. Just you and me."

"Just you and me," She repeats softly, a wistful look on her face. "But what if my cancer comes back?"

"It won't come back, but if it does... If it does, we'll deal with it. Together."

She looks at the photo of the two of us, the silence settling over us as she mulls over my words.

"I would have done it too." She turns to me. "I'd have gone back to that hell if it meant I get to be with you. I never planned to fall in love, Prescott. That's why you were so safe. I didn't even like you for the better part. How could I fall for you, and yet..." She shakes her head. "You snuck up on me, took bits and pieces of my broken heart, and convinced me that I was worth it, just the way I was. Broken and jaded."

I cup her cheeks, pressing my forehead against hers. "You're not broken."

"I was." Her warm breath touches my skin as her hands cover mine. "I was broken, but you helped me put my pieces back together. You helped me learn how to love myself when I didn't think it was possible, and you were never afraid of my darkness."

"There is only one thing I'm afraid of, and that's losing you."

"I'm not going anywhere. Not now, not ever. I love you, Prescott Alexander Wentworth, and I want to give us another shot. Even though all the sneaking around was kind of fun."

The corner of my mouth tugs upward. "So what you're saying is that you want to keep me as your dirty little secret?"

"Never," Jade shakes her head. "I'm done with keeping secrets."

"Good. Because there's no way I'd be able to hide how much I love you."

Skimming my thumbs over her cheekbones, I close the distance between us and press my mouth against hers in a slow kiss. My mouth glides against hers, and it feels like I've come home.

Here in the middle of the gallery that tells her story, *our* story, the story of love and loss, heartbreak and darkness, and we're still standing strong.

Together.

Breaking the kiss, I press my forehead against hers.

"Let's get you home."

And, with her hand in mine, we walk out into the light.

Epilogue

JADE

Late August

"Give me that."

I clasp my hands tighter around the chair, looking up to meet a pair of narrowed, dark eyes. "Are we seriously going to do this again?"

"We wouldn't have to if you'd just be a good girl and hand it over."

"I'm quite capable of carrying that myself. I thought we established that last year."

"We did, but you also have a big hunk of a boyfriend who can carry it for you, so why not use me?" Prescott wiggles his brows, and I can feel my belly tightening at the innuendo.

"Because I have way better ways of using you?"

"You do." He presses a hard kiss to my lips, leaving me breathless. Which gives him just enough time to steal the chair out of my hands as he pulls back. "But you'll start with that chair."

"Chair stealer!" I yell after him.

He looks over his shoulder, a big grin on his face. "But you love me."

"I do."

Oh, how I do.

Grace nudges me with her elbow. "I never thought I'd see you so..."

"Happy?" I offer, shifting my attention to my best friend.

"Sappy."

"What? I'm not sappy."

"You so are," Penny chimes in. She's sitting on the floor, packing my clothes into suitcases. "But it looks good on you. You guys seem so happy."

A smile spreads over my lips. "We are."

After the gallery, Prescott and I started really slow. We got all those firsts we never had. We went out on dates. We kissed in the backseat of his car and dark movie theatres. We talked and got to know one another in a way we hadn't before. He even took me to one of those couple's cooking courses where you cook your meal and have a dinner date after, a miserable failure on our part, but we ended up laughing our asses off afterward. I think we both needed it—this time to help us heal and get to know one another as we are now.

And then last weekend, he took me for a weekend getaway, just the two of us, in a small cottage on the beach to celebrate my birthday, and it was beautiful.

That's when he asked me to move in with him.

The question threw me completely off guard. I'm not even sure why. I knew Spencer had graduated and was drafted to the pros, and Prescott would eventually need to find a roommate now that he was accepted to the med school here at Blairwood. But it never crossed my mind that that roommate could be me.

Then there were the girls. Zane and Rei found a small, one-bedroom apartment not that far away for the two of them, now that they're engaged. He enrolled into a physical therapy program and plans to work alongside Dr. Snow until he gets his master's. And Mason finally convinced Grace to move in with him at his place. Which meant, I'd have this big ass apartment all for myself.

It made sense.

And I wanted it.

I hadn't even realized how much until he asked.

I wanted to live with him.

I wanted to see him every day.

I wanted to wake up snuggled against him.

I wanted us to fail at cooking over the weekends, study together, and go out on dates.

I wanted him.

In every way, shape, and form.

I grab a box of my stuff from the table. "I'm going to take this over," I say to the girls before getting out of the apartment.

Late August heat slams into me the moment I get outside, the bright afternoon sun blinding me. That's why it takes me a moment to realize Prescott is standing out in the parking lot and talking to a woman.

And not just any woman.

His mother.

I watch them for a moment, unsure of what to do. Should I go there and save him? Should I sneak back inside and let them talk?

But before I can overthink it, Prescott turns around, his eyes landing on mine. His smile is stiff as he motions me over.

"Hey, what's up?" I ask as I slide into his open arms and look up at him.

"Jade, this is my mother, Molly Wentworth. Mom, this is my girlfriend, Jade."

The woman offers me her hand, which I take, giving it a firm shake as her eyes go to my short hair.

My hair started growing one month after I was done with chemo, and just recently, it grew enough for me to go to the hair salon and have it cut in a cute pixie style.

"It's so nice to meet you, Jade," she says, a soft smile on her lips. "Are you moving?"

Prescott's arm tightens around me. "She's moving in with me."

"Oh, that's nice. So you've been dating for how long?"

"A year now." Prescott meets my gaze. He must read the question on my face because he says: "Mom left Dad. She's moving to Boston to live with her sister until she finds her own place."

She left him?

Talk about a curveball.

"I just wanted to stop by and check in on Prescott. See how he's doing."

"That's nice of you."

"What it is, is long overdue." Sadness creeps in her eyes for a moment, but she blinks it away. "Maybe we could have dinner sometime? After I'm settled in?"

I rub Prescott's back as he processes her words. I know he hasn't talked to either of his parents since he walked out on them for Christmas. Turning his back on his family was hard, but it was the right thing to do since they treated him the way they did.

"Yeah, maybe," he finally rasps.

I give him a squeeze, letting him know I'm here.

His mom smiles and nods. "I'd love that. I want a chance to get to know you, Prescott. I missed out on so much, but... I'm here now. And I'm sorry." She wipes under her eyes, her attention switching to me. "And you, Jade, of course."

"That's fine. I'm sure you two have a lot to catch up on."

"Too much." She tucks a strand of her hair behind her ear. "Anyhow, I'll let you continue with your work, but I'll talk to you soon, Prescott?"

"Sounds good."

"Okay."

She shifts from one foot to the other. I can see it on her face. She wants to come in and hug him, but Prescott doesn't let go of me, so in the end, she settles for a nod. "I'll see you soon."

We stay in our spot as we watch her walk to a black sedan and drive off. I hold onto Prescott, giving him time to process what just happened.

"Well, I'll be damned."

"Didn't see that one coming?"

"Not in a hundred years."

Letting my hand drop, I turn around, so we're face to face. "Do you know what you are going to do about it?"

Prescott runs his hand over his face. His eyes were still fixed on where his mom had disappeared. "I have no fucking idea. I've been doing so good, I..."

"Hey..." I cup his cheek, returning his attention to me. "You don't have to decide now. Hell, you have every right not to return her call and not to agree to meet her. Not if you're not ready. Not if that's not what you want. It's your choice."

"You'll still love me if I don't meet her?"

"Always." I pull him down, brushing my mouth against his. "I'll love you always."

PENELOPE

A slobbery, wet ball is shoved into my palm. "You're such a good boy, Henry," I praise, wrapping my fingers around the tennis ball. I lift my hand in the air, tossing the ball once again.

There is the familiar sound of Henry's feet as he dashes after the ball, so I wait. Soon enough, he's back, his furry body brushing against the side of my leg as he lies down on the ground next to me, panting hard.

"Tired?"

At ten years old, Henry is still a pretty active dog, and he doesn't show any signs of slowing down in his older age. It's something that I don't take for granted, considering he's been my best friend and companion for the past eight years as he has worked as my guide dog.

I place my hand on Henry's head, scratching between his ears. His fur is thicker, so I make a mental note to give him a good brush tomorrow morning because things will get hectic once classes start on Monday. Although we come early every year to campus so we can learn the best routes to my classes before the orientation week starts, things are always crazy these first few days as we both reacquaintance ourselves with the pandemonium that's the beginning of the semester.

"You ready to go home, buddy?"

The mention of home has his head snapping up with interest, as it always does. I let out a soft chuckle, grabbing his harness off the bench where I had left it earlier. "C'mon, you earned your dinner."

Henry slips into his harness easily, and I secure it before getting to my feet.

The walk back to our apartment is short. There are a lot of reasons why I loved this apartment. The three bestselling factors were that it's dog-friendly, close to campus, and has a dog park just around the corner so Henry can get enough play time where he can just be a dog, and not my eyes, even if it's only for a moment.

As we come to a stop before the front door, I slide my hand into my pocket, pulling out a key, when I hear the soft notes of a guitar playing in the air. I suck in a breath, my whole body going still as I stand and listen. The dark, haunting melody is unfamiliar but so beautiful it makes my heart ache.

Who is playing that?

This is the first time I've heard anybody playing here, and I would have known because this is my third year living in this building. Usually, I was the one playing on my keyboard.

Did somebody new move in? I don't think it's anybody from my class. I've heard their stuff, and it's nothing like this.

It has to be somebody new.

Somebody different.

Just as suddenly as the music starts, it dies down. I stand there and listen, hoping whoever is playing will continue to do so, but they never do.

Maybe it was just a radio?

Shaking my head, I let out a shaky breath and push open the door.

"Apartment, Henry."

Thank you so much for reading Shattered & Salvaged Duet. I hope you enjoyed Jade and Prescott's story as much as I did.

Not ready to say goodbye yet? You can grab their bonus epilogue here.

Penelope's story is coming next! *Kiss Me Tenderly*, the final book in the Blairwood University series, is coming in spring 2023. Find out what will happen when a world-famous rockstar and Penny's childhood crush moves in next door in this good-girl, bad-boy college romance. Pre-order now!

New to Blairwood University? Most of Prescott and Jade's friends already have their story out: Kiss To Conquer (Hayden and Callie), Kiss To Forget (Nixon and Yasmin), Kiss To Defy (Zane and Rei), Kiss To Remember (Grace and Mason) and Kiss To Belong (Maddox and Alyssa)!

Bloggers, bookstagrammers and booktokers join Anna's share team to be the first to know about her upcoming releases and sales.

Want to stay in touch with Anna? Join her reader's group Anna's Bookmantics, or sign up for Anna's newsletter.

ACKNOWLEDGMENTS

I started writing Kiss To Shatter on March 2nd, 2022. On March 24th, I was talking to one of my author friends, and I told her this story was going to be a long one. That was the day I started playing with the idea of turning it into a duet.

And I was right. I knew going this route for Jade's story was going to be risky. I knew this story would not be for everybody. Hell, I even asked my alpha readers if they thought I was making a mistake and if I should just write it as a cancer scare instead of putting Jade through the whole ordeal, but I couldn't do it. I knew deep down in my gut that this is Jade's story, this is her path, and so is Prescott's, and I would be doing them a disservice if I took an easy way out by cutting the story short to make it fit better for the current market.

And I never want to do that.

I don't ever want to settle and give my characters an easy way out.

Because life isn't easy. Life is messy and scary, and it takes until there is nothing else left to give. Life hurts. But life is also beautiful. It's filled with people you love, experiences you'll cherish, and dreams that will come true.

And that's this duet for me.

It's a story—a life story—told in all its devastatingly beautiful glory.

My only wish is that I could have published it in October as I originally planned during Breast Cancer Awareness month. But as we all know, we can't have all we want. What matters is that I managed to publish a story I truly love and cherish, and I hope people will be able to connect to it and learn from it.

Listen to your bodies, ladies and gentlemen; if something feels off, don't let other people, not even doctors, convince you otherwise. You know your body the best.

As always, a huge thank you to Carrie, Melody, and Nina, my alpha cheerleaders, for being there every step of the way these last eight months as I struggled through writing this story, but also to old and new faces of my beta team. Julie and Summer, without whom these stories wouldn't be possible. They've shared their personal experiences with me, for which I'll forever be grateful.

Thank you to my talented cover designer Najla and her team for these stunning covers. And for Kate taking on this project last minute like the champ she is and helping me polish it to perfection.

A big shoutout to my street and promo teams for sharing the news about this release and helping me reach new readers with their hard work.

Most of all, THANK YOU to *you,* my readers. I wouldn't have been here if it weren't for you. I hope you enjoyed Jade and Prescott.

Until the next book.

Xo,

Anna

PLAYLIST

The Rasmus - Justify
Beth Crowley - Battle Cry
Beth Crowley - Savior
Arlissa - Healing
Ruelle - Hold Your Breath
Demi Lovato - Still Have Me
Demi Lovato - Unbroken
Tate McRae - you broke me first
Morgan Berry - Fearless
Bebe Rexha - I'm a Mess
Rymez - Kryptonite (feat. James Arthur)
Ryan Hurd, Maren Morris - Chasing After You
Beth Crowley - Trenches
Beth Crowley - Standstill
Kodaline - Brother
The Rasmus - Odyssey
Julia Ross - You're Not Mine
Dan + Shay - Keeping Score (feat. Kelly Clarkson)
Anson Seabra - Walked Through Hell
Faouzia - Hero

Cimorelli - You're Worth It
Avril Lavigne - Head Above Water
5 Seconds of Summer - Teeth
The Kid LAROI - STAY (feat. Justin Bieber)
Justin Bieber - Ghost
Madison Watkins - Lose To Love
Shawn Mendes - When You're Gone
Mitchell Tenpenny - Drunk Me
Citizen Soldier - Still Breathing
Citizen Soldier - Let Me Let Go
Citizen Soldier - Save Your Story
The Rasmus - Save Me Once Again
Jon Mullins - In a Second
Camylio - monsters
James Arthur - Train Wreck
Daisy Clark - Battle Scars
Taylor Swift - Haunted
Paloma Faith - Only Love Can Hurt Like This
Nate Smith - Wreckage
Taylor Swift - Bigger Than The Whole Sky
Citizen Soldier, Lo Spirit - Limit
Chase Wright - Hurt No More
Dayseeker - Sleeptalk
Laura Marano, Wrabel - Worst Kind of Hurt
Bad Omens - Just Pretend

OTHER BOOKS BY ANNA B. DOE

Blairwood University

College sports romance

Kiss Me First

Kiss To Conquer

Kiss To Forget

Kiss To Defy

Kiss Before Midnight

Kiss To Remember

Kiss To Belong

Kiss Me Forever

Kiss To Tempt

Kiss To Shatter

Kiss To Salvage

Kiss Me Tenderly

Greyford Wolves

YA/NA sports romance

Lines

Habits

Rules

Greyford High

YA/NA sports romance

The Penalty Box

The Stand-In Boyfriend

Standalone

YA modern fairytale retelling

Underwater

New York Knights

NA/adult sports romance

Lost & Found

Until

Forever

Box Set Editions

Greyford Wolves: The Complete Collection

The Anabel & William Duet

ABOUT THE AUTHOR

Anna B. Doe is a *USA Today* and international bestselling author of young adult and new adult sports romance. She writes real-life romance that is equal parts sweet and sexy. She's a coffee and chocolate addict. Like her characters, she loves those two things dark, sweet and with a little extra spice.

When she's not working for a living or writing her newest book you can find her reading books, binge-watching TV shows or listening to music while she walks her shi tsu puppy Tina. Originally from Croatia, she is always planning her next trip because wanderlust is in her blood.

She is currently working on various projects. Some more secret than others.

Find more about Anna on her website: www.annabdoe.com

Join Anna's Reader's Group Anna's Bookmantics on Facebook.

Made in United States
Orlando, FL
21 August 2025

64127064R00270